TREMBLING ON THE BRINK

Based in the mid-1950s and set in the suburbs of London, this nostalgic novel accurately recalls teenage life during those early postwar years.

Covering two years in the life of a young girl with an overprotective mother, *Trembling on the Brink* follows Charis Mitchell and her friends as they blossom into adulthood. In their optimistic world, which revolves around school exams, parties, coffee bars, youth and jazz clubs, the church and dances, they suffer and enjoy the many new experiences and emotions that enter their lives.

TREMBLING ON THE BRINK

Vera M. Black

ARTHUR H. STOCKWELL LTD.
Torrs Park   Ilfracombe   Devon
Established 1898
www.ahstockwell.co.uk

British Library Cataloguing-in-Publication Data.
A catalogue record for this book is available
from the British Library.

This is an entirely fictional story,
and no conscious attempt has been made
to accurately record or recreate
any real-life events.

By the same author:
Iridescent Wings

ISBN 0 7223 3703 5
Printed in Great Britain by
Arthur H. Stockwell Ltd.
Torrs Park   Ilfracombe
Devon

Dedicated to the memory of
my beloved R.G.M.
who provided the tools for the job
and without whose encouragement
I would not have written this book

Contents

SUMMER 1995

A casual onlooker on a certain warm June morning would have observed a middle-aged woman, wearing a blue dress and light jacket, lingering outside a house in Wednesbury Road, but would have given the matter no further thought, not realising that this was the house where the woman had spent the first twenty-five years of her life.

Mixed emotions were crowding the woman's mind as she noted the changed appearance of her former home, and recalled certain events from her past which remained evergreen. She had long debated the wisdom of this return, but, standing as she did at a major crossroads in her life, curiosity had triumphed.

She was saddened that the front garden, so dear to her parents, had become a parking lot, and, where once standard roses had bravely weathered the seasons, a red Ford Mondeo now bloomed. She wondered who had exchanged the old wooden front door for a glass one encased within a modern porch. Double-glazed replacement windows were a further innovation, as was a loft extension which afforded an unassailable view of Wednesbury Road and its environs. She noticed too a prominent security alarm attached to the front wall, and smiled wanly at the thought that the contents of her once modest home now warranted such protection.

Further down the road she stopped again to stare at the large double-fronted house which once had been the home of her school friend, Pam Sperry. The laburnum trees which had given the house its original name had been felled, the entire front garden had been paved over and the house converted into flats.

'I wonder if Pam knows about it,' she thought, but guessed that her former friend would care little, never having been given to brooding.

Tamarisk Villa still stood proudly, resurrecting a wave of nostalgia. It had always been considered the most prestigious house in the road, and its present owners had maintained its glossy facade. As she studied its gracious symmetry, grateful that at least *this* house remained much as she remembered it, the garage doors opened and an elegant Mercedes, driven

9

by an attractive olive-skinned woman reversed down the driveway and backed into the road.

'Not at all like Frances Armitage,' she thought. 'I wonder whether she and Jack are still alive?'

At the far end of the road a few of the original Wednesbury beeches were still standing, but others had clearly succumbed to drought or traffic fumes.

'Youngsters don't need trees to kiss and cuddle under these days anyway,' she mused. 'They're all sleeping together by the time they're sixteen, if not earlier, but it wasn't like *that* forty-odd years ago.'

Later, in Coniston Park, she crossed grass which once had been regularly mown by council workers but now stood a foot high in places, with only a rough swathe cut through it. No rowing boats bobbed on the lake, and indeed the boathouse had been demolished.

'Probably due to vandalism,' she thought sadly. 'How times have changed.'

In the woods beyond the lake she looked eagerly for the little hut which, over forty years ago, had become almost a shrine to the memory of a special, never-to-be-forgotten boyfriend. The hut had gone, but in her imagination it would always be there, half hidden amongst holly and hawthorn bushes.

She spared a thought for her old church, St Luke's, where she had been a chorister, and wondered how much it had changed. However, there was no time to find out, nor to walk down Charters Lea High Street to St Jude's in the Holy Oaks, which had featured even more prominently in her life.

Approximately an hour remained before she was due to rendezvous at Victoria Station — just sufficient time to take the train from Charters Lea into London and then to use the underground.

'I'm glad I came back,' she thought. 'After next week my life can never be the same again, but I wish it were still possible to talk to Daddy and Mummy, Aunt Bee and Vanna. I wonder what they would think of me now? So much has happened; so much has changed, and yet the year when I was sixteen is the one I shall always remember most vividly with all its bitter-sweet connotations. How green I was — how apprehensive — longing for excitement, yet timid and faltering when it came my way; loving, yet resenting, my parents, especially Mummy; anxious to be an adult in some ways, yet so reluctant to cross that swirling river which separated childhood from maturity, that it seemed I was destined always to stand trembling on the brink.'

ONE

Charis Mitchell was fourteen when she guessed correctly that her first real battle with her mother would be over using make-up. Grace Mitchell was slim and sober in appearance, wearing her fine, flyaway hair in a tight bun because she could not bear to look untidy. Her only concession to the cosmetic industry was to dust her cheeks with the merest touch of pale pink powdery rouge to create a subtle glow, because her natural complexion was pale and waxy. Lipstick, however, was taboo because she considered it common and fit only to be used by actresses and fast women. She turned an inconsistently blind eye to the fact that her younger sister, Beatrice, known as Bee, wore it all the time, along with almost all the other ladies of her acquaintance, including those at her church, but Grace remained adamant that she herself would never join their ranks.

Charis had inherited her mother's pale complexion and large eyes, although hers were a deep, greyish-blue, whereas Grace's were brown. Charis's hair was long and straight, the colour of fallen oak leaves, while her features were entirely commonplace.

Charis's friend, Pam Sperry, was exceptionally pretty and took full advantage of her comely appearance, ogling all the boys, who, much to her delight, usually responded enthusiastically with either a wolf whistle or an appreciative wink, gesture or comment. Pam was already wearing make-up out of school, and even a little *in* school, although it was discreet enough not to be noticed by the nuns at Stella Maris. In all this she was positively encouraged by her smart, fashion-conscious mother, Jane, the complete antithesis of Grace.

Leafing through women's magazines, illustrated from cover to cover with photogenic models wearing lustrous lipstick and alluring eyeshadow and mascara, Charis was filled with longing to emulate them— an emotion not shared in any way by her other school friend, Maggie Rigg.

"I don't know why you keep on about it, Mitch," Maggie said one day. "You're quite reasonable to look at, and your hair's nice and silky even if you don't like the colour. You don't get spots — well, not many, and only

11

when you've eaten too much chocolate. You're always on about Pam wearing make-up, but *I* couldn't be bothered to mess about with all that stuff. Time enough when I'm older. I don't think my mother will mind when I want to start, but I don't want to yet."

Pam Sperry thought Grace's ideas desperately old-fashioned, and Charis, of course, agreed.

"You could at least use face powder, couldn't you?" said Pam. "Why don't you ask her about it? Surely even *she* uses that."

Much to Charis's surprise, Grace reacted quite calmly to the suggestion and even went so far as to buy her some Max Factor Creme Puff, which had recently become popular. The shade chosen was Truly Fair, which, Charis thought, sounded far less enticing than Tempting Touch which Pam used, but was nevertheless a step in the right direction.

Grace watched her daughter dubiously applying the compressed powder to her face, and then said, "It makes you look so washed out, child. I'm not so sure it's a good idea after all." Charis looked crestfallen, but again Grace surprised her: "You've inherited my colouring, I'm afraid," she said, "so I suppose you'll have to do as I do. Wait here a moment."

Grace returned from her bedroom a little later carrying a tiny, circular box containing her precious soft-pink rouge.

"Dust this on your cheeks," she said. "But only the faintest touch, mind. Let me show you."

Charis could hardly wait to tell Pam the good news.

"Terrific!" Pam said. "Now you just need lipstick. You can have one of my old ones if you like."

Charis wore it one Sunday morning just before leaving for church with her parents. Even she had to admit that the bright, petunia shade looked garish, but Grace was furious and made her wash it off completely.

"Don't copy Pam Sperry," Grace warned. "I won't have *my* daughter looking cheap."

If Grace considered lipstick common, eye make-up was the epitome of tawdriness in her view, and no amount of pleading would persuade her to let Charis experiment with the pretty blue, green and turquoise eyeshadows which stared up at her appealingly from Woolworth's beauty counter.

Once again, Pam took over: "Try mascara," she urged. "Go on. It would make your eyelashes curl, and your mother probably wouldn't notice unless she looked really hard."

The temptation proved too great. One day Charis smuggled home a small box of brown cake mascara, complete with a dear little brush, and, in the privacy of the bathroom, applied it to her upper and lower eyelashes. Her eyes, already large, looked huge as a result and, wonder of wonders, Grace said nothing.

The battle over lipstick was finally won when Charis's Aunt Bee cajoled Grace into relenting: "After all," said Aunt Bee, "all the young girls wear it these days, and you can't expect Charis to be the odd one out."

"Oh, all right," said Grace wearily, "but only the barest trace. Keep it pale and discreet. If I ever see bright lipstick on you again I shall confiscate it for good, so be warned."

And so, aged fourteen and armed with lipstick, face powder, rouge and the secret mascara, Charis Mitchell launched herself into the exciting world which beckoned beyond her front door.

Grace Mitchell was born in 1906, the second of George and Constance Vanning's four children. Faded sepia photos from her younger days revealed a tall, slim, serious-looking girl with few outstanding features save those large, dark eyes set in an angular face. She left school at fourteen, in common with most of her peers at the time, and joined the City firm of Myers and Hope.

With a sensible eye to the future, she studied shorthand and typing at evening school, an enterprise which paid off handsomely, for she ended up as an efficient, well-respected secretary.

Hugh Mitchell, working in the postal department of the same firm, admired from afar capable, wholesome, no-nonsense Grace, but never dreamed that she gave him more than a passing thought. It was all the more surprising to him, therefore, that when he finally summoned enough courage to approach her, she reciprocated his interest. A protracted courtship was followed by a lengthy engagement, during which time they saved prudently for the future. When Hugh's Aunt Adelaide died in 1934, leaving him a small but useful amount of money in her will, he felt able to put down a deposit on 22 Wednesbury Road, and married Grace the following year.

Donald, Grace's elder brother by two years, had been clever enough to win a grammar-school scholarship — a rare accomplishment in those distant days — and later gained a degree in Divinity at Durham University and became a Church of England priest. Influenced by some of his colleagues at theological college, he leaned towards High Church and, following one or two appointments as a curate and then as an army chaplain during the war, he was finally appointed vicar of a church in Wakefield. Able at last to give full rein to his High Church inclinations, Donald delighted in shocking Grace by using incense and installing statues of the Virgin Mary and various saints. Such practices smacked of Roman Catholicism and were anathema to Grace, who was loyal to the middle-of-the-road church tradition in which she had been raised, and abhorred ostentation.

Hugh and Grace's daughter was born on 15th January 1939. It was Donald, acting as Charis's godfather, who suggested her unusual Christian name, knowing that it meant grace in Greek, thus bonding her in an even closer fashion to her mother. Despite warming to the idea, Grace was at first reluctant to agree, guessing that many people would have no idea that the CH had a K sound.

"So what?" was Donald's reaction. "It will only prove their ignorance, and what does that matter?"

So, in the spring of 1939, a few months after her birth, she was christened Charis Laura at St Luke's.

Hugh had left Myers and Hope and was now employed by the GPO as a full-time postman. He enjoyed the work because he liked being outside in the fresh air and meeting people. Grace, however, considered it far beneath his capabilities. She thoroughly disliked him wearing a uniform because it segregated him from the other men in the neighbourhood, who were mostly white-collar workers. She imagined everyone looked down on them, but this aspect of life did not concern Hugh, who was a quiet and placid man whose favourite pastime was working in his garden or on his allotment.

Hugh's family was small. He had only one sister, Hester, his twin. Their parents were both dead, and Hester was a childless widow who, since losing her husband, Edwin, had lived alone in a pretty house in Sussex. Although missing Edwin acutely, Hester had never been one to bemoan her fate. She surrounded herself instead with three plump cats, colourful ornaments and flowers. Hester, who believed in being nice to people, was always smiling and, like Hugh, was never more contented than when pottering about in her cottagey Sussex garden.

Much loved, sheltered and cossetted by her parents and other relatives, Charis grew up knowing they were proud of her because she happened to be quite bright. Placing great importance upon education, and regretting the sparseness of their own schooling in the second decade of the century, Hugh and Grace, despite the anxieties and deprivations of the war years, lavished much time and patience on their daughter, encouraging her by every means in their power to acquire as much knowledge as possible in a wide range of subjects from an early age. As a result, she could read, tell the time, point out countries of the world on a globe and do simple sums before she even started school at the age of five.

She excelled at her junior school and then, at eleven, passed the three-part scholarship examination, comprising English, Arithmetic and General Intelligence, and secured a place at the school of her parents' choice, the Stella Maris Roman Catholic Convent Grammar School. This had an excellent reputation for achieving university entrances, and an expectation, at least in principle, of turning out well-mannered girls with sound moral values.

That Grace and Hugh had chosen a Catholic school for Charis was something of an enigma in view of Grace's fervent Protestant views. As for Hugh, his interest in churches of any denomination was minimal, although he accompanied Grace with uncomplaining, faithful regularity to matins, evensong, once-a-month Holy Communion and the occasional sung Eucharist at St Luke's. Before making their final decision about Stella Maris, the Mitchells had spoken at length to the principal, Mother Ambrose, who assured them that no pressure would be brought to bear upon their daughter to become a Catholic. So, in the autumn of 1950, Charis had joined the new intake at the convent.

Her first two years there were entirely successful. She was usually placed no lower than third in her end-of-term class examinations, and was praised for her ability in a variety of subjects.

Perhaps because she was an only child, and happy at home, she had never felt a burning need for a close confidante of her own age, but nevertheless Charis soon made friends with buxom, fair-haired Maggie Rigg, who sat next to her in class, and was on fairly amicable terms with most of the other girls in her form. She was called Charis by the staff, but to most of her peers she was known as Mitch.

It was while travelling to and from school each day on the bus that she had begun speaking to Pam Sperry, who was in a parallel form and also lived in Wednesbury Road, and a friendship soon developed.

Once the make-up hurdle had been crossed, Charis decided that she must further emulate her vivacious, flirty young friend, by setting her mind to the acquisition of a boyfriend, and where better to begin than at church?

St Luke's had a large and flourishing choir comprising several men between the ages of seventeen and seventy-five, a similar number of women and girls and a few small boys. Charis joined the choir soon after her fourteenth birthday, but the males and females used separate vestries on Sundays, and at choir practices she was usually monopolised by Patsy Beddowes and Ruth Starr, the girls she sat between. Afterwards, following Grace's strict instructions, Charis always felt duty-bound to catch the earliest possible bus home, so making friends with, or being noticed by, any of the young men was virtually impossible.

Of all the male choristers, Alan Decker was the one who truly appealed to Charis, if only from afar, and she found herself mooning about him more and more. They had never held a conversation, but he had winked at her a few times across the chancel, and once, outside church, had actually called out, "'ello, ducky," accompanied by a cheeky grin, reminiscent of the boy in the Bisto Kids advert. She knew he had left school at fifteen with a somewhat tearaway reputation, and was temporarily employed as a garage mechanic, awaiting his call-up for national service.

She was also mildly interested in Desmond Hoyt, although he was a far less flamboyant character than Alan. Both were nearing eighteen, but while Alan invariably looked slightly crumpled, Desmond's smooth, ink-black hair was always immaculately groomed and his clothes well pressed. His expression was a little stern and serious, and it was well known that he was studiously working towards a place at university.

Charis kept her secret pash on Alan Decker to herself, so Grace was unaware of it and sometimes divulged vital pieces of information about both Alan and Desmond, gleaned from conversations with their respective mothers. The Hoyts were a quietly respectable family; the Deckers less so, according to Grace, chiefly because they spoke ungrammatically and tended to drop their aitches — cardinal sins in her book.

The only boy at St Luke's who displayed any real interest in Charis was fifteen-year-old Colin Crisp, who was not in the choir but would spend most services half hidden behind a pillar, unable to take his eyes off her. Although he looked younger than his years as he had a babyish face, he was really quite handsome in an immature way, with clear pink and white skin, pale blue eyes and silky flaxen hair, but he was unfortunate enough to be afflicted by a stammer and a tendency to blush. Despite these setbacks, he was always anxious to speak to Charis outside church on Sundays, but she found him intensely dull and wished he would leave her alone so that she could concentrate on trying to attract Alan Decker's attention.

Charis was certain that Alan and Desmond belonged to the Greenfinches, St Luke's youth group, which met on Thursday evenings, but it was supposed to be for over-fifteens and, as she was still only fourteen, the situation looked hopeless.

Salvation arrived in the form of Robert Rickard, the youthful, good-looking curate at St Luke's. After evensong one Sunday he collared Hugh and Grace, whom Charis had just joined in the church porch following her stint in the choir and, after the preliminary niceties, turned to Charis: "You're growing up into a very smart young lady," he said. "When are you going to join the Greenfinches?"

"When I'm fifteen, I suppose," she replied, rather hoping that he would notice her darkened, curly eyelashes.

"I thought you were fifteen already," he said.

"It's that lipstick," said Grace, sounding unnecessarily apologetic, and certainly disapproving. "It makes her look older than she is — *and* those high heels."

She still hadn't noticed the mascara.

"But would you *like* to join, Charis?" Robert Rickard continued, unabashed.

"Oh I'd *love* to!"

"Well, if your parents agree, I don't see why we shouldn't turn a blind eye to your age." He turned to Grace and Hugh: "What do you say?"

"If you think it's in order, Mr Rickard, I'm sure it'll be all right," said Hugh, clearly not wishing to scupper the curate's kindly plan.

"I shall be worried about her coming home afterwards," said Grace. "I don't want her wandering around the streets late at night. Choir practice is one thing, it's over by eight o'clock, but Greenfinches must go on much later than that."

"If I personally ensure that she catches a bus around ten o'clock, would that put your minds at rest?" said Mr Rickard.

And so, amazingly, it was agreed.

Like many events in life to which one looks forward, the anticipation was far more exciting than the reality. On Charis's first few visits to the Greenfinches, both Alan and Desmond were missing, but Colin Crisp was a regular member and was delighted to have the chance of playing her at table tennis and joining her for tea and biscuits halfway through the evening. She also played table tennis with Patsy and Ruth, and sat through a series of exceedingly dull talks on the role of young people in the church today, with Colin firmly planted on the chair next to hers. At the end of each evening Colin would stammer: "S . . . s . . . see you on S . . . Sunday then, Charis," and Mr Rickard would escort her to the bus stop.

Then, that April, came an announcement that there was to be a grand social evening in honour of the Queen's Coronation in June. Sub-committees were formed to organise a variety of entertainments, and when Charis arrived at the next Greenfinches meeting she sensed a change in the usually dreary atmosphere. For one thing, two girls she had never seen before were giggling in front of the distorted, speckled mirror in the cloakroom as they applied extra layers of lipstick. She guessed both were about seventeen and they were dressed similarly in flared skirts and short-sleeved jumpers, with colourful sweater-scarves knotted round their necks. As they left the cloakroom they practically collided with Patsy, with whom they exchanged friendly banter.

"Who are *they*?" Charis asked, fascinated.

"Lesley and Geraldine from Reg Bradley's square dance team," Patsy replied. "They came here quite often last year, but I haven't seen them lately."

"Who's Reg Bradley?" Charis asked.

"You'll soon find out," Patsy promised.

Inside the hall the first person Charis noticed was Alan Decker. 'At *last*,' she thought, her heart skipping a little beat and her cheeks reddening. As usual, his tow-coloured hair was flopping over one eye, and his tan corduroys and yellow-and-brown-checked shirt looked a trifle crumpled. Two other girls were engaging him in animated conversation. One had long, dark hair, tied back in a ponytail; the other, also dark, had a bubble-cut, so that crisp curls covered her head like the petals of a chrysanthemum.

Just then, Desmond Hoyt emerged from a side room.

"Don't you think he looks just like a tailor's dummy?" Patsy whispered. "Percy Perfect my mother calls him."

"Come on Des. 'urry along. Let's see yer do-si-do, allemande left and all that," Alan called merrily from the stage, wearing the cheeky grin which Charis always found so appealing.

Patsy was staring at the girl with the bubble-cut: "He's still going out with *her*, then," she observed.

"Who do you mean?" asked Charis, as innocently as she knew how.

"Shirley Croft. She's been Alan Decker's girlfriend for *ages*."

"I've never seen her at church," said Charis, feeling absurdly cheated.

"That's because she never goes," Patsy said. "She's only here because of the square-dancing. She's Penny Reed's friend."

"My head's beginning to spin. Who's Penny Reed for goodness' sake?"

"Des Hoyt's girlfriend. The one in the blue skirt with the ponytail. She used to go to his school — you know, Warbridge Grammar."

It was now Charis's turn to stare. The couples' toning clothes made it clear which square-dance pairs belonged together, but the knowing smirks and winks which Alan and Shirley were exchanging made it patently clear that their relationship went a lot deeper than a dancing partnership.

"How many more are from Desmond's school, then?" Charis asked in an attempt to hide her growing despondency.

"All of them except Alan and Shirley. It started when Reg Bradley introduced them to square-dancing. He was their PT instructor — still is, I expect. That's him over there," said Patsy, pointing out a man in his mid-twenties decked out in a flamboyant stetson. "He's the caller," she went on. "Des and Penny and the others from the school got really keen, so they started going to a square-dance club in Warbridge with Reg. Then they thought it would be fun to start a team of their own, but they needed two more to make the eight, so Penny asked Shirley to join them, and Des asked Alan at the same time. That's how Alan met Shirley, and they've been going out ever since."

"But why did they all start coming here?" asked Charis, still puzzled.

"Des Hoyt suggested it, and Mr Rickard liked the idea. Wait till you see them dancing. They're really good. They've even given demonstrations at the Starlight Ballroom."

"Hi there, everyone," Reg Bradley shouted from the stage. "It's good to be back, and we're hoping to teach you a few square-dance routines so you can all join in at the Coronation party and give your mums and dads some idea what to do. I've been told they've only had old-time dancing at church socials in the past, so this'll make them sit up a bit and take notice. First of all tonight we're going to show you what's in store, so watch closely to see how it's done."

Within seconds the hall erupted with colour from the red, blue, green and yellow of the girls' swirling skirts, and the sound of Reg Bradley's pseudo-American staccato calls rising above loud hill-billy music emanating from a battered-looking record player:

> "Swing 'em, boys, and swing 'em right,
> Swing those girls till the morning light.
> Join your hands and circle all

Halfway round this li'l ol' hall.
Now turn round and circle back
Like a choo-choo train on a mountain track."

When it was over everyone applauded, and then Reg Bradley beckoned to Penny Reed, who joined him at once.

"He fancies her, of course," Patsy whispered.

Charis was inordinately fascinated and inquisitive: "How can you tell?" she whispered back.

"He was always singling her out before, and I've often caught him staring at her with a very strange look in his eye."

"But she's one of his *pupils*."

"*Was* — not any more. She left school last year."

"But you said she was going out with Des," Charis persisted.

"So what?" said Patsy.

Charis was shocked, yet pleased to be party to this spicy information, and kept an eye on Reg Bradley for the rest of the evening.

"Here's how you honour your partner," he was saying, bowing briefly to Penny who, in turn, dropped a neat little curtsey, "and this is the way to do-si-do." Whereupon he and Penny approached one another, passing right shoulders before stepping forward one step and then passing one another back to back.

Further instructions followed, all looking easy enough, but when Reg asked each member of the team to select a new partner, the novice dancers took a while to get into their stride. Charis was overjoyed when Alan Decker chose her. She tried very hard to follow his lead and perform the necessary movements, but it was all so unfamiliar, and she was so dazzled by him that she honoured the wrong corners, turned to the right instead of to the left, trod on Alan's toe and ended up feeling gauche and uncomfortable.

"Not to worry," said Alan with his cheerful Bisto Kid grin. "You'll soon pick it up. We've been doin' it a long time. You can't expect to walk before you can run."

Against the colourful square-dance team, the regular Greenfinches looked like drab little sparrows amongst birds of paradise. They made half-hearted attempts to emulate the team dancers, but their clothes were wrong, their efforts faintly pathetic and the experts were obviously relieved when they were back again with their familiar partners.

"It's early days," said Reg with a grin when the first dance ended in disarray, but Charis had already convinced herself that any faint hopes she might have had of attracting Alan Decker's attention had been dashed for ever.

As for Desmond Hoyt, he was once again dancing with Penny Reed, whose cute ponytail and vivid blue skirt flared out attractively as he twirled her round the hall, and Reg carried on with his well-rehearsed patter:

"Promenade up and promenade down,
Walk your little honey all round town.
Stars shine out in the big black sky,
So honour your partner and say bye-bye.""

Charis was desperately embarrassed, at nine-fifty, when Mr Rickard said it was time to see her to the bus stop. She hoped against hope that Alan hadn't heard or noticed, because it made her feel too infantile, but as they left the hall she heard with miserable certainty the sound of his husky guffaw, accompanied by Shirley Croft's infectious giggle, and imagined — rightly or wrongly — that they were laughing at her.

The Coronation party was a lacklustre affair for Charis. The only time she was at all involved was when, as one of a group selected from the church choir, she joined in singing some patriotic English songs which they had been practising for weeks. Once that was over she sat with her parents and their middle-aged to elderly church friends, drinking metallic-tasting tea, which had been brewed in the oft-used tea urn in the hall kitchen, and nibbling fairy cakes and iced buns prepared by the noble ladies of the congregation, undoubtedly having been chivvied by the vicar's wife.

When Reg Bradley introduced the square-dancing, Mrs Rushwell, a peevish-looking woman sitting at Charis's table said, "I'm surprised Mr Rickard encourages this sort of thing. We've been perfectly happy with old-time dancing before, and Bill and Iris Ward were quite upset when they heard they wouldn't be asked to give a demonstration tonight."

"They always did it so well, too," Grace commiserated. "I don't hold with all this American stuff myself."

Charis, however, felt glad that Bill and Iris Ward had been ditched. They were in their sixties, and although they looked nice when dressed up, and were competent dancers, their old-time routines were terribly dated.

The square-dance team put on a lively and colourful show, and Reg Bradley was soon encouraging everyone to join in. The Greenfinches needed little persuasion, but many of the adults, including Grace and Hugh and Mrs Rushwell, preferred to sit and watch everyone else making fools of themselves and causing great hilarity.

Later, the drama group performed an amusing one-act comedy, during which Colin Crisp, who had been hovering in the background all evening, sat next to Charis and even had the temerity to rest his arm along the back of her chair because they were out of Hugh and Grace's direct line of vision.

At the end of the evening Charis felt misery descending around her as she watched the noisy departure of the glamorous square dancers. Shirley was laughing, challenging Alan with a flirtatious expression in her berry-dark eyes, as he hugged her possessively. Penny walked off in the opposite direction, holding hands with Desmond on one side, and Reg Bradley on the other. All three were enjoying some shared joke, and Charis physically *ached* to be in the shoes of either of the older girls, at the same time realising that she could never hope to compete with them. After all, she thought, how could Alan or Desmond possibly be interested in someone like her; so much younger; so inexperienced and so dull?

Once the national excitement surrounding the Queen's Coronation had died down, Charis began to drift more and more in the direction of Pam Sperry, causing Maggie Rigg to cool towards her, because she had little time for Pam. For her part, Maggie cultivated Wendy King, who lived near her in Halstead and travelled to and from school with her, just as Charis did with Pam.

At the same time Charis began to lose interest in school work, giving up serious study and cutting her homework to the barest minimum. Obstinately, she closed her mind to anything the nuns or lay mistresses tried to teach her, and her position in class soon began to fall, dropping a little lower each time total marks were calculated.

"What does it matter?" said Pam airily. "Who's bothered about all those boring old subjects? I mean, do you *really* want to end up like Louise Heron or Morag McDonald? They never have any fun, and they certainly don't have boyfriends. I'd *hate* to be like them."

Secretly, Charis admired these two studious paragons, but had no wish to be bracketed with them, preferring Pam's easy-going style and lackadaisical approach to anything scholarly. She would often tell Charis spicy tales about people she met at the home of Celia Armitage, whose mother, Frances, organised frequent get-togethers for Celia's friends. Pam mentioned names like Nick and Rosemary, Norman and Eileen, Ronnie, Miranda and even someone with the unlikely nickname Banjo. She said she had been out with at least three boys but was never specific, and Charis had no way of checking whether her claims were true.

On Saturday mornings Celia and her circle of friends, including Pam, would meet at the Zanzibar Coffee Bar, and on Saturday evenings they all went to Holyoaks. This was a very popular, lively youth club attached to the church of St Jude's in the Holy Oaks — so called because a circle of trees in its adjoining graveyard had once been blessed by a bishop. It all sounded such fun. Charis was consumed with envy, wishing that she could be part of it, but knowing it was impossible because Grace would be sure to veto it.

Charis still went to Greenfinches and, not wanting to be outdone, told Pam the odd tale about Colin Crisp, embroidering the details a little for effect. Although she made her friend giggle, she knew her stories were tame in comparison with Pam's.

Christmas of 1953 came and went, and then it was January and Charis's fifteenth birthday. By February, her position in class had fallen to an all-time low at only six places from the bottom. By then she was feeling worried, and not a little ashamed, but was unprepared for what lay in store.

One fateful afternoon, on her return from school, Charis was summoned to the living room where she found Hugh, home unusually early from work, and Grace brandishing a letter: "I wrote to Mother Ambrose about you," Grace announced, "and this is her reply."

"You did *WHAT*?" Charis replied in horror. "You actually *wrote* to the Rice Pudding."

"I will *not* have you referring to your headmistress in that rude manner," said Grace.

"Everyone calls her the Rice Pudding," said Charis, and indeed this was true, for the temptation to bracket Mother Ambrose with Ambrosia Creamed Rice had been too compelling for the majority of giggling schoolgirls at Stella Maris to resist.

"You know very well that I don't *care* what everyone else does. She is the headmistress of your school, and you *must* respect her." Charis pulled a face, and her mother began to read aloud from the letter, "Charis suffers from lack of concentration in class. Perhaps something is on her mind of which we are unaware. We think she may be influenced by a friend or friends in the Beta stream who are, of course, less academically gifted than those in Alpha, but this cannot be the only factor. Fifteen is a difficult age for a girl, but it is of the utmost importance that Charis makes a real effort to regain lost ground so that she attains good results in next year's crucial examinations."

Charis could feel her cheeks flushing crimson, partly with anger; partly mortification.

"What do you have to say?" Grace demanded. "What is the matter with you?"

"Nothing." It was more of a growl than anything.

"Mother Ambrose mentions 'friends in the Beta stream'. I suppose she means Pam Sperry. She's the only Beta girl you mix with, isn't she? I always said she was a bad influence. Why couldn't you have stayed more friendly with Maggie Rigg?"

"I *like* Pam," Charis protested. "She's more fun than Maggie."

"Fun, fun! Is that all you think about these days?"

"I don't *get* any fun," Charis retorted. "It's no fun living here."

"What am I going to do with her?" Grace turned to Hugh in exasperation.

"Let's just calm down," he said. "It's no good getting heated and upset about everything."

At this, Grace exploded: "Oh *YOU*," she said. "Of course *you* wouldn't say or do *anything* to upset anyone. But it's your *daughter* we're talking about. Don't you care if she lets us down after all we've done to bring her up nicely?"

Hugh shuddered visibly: "I don't know what to say."

"*Typical!*" stormed Grace.

At that moment Charis fled from the room, thundered up the stairs, and then, on an impulse, crept halfway down again on tiptoe to eavesdrop on the rest of the conversation.

"How about having a quiet word with Bee?" Hugh was saying. "Charis might take more notice of her."

Grace exploded yet again: "*Bee!* You *know* she and Charis are hand in glove. Always have been. Bee would go along with anything Charis said. It wouldn't be the other way round."

"Perhaps Donald could do something?"

"Donald? *Donald!* I only wish you were right, but when did Charis last show any real interest in church? She's hardly likely to take kindly to advice from a vicar, even if he is her uncle *and* her godfather."

"Then perhaps you'll just have to say your prayers and hope for the best," said Hugh diplomatically.

At this point Grace's tantrum subsided with a sigh of resignation. "Of course, I've *always* placed great faith in the power of prayer," she said, sounding horribly pious, "so perhaps you're right. But I do wish something would happen soon to make Charis try harder."

Sensing that the conversation was at last at an end Charis crept back up the stairs to her bedroom. Of course she loved her mother, but at times like this, when her anger and intransigence were frightening, and her religious sentiments deeply embarrassing, she wondered if she really did. It was worrying and confusing, and she felt enfolded in a blanket of gloom.

Even though Charis was unable to share her mother's firm belief in prayer power, she thought it quite uncanny when someone entered her life at the beginning of the summer term that year who was to make all the difference in the world.

Miss Ingle swung into Four Alpha's classroom on a fine, late-April morning, wearing a pretty lime-green suit under the customary black gown sported by all the graduate lay mistresses at Stella Maris. Glancing at the plaster statue of St Thérèse of Lisieux and the small vase of anemones at its feet, she smiled at the class as everyone stood to attention, as they always did when a member of staff entered the room.

"Good morning, girls," she said brightly, and then, following the usual custom: "In the name of the Father, and of the Son and of the Holy Ghost."

"Amen," they chorused.

The class then joined in a Hail Mary before Miss Ingle told them to sit down. "I'm pleased to meet you all, and I'm looking forward to working with you," she said after introducing herself. "Next year you'll be taking your GCE Ordinary Level exams, of course, so we have one term's grace before we begin the GCE syllabus. I have two ideas in mind to start with.

First, I want you all to write me an essay describing any film or play you've seen, including your own critical opinion of the production. That should give me some idea of your capabilities. Then I'd like each of you to select an English project, and to work on it in your own time throughout the term. For example, it could be a selection of short stories by one particular author, a group of poems, a long epic poem, or perhaps a favourite book. There are endless possibilities. At the end of this term I shall set each of you an individual examination paper based on the special project you have chosen, so think hard about it, girls. If you can't decide what you want to do, come and ask me. Don't be afraid. I shan't bite."

"We have a new English mistress," Charis announced at home later that day. "She seems nice. I quite like her."

Grace and Hugh exchanged glances which spoke volumes; hardly surprising because it was the first time for months that Charis had shown the slightest interest in anything to do with Stella Maris.

Miss Ingle's presence was instantly invigorating, and soon everyone was talking about her. She was so different from the sombre, black-robed nuns, and different again from most of the lay members of staff, being younger, more attractive, but above all approachable. She gave the impression that, even if someone misbehaved, she would deal with that person fairly and on a balanced footing instead of as an insignificant underling, but that remained to be seen and, in any event, no one wanted to displease Miss Ingle.

Charis based her essay on a film she had seen several years before and had never forgotten. It had been singularly unsuitable for a ten-year-old, but Grace had been completely misled over the title: *No Room at the Inn*. Nothing could have been further removed from the comfortable, religious film which she had undoubtedly expected, dealing as it did with the ill-treatment of a group of children by an evil foster-mother on whom they were billeted during the war. Charis had never imagined before that children of her own age could be so neglected and dirty, have nits in their hair and all sleep together, end to end, in an unsavoury bed, let alone be punished by being locked in a freezing outside coal shed. She remembered the film in almost every detail, and had been so influenced by its powerful message and the memory of Freda Jackson's performance as the dreadful Mrs Voray, that when she began to write about it, her mind raced ahead of her pen and she covered several pages within an hour.

Some days after the English exercises had been handed in, Miss Ingle arrived in Four Alpha looking impassive: "I have the results of the first essays you've written for me, girls," she said. "Many of them were very good indeed; some not so good and some excellent. A few of you will need to pay attention to your grammar, spelling and general style of writing, but I'm here to guide you in the right direction if you'll trust my judgment."

Charis was biting the end of her lead pencil so hard that her teeth marks showed in the wood as Miss Ingle continued speaking: "Top marks go to Louise Heron, Morag McDonald and Charis Mitchell. I'd like to talk to those three girls individually for a short while at lunchtime today. Louise, come to the library at one o'clock; Morag at one-fifteen and Charis at one-thirty. I've given the lowest marks, I'm afraid, to Angela Doyle and Bernadette O'Malley, and I'd like to speak to you two as well, perhaps after school today, but only for about five minutes. Wendy King, your essay is borderline, but your spelling needs attention. The rest of the essays were good to average. Nothing for any of you to worry about particularly, but there's always room for improvement of course."

Dazed with her triumph, Charis wondered all through the rest of the morning what Miss Ingle would have to say. She reported at the library at the appointed time just as a smug-looking Morag McDonald was leaving. Miss Ingle was sitting in a quiet corner, well away from where some sixth-formers were doing prep. She beckoned Charis over and invited her to sit down at the small table on which the *No Room at the Inn* essay lay spread out. "You write very well, Charis," Miss Ingle began in a quiet voice so as not to distract the sixth-formers, "and yet I was disturbed by the subject matter. Why did you select such a harrowing film?"

"It's just that I never forgot it. I saw it when I was about ten, and I think it was the contrast between those poor children's lives and my own that shocked me so much."

"Why were you taken to see it in the first place?"

Blushing, Charis explained her mother's faux pas: "She hadn't realised what it was about beforehand, and we went on the bus to the cinema, bought seats in the one-and-nines, and it was too late then because she didn't want to waste the money."

Miss Ingle smiled. "Well, I don't suppose it did you any harm, but I'd like to think you could write about something more pleasant next time. I mean it when I say that you write well. Your work is a good deal better than that of an average fifteen-year-old, and yet I understand from your form mistress that you haven't been doing at all well in your general studies lately. Is that correct?"

"Yes, Miss Ingle." The blush returned with a vengeance.

"Can you explain why, Charis?"

"I don't know. I just lost interest."

"Where do your interests lie now, then, if your school work bores you so much?"

Charis quailed. How could she possibly tell Miss Ingle about her longing for a boyfriend, her wish to look more like Pam, and her overprotective home life? She did not answer.

"I believe you're friendly with a girl in Four Beta. Is that so?"

"Yes, Miss Ingle. Pam Sperry."

"I'll be frank with you, Charis," said Miss Ingle. "I haven't had very

25

much to do with the Beta girls yet, but I think I know Pam Sperry. I'm sure she's a very nice person, but few of the pupils in the Beta forms have much chance of going on to university. You, on the other hand, in the Alpha stream and until recently in the upper half of that stream, stand an excellent chance of becoming truly successful academically. In my opinion, you should concentrate most of your efforts on English, and go on to read it at university."

"I'd always planned to do that," said Charis, "but . . . " she hesitated momentarily, but Miss Ingle had opened the flood gates, and now the words came tumbling out " . . . I used to put my school work first all the time, but Pam started going out with boys, and it made me think I'd like to do the same, only the ones I liked were too old for me and they just weren't interested. Pam never has any trouble getting boys to like her. She's so pretty that they all want to go out with her, but I'm not allowed to go anywhere much to meet anyone, and even if I did I don't suppose any of them would even notice me."

"Oh dear," said Miss Ingle. "I'm beginning to get the picture. If Pam is the girl I'm thinking of, she is indeed very pretty, but you mustn't compare yourself with her, or anyone else for that matter. You are *you*, and you must believe in yourself and make the very best of yourself. None of the Beta girls could have written an essay like yours in a hundred years, and isn't it more important to write well and influence other people by your ideas than to have a pretty face and very little else? Looks aren't nearly as important as you might imagine but, all the same, you are attractive and have an *interesting* face, you know. I promise you, Charis, that your turn will come, and sooner or later someone will single you out and fall in love with you, but you must be patient. You're still very young. Yes, I know Pam is the same age, but then, you see, I'm sure she has no aspirations of going to university. Promise me you'll try to work harder this term, and certainly next year, so that your exam results are good. Then you'll go on to the sixth form and, hopefully, to university eventually. Do I have your promise?"

"Yes, Miss Ingle," said Charis, filled with a sudden surge of resolve. "You do."

After that her work began to show a marked improvement, although she had wasted so much time that it was a struggle to catch up on some of her weaker subjects.

For her special topic she chose Rupert Brooke. She thought he looked so sad and beautiful, and many of his poems touched a chord somewhere inside her. She borrowed books from the school library to learn about his life as well as his poetic works, and found she was able to write about him with sufficient enthusiasm and conviction to gain a staggering ninety-one per cent mark in the end-of-term exam, which placed her at the top of the class in that one subject. Her family were all bursting with pride, and Charis experienced a great sense of personal satisfaction at having achieved something worthwhile at last.

St Luke's was brightly decorated for the 1954 Harvest Festival. Brass vases, filled with carefully arranged Michaelmas daisies and gaudy dahlias, adorned the stone window sills, competing with the softer colours of the stained glass above them, while more elaborate floral displays dominated the chancel steps and the alcoves behind the altar. Bunches of glossy black grapes spilt over the sides of baskets filled with oranges, apples, bananas and pears, and two specially baked loaves in the shape of corn sheaves had been placed upright behind the altar cross.

> "Come, ye thankful people, come,
> Raise the song of harvest home;
> All is safely gathered in
> Ere the winter storms begin. . . . "

From her position in the choir stalls Charis could see almost everyone in the congregation, including her parents, singing the last hymn. Hugh looked smart in his best grey Sunday suit, and Grace was resplendent in her favourite hat — a head-hugging light-green creation which, both in colour and texture, reminded Charis of the outer casing of an almond.

When the hymn ended, the choir filed out of the chancel and into the ladies' vestry where Patsy Beddowes collared her: "Are you going to the Harvest Supper on Wednesday?" she asked.

"I suppose so," Charis replied.

"You don't sound very keen."

"Well, it won't be very exciting, will it? I mean, those church things never are."

"You wouldn't have said that when Alan Decker was around."

"What makes you say that?"

"You used to have an almighty crush on him, didn't you?"

"How did you know? I never told you."

"You didn't need to. It was obvious."

Patsy laughed merrily, and Charis blushed: "Well, what if I did?" she said. "He's long gone, and I've got other things on my mind now."

"Such as?"

"Well, there's just a chance that I may be invited to a party soon."

"A party? Whose party?

"You don't know her. Celia Armitage. She's in my form at school. She lives in my road."

"Why don't you know for certain if you're going?"

"My friend, Pam, told me Celia hadn't made up her mind about numbers yet, and at least my name was mentioned. I'd love to go. Celia knows crowds of people, and I'd really like a chance to meet them."

"When you say people, I suppose you mean boys," Patsy observed, correctly.

"How on earth did you guess? Well, boys are a bit thin on the ground here, aren't they?"

"Almost non-existent. Oh well, keep me posted, won't you? See you on Wednesday."

Colin Crisp was, as usual, hovering outside, and obviously waiting for Charis.

'Oh rats,' she thought. 'I simply can't be bothered with him today.'

"H . . . h . . . hello, C . . . C . . . Charis," he began, with his customary blush. "I'm afraid I c . . . c . . . can't walk w . . . with you to the b . . . bus today. I've g . . . got to g . . . go home early. We've g . . . got c . . . c . . . company."

'Thank goodness for that,' she thought, but she said as nicely as she could, "Oh well, never mind. See you sometime."

By the time Charis arrived at the bus stop her parents were nowhere to be seen. She guessed they had either caught an earlier bus or someone had given them a lift home by car, so she was left to wait alone, with only her thoughts for company.

TWO

In Five Alpha, Charis's form at Stella Maris, it was now common knowledge that Celia Armitage was planning a Guy Fawkes party to coincide with her sixteenth birthday, but still no one knew exactly who was to be invited.

Charis stood in awe of Celia, who was mature for her age and blessed with more common sense than most of the other girls. Although both girls lived in Wednesbury Road, Charis scarcely knew Celia, but since her friendship with Pam Sperry had developed, Celia had drifted into the picture because she and Pam had been neighbours all their lives, and their parents were old friends. Charis was aware that both families were well off, but she felt much more comfortable with Pam, who lacked Celia's finesse and more easily bridged the gap between affluence and Hugh and Grace's financial inferiority.

Charis woke early each morning feeling apprehensive, as she was still uncertain whether or not she would be invited to the party. She wanted to go, if only to feel accepted by Celia, but the social implications scared her. Charis suspected Pam of knowing more of Celia's intentions than she was prepared to divulge, for she had even hinted that if a certain Miranda Gates was unable to go to the party, Charis might well be invited to take her place. Being a substitute was hardly flattering, but Charis decided it was better than nothing and continued to live in hope.

Roughly a week before Guy Fawkes Day, Celia finally approached her: "You've probably heard about my party by now," she said with a nonchalant little laugh. "Would you like to come? We're having fireworks, of course, but you don't need to bring any. We'll have more than enough as it is."

Charis was thrilled to distraction, but thanked her and accepted as calmly as she could in an effort to disguise the extent of her relief and excitement.

Later she discussed the forthcoming event with Pam, and the all-important question of clothes.

"I've got a new dress," Pam said proudly. "My parents were planning to buy me one for Christmas anyway, so they let me choose it early. It isn't a winter dress though. It's silk, but Celia said we'd be watching the fireworks from the conservatory, so I shan't feel cold."

"Who else will be there?" Charis asked, feeling envious of Pam's good fortune.

"Mostly the Holyoaks crowd," said Pam. "Barry Duggan, of course, because he's Celia's boyfriend, and Norman Fairway, Ronnie Costello, Rosemary Gordon and Nick Buchanan. I expect Celia's cousin, Eileen, will be there too, but I hope they haven't invited her younger brother, Teddy. He's *awful*! The only people from school will be you, me, and Babs Randle with her boyfriend. Celia invited Louise Heron and her brother, but they couldn't come."

Charis felt highly honoured to be placed on a par with Pam and Babs, the latter having been Celia's closest friend at school ever since the first form. She wanted to know more about Holyoaks too and wished she could go there, but as it was attached to St Jude's, well known for being High Church and therefore totally discredited by Grace, it seemed unlikely that she would ever be allowed to join.

Charis wondered how her mother would react to her invitation, and if (heaven forbid) she would prevent her from going to the party, but Grace sounded quite pleased: "Celia Armitage? Oh yes, she's the girl who lives down the road at Tamarisk Villa, isn't she? I've often wondered what it was like inside that big house. You'll have to tell me all about it. I expect you'll meet some classy people there."

"I shan't know anybody except Pam and Babs Randle," said Charis suddenly feeling anxious. Babs, a haughty girl with a frosty manner, had never made any overtures of friendship towards her, and, in turn, Charis had never particularly liked her.

"From what I've heard, the Armitages are a highly respectable family," Grace continued. "Celia's father is a bank manager, you know, and her mother always dresses so tastefully. People like that have good manners and style. I'm sure they'll make you feel at ease."

"I hope so. Anyway, even if they don't, I'll have Pam to talk to."

Grace sniffed: "I've never been too happy about that girl," she said. "She's always seemed a flighty little thing to me, and her mother isn't at all like Mrs Armitage. Look at those vivid colours she wears. So *common*."

The only remaining problem was what to wear, so, while her mother was talking about clothes, Charis took the plunge: "Do you think I could possibly have a new dress?" she wheedled, guessing that the answer would be a resounding "No."

"Aren't you forgetting the one you wore to the Harvest Supper at church," Grace said at once. "That's a lovely dress and really suits you."

Charis yearned for something prettier and more dramatic than the sober, greyish-blue frock which had been Grace's choice when she had seen it in the July sales. It made her feel dull and dowdy: "Oh Mummy . . . *please* couldn't I have something new? I never liked that one much anyway."

"Now look, Charis, you know perfectly well we don't have money to burn. The blue dress is perfectly suitable and that's an end to it. We had enough trouble before finding something that wasn't too desperately expensive."

There was only one avenue left to explore: "Couldn't I ask Aunt Bee to buy me one?"

"Absolutely *NOT*," said Grace. "I'm surprised and ashamed that you would even think of such a thing. I will not have you pestering Bee like that. Any more nonsense out of you, my girl, and you won't be going to the party at all."

On the evening of the party Charis sat in her bedroom wearing the despised blue-grey dress, nervous at the prospect of meeting so many new people in a strange house, and hoping that she would not be tongue-tied. She dabbed a little Evening in Paris behind her ears from the small, royal-blue bottle someone had given her for Christmas the previous year, and then picked up a canister of the latest innovation on the market — a hairspray by Max Factor called Top Secret, which Aunt Bee had been cajoled into buying her. Cautiously removing the lid, she aimed the nozzle at her head, only partially succeeding in covering her hair with the invisible haze, since most of it speckled the wallpaper above the dressing table with an array of tiny wet dots. Finally, she collected her handbag, making sure that the pastel-coloured handkerchiefs she had bought for Celia were securely inside in their pretty gift wrapping. It had been difficult deciding what to buy when pocket money was in short supply, but the handkerchiefs were fairly inexpensive. Pam's present, Charis knew, was a miniature china dog — a replica of Ross, Celia's Scottie.

"Have a nice evening, sweetheart," said Hugh, fondly appraising his daughter as she stood in the hall in her outdoor coat. "You look really special."

She glowed with pride.

"Be sure you're home by half past ten at the very latest. Half past ten, mind. Don't forget," Grace said with a note of warning.

Charis walked very slowly down the road to call for Pam, deliberately taking her time so as to postpone the moment when anticipation and apprehension would finally merge. Fireworks were exploding all around with ear-splitting cracks and thunderous booms, accompanied by the whoosh of rockets streaking across the sky, and cascades of multicoloured stars, while the night air was charged with the smell of acrid bonfire smoke rising from numerous back gardens.

In common with all the other houses at the far end of Wednesbury Road, Pam's, The Laburnums, was detached, spacious, double-fronted and gabled, with a gravel pathway leading to a solid oak door.

Charis had met Pam's mother, Jane, only on a few previous occasions, and had always found her intimidating. Tonight, heavily made-up and smoking a cocktail cigarette wrapped in cerise paper, she opened the door and greeted Charis with cool cordiality. An expensive fragrance wafted down the stairs in advance of Pam who, decked out in her new emerald-green silk dress with a low-cut, heart-shaped neckline and a neat little matching bolero, had never looked more fetching. Small gold earrings and a gold necklace glinted in the light, and, yet again, Charis knew only too well that it was impossible to rival Pam — impossible to look even one half as good — and her spirits sank.

"I needed a new bra to wear with this dress," Pam confessed with a sexy laugh as the door closed behind them. "Even then there wasn't enough of me to fill it properly, so I've had to stuff it with a couple of hankies. I hope they don't show."

As they approached Tamarisk Villa they could hear music, male voices and laughter. Opening the door Celia welcomed them warmly and Charis secretly admired her well-cut dress, the colour of burgundy wine, its scooped neckline and three-quarter-length sleeves edged with generous ruffles of cream lace. Behind her, a wide flight of thickly carpeted stairs rose from the centre of a large, parquet-floored hall on which Chinese rugs formed oval islands.

Frances Armitage joined her daughter to greet Charis and Pam, while Ross barked gruffly and snuffled round their ankles as they left their coats in a downstairs cloakroom, before being ushered into the lounge to be introduced to the other guests.

Several young people were grouped in a comfortable, spacious room, its pale walls, ceiling and furniture creating an impression of abundant light. Jewel-bright cushions were scattered on cream leather settees and armchairs, and Charis felt her high-heeled shoes sinking into the rich pile of the pale carpet.

She sensed at once that all these people were surrounded by an invisible aura, a heady mixture of wealth, confidence and savoir faire, setting them on an altogether higher plane than the one she inhabited, yet she experienced an urgent and overwhelming desire to be accepted by them and to join their ranks.

Celia reeled off her friends' names too quickly for Charis to remember them all, but she noticed Ronnie Costello at once, for Pam had already described him in some detail. It was difficult to ignore him anyway, since his appearance was strikingly different from any of the others. He was small, slim and exotic; his skin the warm colour of an apricot; his eyes deep-set and dark. His hair was short, curly and black, but his most unusual feature was a neatly trimmed black beard. Dressed in a black polo-necked sweater, he was tossing peanuts into the air and catching them in his mouth with some expertise. Charis was fascinated.

"Look at my birthday present from Barry," said Celia, lifting her slender wrist to display a silver bracelet from which dangled a selection of appropriately feminine, jingling charms: a kitten, a dainty shoe, a little jug, a bell. "Isn't it pretty?"

Barry Duggan was tall, with corn-coloured hair, combed back from his forehead in corrugated waves. He had a thin nose and lips and piercing blue eyes. He and Celia made an attractive couple, but he did not appeal to Charis in the physical way that Ronnie did.

"What will you have to drink, young lady?" asked Celia's father, a large, prosperous-looking man with a charming manner.

Charis hesitated. In her home alcohol made its appearance only at Christmas, and even then it was strictly limited.

"I can recommend the punch," Jack Armitage continued with a grin. "I made it myself, but it's not too lethal."

"What's in it this time?" asked Pam, confident and familiar with her friend's father. "I had some of your punch once before. Is it the same?"

"I ring the changes," said Jack. "This one is absolutely right for a chilly November evening. Try it."

The two girls followed him to a polished sideboard on which stood a large bowl filled to the brim with a steaming, reddish-gold brew. Jack Armitage ladled it into tumblers and they sipped cautiously. It was hot, spicy and delicious.

Babs Randle acknowledged Charis with a cool, fleeting smile and a nod. She and her boyfriend, Steve Parish, were stationed beside an electronic record player, the first Charis had ever seen at close quarters. It held eight records at a time, suspended on a spike in the centre of the turntable, and changed them automatically.

At her home there was only a heavy, old-fashioned, wind-up gramophone with an ancient, moth-eaten green baize turntable. Once a record had been played the steel needle had to be changed to avoid damaging the surface of the next. Her parents had no modern records; only those dating back to the 1920s and 30s, featuring classical music or the kind of songs performed at seaside concerts.

Most of Celia's guests had brought a few records of their own, and something bold, fast and rhythmic was now being played. It was vaguely familiar to Charis: "What *is* that tune?" she asked Pam.

"'American Patrol', I think."

"Good old Glenn Miller, but a bit dated now," said Ronnie Costello, suddenly materialising behind Pam. "I know his music's been popular ever since the war, but traditional jazz is the thing these days."

He spoke softly, his voice slightly higher in pitch than Charis would have expected, but decidedly masculine and very attractive.

"Do you mean the kind of stuff Louis Armstrong plays?" said Pam.

"That's right. He's brilliant, of course, but some of the English jazz bands are really good too. Haven't you heard of Humphrey Lyttelton?

Chris Barber? Ken Colyer?"

Pam and Charis looked blank.

"You will," said Ronnie, and then left them with a funny little bow as a very attractive girl arrived.

"That's Miranda Gates," said Pam. "You know, the one I mentioned before."

Charis was gratified that Miranda's acceptance had not after all jettisoned her own invitation to the party, and took a good look at her. She was petite and elfin, with a fascinating little bird-like nose, dainty feet and short, sculpted black-brown hair, brushed forward over her ears to frame her face.

Ronnie kissed Miranda's right cheek, then her left, and whispered something in her ear.

"Is she his girlfriend?" Charis asked Pam in a low voice.

"I'm not really sure. She certainly used to be, but he gets around and no one ever knows exactly who his latest is. Why? Are you interested?"

Charis blushed: "No, of *course* not. I just wondered."

The record changed.

"'In the Mood'," said Pam, with a saucy grin. "Are *you* in the mood, Mitch?"

"More punch, girls?" asked Jack Armitage.

Charis allowed her glass to be refilled to the brim.

"We'll be having the fireworks soon," Jack promised. "They're all ready, but I didn't want to set them off too early on."

Frances Armitage, a vivacious older version of her ash-blonde daughter, mingled easily with Celia's friends, the boys in particular warming to her charm: "Did you pass your driving test, Norman?" she asked a fair-skinned youth with a thatch of light hair.

"Just this week. What a relief! Now I'm waiting till my dad buys a new car and then I'll get his old one."

"Well done! Celia can't *wait* to start lessons. She's been watching Jack and me drive the car all her life, of course, so she already has some idea. Let's hope she'll do well." Frances turned to Pam and Charis as they stood by the sideboard: "I love your dress, Pam. What a marvellous colour! And yours too, Charis. Doesn't it do nice things for your eyes?"

Charis glowed. People rarely paid her compliments and this one boosted her confidence at once.

"Firework time," Jack Armitage announced at last. "Is Ross out of harm's way?"

"Yes. Shut in Celia's bedroom," said Frances.

Everyone trooped into a conservatory filled with terracotta pots of over-wintering plants. Some were arranged on long trestle tables; others stood on the floor. There were a couple of watering cans, empty flowerpots and a few garden tools stacked in one corner, and a trug basket, containing gardening gloves, a ball of string, secateurs, a trowel and a hand fork, standing on a low wooden table in another.

A flick of a switch plunged the conservatory into almost total darkness, the only light now coming from two Chinese lanterns suspended from a nearby tree and shining through the glass roof. The garden beyond was shrouded in darkness. Jack's shadowy figure was just recognisable as he picked his way over the lawn, aided by torchlight.

Everyone crowded forward to gain the best view of the impressive display that followed. Roman candles burst into red and green stars; rockets shrieked and whistled as they raced fiery-tailed across the night sky; Catherine wheels spun dizzily on tree trunks, and explosions of varying intensity were followed by cascades of technicolour stars, zigzags and tiny dots of light like confetti.

Charis was charmed: "Isn't it *lovely*?" she said, thinking that Pam was beside her.

"A pretty good display," a quiet voice answered and, turning, she found Ronnie Costello there instead. "Are you Charis?" he asked. "I suppose you are, as you arrived with Pam."

"Yes. How did you know my name?"

"I heard you'd been invited, but I haven't seen you around before."

Frances was mingling with the guests, and soon approached Ronnie and Charis: "Here, have some sparklers. They're *so* pretty."

The indoor fireworks made wild patterns of fizzing white light as they were waved around, but suddenly, shockingly, a banger exploded with a deafening retort inside the conservatory, followed by a series of short, sharp cracks as a handful of jumping jacks leapt across the floor on a crazily unpredictable course. Shouts and screams added to the general pandemonium. Garden tools and flowerpots were sent clattering noisily to the ground as people tried to escape from the leaping fire crackers in the limited, darkened space.

In that moment of minor panic, a girl standing just to Charis's right turned round sharply in blind confusion, cannoning into her with such force that they both went flying. Dazed and shocked, they tried to stand up together, but in so doing the other girl trod on the hem of Charis's dress and there came the sickening sound of tearing material.

"Are you OK, Charis?" asked Ronnie as he helped her to her feet. "I'd like to know what crazy fool started all this. What a prize idiot!"

Within seconds of the incident the conservatory was flooded with light, and Jack and Frances Armitage, clearly irritated, were checking on everyone's well-being. Their own nephew, Teddy Clack, was denounced as the culprit by his furious elder sister, Eileen (the girl who had collided with Charis), and made to apologise in front of them all.

"Can't think why he was invited in the first place," muttered Ronnie. "Younger than the rest of us, and always playing up."

"Is everyone all right now?" asked Frances. "It's such a pity that one stupid, thoughtless action can cause so much mayhem, but don't let it spoil the evening. Let's forget all about it, shall we? Time for supper now anyway, and I'm sure you're all ravenous."

Charis was imagining how her own mother would have reacted in a similar situation, and knew she would have been absolutely livid. She doubted whether Grace would have acted with the same restraint as that shown by Frances Armitage, and would probably have smouldered for the rest of the evening.

As for her dress, she dreaded to encounter the damage, quailing as she anticipated Grace's vexation, and it was only after this disturbing thought that she remembered with a faint rush of excitement that, for a few moments, Ronnie had actually been holding her hand.

Pam joined Charis in the dining room where bridge rolls, crustless sandwiches, vol-au-vents, various dips, sausages on sticks, potato crisps, and an interesting selection of cakes and biscuits were arranged on a large table.

Ronnie Costello had crossed to the far side of the room, and was talking to Miranda Gates as they stacked their plates with goodies.

"What a fuss!" said Pam. "What happened to you? I bumped into the watering cans and sent them flying. I told you how awful Teddy Clack was, didn't I?"

"My dress got torn. Look, it's ripped near the hemline. My mother will go absolutely *mad*."

"Don't tell her then. She won't notice it tonight, I shouldn't think, and you could probably get it mended without her knowing."

"Perhaps Aunt Bee would do it for me," said Charis, wondering why the idea hadn't occurred to her before. Aunt Bee was a dab hand with the needle and it wouldn't be the first time they had shared a secret.

"What was Ronnie saying to you?" It was clear that Pam missed little.

"Oh, nothing much. Just how silly he thought Teddy was."

When most of the food on display had disappeared, Frances, with a proud flourish, carried in Celia's birthday cake. Covered in white icing sugar, it was decorated with tiny pink shells, sixteen lighted candles, and the message 'Happy 16th, Celia' in pale-pink lettering. Everyone cheered when Celia extinguished all the candles at once, and then Frances cut neat slices of cake, handing them round to everyone.

At the same time, Jack Armitage uncorked a bottle of champagne with a victorious pop: "It isn't every day my daughter is sixteen," he said, "and a little of this isn't going to harm anyone."

"I don't like that stuff," Pam whispered, making a wry face.

"I've never tried it," Charis admitted.

The bubbles irritated the inside of her nose, and she disliked its sour, astringent taste, but at the same time enjoyed the challenge of experiencing something new.

By then it was half past nine. Charis and Pam trooped upstairs with some of the other girls to powder their noses and tidy their hair in the Armitage's master bedroom, while the boys used the downstairs cloakroom.

"I could *murder* my brother," said Eileen Clack. "I was so embarrassed I could have died."

"Jack and Fran weren't too pleased either," said Babs. "I don't suppose they'll invite him to another party until he's older."

"I wouldn't let him come, even if they did," said Eileen.

"Mitch's dress got torn," said Pam.

Charis blushed fiercely, further embarrassed by Pam's use of her nickname: "It's nothing," she said. "Really, it's nothing."

"I'm terribly sorry," said Eileen. "I'm afraid it must have been me who trod on it, but it wasn't my fault about the fireworks. I spend my life apologising for Teddy. One of these days he'll grow up, I suppose."

From downstairs came the sounds of dance music and popular songs. The girls rejoined the rest of the party grouped round the shiny, wood-block hall floor, where the rugs had been removed and dancing had already begun: Ronnie with Miranda; Barry with Celia.

"I like quicksteps," said Norman Fairway hovering close to Pam. "Care to dance?"

Charis watched admiringly from the doorway of the lounge as he swung Pam away. They had been taught the basics of ballroom dancing at special classes after school, taking it in turns with other girls to learn the men's steps so that everyone could join in. The nuns at Stella Maris had been wise enough to realise that a knowledge of ballroom dancing was a social necessity, but so far Charis had never had the opportunity of putting what she had learnt into practice.

She hoped desperately, yet rather dreaded, that one of the boys would ask her to dance, but when the quickstep ended Jack Armitage said, "Let's have a ladies' excuse-me now. Each time the music stops I want all the girls to find different partners. OK?"

It was a waltz.

Steve was with Babs; Norman with Pam again; Barry with Celia; Nick Buchanan with Rosemary Gordon, who had a soft-featured, kittenish face; Ronnie with Eileen this time; Jack with Miranda; only Teddy Clack was left.

'I can't bear it,' Charis thought, but even at that moment Teddy grabbed her roughly and propelled her on to the floor. He danced like a square, wooden box on legs which marched rather than glided, pumping her arm up and down at the same time, while perspiration streamed down his red cheeks from the sheer exertion. Frances was in charge of stopping the music and when she did so, Charis was hugely relieved.

"All change," Frances called. "Don't forget, only the girls have a choice of partner."

Jack Armitage was the nearest male, so Charis approached him timidly: "Delighted, my dear," he said, and swept her off expertly as the music restarted. "Are you enjoying yourself, despite all that earlier kerfuffle?"

"Very much, thank you," she whispered, at the same time watching Ronnie's every move as he danced now with Rosemary.

The music stopped again. This time Ronnie was nearby and Charis seized the opportunity: "Excuse me," she said shyly.

They were exactly the same height. The hand that held hers was pleasantly dry; the other pressed gently into her back. She rested her left hand on his shoulder and was immediately conscious of the softness of his sweater and the warmth from his body penetrating the wool. Ronnie danced lightly. He said nothing, but the thrill of his closeness was unbearably exciting.

There were no more partner changes, and another record began without an interval. This time it was 'Unforgettable' — a song that Charis had always loved.

As Nat King Cole's velvety voice suffused the atmosphere, Charis felt more and more drawn to Ronnie, while the incredibly romantic words of the song expressed exactly the wild, unfamiliar feelings she was now experiencing.

Dance steps were abandoned as the slow, dreamy music demanded little more than slight movement. Someone switched off the hall light, and in the sudden dimness Ronnie rested his cheek gently against hers — his skin warm, his beard not bristly as she would have expected, but pleasantly silky. It was like heaven, thought Charis. Bliss, bliss, sheer bliss.

At last the record ended, and the lights were bright again. Ronnie squeezed her hand as he had in the conservatory, and then the magic faded.

It was ten forty-five before Charis realised the time: "I'll have to go," she said anxiously to Pam, whose smug expression in no way concealed her delight that Norman Fairway was clearly smitten by her charms.

"Oh, must you?"

"Be *home* by ten-thirty, my mother said, and it's way past that already."

Charis explained briefly to Frances Armitage that she would have to leave right away.

"Oh, not yet surely, dear?" Frances replied. "We were planning to serve coffee at eleven o'clock just before the end of the party. Couldn't you stay till then?"

"No, I promised. I really must go right away."

"Well, if you're sure. I'll get Jack to run you up the road in the car."

"Don't worry, Fran. I'll take care of her." It was Ronnie. "Come on, Charis. Where's your coat?"

Dazed by this unexpected turn of events, she thanked Frances, Jack and Celia for the evening and said hurried goodbyes to Pam and a few of the others before following Ronnie down the Armitage's front path.

"Do you always call Mrs Armitage Fran?" she asked, impressed by his daring.

"Of course. Good old Fran," he said with a chuckle. "I've known her a while, and she doesn't mind at all. She's a real honey. You live nearer the other end of Wednesbury, don't you?"

Charis wondered how he knew, but did not pursue it.

"Have you enjoyed yourself?" he asked.

"Oh *yes*! If only I didn't have to go home yet. I loved the dancing. It was . . . just wonderful," she replied, wishing she could find a more appropriate word, and that this conversation, this entire evening, could last for ever.

By then they were strolling under some trees, known locally as the Wednesbury Beeches, where it was dark and secluded.

"You're a sweet, shy thing," Ronnie said. "How about a nice goodnight kiss before we get to your house?"

His arms were round her and his slightly open lips touched hers in a gentle, undemanding way, carrying with them an unfamiliar, teasingly bittersweet taste, vaguely reminiscent of geraniums mixed with cigarettes. He hugged her against him warmly, kissed her long and sweetly again and then released her, leaving her breathless and delighted.

"Didn't you expect me to do that?" he asked.

"I . . . I don't really know, but I'm awfully glad you did," said Charis, and then blushed at her temerity.

He laughed, but not unkindly.

It was another ten minutes before they were standing outside her house. She wondered if he would kiss her again, and hoped quite desperately that he would, but at that moment the front door opened and, to her horror, Grace emerged and strode briskly down the path to the gate: "Come in at once, Charis," she said crossly, ignoring Ronnie completely. "At once! Do you know what time it is? I asked you to be home by ten-thirty and you're at least an hour late. It simply isn't good enough."

Charis was speechless with embarrassment as Ronnie simply raised his eyebrows, gave another of his funny little bows, turned on his heels and walked back in the direction of Celia's house. Charis's evening was ruined; her humiliation absolute.

Christmas came and went, and on a wintry Saturday morning in the January of 1955, Charis was sitting in her bedroom, huddled as closely as possible to a one-bar electric fire, and balancing a handsome leather-bound diary on her knee. This had been a Christmas present from Aunt Bee and had a full page for each day of the year. It was altogether larger and more important looking than any she had owned before, and she was determined to write it up on a regular basis, unlike her feeble attempts in the two preceding years when her diaries were thin and small, with room only for the briefest of notes.

Charis hoped that this would be a memorable year and, although it was only eight days old, she kept wondering what lay ahead and whether perhaps, at last, she would meet someone really special. She would soon be sixteen, but so far her love life had been distinctly unexciting and devoid of romance.

For the past two months, though, she had thought of no one but Ronnie Costello, and today there was just the chance she would see him again. The idea scared and thrilled her so much that it made her catch her breath and feel shivery, although the latter sensation was more likely due to the low temperature of her bedroom.

The house was warm downstairs, heated by the kitchen stove and a coal fire roaring in the living room, but in Charis's bedroom it was difficult to allay the chill. She leant forward to peer in her dressing-table mirror before applying her make-up, rummaging in her floral cosmetic purse for her creme-puff compact. Her new lipstick, Petal Pink, had come from Woolworth's and was encased in a small, cheap-looking gilt tube. She was now on her fourth block of mascara, but her mother still had not noticed how much darker her eyelashes had become, which was a miracle.

She could hear Hugh shovelling coal from the outside bunker to replenish the living-room fire, and Grace in the kitchen fussing over Dizzy, their tabby cat. Grace had been cooking a cod's head for him in the special saucepan reserved for such delicacies, and the unpleasant odour of warm fish still lingered.

The weather had been bad, and Charis could not decide which outdoor shoes to wear. She had to make do with ugly black lace-ups with thick crepe soles for school in the winter, but this morning it was vitally important to look as smart as possible, so she decided to throw caution to the wind and chance her black high heels. Almost ready, she ran a comb through her hair, buttoned up her bottle-green coat and switched off the electric fire before venturing into the smallest of the three bedrooms where she could watch out for Pam's approach.

Outside, in Wednesbury Road, grubby cushions of snow lay piled at the side of pavements coated with ice and slush.

"Charis!" Grace called suddenly from downstairs. "Which shoes are you wearing?"

Charis groaned, anticipating a battle: "My black ones," she said, hopeful that Grace would think she meant the lace-ups.

"*Not* the high heels I hope? You're surely not going out in this weather wearing those? You'll slip on the ice."

To her dismay, Charis heard her mother's footsteps on the stairs just as Pam's familiar figure appeared in the distance, accompanied by Celia. Although Charis admired Celia enormously, her heart sank at having to compete with her as well as with Pam, for the former's trump card was impeccable grooming, while the latter's remained her devastating prettiness.

At that very moment Grace produced a pair of ghastly galoshes, which looked as though they had come out of the ark.

"Come along now, Charis, be sensible. Change into these to please me."

Charis, caught in the throes of turbulent adolescence, was rarely given to pleasing her mother, and today was no exception: "I'm *not* wearing those. They're *awful*. Anyway, that's Pam at the door now, and there isn't time to change."

Charis ran downstairs, opened the door and admitted a gust of frosty air.

"Ready?" Pam asked, smiling brightly.

"She thinks she's going out in those high-heeled shoes," Grace called crossly from halfway down the stairs, before Charis had time to answer Pam. "I've never heard such nonsense. She'll fall and break her leg on those pavements. Can't *you* make her see sense, Pamela?"

"It *is* pretty slippery," Pam admitted, but noticing Charis's fierce grimace in the direction of the ancient galoshes, tactfully she said no more.

Celia was waiting patiently at the gate, her feet clad elegantly in smart ankle boots with slightly raised heels. Pam, equally smart, was sporting brand-new sheepskin boots, calf-length and warmly lined.

Wearing a vexed expression, Grace thought for a moment and then said, "I know — how about Aunt Bee's boots? She left them here last week for your father to mend, and they're ready. You wouldn't mind wearing those, would you? You take the same size."

Celia, glancing questioningly at Charis's front door, rubbed her gloved hands together to keep warm, her breath forming wispy clouds. Grudgingly, Charis conceded defeat and zipped up Aunt Bee's ankle boots, which were made of brown leather with a little cuff. They made Charis feel dumpy and old-fashioned, but they were at least an improvement on the galoshes, and there was no time for further delay. She closed the door behind her and cautiously followed Pam down the treacherously glazed path to the gate.

"Are you going to the Zanzibar too, Celia?" Charis asked, not quite knowing whether she wanted the answer to be in the affirmative.

"It's doubtful," said Celia. "My mother wants me to get her a few odds and ends from the High Street, and then we're going to London to the Harrod's sale."

Celia was wearing an expensive-looking raincoat, with a wide belt and a matching rainproof sailor hat. With the exception of the Stella Maris regulation school beret, Charis never wore hats, regarding them as suitable only for mothers, aunts and old ladies, but she had to admit that the sailor hat looked very smart on Celia, sitting neatly on her short, ash-blonde hair.

Pam's coat was black with a nipped-in waist, fur collar and cuffs. A few

41

of her dark curls had escaped from under a cherry-red Kangol beret, and her smile revealed even teeth, enhanced by bright lipstick. As usual, Charis felt like the poor relation, but she was determined to go ahead with her resolve to brave the Zanzibar Café, the popular Saturday morning rendezvous for the cream of the local youth, whom she was about to confront for the first time since her humiliation on Guy Fawkes Day.

"I'll leave you two here," said Celia at the top of the road, where it forked into two streets of shops. "I may join you later for a little while, but I don't think I'll have time."

Charis was shivering again — partly with apprehension; partly with the chill of the raw, January morning. Pam, in complete contrast, was relaxed and grinning as they neared the Zanzibar Café, its windows so steamy that it was impossible to see inside.

"Don't worry, Mitch," said Pam. "He may not be here."

'Clearly,' thought Charis, 'she doesn't understand how much I *long* to see him again, almost as much as I dread it.'

Pam pushed open the glass door and a gust of warm, smoky air rushed out to meet them. High-backed wooden booths lined the entire length of one side of the café, and half the other side as well. Each booth comprised bright-red padded bench seats and yellow-topped tables, but the main feature of the café was a vivid mural covering the entire left-hand wall. It created the atmosphere of a tropical island, complete with palm trees, white sand, blue sea and brightly clad natives. The counter, on the right-hand side of the café opposite the mural, was stacked with tiers of cellophane-wrapped sandwiches and slices of cake perspiring behind perspex casing which, in turn, stood alongside stainless-steel coffee machines and large domes containing soft drinks.

Two ladies — one young; one middle-aged — were serving behind the counter. Business was brisk, and they looked harassed as they took money and gave change.

The café was packed with young people, mostly unknown to Charis but, huddled into one of the booths at the far end, she recognised Rosemary Gordon's heart-shaped face under a white angora beret, and the boy she remembered as Nick from Celia's party. The two of them were deep in conversation and oblivious to anyone else.

Pam handed Charis a mug of coffee, and they looked round for a seat.

"Can you see who else is here besides Rosemary and Nick?" asked Charis.

"I think Babs and Steve may be at the back too," said Pam, but Charis could tell she was only interested in whether or not Norman Fairway would put in an appearance.

"Are you going out with Norman tonight?" Charis asked her.

"Yes. We're going to a film at the Regal in Upsvale."

"Oh! You're not going to Holyoaks then?"

"We don't go *every* Saturday. There *are* other things besides Holyoaks, you know."

"But Celia goes every week, doesn't she?"

"She used to, but that was before she started going out regularly with Barry."

"How about the others? Do they always go?"

"I shouldn't think so, but it's still a good place to meet people. You should join, Mitch. You really should."

"Fat chance."

Since Celia's party, Charis's social life had been severely curtailed. She knew this was partly because Grace and Hugh were anxious for her to do well in the GCE exams in the summer, but she also suspected that Grace was suspicious about what might have happened with Ronnie Costello, and wanted to keep her daughter away from temptation.

"Have you done your holiday prep?" Charis asked Pam, remembering with gloomy shock that the return to school after the Christmas holidays, and the prospect of mock GCE exams, was looming.

"Oh, don't remind me," sighed Pam, whose interest in anything scholarly was exceedingly remote. "I've left it all till the last minute, as usual, and I don't know where to begin. Matty will have my guts for garters."

"Do you think she *wears* garters?"

They exploded into a fit of girlish giggles. Matty was Sister Matthew, Pam's elderly form mistress.

A little later, the door of the Zanzibar swung open and Norman Fairway hurried inside. Pam sat up straight and waved to catch his attention before he ordered his coffee and carried it over to their table.

"God, isn't it *cold!*" He rubbed his broad, pink hands together before warming them on the coffee mug, and pecking Pam on the cheek.

"Are we still going out tonight, Norm?" she asked.

"Yup. It starts at seven o'clock. I'll call for you at six-thirty, and I've got a surprise for you."

"What? *What?*"

"Wait till tonight."

"Oh you are *mean!*"

The door opened again to admit a slightly built male figure. Charis glimpsed curly black hair, a red and black striped scarf, a little black beard, a cigarette, and thought she would *die*. It was the first time she had seen Ronnie Costello since the fateful night of Celia's party, but she had thought of him so often and with such longing, and there he was, only a few yards away and looking just as irresistible as before.

Standing at the counter, he turned round halfway and acknowledged them, "Morning, girls. Morning, Norm. Everything OK? Lemon tea, please?"

Charis wondered how he could act so coolly and naturally when she

43

was prickling with discomfiture?

Tea in hand, he stopped by their table, pulled a rueful face for Charis's sole benefit, and then asked Norman and Pam about their plans for the evening. In less than a minute he was ambling off to join the shadowy group at the far end of the café, leaving Charis to face the unpleasant realisation that, despite being nearly sixteen, she would have a long, hard road to travel before anyone as desirable as Ronnie Costello would give her a second glance.

Early on a Sunday morning in February, Charis was wide awake and debating which would be the best way of avoiding church later on. She had used headaches, colds and feeling tired a little too often, so perhaps homework was the only plausible excuse left to her. Grace always looked reproachful and sad when her daughter missed Sunday services, but since Celia's party, Charis's mind had been fixed on far more earthbound matters, like her yearning for Ronnie Costello. Colin Crisp was another reason why she preferred to stay away, because he still pursued her whenever possible, and had sent her a card for her sixteenth birthday; an occasion so far removed from Celia's glittering celebration as to be a world away.

For a start Charis had never thought it much fun having a birthday in January. This year it had fallen on a Saturday, but it made no difference as Christmas was long forgotten, and nothing was festive any more. The weather was usually freezing, and there was never any question of a party. Grace was a very good cook and tried to make it a special day this year by producing a lovely iced fruit cake which had taken pride of place on the tea table, but only she and Hugh had been there to share it with Charis because Grandma Vanning (always known as Vanna) had been ill with bronchitis, and Aunt Bee had stayed at home to look after her.

Charis had relived the events of Celia's party many times, along with the unsatisfactory aspects of recent weeks when, despite going to the Zanzibar Café with Pam on most Saturday mornings, no one from Celia's exalted group had ever paid her the slightest attention, and Ronnie had only been there on her first visit.

Pam, on the other hand, had been having plenty of fun, with Norman Fairway taking her to Holyoaks, to local dances and to the cinema. More recently, he had been driving her further afield in his father's old car — the surprise he had had in store for her on the January morning when Charis had first ventured into the Zanzibar. Charis had thought Norman was really smitten with Pam, so the previous day's startling news that he had ditched her in favour of someone else had come as a great surprise.

Pam's reaction to his sudden defection was irritation rather than sorrow: "I was never all that keen on him anyway," she insisted when she told Charis the news. "I always thought he looked a bit soppy, and his hands were like slices of pink ham. Oh well, his new female's welcome to him. Good riddance! He was a drip, and he didn't have a clue how to kiss properly either."

Charis wondered how to recognise a proper kiss, but was determined not to reveal her ignorance. She simply murmured sympathetic words, while secretly reliving Ronnie's gently tantalising kisses under the Wednesbury Beeches. How would *they* rate in Pam's opinion? It gave her a moment of superiority knowing that she had kept them a secret from Pam, although, of course, she had had to reveal the evening's humiliating finale.

"Charis! Time to get up. Come along now, or you'll be late for church." — Grace's voice — the voice of doom.

Now Charis had only a few precious minutes to decide on an excuse which, she now knew, would almost certainly have to be homework. Actually she thought it would be perfectly honest and legitimate because she was anxious to finish her Julius Caesar essay, ideas for which had been gathering momentum in her mind ever since Friday's English lesson, given by the ever-fascinating, ever-surprising Irene Ingle.

Charis still marvelled at Maggie Rigg having had the pluck to ask Miss Ingle to divulge her Christian name. The entire class had held its breath, half expecting Maggie to be dismissed from the room, if not from the school, but Miss Ingle had simply laughed and spelt it out: "I R E N E — Irene. Please note, girls, that I pronounce it *Ireenee*, not *Ireen*. I'm aware that many people choose the other version, and of course that's entirely up to them, but *Ireenee* is more correct. I am always reminded of *The Forsyte Saga*, and simply cannot imagine Irene Forsyte being called *Ireen*. It would be a complete travesty."

Charis was pleased to have her own ideas on the name sanctioned by Miss Ingle. Ireen or Reenee always evoked images of stout, middle-aged ladies with permed, frizzy hair and accents which Grace would deplore. Ireenee on the other hand, perfectly suited Miss Ingle, who was slim, willowy and graceful and wore her corn-coloured hair in a long pageboy style.

Bernadette O'Malley, a timid little mouse of a girl with a silly schoolgirl crush on Miss Ingle, had been swift to demonstrate her ignorance: "Please, Miss Ingle, what's *The Forsyte Saga*?"

Miss Ingle had momentarily raised her eyes to the ceiling before saying; "Oh girls, girls, don't you know *ANYTHING*? *The Forsyte Saga* is a series of books written by John Galsworthy about an affluent and influential English family. I guarantee that you'll love it, but perhaps not until you're a little older. In the meanwhile, back to Julius Caesar, and don't forget I'm Miss Ingle to you *AT ALL TIMES*. Is that clear?"

Charis had longed to boast that, although she had never read the book, she knew quite a lot about *The Forsyte Saga*, having listened to it with her parents when it had been serialised on the wireless years before, but such an outpouring of pride would have been unthinkable.

At the breakfast table Charis endeavoured to excuse herself from church: "I don't think I'll have time to go. I still have my essay to finish, and learn loads of French vocab. We're being tested on it tomorrow."

Grace and Hugh exchanged glances.

"You should have done more homework yesterday," said Grace. "I told you not to go down to Pam's."

"She needed some help with her Maths," Charis protested, "and I wasn't there all that long."

Of course, they had spent much longer discussing Norman Fairway than quadratic equations, but Charis did not intend to enlighten her parents on that score.

"The service shouldn't be very long today," Grace coaxed. "The vicar's away, and you know how short Mr Rickard's sermons usually are."

Charis swallowed a piece of toast and marmalade, and recalled the moment when Pam had told her that her short-lived romance with Norman had floundered. In discovering that even Pam was not always lucky with her boyfriends, Charis had experienced a mean moment of triumph, an emotion which, she supposed, a true friend would not have entertained. This uncomfortable thought shamed her into deciding that she probably *ought* to go to church to make amends for her lack of generosity, and so, after all, she gave in quietly.

THREE

One memorable afternoon in late February, just before half-term, Celia Armitage invited Charis to join Holyoaks. The two of them had been travelling home together regularly on the bus since Pam had palled up with Polly Phillips, a girl in her own form, with whom she was usually so deep in whispered conversations, punctuated by much sniggering, that she was rarely ready to leave for home at the same time as Charis and Celia.

Thrilled and delighted, Charis hesitated for a moment before replying, "I'd simply *love* to go there, but I'm not sure my mother will let me."

"Why ever not?" said Celia. "It doesn't seem unreasonable to me. You're sixteen now, aren't you? Why don't you ask her? I started going to Holyoaks when I was *fifteen*, and so did Pam."

"Yes, I know, but your mother and Pam's are, well, different from mine somehow."

Celia smiled politely, and Charis wondered, not for the first time, how much she knew about the aftermath of her famous party.

"I don't know why, but there seems to be a big difference between being only fifteen and then being sixteen," Celia said. "It sounds older somehow, and you feel older too. Don't you think so?"

"I was *longing* to be sixteen," Charis admitted, "but so far it hasn't made any difference at all."

As they walked down Wednesbury Road, Celia said, "Why don't you ask your mother right now about joining Holyoaks? You can tell her it's held in the church hall, just next door to St Jude's, and it's very respectable. Don't get cross with her if she refuses at first. Just take your time, be persuasive, and I'm sure she'll let you go in the end. You can come with me to start with, but scores of people go so you'll have plenty of opportunities for making friends, and I'm sure it won't be long before you meet someone you like."

"It sounds so much better than the youth club at *my* church," said Charis. "Not that I go to that one any more."

"Where was that?"

"St Luke's."

"That's at Ockley, isn't it?"

"Yes. My parents like that church, and I've always been with them. I like it too, actually. At least, I *used* to."

"Has it changed, then?"

"No, but I suppose *I* have. Sometimes I don't think I believe in anything much any more, but I'm in the choir and everyone knows me and my parents, and it would upset them dreadfully if I left."

"It would be a pity to leave anyway," said Celia. "My parents never go to church, but what I've learnt from the nuns at school makes me think there must be something worthwhile about religious beliefs, and I've been to services at St Jude's from time to time. Babs and Steve go there regularly. It was Babs who introduced me to Holyoaks, but you don't have to belong to the church to join the club, which is just as well because I don't think many of the boys would go under those circumstances."

"How about Ronnie Costello?"

"Ronnie?" Celia smiled. "Somehow I can't see him in church, can you?"

Charis had to admit that she could not. He looked far too . . . what was the word her mother was so fond of using when describing people like him? Worldly? Yes, that was it, but oh how fascinating — how exciting! She shivered.

"What's the matter?" asked Celia gently. "Do you like Ronnie, or something?"

"*Like* him? I think he's *super!*" Charis hesitated a moment before continuing shyly, "Oh Celia, did he ever say anything about what happened after your party?"

"I heard your mother wasn't too pleased because you were late home," Celia admitted, "but I'm quite sure Ronnie didn't tell everyone. Whatever else he may be, he isn't mean. I suppose I shouldn't say this, but if you told Pam, *she* might have spread it around."

"I never thought of that. I *trusted* her."

"Well, it's all in the past now, anyway. I'd forget about it if I were you. We all get upset about things sometimes, but it doesn't do to dwell on them."

By then they were outside Charis's house: neat enough, but just an ordinary semi-detached property, and in every way inferior to Tamarisk Villa.

"Now don't forget," Celia instructed. "Ask your mother about Holyoaks. The sooner the better."

Grace, her clothes protected by a floral wrap-around apron, was washing up various bowls, the egg whisk and other utensils when Charis breezed into the kitchen.

"I've been busy baking all afternoon for Vi tomorrow," said Grace, drying her damp hands on the striped kitchen towel. "Have you had a good day at school?"

"Miss Ingle gave me 8 out of 10 for my English homework, but Louise got 9. I just can't outshine her."

"Well, you did last year when you came top in that special exam, and 8 out of 10 is very good."

"What's for tea, Mummy?" Charis was ravenous, as usual.

"Egg, chips and peas. Will that do?"

"Super! I'm *starving*. Is Aunt Vi coming to lunch as well as tea tomorrow?"

"Yes, of course. She wouldn't miss lunch. You know how much she enjoys the way I cook fish and chips, so we'll be having fried plaice. There'll be pancakes for dessert as it's Shrove Tuesday, and I've made jam tarts and scones for tea. I expect she'll still be here when you come home from school."

Charis had mixed feelings about her mother's old friend, Violet Leyton, who could be very nice, but on other occasions offhand, difficult, or, to use Grace's description, tricky.

With Grace in an unusually good mood, Charis decided to take the plunge with her bold request: "Celia asked me just now if I'd like to go to the Holyoaks Club at St Jude's with her. Do you think I could?"

Grace frowned momentarily and then said, "Well, I don't know about that. I had an idea you'd be wanting to go there sooner or later, but Daddy and I don't want you to get involved with that church. It isn't at all like ours. It's *very* high indeed, like Uncle Donald's. They call their vicar Father, and I believe they even have statues and incense, and at least six candles on the altar."

Charis had secretly attended Mass with some of her Catholic classmates in the chapel at Stella Maris on several occasions and did not share her mother's aversion to Roman practices. In fact, she positively enjoyed them, thinking that statues, incense and ceremonial added enormously to the appeal of the service. Grace would have been horrified if she had known, so Charis wisely kept her in the dark.

"Celia says you don't *have* to belong to the church. You can just join Holyoaks without any bother," said Charis, mentally keeping her fingers crossed.

"It seems rather odd. I'd have thought they would have wanted their own people at the club. Why don't you go back to the Greenfinches?"

It was some time now since Charis had been there, and she had no intention now of ever returning: "Oh Mummy, it's so *dead*. No one interesting goes there any more and I'm so fed up with Colin Crisp. He won't leave me alone."

"I've noticed," said Grace. "Daddy and I have nothing against him, but he doesn't seem very bright. Not the type of boy we'd like you to go out with seriously. We always hoped it would be Desmond Hoyt."

"*DID* you?" Charis was most surprised by this information.

"Knowing his parents made a difference, of course. They were such a nice family and we were all at the same church, which was very important to us. I suppose he was just that much too old for you, but later on a gap of four years is nothing."

"Do you ever hear anything about him?" Charis asked, more out of politeness than interest since any vague feelings she had ever harboured for Desmond were long gone, and she had always preferred Alan Decker anyway.

"He's doing very well at university. He has one more year there, and then, I suppose, he'll have to do his national service."

"What will he do eventually?"

"Teaching, Mrs Hoyt thinks. Probably Classics. He's such a *gifted* young man. We'd like you to meet someone with a good brain, you know."

The idea that her parents, particularly Grace, had even *thought* about her having a boyfriend was entirely new and surprising, but far more urgent matters were on her mind at that moment.

"*Can* I go to Holyoaks with Celia then?" she asked again. "*Please* let me, Mummy."

Grace hesitated, but not for long: "Oh well, I suppose so," she said, "since it's Celia who's invited you. She seems a sensible, level-headed girl."

"Oh *thank you*," said Charis, and rushed over to give Grace a hug, which nearly toppled her.

"Careful now," she said good-naturedly. "Don't crush me to death before I've fed Vi tomorrow."

"Can I phone Aunt Bee and tell her I'm going to Holyoaks?" said Charis, feeling somehow that this action would confirm Grace's agreement.

"If you like," said Grace, "but don't keep her too long."

Charis rushed off to speak to her beloved auntie.

Bee was three years younger than Grace, and her complete opposite. Grace was slender; Bee was rotund. Grace would brood; Bee was the eternal optimist. Grace was a regular churchgoer; Bee was not. As Charis grew up, she heard snippets about Bee's early years, but there were some areas of her life which were veiled in secrecy.

After leaving school, Bee had become a shop assistant in one of the London department stores. It was there that a certain Mr Sackville, one of the managers, had taken a fancy to her twinkling blue eyes and sunny disposition, and had singled her out for promotion to a clerical position with enhanced wages. Her benefactor had retired soon afterwards, but by then she was settled in a job she enjoyed, and spent her leisure time as a teenager and in her twenties being courted by a string of admirers. This capricious behaviour continued until she met dark-eyed Larry Brown, who stole her heart completely. Bee and Larry became engaged four years after Hugh and Grace married, but before they were able to make arrangements for their wedding Larry was killed in a wartime air raid. Grace told Charis that Bee had kept her intense grief very much to herself, but there were to be no more serious love affairs, and Bee remained single.

The last of the Vanning brood was Freddy, born in 1910. Charis knew very little about him as their paths had never crossed. She was told that he had been a chubby, freckle-faced, happy little boy, who grew into a handsome young man with the same sunny personality as Bee. He was adored by everyone and developed an eye for a pretty face from his early teens. He broke the hearts of all the girls he pursued, and was a constant worry to his parents. His main interest, apart from the opposite sex, was motor cars, and no one was surprised when he took up employment with an automobile company. He worked there until the outbreak of war when, aged twenty-nine, he joined the army. Very soon after being demobbed in 1945, Freddy married his most recent conquest, Isobel Sydney, of whom the family, particularly Grace and Donald, disapproved because she was a glamorous divorcee. Freddy and Isobel moved to Rochester in Kent, well out of the family orbit, and thereafter the Mitchells heard from them only at Christmas time.

The Vanning family had originally occupied an old, shabby, rambling Victorian house in Upsvale, but once Donald, Grace and Freddy had left home its size became impractical, so George, Constance and Bee moved to a much smaller terraced property. George died from natural causes early on in the war, so Charis never knew her grandfather. Then, in the late 1940s, Bee and Constance moved again due to a completely unexpected change in their fortunes, made possible by the demise of one Henry Gander.

The Ganders had been linked in friendship to the Vannings for many years. Henry and his wife, Doris, owned and ran a handiwork shop specialising in knitted and embroidered goods, and were both particularly fond of Bee. Then, during the severe winter of 1947, 'poor old Doris', as Bee described her, caught a bad cold which turned to pneumonia and led to her death. Once Henry began to recover from his loss he turned to Bee for help and support, knowing that she had considerable experience in the field of accounts. This led to him asking her to assist him in the financial side of running the shop instead of continuing at the London store, to which she had returned after VE day, following her wartime job in a munitions factory.

Around that time, Constance Vanning's arthritis worsened, and Bee was becoming disenchanted with travelling to and from London on crowded trains from Upsvale. She also felt that she needed more time to look after her mother, and so she made a snap decision to accept Henry's offer. Much to everyone's surprise, when Henry himself died a few years later, he left the shop, the flat above it and the bulk of his money to Bee. No one asked why, but they knew the Ganders were childless and had always favoured Bee, so they closed ranks and accepted the situation as Bee and Constance moved into the roomy flat over the shop. Bee renamed the shop The Beehive. Gladys Grove, the fragile spinster who had worked there for many years and was also devoted to Bee, stayed on and was perfectly willing to keep an eye on Constance whenever Bee wanted to take time away.

Pam was cool and casual about Charis joining Holyoaks, dismissing it as though it were already passé to go to the most prestigious club for young people in the neighbourhood. She had grown much more adventurous of late, often going to dances at the Starlight Ballroom in Upsvale with Polly Phillips. They had both met boys who had taken them home afterwards, and Pam skilfully doused Charis's momentous news with tales of her amorous adventures with one Trevor Quinn: "He was very fast . . . *YOU KNOW!*" she said, in the privacy of a booth at the Zanzibar one Saturday.

"What did he do?"

"Put his hands under my jumper and had a feel, and stuck his tongue in my mouth."

"I don't think I would have liked that," Charis said, feeling peculiar.

"It's called French kissing and it's much nicer than you'd think," said Pam. "Of course, it makes a difference if you really like someone, and I *do* like him. He's twenty-one."

Charis felt curiously tight and tense inside. Her limited knowledge of lovemaking came from tame romantic films she had seen, all of which had been carefully vetted by Grace beforehand to make sure they were suitable. Her mother took more interest in the content of films since the *No Room at the Inn* episode, and Charis had never yet seen a film with an X certificate. Pam, though, had managed to make herself look old enough to be admitted to *La Ronde*, following which the two girls had shared many a salacious conversation. Charis had also been pleasantly disturbed by titillating passages she had read in novels smuggled home from the local library and hidden under her bed, such as Pierre La Mure's *Moulin Rouge*, but now, all she could think to say was, "I hope he didn't notice the hankies you stuff in your bra."

Pam smirked: "You're behind the times," she said. "I don't need hankies any more. I've got two new bras: Berlei uplift with some built-in padding. They're *super!*"

"When did you get them?"

"My mother bought them for me. She guessed I could do with them."

Charis felt a great burning envy, recalling the time three years ago when, aged thirteen, she had quavered for *months* before asking Grace if she might have a bra — the first she had ever worn. True, her mother had been very understanding and had bought her two Marks and Spencer 32As, which were cheap enough, but Charis knew for certain that Grace would never have dreamed of even *suggesting* anything as daring and provocative as padded uplift bras, let alone buying them.

Celia sounded pleased when Charis told her the good news about being allowed to join Holyoaks: "When would you like to start?" she asked.

"Soon, but I'm not sure *exactly* when. I'll let you know," said Charis. She needed time to plead with Grace for something new to wear, and to have something done to her hair which was halfway down her back and becoming more and more unmanageable. "I wish my hair looked like yours, Celia," said Charis, envying her chic, modern style. "Which hairdresser do you go to?"

"Oh, that Italian place in Upsvale — Luigi's. Luigi himself cuts it for me, but it has some natural wave, so that's all I have done."

"Yours *always* looks so nice," said Charis. "Is it very expensive at Luigi's?"

"Seven and sixpence for a cut," said Celia.

Mr Forbes, the elderly gentleman who had been trimming Charis's hair since she was a toddler, charged only half a crown. His shop was clean but gloomy, old-fashioned and, Charis guessed, poles apart from Luigi's glamorous salon.

"Seven and six!" Grace exclaimed when Charis told her. "Daylight robbery! Your hair certainly needs cutting, but it won't be Luigi's for you, my girl. You'll have to go to Mr Forbes as usual."

Waiting her turn at the hairdresser's, Charis leafed through the usual pile of dog-eared women's magazines, turning the pages nonchalantly in search of interesting titbits and intriguing agony letters. Halfway through one of the more colourful periodicals she came across an article entitled:

Why be a Mouse?
Brighten up your appearance.
Make a statement.
Start living.

It was clearly written for people with nondescript colouring, and gave some stimulating ideas on choosing flattering make-up and clothes. Charis read on fascinated, and found herself yearning to wear something in a striking colour that would make people notice her instead of fading into the background as she usually did. Certain that she had made a momentous discovery, she was reluctant to part with the magazine and took it with her into Mr Forbes's cubicle.

"How are you today, Mr Forbes?" she asked politely.

"Mustn't grumble. A few aches and pains, but that's the penalty of getting old."

Charis made sympathetic noises before continuing, "I hope you don't mind my asking, but there's *such* an interesting article in this magazine. Do you think I could tear it out and take it home to keep?"

"Let's see," he replied. "That was one of last week's wasn't it? The new batch are due in tomorrow. Yes, I don't see why not. Help yourself."

Charis thanked him, and was soon sitting in front of the mirror with a white towel draped round her shoulders: "Just look at my hair," she groaned. "I used to like it long, but it grows awfully fast, and I don't think it really suits me. I wish I could do something different with it."

"You and your hair," said Mr Forbes with a chuckle. "I've never known anyone to be so unhappy with their crowning glory as you are."

"Crowning glory!" Charis snorted. "That's a joke. Honestly, I'm so *bored* with it. Couldn't you make it look a bit more interesting?"

Tut-tutting, Mr Forbes studied her face and profile for a little while before lifting up her long light-brown tresses and pushing them outwards at the sides: "I think a shorter style would suit you," he said. "You could do with a light perm, but I don't suppose your mother would approve of that, would she?"

"I don't know. How much would it cost?"

"Two guineas," said Mr Forbes.

Charis sighed.

"Well, let me style it for you anyway," he went on, "and we'll think about a perm another time." Snip, snip, snip. He was taking off the ends of her hair until it was shoulder length. "A little bit more, I think," he said, and continued with the trim until her hair at the sides of her face was level with her chin. Then he concentrated on the top and front, and she ended up with a neat little bob and a delicate fringe. "All you need now is a colour rinse to bring out your highlights," said Mr Forbes. "Your mother could do that for you. I can let you have one if you like. Let's see." He flicked through some sachets in a little drawer beside the basin and handed Charis one called Golden Haze: "Here you are. I won't charge you for it, but tell your mother I suggested it, and next time you can get one from Boots."

Grace's reaction was encouraging: "No one could have cut your hair better," she said. "It looks nice, but it'll take some getting used to, being shorter and with that fringe too." Charis was doubtful about how her mother would react to the colour rinse, but all she said was, "Well, I suppose it might be a good idea. I trust Mr Forbes. He knows what he's talking about, and perhaps your hair could do with a lift."

"I hardly recognised you, Mitch," said Maggie Rigg, when Charis arrived at school with her new hairdo. "Isn't it nice? Really attractive. And I do like your fringe."

Maggie had changed from the dumpy, rather prosaic youngster of earlier years into a supremely confident, attractive sixteen-year-old, and their friendship had blossomed once more now that Pam had become so attached to Polly Phillips.

Charis glowed in the warmth of Maggie's praise, but was still one step away from complete contentment as she desperately wanted something new to wear when she made her debut at Holyoaks, and guessed this would mean a further battle with Grace.

She saw the very thing in the window of Brooks' Ladies' Fashions in Upsvale when she and Grace were on their way to visit Aunt Bee and Vanna one Saturday afternoon. It was a high-necked red jumper, relieved by a white yoke, on which four small red buttons had been stitched by way of decoration.

"It's a nice enough style," Grace conceded, "but I don't know about red. Soft, gentle shades are more flattering and ladylike."

Charis was remembering the magazine article and its words of wisdom about making an impact in brighter colours. She decided to be diplomatic: "I know you never wear red yourself, Mummy," she said, "and perhaps *bright* red wouldn't look too good, but that jumper's a pinky sort of red. I think it would suit me, and I'd really love to have something like that to wear when I join Holyoaks."

"You could always wear your navy-blue jumper, of course," said Grace.

"Well, yes," Charis admitted, stifling an inward groan, "but there's a darn in the sleeve." She was still staring at the red jumper in pure enchantment, reluctant to move away: "It would look just perfect with my grey skirt," she continued persuasively.

"Come *along*, child," said Grace, clearly growing impatient. "We're already late, and you know how Vanna worries."

No further mention was made of the matter, so it came as the greatest surprise when Charis arrived home from school the following Wednesday and discovered a large paper bag lying on her bed. Inside, carefully wrapped in rustling tissue paper, was the coveted jumper, and she was so thrilled that she flew downstairs immediately to thank Grace.

"You should really be thanking Bee," said Grace. "I mentioned it to her on the phone and she was all in favour, so she bought it for you and we went halves on it."

Charis was ready by six-thirty the following Saturday evening, and waiting eagerly for Celia to call for her. The red jumper was a perfect fit and suited her well, cheering up her old grey skirt. Her black high heels and bottle-green outdoor coat completed her ensemble, and she felt really grown-up and pleased with her appearance. Her newly-styled hair had taken on a golden sheen after the colour rinse, and she had applied her make-up with the utmost care so that nothing was smudged or uneven, especially the mascara.

Celia looked as neat as ever in a light-beige coat, under which Charis noticed she was wearing a hyacinth-blue jumper and a beige and blue tweed skirt: "Barry's meeting us at the station bus stop. I hope you don't mind if he comes with us," she said.

"Of course not," Charis replied in the highest of spirits.

It was mild for mid-March. Illuminated by the street lamps, daffodils and narcissi in numerous front gardens along Wednesbury Road were swaying and nodding in the gentle breeze, some of the prunus trees were already lavishly starred with blossom, and a sharp, fruity scent emanated from bushes heavily hung with the deep-pink clusters of flowering currant. Charis loved the spring, and told Celia so.

"Me too. Everything looks so fresh and green and coming to life again after the winter."

Barry Duggan actually grinned at Charis: "You decided to risk it, then?"

"It isn't risky, is it?"

"Everything new is a risk. You may *hate* it. You may not. You don't know who you might meet, either. *That's* a risk too."

Celia rebuked him: "Don't put her off, Barry. I'm sure she's going to enjoy herself — aren't you, Charis?"

Celia always used her real name, which she appreciated. She did not much want to be known at Holyoaks as Mitch.

"I hope so," she replied.

"I think old Banjo Wilkinson might be there tonight," Barry said a moment later.

It was a while since Charis had heard that strange name, and she noted Celia's reaction — an immediate grimace: "*Banjo?* I haven't seen him for *months*. Where's he been hiding? I'd almost forgotten him," she said.

"I met him just the other day," said Barry. "He's still very keen on jazz. He was telling me he goes to London clubs as well as that one over at Warbridge. Apparently they get some good bands there, but the London ones are better."

Charis was puzzled that anyone should be called Banjo, and asked them why.

"It goes back a long way," Barry explained. "His name's really Joseph, but of course his family called him Jo. Apparently he was given a toy banjo as a toddler and someone saw him strumming away, making a fine old row, so the Jo turned into *Banjo*."

The first thing Charis noticed about St Jude's hall was its size in comparison with the drab little parish hall at St Luke's. It was a two-storeyed building, which they entered through double doors at the front. On the left of the entrance lobby a flight of stone steps led, she supposed, to the upper hall, and on the right stood a small kiosk complete with counter. This was manned by a fair-haired young man of about twenty, who was introduced to her as Leo Crewe.

"Leo's on the committee," Celia told Charis as they left their coats in the cloakroom. "You have to be on St Jude's electoral roll to qualify for a committee post, but anyone can be an ordinary club member as long as they have a proper introduction."

The walls inside the hall were painted in cream emulsion from the top to the halfway point, and in a dark-brown gloss, like Bournville chocolate, downwards to the floor. Tables and chairs grouped round the perimeter were occupied by scores of young people ranging in age from about fifteen to nineteen. A stage dominated the far end, fringed with dark-brown velvet curtains drawn back to display a large table supporting twin record players and a pile of records.

Celia nodded to a door on the left: "That leads to the annexe, used as the games room," she said, "and the one on the right is the kitchen."

Barry and Celia escorted Charis to a table where their friends were gathered. Rosemary Gordon, wearing a fluffy pink jumper and looking more like a chocolate-box kitten than ever, was being fussed over by Nick Buchanan, while Babs Randle and Steve Parish were absorbed in a record catalogue. They greeted Celia and Barry warmly but, as usual, were cool towards Charis, who immediately felt shy and isolated.

"I'm much more interested in English bands than I used to be," Steve was saying.

"Glenn Miller's still my favourite," said Babs, "but, I grant you, Chris Barber and the others have got something really special going for them."

"I wouldn't mind going to Warbridge Jazz Club one Saturday," said Celia. "How about it, Barry?"

"You surprise me sometimes," he replied. "I wouldn't have expected you to be interested in a place like that."

"I've been converted," said Celia. "Those jazz records Ronnie lent me were sensational."

"Playing records is one thing, but actually hearing a live band would be terrific," said Steve. "Why don't we all go together?"

"We've already been," purred Rosemary. "Didn't we tell you? I've never felt so hot in all my life."

"You never looked so hot either, sweetheart," said Nick indulgently, "but we had a whale of a time there."

Already, thought Charis, they were all several steps ahead of her. There she was, feeling frightfully grown-up because she had been allowed to join this prestigious club, but now everyone was champing at the bit to progress to more exciting forms of entertainment. It was bewildering but, despite her shyness, she resolved to enjoy every moment of the evening if she possibly could.

"Shall we play table tennis while we're waiting for the dancing to start?" said Celia. "Are you any good at it, Charis?"

She was, having played it so frequently at St Luke's. She knew it was something she could do without having to worry, so she readily agreed to join in.

"Let's have a mixed doubles, then. You partner Charis, Barry, and I'll rope in someone else to partner me."

The annexe was cacophonous with bouncing ping-pong balls, voices shouting out scores, and the clink of billiard cues. A darts match was in progress near the far end, four people were playing cards at a table with a green baize top in a nearby corner, and there was even a shove-halfpenny board tucked away at the back.

"How long will you be?" asked Barry of a couple playing table tennis.

"Nearly finished. Hang on."

Five minutes later the table was theirs, and Charis was able to demonstrate her prowess at the game, helping to score a convincing win for herself and Barry.

A bespectacled youth had been watching the game throughout, frequently calling out, "Good shot! Well done!" whenever Charis scored a point.

When the game ended he approached her: "You're good at table tennis," he said. "You must have had a lot of practice."

"Yes, I have, but I used to be hopeless."

"You're new here, aren't you? What's your name? I'm Tom Potterfield."

"Charis Mitchell. Yes, it's the first time I've been here."

"Pleased to meet you, Charis," he said. "Oh, good! I think the dancing's about to start. Will you come through and have the first one with me?"

Tom Potterfield swung Charis round the hall, dancing to a recording of 'Mr Sandman'. She studied him at close quarters, taking in kindly brown eyes behind ugly wire-framed National Health Service spectacles, dry lips which looked chapped and flaky, a cheerful smile, revealing slightly uneven teeth, and one or two minor red marks on his face where, she guessed, pimples had recently erupted.

"Are you still at school?" he asked.

"Yes. Stella Maris at Kemsworth."

"I know the one. I suppose you're a Catholic, then?"

"Good heavens, no. I'm C. of E."

"Me too. St Jude's is my church, and I'm at school at Eden House Grammar," he said.

Charis had heard that this was the school attended by Nick, Steve and Barry, and knew it had a first-rate academic record.

"Are you in the sixth form?" she asked, wondering how old he was.

"Yes, the lower sixth. I take GCE Advanced Level next year. How about you?"

"Five Alpha. GCE Ordinary Level this year, worse luck."

"What are your best subjects?"

"English, without a doubt, is my very best, but I'm not too bad at Maths and tolerably good at Art. How about you? What are you taking at

Advanced Level?"

"Maths, Science, Biology and Physics with Chemistry. I want to be a chemist, you see."

"Oh, do you? How interesting!"

Charis was pleased to find how easily she was chatting to Tom in so short a time.

'Mr Sandman, send me a dream.' The quickstep came to an abrupt end.

"I hope they play another one," said Tom. "I like quicksteps best of all. Waltzes are so slow, and I'm not too sure how to do the foxtrot properly."

"Carry on dancing," called Greg Duffy, the Holyoaks leader.

"Sounds like a Rosemary Clooney record. That'll do," said Tom, as 'This Old House' began. "Would you like to dance again?"

"Very much."

"Where do you live, Charis?"

She told him.

"You said you were C. of E. Which is your church?"

"St Luke's in Ockley."

"Really! Isn't that strange? I live in Ockley but I go to church here, and you do just the opposite."

After they had circled the hall about twice, a newcomer sidled over to the table where Babs, Steve, Barry and Celia, who had yet to dance, were deep in conversation. Charis's first impression was of a large fellow who could almost be described as ugly, yet, when she noticed his wide smile, his whole face became amusingly animated. As he talked he kept an eye on the couples dancing by, and when Charis spun past with Tom he looked her up and down as though making a rough assessment and then whispered something to Steve, who was nearest to him.

At the end of the quickstep Tom said, "I've promised someone a game of table tennis. Would you like to come and watch?"

Charis thanked him but declined, thinking that she ought to return to the others out of courtesy to Celia.

"I'll see you later then," he said, and strolled back towards the annexe.

The stranger was still standing beside Celia's table when Charis returned: "Well, he*llo*!" he said. "Where have *you* been all my life? What's your name? What's your phone number?"

"Hang on, Banjo, give the poor girl a chance," said Barry, and then introduced them.

"My *friends* call me Banjo, so you *certainly* must," he said. "Isn't she a poppet?" he remarked to the others at the table. "Are you going to dance with me?"

"If you'd like me to."

Just at that moment Greg Duffy announced a Paul Jones.

"She's been saved — temporarily," Steve Parish muttered.

Two circles formed, with boys on the outside, girls on the inside, and everyone marched round to the strains of 'A Life on the Ocean Wave'. When the music stopped Charis was opposite Nick Buchanan.

They danced awkwardly. Charis sensed Nick's eyes following Rosemary Gordon round the hall as she waltzed off in someone else's arms, and wondered whether anyone would ever show such singular interest in *her*.

After two further partner changes, Charis came face to face with Banjo Wilkinson, and the dance happened to be a foxtrot.

"I'm not too sure how to do this," she confessed.

"Not to worry, sweetie," said Banjo. "Just follow me."

He led her well, refraining from exaggerated steps, so that she soon began to relax and enjoy herself, stealing several furtive glances at him. She decided the best adjective to describe his face, nose and mouth was 'wide'. His eyes were of a nondescript colour, shadowed by untidy eyebrows which lent his expression great mobility, since he was constantly raising them either separately or together, but the smile he flashed at her was, as she had observed from the outset, the single characteristic which transformed him into a vibrant personality with an appetite for life.

"What a fabulous colour," said Banjo, eyeing her new jumper.

"Do you like red?"

"As a matter of fact it's my favourite, and it looks marvellous on you," he remarked, and then, with a frank stare at the gentle rounds of her slight bosom he added, "I like what's inside it too! I say, do you come here often?"

"This is my first time," she replied, thinking that surely he must already know that.

He roared with laughter: "You're clearly not a *Goon Show* fan."

Charis was mystified. Of course she had heard of the *Goon Show*, but had never listened to it on the wireless, as Grace and Hugh had dismissed it as utter gibberish after tuning in by mistake one evening.

"How do you know?" she asked innocently.

"I shan't tell you. Start listening and you'll soon find out."

After the Paul Jones there was a waltz.

"Again?" asked Banjo, and this time he held her much closer, so that she remembered the blissful evening when she had danced with Ronnie Costello. Banjo joined in with the crooner on the record, singing so close to her ear that it made her shiver. His hand was pressing firmly into the lower part of her back so that she was moulded even closer to his heavy body, and she experienced a mixture of excitement and an annoying, nagging anxiety. When the record ended he took her hand, which, like the rest of him, was larger than the norm, and led her back to the table where the others were assembling once more.

Refreshments were available halfway through the evening.

"I'll show you the kitchen, Charis," said Celia. "I've taken everyone's orders, so will you help me carry the trays back, please?"

Away from the others Celia said, "Banjo Wilkinson has his eye on you."

"Has he? Do you really think so?"

"It looks like it, doesn't it? He can be great fun, but if I were you I'd keep your distance for the time being."

"Oh. Why?"

Celia hesitated momentarily, "He has a bit of a reputation, you know."

Charis sighed. She was flattered by his interest, yet here was Celia, whom she truly admired and respected, trying to give her some kind of veiled warning. She wondered how the evening would progress.

Carefully carrying one of two trays of tea and biscuits, Charis followed Celia back to their table. By then, Banjo had Rosemary Gordon on his lap and was nuzzling the back of her neck.

"Yum, you gorgeous thing," Charis heard him saying as Rosemary tried to struggle free, but when he saw Charis he changed his line to, "That'll do now, Rosie. It's very naughty to seduce me like that the minute old Nick's back is turned."

"Shut *up*, Banjo," said Rosemary, smoothing down the folds of her skirt. "No one's safe with you around."

After the tea interlude a snowball waltz was announced.

"What's that?" Charis whispered to Celia, ashamed of her ignorance.

"It begins with one couple, and when the music stops they have to choose new partners until everyone's dancing."

Two couples; then four; then eight — by the time there were sixteen Charis noticed that Tom Potterfield was one of them, and at the first opportunity he asked her to dance again.

"Banjo's been monopolising you," he said, sounding reproachful.

"Do you know him well?" she asked.

"He's at my school. In the upper sixth."

Again she noticed Tom's brown eyes and their particularly kind expression. What a pity he wasn't more exciting though, she thought. She was *itching* to dance with Banjo again, even as Tom waltzed her round the hall.

"Will you be here next week?" he was asking.

"I expect so. I certainly *hope* so."

"Good!"

The music stopped, but now nearly everyone was dancing and there were certainly not enough people left to double up again.

"Right. We'll carry on with a gentlemen's excuse-me," Greg called from the stage.

"Excuse *ME*!" It was Banjo. "How did you enjoy dancing with old Potty?" he went on, pressing Charis hard against him.

"It was nice. *He's* nice," Charis replied, thinking how inane she must sound.

"*Nice?* Old Potty, *NICE?*" Banjo roared with laughter. "He's just an old swot. Never goes out with anyone. Never lets his hair down. Never does anything except study."

"He told me he wants to be a chemist." Charis sensed a need to defend Tom in some measure. "He'd have to work hard for that, wouldn't he?"

"Oh needle nardle noo," Banjo chanted. "Don't let's talk about him. This is *much* too good to waste time on old Potty."

The record being played was 'Softly, Softly', sung in a breathy little voice by Ruby Murray, who was enjoying great success with that particular number.

Again Banjo joined in, whispering the sugary, sentimental words closely into Charis's ear. "Can I see you home afterwards?" he asked.

At once she recalled the indignity of the Ronnie Costello incident, even before she remembered Celia's mild warning. Would Grace be lying in wait and come storming down the front path again? The prospect was too ghastly to contemplate, so hastily she devised a compromise: "Just as far as the station."

"Where do you live then?"

"Wednesbury Road."

"How far down?"

"Not far."

"Well, why can't I walk with you all the way?"

Charis was tongue-tied, not wishing to disclose her very real concerns about Grace's potentially embarrassing behaviour.

By then Ruby Murray was almost at the end of the song and time was running out for Charis in her efforts to think of a plausible excuse. Finally she decided that honesty was probably the best policy: "I have a difficult mother," she said simply.

"Oh I *see*," said Banjo. "That's what's known in the business as Mumtrub. I've met it before, but not *that* often, fortunately. OK. Just to the station *this* time, if you insist."

He danced with her for the rest of the evening, the last waltz beginning just before ten o'clock. She was surprised when the hall lights were extinguished, and those on the stage dimmed to a soft glow. At the darkest part of the hall, near the back, Banjo stopped dancing and kissed her, pushing his tongue forcefully between her lips and into her mouth. She was virtually glued to him, and then remembered how odd she had felt when Pam Sperry had described French kissing with Trevor Quinn: 'How silly of me,' she thought now, slightly shocked at herself, and then, as Banjo kissed her again, she found herself responding readily and actually enjoying it.

When the last waltz ended the lights came on again and there was some hasty shuffling and disentanglement.

"We'll end as usual with a short prayer," said Greg Duffy. "Father Kellow isn't here tonight, so I'll do the honours instead. Let's all be quiet now."

"Who's Father Kellow?" Charis whispered.

"The vicar," said Banjo, describing an imaginary halo round his head and gazing heavenwards.

It seemed a little inappropriate to be offering a prayer, however short, after the enticing pleasures afforded by the last waltz. Banjo suppressed irreverent snorts and giggles as Greg read a collect from the service of evensong.

In the ladies' cloakroom Celia said, "I suppose Banjo's seeing you home."

"Just to the station."

"Well take care, Charis. I'll see you on Monday. Good night."

"Good night, Celia, and thank you so much for introducing me. I've had a marvellous time."

Celia smiled, "Don't forget what I told you," she said.

Buttoning up her outdoor coat and shivering involuntarily, Charis found Banjo waiting for her outside the hall.

"Shall we walk or take the bus? Oh, let's walk," he said without waiting for an answer. "After all, it isn't that far, is it?" He put his arm round her, making her feel warm, wanted and undeniably excited: "Why haven't you been down here before?" he asked.

"No one invited me."

"Where have you been hiding yourself then?"

"I haven't been hiding."

"Well, where did you go to have fun?"

"*FUN!*" she spluttered. "I haven't had much fun at all, actually. I used to go the youth club at St Luke's, but it was awfully dull there."

"I don't know that one, but thanks for telling me. I'll give it a miss," said Banjo.

"Barry Duggan said you go to jazz clubs. *Do* you?"

"Oh yes, more often than not. Much more exciting than silly old church clubs. Oh, sweetie, don't let's talk. You *do* something to me you know. Come here."

By then they were passing a recreation area set back from the houses and shops along the main road. Banjo led her down an asphalt pathway to the cover of some trees and pushed her gently up against the trunk of one of them.

He kissed her even more enthusiastically than in the last waltz, and then unbuttoned her coat. Charis was very unsure what was expected of her, but sheer curiosity prevented her from stopping him. The next moment, in exactly the same way that Pam had described her experience with Trevor Quinn, his hands were inside her coat and fondling her breasts, first outside and then inside her red jumper. She began to feel trembly, realising that *at last* she was on the verge of discovering grown-up experiences which, so far, she had only read about in novels.

"Aren't you gorgeous?" Banjo whispered, continuing his exploration.

Charis supposed they stayed there for less than ten minutes, but it was long enough for Banjo's caresses to have shifted her bra into completely the wrong position, which made it feel most uncomfortable.

"Wasn't that nice, you little temptress?" he said, buttoning up her coat again, before adding, "I could stay here for *hours*, but I suppose that's not a very good idea."

As the lights of the station came into view Banjo said, "Give me your phone number and I'll call you during the week. I don't think I can wait until next Saturday to see you again."

Charis had been wanting to hear words such as those ever since she had hankered after Alan Decker in what seemed like another era: "It's Charters Lea 6507." She spoke distinctly so that there could be no mistake. "Will you remember?"

"It's written on old Banjo's heart," he said.

Charis floated down Wednesbury Road on winged feet and remembered just in time, once she had rung the front doorbell, to wriggle herself back properly inside her bra so that no suspicious looking bumps would be visible when she took off her coat.

Hugh opened the door: "Oh, you're back already, sweetheart," he said. "We wondered if you'd be later."

"How did you get on?" Grace called from the sitting room. "Come and tell us all about it."

Charis could not help thinking that if only her mother knew what she had been up to, she would have had far more cause for worry and complaint *tonight* than on the evening of Celia's party, when the walk home with Ronnie Costello had been so innocent.

'What the eye doesn't see . . . ' she thought to herself as she gave her parents a bland account of the evening, and a glowing description of Banjo Wilkinson.

In bed later that evening though, Charis was assailed by warring emotions. Although Banjo had seemed very interested in her, she still felt mixed up about what had happened on the way home. Should he have done that? Should she have let him? She resolved not to tell anyone about it so there would be no one with whom to compare notes, and she would have to live with any guilt feelings for the time being. It wasn't anything really *dreadful*, but quite naughty, she supposed. She had enjoyed it, which made her feel uncomfortable, and she blushed as she lay back against her pillows.

FOUR

On the Sunday morning after meeting Banjo, Charis went to church with a slight headache and a mixed-up feeling inside after a disturbed night. His attentions at Holyoaks and his behaviour on the way home convinced her that he was interested, and she had to admit that she found him fascinating and exciting. At the same time she still felt guilty because she had not stopped him fondling her, and all through matins she felt increasingly uneasy as she sang Lenten hymns and listened to a sermon about sin and repentance. Once the service was over, however, she allowed herself to relive the intimate moments of the previous evening with renewed delectation, and was anxious to tell her friends in the choir about her debut at Holyoaks, omitting the spicy parts.

"How was it? I've heard it's good there," said Patsy Beddowes as they stood outside church.

"More than good. *Super!*"

"Did you meet anyone?"

"Well, yes, I did actually."

Colin Crisp was hanging about as usual, and undoubtedly eavesdropping on their conversation, which made Charis feel vastly superior, if a trifle mean.

"What's his name?" asked Patsy.

"Joe," said Charis, not yet wishing to divulge his unique nickname. "He walked me to the station afterwards."

Colin looked crestfallen, but Charis was riding high on a cloud of triumphant pride, and virtually ignored him.

"Has he asked you out?" said Patsy.

"He said he'd phone me."

"Wh . . . what's so different about Holyoaks then?" Colin asked later, tagging along with Charis to the bus stop.

"Everything," she said. "They have ballroom dancing, and crowds more people than we ever had at Greenfinches, and it's all much more grown-up and sophisticated."

Charis had always considered Colin Crisp the least sophisticated boy in the world, but now, dazzled by Banjo, *anything* Colin might have to offer was totally eclipsed. She wished he would go away and leave her in peace, but instead he shocked her: "Well, p . . . p . . . perhaps I'll come along t . . . too and see for myself," he said.

"You'd *hate* it, Colin!" Charis said firmly. "It just wouldn't be your kind of thing. Anyway, you'd need someone to introduce you, and I'd be there with Joe, so you couldn't very well come with me. You'd be on your own, and — another thing — you can't dance, can you? I'm sorry, Colin, but it really wouldn't be a good idea, believe me."

Colin pulled a rueful face because it was true he couldn't dance, but by then they were at the bus stop where Grace and Hugh were waiting, so, much to Charis's relief, the conversation dried up.

On the way to school the next day Pam quizzed Charis about Holyoaks.

"I had a super time," Charis said, "and Banjo Wilkinson danced with me nearly all the evening, and walked me to the station."

Pam raised her eyebrows: "*Him!*" she exclaimed scornfully. "He's always on the lookout for someone new. The number of girls he's been out with you wouldn't believe. He never stays with any of them for long though. Love 'em and leave 'em, that's *his* motto." Charis was thrown off balance, unsure how to respond to this onslaught, but Pam continued mercilessly, "He used to be crazy about Miranda Gates. He went out with her for longer than most, as a matter of fact, but *she* was the one who did the packing up that time, which didn't please Banjo at all. As for Rosemary Gordon, he can't keep his eyes off her, or his hands, even though she's going steady with Nick."

Charis recalled the way Banjo had been nibbling the back of Rosemary's neck, and began to feel doubtful about him. She wished Pam had kept quiet, but it was too late now.

"He promised to ring me," Charis confided.

"Pigs might fly," said Pam over her shoulder as she wandered off down the corridor to Five Beta.

Maggie Rigg and Wendy King bombarded Charis with questions too.

Charis told them as much about Banjo as she chose, drawing the line at divulging the spicier aspects.

Wendy King looked wistful: "I wish I could join your club," she said. "Do you think I could?"

Maggie's protégé was a harmless, sweet little thing, who lived an even quieter social life than Charis's had been until recently.

"I can't really call it *my* club yet, but I don't see why you shouldn't come along, Wendy," said Charis. "I'll ask Celia about it, shall I?"

"No, don't do that," said Wendy quickly. "Not yet, anyway. Let me think about it first. Celia's so sure of herself that she makes me feel all fingers and thumbs."

"She's very nice when you get to know her," said Charis, "but I can understand how you feel. I used to think the same about her."

"I wouldn't mind joining either," said Maggie, "Celia or no Celia. But it's a good way from where Wendy and I live. Maybe in the summer when the evenings are lighter."

"I'd *love* that," said Charis, thinking how much her confidence would be boosted by having someone like Maggie with her at Holyoaks.

"When do you think this Banjo person will phone you then?" Maggie asked.

"I don't know. Soon, I hope."

When Wendy had gone off to the school canteen, Maggie and Charis settled down to one of their usual home-made sandwich lunches. It was then that Charis decided to quiz Maggie about the *Goon Show*: "I must ask you something, Maggie," she began. "Banjo said 'Do you come here often?' and then laughed when I answered, and said I obviously wasn't a *Goon Show* fan. What do you think he meant?"

"You mean to say you don't *know*?"

"That's why I'm asking you, idiot."

"It's a catchphrase. They're always saying it. You're supposed to answer 'Only in the mating season'," said Maggie with a saucy laugh.

Charis blushed, wondering why it was funny: "Well, how was I to know? I don't listen to the *Goon Show*."

"You'd better start before you get any more catchphrases thrown at you. Another one that's popular is 'Do you play the saxophone?'"

"There's surely no answer to that?" said Charis.

"Oh yes, there is. You say 'I'm trying to give it up', but you have to put on a Goonie kind of voice. It's no good my telling you. Listen to a few *Goon Shows* and you'll soon get into it. I did, but it took me a while."

"My parents think it's silly."

"*All* parents think it's silly. They don't understand it. It's too quick for them. That's what makes it special for people our age. It was my brother Bernard who got me interested. Honestly, Mitch, it's essential to cotton on to it."

When the bell rang for the end of the lunch break, Maggie groaned: "Do you realise it's double Latin now?" she said, pulling a mournful face. "Of all the subjects, I think Latin is the most awful, don't you?"

Charis was in full agreement, for not only was it a dry subject, but the nun who taught them — Sister Catherine — had a tedious voice and was very unattractive, with pebbly glasses and whiskers sprouting from her chin. The two girls dawdled down the corridor leading to Five Alpha, bracing themselves for an hour and a half of translating passages from Caesar's Gallic Wars.

Monday night; Tuesday night; Wednesday night — on each of those evenings, Charis waited in a state of high tension for a phone call from Banjo, and on each evening was disappointed. When it looked as though Thursday night was also to prove fruitless, she flung herself down on her bed at half past eight, battling against tears of frustration and pent-up anxiety until she unwittingly fell asleep.

She was woken at nine-fifteen by Grace shaking her and calling, "Wake up, Charis! Hurry up! It's that new friend of yours — Joe Wilkins or Wilkinson, is it? He wants to speak to you on the phone."

Disorientated at being roused so suddenly from sleep, Charis stumbled down the stairs to the telephone in the hall: "Hello," she said trying to sound alert. "Is that you, Banjo?"

"None other," he replied. "And how's my naughty little temptress this evening?"

"I'm just fine," she answered, hoping that Grace was safely out of earshot.

"Sorry I couldn't phone you earlier," he went on, "but I've been tied up one way and another all this week. Are you still going to Holyoaks on Saturday?"

"Well — yes," she said, still trying to convince herself that she was having this conversation.

"Good, good. I'll see you there then. Don't be late. Old Banjo will be waiting for you."

"I shan't be late, I promise," said Charis, thinking how odd it was that her mood could have changed so quickly from bleak despair to high elation just because of a brief phone call.

"Till Saturday then," said Banjo, and rang off swiftly.

On the Friday Celia said, "I'm not going to Holyoaks this week, Charis. I'm sorry, but it's Eileen's birthday and she's having a party."

Charis was crestfallen for a moment, but Pam saved the day by saying, "Trevor wants to see what it's like, for some strange reason. I can't imagine why he thinks it'll be better than a proper dance at the Starlight Ballroom, but we decided to make it tomorrow, so at least *we'll* be there."

"Oh good," said Charis. She had yet to meet Trevor Quinn and had often wondered what he was like. "Banjo rang me last night," she added proudly.

Once again she noticed an odd shadow cross Celia's face, but all she said was, "You won't be on your own after all then. I hope you have a good time."

The vexed question of clothes came up again when Charis rebelled against wearing the same outfit on two consecutive Saturdays.

"You are *impossible*," said Grace, sounding really cross. "All that fuss about wanting that red jumper, and even now you're not satisfied. I suppose you'll never wear it again."

"Of *course* I shall wear it — *lots* of times, but not *tomorrow*."

"I just don't understand you, child. *Why* not?"

"Oh, you're so *stupid*, Mummy!"

"Now, now, Charis. That'll do," said Hugh. "Don't be rude to your mother."

It was rare for her father to correct her, so on the occasions when he did so she took notice.

"I'm sorry," she said. "It's just that all the other girls always seem to have more clothes than I do, and it'd be nice to have a few more alternatives. I *can't* wear the same thing week after week."

"Genuine people don't worry about the clothes people wear; it's the character of the person inside that matters," said Grace sagely. She herself had a severely limited wardrobe, but then she rarely went anywhere exciting, and Charis felt light years away from her mother's strange notions.

During the evening Aunt Bee phoned, and after she had spoken to Grace it was Charis's turn.

"Hello, pet," said Aunt Bee. "How are you?"

"OK, thanks, Auntie." Grace did not approve of 'OK' and, as Charis caught her mother's disapproving look, she hastily corrected herself: "Sorry. All right, I mean."

Aunt Bee giggled in safety at the other end of the line: "And are you off to that club again tomorrow?"

"Yes, and I'm meeting Joe, the boy who was there last week. There's only one problem though, Auntie. I don't know what to wear. Mummy says I ought to wear the red jumper again, and I suppose I should really, but I *wish* I had just one more best one so that I could have a change."

"Of course you do, pet," said ever-understanding Aunt Bee. "Let me think a moment. You know, there's a hand-knitted jumper in my shop to show people how the pattern looks when it's made up. I think that might suit you, pet. Would you like to come over tomorrow afternoon and try it on?"

"Oh, Auntie, you're *marvellous*!" Charis cried. "What colour is it?"

"Wait and see. I'm sure you'll like it."

Grace raised her eyebrows, guessing that Charis was being spoilt by Aunt Bee, as usual, but she said nothing.

The jumper was white, with a polo neck and a single band of diamond shapes in striking shades of emerald-green and royal-blue across the front. It fitted well, and Charis hugged Aunt Bee and Vanna delightedly before hurrying home with her trophy and changing into it in readiness for the evening.

"I don't like it as much as the red one," said Grace, "and I never did care for a polo neck; it makes you look like a bottle."

"Oh, Mummy — *honestly!*" said Charis amused by the imaginative description, but too thrilled by the prospect of the forthcoming evening to take anything too seriously.

Pam and Trevor were going to Holyoaks directly from his home in Halstead where they were spending the afternoon together, engaged, Charis imagined, in questionable activities, so she went to Holyoaks alone. After only one previous visit this took a certain amount of courage, but she was helped enormously by the knowledge that Banjo would be waiting for her inside.

Once she had been welcomed by Leo Crewe, paid her sub, and hung up her coat, she was thrilled to see Banjo. He had clearly just told a joke to a group, including Nick and Rosemary, who were all giggling. He was wearing a chunky grey pullover and a pair of navy trousers, his comical, mobile face attracting her as surely as it had before.

"Cuddly Charis," he said, eyeing her new jumper. "As gorgeous as ever. My special sweater girl."

She blushed, remembering the previous week's experiences.

"Come and join the mob," said Banjo. "I've promised someone a game of billiards, but I'll be back with you as soon as the dancing starts."

As well as Nick and Rosemary, the mob comprised Steve, Babs, Norman Fairway, two strangers, and the exotic Miranda Gates, whom Charis had not seen since Celia's party. She smiled at them timidly, still shy of them all, and wondering at the same time how Pam would react when she arrived with Trevor Quinn and found Norman there with, presumably, his new girlfriend.

Miranda had never spoken to Charis before, but tonight was different: "You were at Celia's party last year, weren't you?" she said with a captivating smile. "I remember you, but I'm awfully sorry I can't recall your name." Charis told her, whereupon Miranda said, "How could I have forgotten when it's so unusual and pretty? Of course, you're at school with Celia, aren't you? Do you know if she'll be here tonight?"

"No. She's gone to a party — her cousin Eileen's."

"Oh yes, she did mention it some time ago, now I come to think of it. Oh well, I'll give her a ring tomorrow. This is Roger Drayton, by the way."

Miranda's friend was good-looking, with neatly cut dark hair, clear blue eyes and strong features. He smiled briefly at Charis as Norman said, "And this is Jackie."

Charis studied Norman's new girlfriend with interest, thinking how ordinary she looked in comparison with Pam. Jackie had long mousy hair, swept back from her forehead but falling straight like twin curtains on either side of her pale face. Black-framed spectacles kept slipping down the bridge of her finely chiselled nose, and she wore very little lipstick.

"Jackie, Roger and I are all at Mundy Park College," said Miranda. "Roger's doing Engineering, but Jackie and I are learning to be secretaries.

We'll have to take RSA Shorthand and Typing exams soon, but the thought of them isn't nearly as worrying as subjects like French and Maths used to be when we were at school; at least that's what *we* think, isn't it, Jackie?"

"Where do you want to work eventually?" asked Rosemary.

"Anywhere they'll have us — right, Jackie?" laughed Miranda. "I'm not too fussy, and once we become qualified secretaries there'll be hundreds of opportunities."

All of a sudden Norman Fairway sat bolt upright and said, "Oh no, look what the cat's brought in. It's Pam Sperry, or Spam Perry or something — I've quite forgotten," and everyone turned to witness the arrival of Pam and Trevor.

Pam was wearing a tight black dress and a chunky gold necklace. Her hair, curled in its usual style on one side of her face, was swept back severely on the other side with a comb. As she walked across the room she swung her hips seductively, their movement matching that of the golden hoops dangling from her ears: "Hi, everyone," she said with an impudent take-it-or-leave-it expression on her pretty, heavily made-up face. "This is Trevor Quinn."

Muttered greetings were exchanged all round, except from Norman, who averted his gaze and stayed ominously silent. Charis thought that Trevor's black greasy hair and sallow complexion made him look like a gypsy and he spoke with a distinctly Cockney accent, which Grace would have deplored. She wondered what Pam found attractive about him, before remembering the French kissing and wandering hands; and he had an undeniably sexy look about him.

Greg Duffy was busy shuffling records on the table beside the twin record players on the stage and, moments later, the dancing began and all the couples near Charis promptly took to the floor.

Wondering what had happened to Banjo, she was just beginning to feel awkward and lonely when Tom Potterfield materialised: "I'm really glad you're here again," he said as they danced. "Have you had a good week?"

"Not bad," said Charis, remembering the miserable evenings she had spent waiting for Banjo to telephone.

"Apart from school work and such, what do you like doing in your spare time?" asked Tom.

"Reading books mostly and playing with my cat."

"You've got a cat?"

"Yes. A tabby."

"I like cats. Ours is black and white."

"Called?"

"Domino, for obvious reasons."

Charis smiled. "Mine's called Dizzy because he was such a crazy kitten and always running round in circles," she explained.

Tom laughed, "I thought it might have had something to do with Dizzy

71

Gillespie," he said. "Do you know who I'm talking about?"

She shook her head.

"Jazzman," he said. "Do you like music?"

"I like this tune we're dancing to."

"I mean *real* music — classical."

"I'm not really sure. I don't know much about it, but I think I'd find long symphonies and things a bit boring."

"You don't go to concerts then?"

"No I don't, I'm afraid."

"We have a couple of music clubs at my school," said Tom. "I belong to the classical one, but there's a jazz one too."

"*Is* there?" said Charis, visualising the unreal scenario of raucous jazz music being played in the hallowed precincts of Stella Maris, where ballroom-dancing lessons had been accompanied by nothing more exciting than the highly respectable, strict-tempo music of Victor Sylvester.

"Our Music master is a man of hybrid taste you see," Tom continued. "He brings along all the best records — classical and jazz — and tells us about them so that we learn to appreciate them."

"When do you meet?"

"After school. Classical club on Tuesdays; jazz on Thursdays. I've been along to the jazz one too, but it just isn't my kind of music."

As Tom was speaking Charis noticed heads turning towards the entrance. At first she could not see who had arrived because other dancers were blocking her view, but she was elated when she discovered it was Ronnie Costello.

"Is something wrong?" Tom asked.

"No. Why should there be?"

"You seemed to tense up all of a sudden."

"Did I? Sorry. I've just seen someone I know, that's all," said Charis.

The record ended and Tom said, "I'd like to dance with you again later. May I?"

"Well, yes, but I'm really supposed to be here with Banjo," she said.

"Oh, are you?" He looked disappointed. "Well, perhaps if there's an excuse-me."

"*Ronnie!*" Miranda was smiling warmly at him and looking all aglow as Charis rejoined the group, "You haven't been here for ages. I didn't think you were ever coming back."

"How could I stay away any longer from all you gorgeous girls?" said Ronnie in his characteristically quiet voice. He was in the same soft-textured sweater he had worn at Celia's party, and looked small, warm and curiously vulnerable, like a furry woodland animal. Turning towards Charis he said, "So we meet again. How's life treating you these days?"

Just then Banjo emerged from the annexe.

"What's *he* doing back here?" said Ronnie with a frown.

"Ask Charis," said Nick. "It's his second week in a row."

Ronnie raised an eyebrow: "No need. I get the picture."

Banjo came directly to Charis's side, put an arm round her waist and gave her a possessive squeeze. Ronnie glowered at him, the hostility between them almost tangible.

Waltzing together moments later Banjo said: "Do you know Costello?"

"Yes. I met him at Celia's birthday party last November."

"He's an oddball. Bit of a loner. Doesn't get on with his old man either."

"Why not?"

"Totally different types. His old man wants him to go into the family business, but Ronnie's got other ideas."

A sudden notion crossed Charis's mind: "If you don't mind my asking, why weren't you at Celia's party?"

"Now there's a leading question," said Banjo. "The simple answer is I wasn't invited. They left poor old Banjo out in the cold. Speaking of cold, that's the word to describe Celia. Cold as ice. Not like you, gorgeous, nor Celia's mother. Now there's a *really* sporty lady."

Peering over Banjo's shoulder, Charis watched Trevor dancing with Pam, her arms round his neck and both his arms circling her waist instead of in the conventional hold. Roger and Miranda were deep in conversation, and Nick and Rosemary were dancing cheek to cheek. Ronnie was smoking a cigarette and watching the dancers through narrowed eyes.

"Changing the subject completely, it's the Boat Race next Saturday," said Banjo.

"Oh yes, I'd forgotten. Are you Oxford or Cambridge?" Charis enquired, hoping he was Oxford.

"Cambridge, of course. I always back winners."

"That's a pity. I'm Oxford."

"More fool you," said Banjo. "They're hopeless! I'll never forget the time they sank. 1951, wasn't it? Did you see it on television? It was the funniest thing ever."

Charis was too ashamed to admit that there had been no television at her house until quite recently.

"Anyway," Banjo went on, "I'm going up to town to watch it. Why don't you come too? Afterwards we could bodge around in London, have a bite to eat somewhere and then go on to a jazz club in the evening. How about it?"

Charis pictured Grace's reaction and her almost certain veto, but so flattered was she at being invited that she delayed the evil moment: "That sounds fun," she said enthusiastically.

"You'll come then?" said Banjo.

"I'd like to very much."

The dancing continued — another quickstep; a foxtrot; the Gay Gordons. After whirling round to the strains of a lively Scottish reel, everyone was ready for the refreshment break, during which Banjo said, "Anyone interested in seeing the Boat Race next Saturday?"

Charis tried to conceal her disappointment that Banjo intended to make it a group venture instead of a private date with her alone.

"Wouldn't mind," said Nick. "How about it, Rosie?"

"Where would we watch it from?"

"Barnes Bridge perhaps, or at the finish at Mortlake," said Banjo.

"I'd like to go," said Pam. "Wouldn't you, Trev?"

"Dunno," said Trevor. "I'll think about it."

"Count me out," said Ronnie shortly.

"And us," said Norman. "Jackie and I have other plans."

When Roger and Miranda returned with the refreshments Banjo asked them too. Roger, in particular, sounded enthusiastic — the more so when Banjo mentioned the evening visit to a London jazz club, but Miranda was non-committal.

"How many Oxfords? How many Cambridges?" asked Banjo.

Nick, Trevor and Charis were the only supporters of the dark-blues, but it was decided that the allegiances of the group would be sufficiently split to make watching the race exciting enough. Charis was increasingly certain that she would not be there, and the idea overshadowed the rest of the evening.

Later there was a snowball waltz, in the natural course of which Ronnie walked deliberately up to Charis and, ignoring Banjo completely, asked her to dance.

"It doesn't seem like four months since we danced at Celia's party," he said. "I was sorry you got into trouble afterwards."

"I've almost forgotten about it now," said Charis, "but it was horrid at the time."

"Are we friends?" asked Ronnie.

"Of course," she replied, all aglow, and noticing for the first time his long, curly eyelashes.

"Not shy of me any more?"

"No."

"Good. What are you doing getting mixed up with Banjo?"

"I like him."

"I can tell that, but he's not a very nice person, so be careful."

Charis began to feel slightly annoyed, although she was thrilled by Ronnie's proximity, finding herself more physically attracted to him than she was to outsized bumbling Banjo, whose feet, she had observed, were as large and wide as the rest of him.

"You're beginning to sound like my mother," she said.

"Oh I *hope* not!" Ronnie laughed.

"What have you got against Banjo?" she asked.

"That would be telling," said Ronnie, "but Celia can't stand him either.

Perhaps you'll find out from her some time. I mean what I say, you're a nice girl, Charis, so just be careful."

Walking home afterwards, Banjo once again led her to the dark protection of the trees in the recreation ground, but this time he progressed a little further by undoing her bra and fondling her breasts, unhindered by its protection. She felt her nipples stiffen under his touch and enjoyed the way he kissed her, responding enthusiastically to his slippery, probing tongue. It was thrilling too to be held so close to his large, heavy body, and feeling a large, mysterious protuberance pressing into her through her skirt.

"I think I'm falling in love with you," he mumbled against her ear. "How do you feel about me, sweetie?"

"I don't really know. You're nice," she said at first, feeling embarrassed and uncomfortable, then, completely out of her depth, she added, "but, yes, I'm sure I'm in love with you too."

His breathing became very heavy as he kissed her again, pulled her against him in an even tighter embrace, and finally released his grip.

"That was absolutely wonderful," he said panting, "but you've got me all hot and bothered, you saucy little temptress. I suppose I'd better get you home. We don't want any Mumtrub do we? Wait till next Saturday, gorgeous, and then we'll make time to be on our own for a lot longer so we can have extra fun and games like this and more besides." He laughed naughtily, stroking her breasts and playing with her dangling bra strap: "I'm an expert at getting these things unhooked," he said, "but not so good at doing them up again. I'll leave that to you."

That evening Charis allowed him to walk her to her house, relieved when he made no attempt to kiss her at the gate.

"I'll give you a ring about meeting next Saturday," he said. "I just can't *wait* to have you to myself again."

"Nor me," she answered.

Indoors, Charis took the plunge and told Grace about Banjo's plans. The veto was every bit as swift and final as Charis had feared: "Certainly not. I won't have you wandering round London all day with someone we don't know, and going to some dreadful dive in the evening. What were you thinking of agreeing to it in the first place? Who *is* this Joe Wilkinson anyway? If he's the type of person who enjoys going to a *jazz* club he just isn't a suitable friend for you. What a pity Celia wasn't there with you tonight. Surely *she* wouldn't have been prepared to go along with what he suggested."

Charis refrained from telling her either that Celia liked jazz or that she loathed Banjo.

"Why won't you ever let me do anything?" she demanded crossly.

"You wanted to join Holyoaks and I let you. Isn't that enough? You've only been going there for two weeks, after all."

"Pam's going to the Boat Race anyway," said Charis, "at least she said she was, and I can't see *her* mother stopping her."

"What Pam Sperry does is no concern of mine," said Grace sharply. "*You* are my daughter, not Pam Sperry, and I tell you for the last time, you are *not* going to London next Saturday."

Charis stormed up to her bedroom, listening to her mother's exasperated voice relaying the news to Hugh, and his "Oh dear . . . " followed by his usual sigh when battle was in progress between his wife and daughter.

Charis was thankful that she was there to answer the telephone herself when Banjo rang.

"All set for some high jinks on Saturday, sweetie?" he asked brightly.

"I don't know how to tell you," she said, "and I'm terribly sorry, but I shan't be able to go with you, after all."

"Really? Oh, that's a pity." He sounded a little put out, but certainly not devastated.

"I truly am awfully sorry."

"Was it Mumtrub?"

"Yes."

"Oh well, there's not much more to add, is there?" he said with a note of awful finality. There was a moment of silence on the telephone before Banjo said, "Cheerio then, sweetie. See you some time," and hung up.

Charis existed miserably for the remainder of the week, thinking constantly about Banjo and their ill-fated relationship.

On the Friday morning her unhappiness was compounded by Pam Sperry: "Trevor thinks the Holyoaks crowd are toffee-nosed," she said, "and he doesn't want to go to the Boat Race after all, so I asked Polly if she'd come with me instead. She was keen and Banjo said it was fine with him."

Polly Phillips had the reputation of being fast. Her full glossy lips always looked as though she was pouting, and her black hair was straight, shiny and thick, cut in a fringe and bobbed so that she resembled a Japanese doll. She made the greatest possible use of her large prominent eyes, which were a curiously light shade of green, ogling all the boys in her vicinity whenever the opportunity presented itself. She also flaunted a curvaceous figure, and Charis visualised Banjo, and probably all the other boys in the party too, feeling tempted by such irresistible charms, and guessed her own chances of ever going out with Banjo again were virtually nil. According to Pam, those in Banjo's Boat Race jaunt would now be Nick and Rosemary, Roger and Miranda, Polly and herself, and at least two others.

Charis wondered how to survive the coming Saturday. Her damaged pride would not allow her to go to Holyoaks without Banjo, so she braced herself for a cheerless evening, during which her imagination ran riot, clouded by fermenting anger against Grace, whom she saw as the root

76

cause of her present unhappiness, and rampant jealousy of all those within Banjo's hedonistic clique.

Pam relayed the outcome of Boat Race day to Charis by telephone: "We had a *fantastic* time," she began brightly. "We went to Mortlake to see the finish, and I cheered good old Cambridge like mad. Everyone wore mascots pinned to their coats. Ours were little men made out of navy-blue or pale-blue wool, but we could have got miniature pairs of oars or blue rosettes. There was a terrific atmosphere and Banjo was terribly funny. He was cracking jokes all the while and making everyone die laughing."

"I can imagine," said Charis bleakly. "Did he say anything about me?"

"Not that I can recall," said Pam. "Anyway, when the race was over we went back to London and had something to eat at a Lyons Corner House."

"How about the jazz club?"

"It was *fabulous*! Terrific music."

"Was there dancing?"

"Not *ballroom* dancing, but people did a special kind of jive. Polly and I joined in. We were quite good at it. Banjo seemed to think so, anyway."

Charis dreaded the answer to her next question: "What happened at the end?"

"Are you sure you want to know?"

"No, but tell me all the same."

"Well, we all came home together on the train. It wasn't all that late. We were back at Charters Lea by about half past eleven. You won't like what I'm going to tell you, but Banjo obviously took a fancy to Polly, and he went off with her. You know what he's like — always on the lookout for someone new." Charis gulped back tears as Pam went on: "The other funny thing was that Miranda didn't turn up after all, but Roger Drayton did, and — well — he took *me* home. Apparently, during the past week, things went a bit cold between them and he's asked me to go out with him now. Isn't it strange how much can happen in just a short time?"

Charis said nothing because she was still trying not to cry.

"I was getting fed up with Trevor, anyway," Pam continued. "He didn't fit in very well with my friends, and my parents didn't like him at all. Roger's much more interesting, and he's better-looking too."

When Pam rang off Charis retreated to her bedroom, imagining the intimate details of Banjo and Polly's homeward journey. She guessed he would have enjoyed exploring inside Polly's bra more than he had in hers, as Polly was well endowed and at least three sizes larger. She wondered too how Polly would have responded. If she was at all like Pam, and Charis was pretty sure she was even more adventurous, Banjo wouldn't have been the first boy to have played around with her, and Polly would have welcomed his advances without question.

Charis was tangled up in such a web of envy and bitter disappointment that she was at a loss to know what to do. The only small crumb of comfort was that it had been Polly rather than Pam whom Banjo had fancied, for the idea of Pam enjoying Banjo's attentions and becoming his girlfriend would have been ten times harder to bear.

As the days went by Charis began to feel a little less despondent.

She was supported by Maggie Rigg's loyalty and friendship: "Someone who could drop you like that isn't worth knowing, Mitch," she said. "If he really liked you, he would have suggested taking you somewhere instead of London."

"Yes, but everyone else was in on it, and all the plans were made for meeting. He couldn't cancel everything just because of me."

"Maybe not, but he could certainly help getting mixed up with Polly."

"I can't bear looking at her," said Charis bitterly.

"No one likes her much — not the girls at school, anyway," said Maggie. "I shouldn't let her worry you. Try to forget Banjo. There are plenty more fish in the sea. There must be lots of nice boys at Holyoaks. Are you going back this week?"

"I can't face it," Charis admitted. "Supposing Banjo was there with Polly. It would be unbearable."

Celia was sympathetic too: "I did try to warn you," she said. "He's one of the most fickle characters I've ever met; not a nice person at all."

"Will you be going to Holyoaks this week?" asked Charis.

"I'm afraid not," said Celia. "Eileen and I are going to Warbridge Jazz Club with Babs and Steve."

"Not Barry?"

Celia shrugged: "Things aren't too rosy between us just now," she said.

Charis was astounded. Barry and Celia had been a positive institution for little short of a year.

"What happened?" she asked, wondering whether she ought to pry.

"I was simply getting bored with him," said Celia. "He had such fixed ideas about everything, and never wanted to try anything new. I very much wanted to go to the jazz club, just to see what it was like, but he wouldn't take me there, so I made other arrangements and, of course, that made him cross."

"I'm awfully sorry," said Charis. "I always thought you two were the perfect partnership."

"Barry was getting far too serious," said Celia. "It worried me. I didn't want to be tied to him — after all, I'm only sixteen."

"I wish someone would get serious about me," said Charis, aware that she sounded wistful. "If only I'd been allowed to go on that Boat Race trip with Banjo, who knows?"

"I don't think Banjo could be serious with *anyone* for long," said Celia.

"But I liked him *so* much, and I really thought he liked me too."

"What do I have to say to convince you that he's not a very nice person?"

said Celia. "Look, I'll tell you a secret, but you must promise never to breathe a word to anyone else."

"I promise," said Charis, immediately curious.

"It was some time ago now, but it was at one of the parties at my house. Banjo was in the picture then. He'd been trying to get me to go out with him, but I wasn't particularly interested and it annoyed him. The party was nearly over. Some of us were dancing, but my mother went into the garden to call Ross. Banjo followed her out and made a pass at her, but unfortunately for him my father saw what was happening. He was absolutely livid and told Banjo to leave at once. As you can imagine, he was never invited back, and I can't bear to be anywhere near him now."

"He made a pass at your *mother*? What on earth did he *do*?"

"He was kissing and cuddling her under our cherry tree."

Charis was deeply shocked, yet gratified that Celia had trusted her enough to confide in her. At the same time she remembered Banjo's description of Celia as 'cold' and of Frances Armitage as 'a really sporty lady'. These were matters which she would keep to herself for all time, yet she found herself speculating on how Frances might have reacted to Banjo's advances had Jack Armitage not intervened, for she was undoubtedly a very attractive woman, whilst Banjo, despite being her junior by many years, was clearly well versed in the art of seduction.

Charis stayed at home on the Saturday evening following the Boat Race debacle, and then school broke up and Holyoaks closed for Easter. Pam's new relationship with Roger Drayton blossomed, and Celia's break with Barry became permanent when she met Mark Earle, a medical student from Guy's Hospital, at Warbridge Jazz Club. As for Charis, it was like being back in the boring old days before her first visit to Holyoaks. Life seemed unbelievably dull, and would probably remain so.

Following sung Eucharist at St Luke's on Easter Sunday morning, while Charis was walking to the bus stop as usual with Colin Crisp, he happened to ask her about Holyoaks, and she told him there had been no meeting the previous evening because of Easter.

"H . . . how about that person you met there?" he said. "Are you st . . . still s . . . seeing him?"

Charis rather wished she could tell an outright lie, but she compromised with, "Not really. It was never at all serious."

It was then that Colin asked her to meet him for a stroll in the park the next day and, when she agreed, due solely to a feeling of hopeless desperation, he was so surprised and delighted that his expression was quite comical. He would call for her at two o'clock, he said.

On Easter Monday, Hugh was taking advantage of the fine spring weather to mow the back lawn. Charis could smell the sweet, damp, green scent of freshly cut grass, and hear the whirring, grating sounds of the blades as he guided the mower up and down to make beautifully straight lines. She could just make out Dizzy, safely out of harm's way at the far end of the garden, and could imagine him blinking sleepily in the sunshine as he lay halfway under a blackcurrant bush, one eye on the lookout for any passing sparrow or blue tit.

Next door, at No. 24, Arthur Farrow was pottering about in his greenhouse, while his wife, Emily, was pegging out washing as she always did on Mondays, even when it was a bank holiday. They were a dumpy, severe-looking couple in their sixties — ardent chapelgoers who mostly kept themselves to themselves, but were not averse to making critical comments on occasion. Arthur Farrow had been a departmental manager in a small insurance company, retiring with enough pension and savings to enable him and his wife to live in modest comfort.

The neighbours on the other side were the Walsh family, comprising father, mother, and twenty-year-old daughter, Beverley, all of whom had gone away for Easter. Ned Walsh worked in the head office of an electrical firm, whilst his wife, Cynthia, a breezy, capable woman, was much involved with the local branch of the Women's Institute. They also had a married son called Gary, who had taken up the army as a career.

As Charis leant out of her bedroom window overlooking the garden she recalled a recent conversation between her parents on the topic of neighbours: "Everybody in this road has more money than we do," Grace had begun.

"Does it matter? We manage quite well," Hugh replied.

"Oh yes, we *manage*, but no one else has to scrimp and save the way we do, and no one else's husband down here wears a *uniform*."

"We've talked about this *so* many times," said Hugh. "I can't see what difference it makes. We get along well with everyone. No one is unpleasant to us."

"How about the Farrows?" said Grace. "I've never been comfortable with *them*. Don't you remember when our apple tree was overhanging their garden and he sawed the branch off and threw it over the fence? *And* he did the same with the windfalls, and never said a word."

"Well, of course, that's the law. He didn't do anything wrong."

"I know that, but it wasn't very friendly."

Discussions of this nature were a fairly regular occurrence which Charis thoroughly disliked. Ever since she could remember Grace had harboured feelings of inferiority because of Hugh's job, engendered because everyone else's husband in the near vicinity worked in banking or insurance or the civil service.

"We're conspicuous in Charters Lea because of your uniform," Grace continued. "We're stamped 'working class', and everyone looks down on us."

"I just don't think that's true," said Hugh. "Most people treat us exactly the same as they do everyone else."

"If they do, it's only because we know our place. We're quiet and respectable, and we've ensured that Charis speaks properly and behaves herself. That's all very well but, underneath it all, the people round here still think we're a lower class than they are. I wouldn't mind betting that most of them wonder how we ever managed to afford a mortgage for this house in the first place."

"It's none of their business, of course," said Hugh, "but it wasn't a crime for Adelaide to leave us money in her will, was it? If she hadn't, we wouldn't be living in this district at all. You wouldn't have been happy in a small house in Halstead, and that's for sure."

Charis and Hugh were used to Grace's periodic outbursts of dissatisfaction which, as on that occasion, usually ended with an uneasy truce.

Charis always tried to be polite to the neighbours, although she did not like the Farrows any more than did Grace. The Walshes were more approachable but, even so, their paths rarely crossed.

In the kitchen downstairs Grace had transferred rounds cut from a flat oval of rolled-out pastry to a baking tray, and was carefully placing apricot jam in the centre of each one.

'Just like the Queen of Hearts,' thought Charis, not daring to interrupt as she slipped past her mother and stepped outside to see how Hugh was progressing with the lawn.

"Nearly finished, Daddy?"

He straightened his back and mopped his forehead with a large handkerchief: "Just the edges to be done and some weeding," he said. "Feel like helping?"

"OK."

"Good thing your mother didn't hear you say that!"

"Why is she so fussy, Daddy? *Everyone* says OK."

"She thinks it's American and a bit common. She wants you to speak like a lady. You know that."

"But even *Celia* says OK."

"I expect she does, but your mother doesn't like it, so try not to say it when she's around."

Hugh winked at her sympathetically: "Go and get the trowel. I left it on the table outside the back door. Have a go at getting rid of that chickweed in the rose bed, will you?"

Dizzy ambled down the lawn to investigate, and an appetising baking smell issued from the kitchen. Charis knelt on an old piece of sacking, sat back on her heels and began to attack the weeds, which lifted out easily as she dug under them with the trowel. For the umpteenth time since the previous day she asked herself why on earth she had finally agreed to see Colin Crisp of *all* people, and how it could be that so much had changed in the space of just a few short weeks.

Coniston Park was very popular. As well as a shallow pond where children could float their toy yachts, there was a large boating lake for adults, some swings and roundabouts, several tennis courts, well-maintained flower beds, a sizeable wooded area and wide stretches of open grassland.

As Colin and Charis dawdled on one of the paths to watch children playing with kites, Colin said, "It was n . . . nice of your mother to ask me back for tea. I've always liked her — *and* your father, of course."

Was he being truthful, or merely polite? Charis wondered.

"She can be OK sometimes, but I wasn't even *speaking* to her last weekend," she said.

"Weren't you? Why was that?"

"Oh, never mind."

"D . . . don't you get on with her?"

"Not always. She stops me doing things."

"It's my *father* who st . . . stops me. My m . . . mother is very understanding."

"I don't know your father. Why doesn't he come to church?"

"He's an agnostic, but he d . . . doesn't mind my mother and me going to St Luke's just as long as he doesn't have to."

By then they were by the lake, which was crowded with boats containing groups of up to four people.

"Shall we take a b . . . boat out?" said Colin.

"Definitely not," Charis insisted. "I can't swim, so I can't afford to risk it."

"You really *m . . . mean* you can't swim? That's amazing. I've b . . . b . . . been swimming since I was about five."

"My mother never wanted me to learn, and I can't say it's ever appealed to me either."

Just then Charis heard familiar laughter and, to her dismay, saw Banjo playing the fool in one of the boats for the sole benefit of Polly Phillips, who was alternately giggling and shrieking as he stood up and balanced on one leg.

"What a s . . . silly thing to do," said Colin, unaware that Banjo had been the other party in Charis's recent relationship. "He deserves to fall in."

"Hear, hear," she agreed fervently.

Almost at the same time the man in charge of the boats shouted through a loudspeaker: "That's enough of that, No. 4. No standing up in the boats. No horseplay. Any more nonsense and there'll be a fine to pay."

Charis winced as she recognised one of Banjo's well-rehearsed *Goon Show* responses — a convincing take-off of Bluebottle — "Shut up, Eccles!" followed by Polly's admiring giggle.

Later, despite despising Banjo for playing the fool on the boating lake, she was assailed by waves of envy as she observed him walking, closely entwined with Polly, in the direction of the woods. She felt a painful, desperate longing to experience once again the thrill of his large exploring hands and his probing tongue in her mouth. Meanwhile, baby-faced, fair-haired little Colin padded along beside her, not attempting even to hold her hand although, even if he had tried, she would probably have snatched it away in sheer frustration. The gap between Banjo's enticing boldness and Colin's inexperience and temerity was immeasurable, and the whole afternoon had been so utterly pointless that she vowed it would be her first and last date with him.

"Oh, come on, let's go home," she murmured flatly.

FIVE

Holyoaks reopened on the Saturday after Easter, but Charis stayed home again, still too mortified to put in an appearance. She returned to school for the summer term the following Monday morning, and found Celia and Pam waiting together at the bus stop. Slightly out of breath from running because she was late leaving home, Charis joined them as they were recounting recent events.

"Mark and I went to Warbridge Jazz Club again," Celia was saying. "It's fairly respectable, but incredibly noisy. Phil Duke's band was playing. They're getting very popular. I've even heard them on the wireless."

"We were at Holyoaks again," said Pam.

"Who was there?" asked Charis, rather dreading the reply.

"Not Banjo, if that's who you mean. Holyoaks isn't exciting enough for Polly, so there's not much chance of them turning up there very often."

Encouraged by this news, Charis spent much of the morning debating whether or not she had sufficient courage to return to the club on her own, but her mind was made up by Maggie at lunchtime: "I've been thinking, Mitch," she said. "Now that the evenings are lighter I might join you one Saturday at Holyoaks, if you think it would be OK."

"I'd *love* you to, Maggie," said Charis. "Why shouldn't it be OK?"

"Well, because I'm a Catholic and all that. They wouldn't bar me, would they?"

"Of course not, but how would they know? You don't have to fill in any forms or anything. You just turn up, but I think you have to go with someone who's already been a few times. I suppose I might be able to introduce you."

"Well, how about next Saturday, then?"

"I've been trying to pluck up courage to go back, so that settles it," said Charis. "How did you guess?"

"Feminine intuition," said Maggie. "Besides, I said before that I'd like to join you in the summer, didn't I?"

"Yes. So did Wendy, now I come to think of it. What shall we do about her?"

"The more the merrier," said Maggie. "Let's ask her now."

When Charis went home that evening, Grace opened the door looking grave: "Vanna's in hospital," she said. "Bee telephoned this afternoon to say she'd had a fall at the flat. She's being X-rayed to see if there are any broken bones."

Charis was shocked and very upset. Vanna was a dear old lady, and she couldn't bear to think of her being ill or, unimaginably, dying: "How awful," she said, feeling weepy. "Do you think she'll be all right?"

"God willing," said Grace. "We must pray for her, and leave her in His hands."

When Hugh came home from work they all went to Halstead General Hospital where they were directed to the geriatric ward. It was much too hot and there was an unpleasant odour of disinfectant and urine, which made Charis feel sick. Aunt Bee was sitting in a chair by Vanna's bedside, looking unusually sad, but she smiled wanly as they approached.

"I've been beside myself with worry," said Grace. "How is she?"

"We're still waiting for the X-ray result," said Bee, "and of course she's very shocked. They sedated her and she's sleeping now. Hello, pet. Hello, Hugh."

Again Charis felt close to tears, but held them in check while she listened to the adults speculating on Vanna's chances of recovery.

She thought about the last time she had been to the flat that Aunt Bee and Vanna shared. The furniture was old-fashioned and there were many Victorian objects from their former home, but it was a cosy little haven which Charis always enjoyed visiting. She adored her aunt and grandma, and was in turn the apple of their respective eyes.

"Hello, my dears. Ready for a cup of tea?" Vanna had asked, as she always did as soon as anyone arrived at the flat.

She invariably kept three kettles constantly filled with water so that one or other of them had either recently boiled, was actually boiling, or was just about to.

"All you ever think about is tea, Mother," said Grace. "I'm sure it doesn't do you any good to drink so much of it."

Aunt Bee had been setting cups and saucers on a tray and arranging cakes and biscuits on a plate. Those had been lovely, but the conversation had hinged on topics which Charis found exceedingly dull. Grace had spent ages telling them the latest news about Uncle Donald, who had been having problems with his new curate, and Aunt Bee had elaborated on a serious operation recently undergone by Gladys Grove's sister.

'Operation!' Charis thought now with horror. 'Oh, dear God, don't let Vanna need an operation.'

The ward sister arrived, accompanied by a young doctor wearing a white coat.

"Are you all family?" he asked briskly.

"Yes, we are," said Bee. "What's the verdict, Doctor? Do you think our mother will pull through?"

"Good news," said the doctor. "No broken bones, but Mrs Vanning is in considerable shock. We'll need to keep her under observation for a few days at least. No more than two visitors at a time, please, from now on, and the hours are six until eight in the evening. As you see, she's sedated now and I think perhaps it might be better if you left. You really can't help her by staying, and she needs to rest."

Grace, Aunt Bee and Charis dropped light kisses on Vanna's pallid, wrinkled cheeks, while Hugh stood at the foot of the bed looking awkward. As they left the ward Charis glanced briefly at some of the other beds with their wizened occupants, and was guiltily thankful when they were standing in the light and airy hospital lobby once more, away from the aura of death and decay.

The adults were making arrangements as to when they would next visit Vanna when, to her complete surprise, Charis noticed Tom Potterfield walking briskly down the hospital staircase.

"Charis!" he exclaimed as soon as he saw her. "Fancy meeting you here. What's going on?"

She explained, while her parents and Aunt Bee stopped their conversation to appraise him.

Tom was suitably sympathetic about Vanna, and Charis, in turn, asked him why he was there.

"It's one of the chaps in my form," he said. "Poor old Paul Williams broke his arm playing tennis, so some of us are taking it in turns to visit him."

"Aren't you going to introduce us to your friend, Charis?" said Grace.

"Oh yes, of course. Sorry," said Charis. "These are my parents, Tom, and my aunt, and this is Tom Potterfield from Holyoaks."

He looked neat and tidy in his Eden House blazer, a pair of well-pressed flannels and nicely polished shoes. With his kindly brown eyes behind the owl-like spectacles, which made him appear even more intelligent than he undoubtedly was, Charis guessed that he epitomised the kind of boy most parents would regard as a suitable friend for their daughters, and she was swift to observe Grace's approving eye and Hugh and Aunt Bee's friendly smiles.

"Stay and talk to Tom for a little while if you like, Charis," said Grace. "We're walking to the bus stop to see Bee on her way, so we'll wait for you there and then we'll go home on the train."

"Do come back to Holyoaks soon," said Tom, before leaving Charis some five minutes later. "I've really missed you."

"I was *hoping* to be there this coming Saturday," she said, remembering sadly the happy plans she had made with Maggie and Wendy, "but I may not be able to now that my grandma's in here."

"No, of course," said Tom. "Well, Holyoaks won't go away, so I hope it won't be long before you're back."

Aunt Bee had caught her bus and gone home to Upsvale by the time Charis rejoined her parents. She was sorry not to have said a proper goodbye to her aunt, who was very special to her and with whom she had shared quite a few confidences over the years.

For one thing, Charis had told her about her pash on Alan Decker when she was fourteen, and her despondency when she had learnt about his girlfriend, Shirley Croft. Also, there was the continuing saga of Colin Crisp, for whom, Charis thought, Aunt Bee tended to feel a certain compassion, while fully understanding Charis's antipathy towards him. Then there had been the aftermath of the firework incident at Celia's party, when Charis had smuggled her torn dress into Aunt Bee's shop after school one dank November afternoon, in the hope that her aunt could mend it as invisibly as possible.

"What will Mummy say about you being home late today?" Aunt Bee had asked anxiously, because the bus journey from Stella Maris in Kemsford to Upsvale lay in the opposite direction from Charters Lea.

"Oh, I'll say I had a detention for talking," Charis had said, surprising herself as much as her aunt with her duplicity. "How long do you think it'll take to mend it?"

"I'll have to wait until Vanna goes to bed, if you don't want her to know either."

"Better not tell her. She might let it slip out to Mummy some time."

Aunt Bee had raised her eyebrows: "I don't like to think of you deceiving your mother, and I don't like doing so myself for that matter."

"I know, but Mummy makes such a fuss about everything, and it just isn't worth the trouble."

Aunt Bee usually closed the shop at noon on Saturdays, so Charis had called round to collect the dress on a Saturday afternoon, carrying a large shopping bag so that the parcel could be slipped inside without Vanna knowing. Fortunately for everyone the cunning ploy worked out exactly as Charis had hoped, and Grace never did discover what had happened to the dress.

"How did you think Mother looked?" Grace said on the way home.

"Difficult to tell while she was asleep," said Hugh.

"Thank goodness there aren't any broken bones," Grace went on, "but the shock of it worries me. Shock can cause all kinds of problems, particularly at Mother's age. Supposing her heart gives up?"

They rambled on, weighing the pros and cons, but later that evening, after they had all had beans on toast for supper, Grace said, "What a coincidence meeting that nice young man at the hospital! Wasn't he charming? Didn't you think so, Hugh?"

"He was indeed," said Hugh. "You never mentioned him before, did you, Charis?"

"I've danced with him a few times, that's all," she said, remembering Banjo's disparaging remarks about 'old Potty'.

"He reminded me a bit of Desmond Hoyt. Not to look at, I mean, but the same type," said Grace. "I'd be quite happy if you were going out with someone like that. I can't imagine *him* expecting to drag you up to London to take you to some dreadful dive, and I see he goes to Eden House. I expect he's very clever."

"He wants to be a chemist," said Charis, "but lots of the Holyoaks boys are at Eden House too."

She decided to keep quiet about Banjo being one of them.

"Perhaps it's time you went back to Holyoaks," said Grace surprisingly. "Once, please God, Vanna's back on her feet, of course."

News of Vanna improved as the week passed. The hospital gave her a walking frame to help her regain her confidence after the fall, and it looked as though she might be discharged sooner than anyone expected.

Donald telephoned Grace from Wakefield to hear the latest news of his mother, but the next time Charis visited Aunt Bee on her own at the flat, her aunt told her that Freddy had rung from Rochester, because she was the only family member he would speak to.

"It was always Donald and Grace, the serious ones, who got along well together," said Aunt Bee. "Freddy and I were younger and we both took life lightly. We thought Donald and Grace were awfully unexciting and we used to giggle about them behind their backs. We loved them dearly, of course. I mean, they were our brother and sister, but Freddy and I were much closer to each other than to the others."

This rekindled Charis's interest in her erring uncle, and she persuaded Aunt Bee to divulge a little more of the family history: "Well, I've told you most of it before, pet," she began. "Freddy always liked pretty girls, and after being away so long in the war he was on the lookout for someone as soon as he was back in Civvy Street. I shouldn't tell you this, I suppose, but he went a bit wild while he was out in Egypt. They have all kinds of naughty goings-on out there, you know, and I'm sure he enjoyed himself whenever he could, if you know what I mean."

Charis nodded, only half comprehending her aunt's insinuation: "Where did he meet Aunt Isobel, though?" she asked.

"Oh, at some nightclub in London, I think. She was still married at the time, but not happily. Mind you, we always thought she was the guilty party, and we're sure Freddy wasn't the first man she'd been with during her marriage. Anyway, she really fell for Freddy, and I'm not at all surprised — he was *so* handsome. Still is, I expect, although I haven't seen him for years. He was cited in the divorce case, and they got married as soon as they could."

"I've never seen her. Have you got a photo?"

"Somewhere, pet. Let me see."

Aunt Bee rummaged through the drawer where all the photos were kept, and finally handed Charis a black-and-white studio portrait of Isobel. She was gorgeous to look at, with perfectly even features, shapely lips emphasised with dark lipstick, and a mass of black curly hair.

"Wow!" said Charis.

"I know," said Aunt Bee. "Who could blame him?"

And they both giggled.

By the weekend Vanna's condition was no longer giving rise to concern, so Charis was able to go back to Holyoaks after all, and met Maggie and Wendy at Charters Lea Station.

Maggie was taller than Charis and considerably more curvaceous, with large bones which made her look slightly plump. Fine flaxen hair curled round her shoulders, and she had light-blue eyes and a flawless skin. She was wearing pink, which made her look like a rose in full bloom. Little Wendy, with her neat thatch of straight honey-coloured hair, was in a plain cream dress with a simple red belt and matching red shoes.

"I'm really excited," said Maggie. "You've told us so much about Holyoaks I can hardly believe we're actually *going* there at last."

"I'm scared to death," said timid Wendy, "but I'm sure I'll enjoy it even so."

Leo Crewe was, as usual, collecting subs at the door: "Welcome back!" he said to Charis. "I wondered what had happened to you. Are these two new recruits?"

Charis introduced them, observing that while Leo glanced only briefly at Wendy, his eyes lingered on Maggie, for whom he reserved a specially warm smile.

They left their cardigans in the cloakroom and ventured into the main hall, where a lively quickstep was already in progress. Maggie began tapping her feet. She loved that kind of music and was itching to dance, but everyone who intended to join in was already partnered.

Charis noticed a few familiar faces, Ronnie's amongst them.

"That's Ronnie Costello," she whispered, having long ago given them a detailed description of his attributes.

"Isn't he *gorgeous*?" said Wendy, her eyes following him in obvious admiration as he danced round the floor.

During a snowball waltz Charis was gratified when Ronnie headed towards her and, in his quiet way, asked her for a dance. From the corner of her eye, she saw Maggie and Wendy raise their eyebrows and felt absurdly proud.

"You've brought some of your friends tonight then," said Ronnie. "I'm glad about that. I thought you were rather out on a limb when you were here before with Banjo and the rest of the mob. Are they from your school?"

"Yes. Maggie — the tall one — is my best friend, and the other one is Wendy."

"Where does Pam fit into the picture?"

"Well, I'm still friendly with her too, but now she goes out with Roger Drayton all the time I don't see so much of her."

"I'm glad you stopped seeing Banjo," said Ronnie.

"Are you? Why should it matter to you?"

"You're far too nice to string along with him. His current floozie is much more suitable, in my view — two of a kind, they are."

"Do you mean Polly Phillips?"

"The one with eyes like poached eggs in saucers. I don't know her name."

"Yes, that's Polly Phillips," said Charis, giggling at Ronnie's description, which reduced Banjo's relationship with her to a mere triviality.

The music stopped.

"Thanks. I'll probably see you again later," said Ronnie, and sauntered off in search of another partner.

Before long, Tom Potterfield emerged from the annexe, and was soon dancing with Charis: "How's your grandma?" he asked kindly. "I was pleased to meet your parents, but sorry it wasn't a happier occasion. Are you an only child, Charis?" he added a little later.

"Yes. Are you?"

"I have a brother, Vernon. He's twenty-four, married, and lives over at Mundy Park."

"You told me you go to St Jude's," said Charis. "Do your parents go there too?"

"Oh yes. It's been our church ever since I can remember. My brother met his wife, Joyce, there."

"I've heard it's High Church. Is it?"

"You could say that," said Tom, but he did not enlarge any further on the subject. A moment or two later, Tom said, "What does your father do, Charis?"

Conditioned by Grace to regard Hugh's job as somehow demeaning, Charis hesitated for a moment as she always did when anyone posed this question: "He's a postman," she said, feeling a blush coming on, but Tom neither drew back in disdain, nor even registered particular surprise.

"That must be an interesting job in some ways," he said, "except for negotiating fierce dogs. Has he ever been bitten?"

"Not seriously, but small dogs like corgis tend to snap round his ankles sometimes. He quite likes dogs, though, so they don't worry him too much."

"My father's an accountant," said Tom. "He works for an international company based in London. Deadly dull in my opinion, but he was always good at figures."

Later, after Charis had introduced Tom to Maggie and Wendy, he said, "I'll be back soon. I just have to see Greg about something."

When he had gone a blissfully smiling Wendy said, "I danced with Ronnie. Did you see me?"

"Couldn't miss you," said Maggie, laughing. "Don't forget I was right beside you when he asked."

Charis had never paid much attention to Leo Crewe because she usually saw him only at the entrance. Tonight, though, he put in an appearance in the hall much earlier than usual. He was quite tall with fine, floppy, fair hair, a Roman nose and a limp. With some difficulty he climbed the stairs to the stage, joining Tom, Audrey and Greg Duffy, who appealed to everyone to stop talking for a moment and to give him their attention.

"Just one or two announcements," said Greg. "I expect you all know we held our AGM this week, and I'd like to tell those of you who weren't there about a few changes on the committee."

"*I* didn't know about the AGM," Charis whispered to Maggie.

"Well, you haven't been here for ages, so that's not surprising," Maggie whispered back.

"Leo's been our cashier for a long time," said Greg. "It's meant that he hasn't had much chance to dance or play billiards or table tennis, so we're giving him a break this year. Audrey's replacing him, taking turns with Tom — one week on; one week off. That seemed a fair deal to us. I'm still the leader, for my sins. . . . "

This statement was greeted with cheers, groans, guffaws and clapping.

"Audrey remains secretary; Steve Parish has been elected treasurer, and Tom's our new admin officer, as well as helping on the door, so that'll keep *him* out of mischief."

Amidst general laughter Maggie said, "So that's why Tom went up on the stage with the others. He clearly has hidden talents."

"Now a word about our record collection," said Greg. "It's beginning to get a bit out of date, so we thought some of you might like to bring in a few of your own records to ring the changes — tunes we can dance to, of course. We'll check them out first, and if they're suitable we'll use them. We'll be very careful, but I promise you'll be reimbursed for any breakages, so think about it and see what you can come up with."

"What a good idea!" said Maggie. "Don't you think so, Mitch?"

"Yes, but I haven't got any," said Charis, wishing that she had.

"Well *I* have," said Maggie. "I spend nearly all my pocket money on records. I'll bring some next week."

"Do you really want to come back next week, then?"

"Just try stopping me," said Maggie. "I really like it here."

"So do I," said Wendy.

"Finally, a word about the refreshments," Greg continued. "We've roped in twelve gallant volunteers to do them on a rota basis, so with two of them in the kitchen each week they'll only have to be on duty one week in six. The programme of outside events will be available as soon as Tom's had time to finalise it and get it duplicated, and, as usual, I'm sure you'll find there'll be something to interest everyone."

When Greg had finished speaking and the applause had died down, the dancing continued.

It was a particularly jolly evening. At one point, they played a version of musical chairs during which, when the music stopped, everyone had to rush to the nearest available chair and sit on it with their partners on their laps. Tom partnered Charis, Maggie was asked by someone Charis didn't know, and Wendy romped round the hall with a tubby fellow who turned out to be called Ken Purchiss. It was Wendy and Ken who were the last remaining couple when the game ended, for which they received prizes: Wendy's a box of bath cubes; Ken's a packet of handkerchiefs.

Tom promptly asked Charis for the next dance, but after they had taken to the floor she noticed Ronnie asking Wendy, and found herself burning with a mixture of envy and curiosity. Leo was dancing with Maggie, and despite his limp was managing quite well, sharing a joke with her at the same time.

Everyone kept their partners as another waltz followed, during which Tom maintained a steady flow of earnest conversation revolving round his election to the Holyoaks committee; the latest news about Paul Williams's broken arm; forthcoming exams and even politics. Charis answered him woodenly, wondering why she was stuck with someone so prosaic, when quiet little Wendy had so easily attracted Ronnie, with all his elusive charms. Perhaps it was because Wendy was a mere five foot two inches tall, the perfect height for Ronnie, and this idea comforted her a little. Tom was still extolling the virtues of the local Conservative MP when the waltz finished and they joined up with Ronnie, Wendy, Maggie and Leo.

"Let's do this one, Charis," said Ronnie when the next record began. "Yes, I *know* it's a foxtrot, but that doesn't matter. We can manage."

Tom, foiled by Ronnie, automatically turned to Wendy, and Leo once again asked Maggie.

"Tom Potterfield seems interested in you," Ronnie observed. "Do you like him?"

"There isn't anything about him *not* to like," Charis replied.

"But he's not as challenging as, shall we say, Banjo Wilkinson?"

She bristled.

"Don't be upset. I'm not being judgemental," said Ronnie, "but I observe people from afar, and I think you are a young lady who enjoys a little excitement."

"Well, what if I am?" she protested, spiritedly. "Life at home isn't exactly very sparkling. I joined this club to have some fun, but it's been in pretty short supply on the whole."

Ronnie laughed: "I have a feeling that something is just around the corner for you," he said. "You've changed since the first time we met, you know. Not nearly so shy, for instance, are you?"

A soft flush spread over her face as she basked in the sunshine of his approval. She wondered why she had always been so attracted to Ronnie, despite his slight stature, when Colin Crisp, also skinny, made her want to run in the opposite direction. Ronnie was so *warm*: his skin; his eyes; his body. Whenever she saw him she wanted to hug and kiss him, and that, she supposed, was the real secret of having sex appeal.

All too soon it was the last waltz when, eager to be partnered again by Ronnie, Charis was forced instead to watch him dancing it with Wendy. Leo had stayed with Maggie all the evening, and the two of them joined the other dancers as, inevitably, Tom claimed Charis and the hall lights were dimmed.

Shadowy figures stopped often to kiss. Tom, however, danced the last waltz in the same way as any other, making no attempt either to kiss Charis or to hold her any closer. This neither surprised nor disappointed her, for, as Ronnie had so accurately observed, she found him singularly unexciting, dubbing him mentally as an intelligent version of Colin Crisp. She was aching chiefly for Ronnie, yet she would have settled for Banjo — indeed, for anyone who could have alleviated the intense desire which welled up inside her. It was difficult to suppress her envy of Wendy, with whom Ronnie was probably at that very moment dancing cheek to cheek. Remembering the surprising silkiness of his beard against her face and his undemanding kisses, which, although gentle, had held such blissful promise, she wondered how to control the ominous lump in her throat as Tom danced her round the darkened hall, completely unaware of her turbulent emotions.

"Wow!" said Maggie, afterwards. "*What* an evening! It's fairly taken my breath away. Thanks a million for introducing me to this place, Mitch. I can't remember when I last had such a good time."

Wendy was silent — dazed.

"What did you think of it, Wendy?" Charis asked, yearning to quiz her about Ronnie.

"Wonderful," said Wendy in a dream. "Perfect. I just loved it."

"Leo said he'd meet me here next week," said Maggie. "He was so funny; very Goony, actually. Lots of 'Do you play the saxophone', and all that. Fortunately he liked my well-rehearsed replies. Although I say it myself, I do think I take off Eccles to a T."

"I don't know Leo very well," Charis admitted. "As Greg said, he's usually been missing for much of the time because of collecting the subs."

"My lucky night, then," said Maggie happily.

"What did Ronnie have to say?" Charis asked Wendy, unable to contain her curiosity any longer.

Wendy smiled serenely: "He's seeing me here next Saturday too," she purred. "I think he's absolutely lovely."

Constance Vanning was discharged from hospital one week and three days after her fall. Using the walking frame, she began to regain her confidence, and life at the flat began slowly to return to normal, much to the relief of the entire family.

At Stella Maris, that week dragged interminably. Exam revision was a necessary evil, undertaken only as a last resort, because Maggie, Wendy and Charis were totally preoccupied with how their fortunes might change at their next visit to Holyoaks.

On the Friday Wendy was absent from school.

"I wonder why?" said Maggie. "She was fine yesterday."

"I hope she'll be around tomorrow," said Charis. "She'll be very upset if she can't go to Holyoaks with us."

"Well, *I'll* be there, anyway," Maggie promised, "come hell or high water."

Wendy rang Charis the next morning: "It must have been something I ate," she said, sounding very subdued. "I was violently sick all day yesterday, and today I feel really washed out. My mother won't let me go out, but I don't think I could, anyway; my legs are all wobbly."

"Oh, Wendy, I *am* sorry," said Charis, genuinely enough, although the thought of Ronnie at Holyoaks without Wendy was exciting. "Does Maggie know?"

"I would have rung her, but I wanted to let you know first because of Holyoaks. Could you tell her for me?" said Wendy. "I'm so worn out I just want to go back to bed."

When Charis met Maggie at the station that evening, Maggie was clutching a carrier bag containing gramophone records. She was wearing a pale-yellow frock, her generally creamy appearance once again resembling a rose in full bloom.

"I've brought 'Stranger in Paradise', 'Cherry Pink and Apple Blossom White', 'The Naughty Lady of Shady Lane' and 'Let Me Go Lover'. I hope Audrey and Greg approve," she said.

"They sound fine to me. Just as long as we can dance to them."

"I can dance to *anything*," said Maggie exuberantly.

Arriving at the hall Charis was momentarily surprised to see Tom collecting the subs, until she remembered the previous week's announcement. "How do you like your new job?" she asked.

"It's fine," said Tom, "but I'm going to miss dancing with you this week. I hope there'll be a chance later. I'll probably be able to pack up here after, say, nine o'clock."

Maggie strode confidently up the stage steps to hand over her records to Greg Duffy, who clearly approved of them, judging by the smiles they exchanged. On her way back, Leo Crewe waylaid her and asked if he could sit with her. He could barely take his eyes off Maggie, and familiar pangs assailed Charis as she wondered if anyone would ever be so obviously attracted to her.

Greg's first selection was 'The Naughty Lady of Shady Lane'.

"Oh good! One of mine," said Maggie.

"I like that song," said Leo. "It's cute. I like the way you don't find out until the very end that the naughty lady is really a baby."

"My mother said it reminded her of when *I* was a baby, because I was her first daughter," said Maggie. "Actually my father bought it for her because she liked it so much. She's dotty about babies. She must be, after all, seeing she's had so many."

"I'd love to dance this with you, Maggie," said Leo, "but quicksteps are out for me. I can only manage waltzes and slow foxtrots because of the old gammy leg."

"That's OK," said Maggie, skilfully hiding her disappointment. "What's up with your leg, if you don't mind my asking?"

"What's up my leg?" teased Leo. "Nice young ladies don't ask questions like that."

"Idiot!" said Maggie. "I said up *with* your leg."

"I had polio when I was a kid," said Leo. "Fortunately I only had a mild dose, but it left one leg a trifle wonky."

"Poor old you," said Maggie.

Charis admired Maggie's composure and the easy way she was able to converse with Leo.

"How about national service?" Maggie was saying.

"Oh, it got me out of that," said Leo. "I suppose it was something to be thankful for that I never met a Major Bloodnok!"

Maggie laughed: "My brother Bernard would be envious," she said. "He's doing his national service right now down in Aldershot and hating every minute of it."

"He has my sympathies," said Leo.

"Where do you work, Leo?" Maggie asked next.

"I'm in the civil service. Ministry of Works, actually."

"If you don't want the works, don't muck 'em about, eh?"

"Couldn't have put it better myself," said Leo.

At that moment, Ken Purchiss, Wendy's partner in musical chairs the previous week, ambled over.

"Care to dance?" he asked Maggie casually.

Maggie glanced briefly at Leo as if to gauge his approval.

"OK," he said. "Off you go, but come back, won't you?"

When Maggie had gone, Leo said, "*What* a super girl! Isn't she fun? I'm so glad you brought her along."

95

"She's my best friend," said Charis.

"Yes, I know. She told me."

It was later, while the 'Tennessee Waltz' was being played, that Ronnie arrived and, like Maggie, went up on stage immediately to hand over some gramophone records. A few moments later he was joined by Miranda, radiant in a royal-blue dress scattered with little white stars.

"Who is that fascinating femme fatale?" asked Maggie.

"The delectable Miranda Gates," said Leo, before Charis could answer. "She used to go out with Ronnie, but that was a while ago."

"He's still interested by the looks of it," said Maggie, as Ronnie and Miranda melted into each other's arms and waltzed round the room in enviable harmony.

"Just as well Wendy isn't here," said Charis, out of Leo's earshot. "She would be quite upset, don't you think?"

"She was certainly smitten with Ronnie last week," said Maggie. "Oh well — what the eye doesn't see . . . "

Steve, Babs, Nick and Rosemary were sitting together at a table on the opposite side of the hall near the stage. They were joined later by Ronnie and Miranda, Norman Fairway and Jackie Wiseman.

"All that crowd with Babs are Celia's friends," Charis explained to Maggie. "I met most of them at her party except for Jackie. Norman started going out with her after he and Pam split up."

"Yes, I remember," said Maggie.

It was immensely satisfying to be with Maggie and Leo. Charis felt that she was making a statement that she had her own set of friends now, and had no need to be tacked on to Celia's group, all of whom, with the notable exception of Ronnie and Miranda, maintained an air of superiority over everyone else.

Ronnie and Charis came face to face during a Paul Jones later on: "Where is your charming little friend tonight?" he asked.

"Wendy? Oh, she's not well. She ate something that didn't agree with her."

"Upset tummy. Oh dear. I'm sorry to hear that."

"I expect she'll be back next week," said Charis.

"I hope so," said Ronnie as the Paul Jones circles were reformed and their conversation came to an enforced end.

Ken Purchiss asked Maggie for another quickstep later on, but Maggie declined, so he turned to Charis instead. Only mildly offended at being his second choice, she accepted.

"Where's that pretty girl with the fair hair you were with last week," he asked her almost at once.

"Wendy? Oh, she's not well. She'll be back next week, I expect."

"Good. I thought she was nice."

They danced in silence for a while, and then he said, "Have you seen

The Glenn Miller Story?"

"No," she replied. "Have you?"

"I went when it was first released in London. It was *fantastic*. It's on locally next week so I'm going again."

"You *must* have liked it."

"I've got all Glenn Miller's records," said Ken proudly. "I think his music is the tops."

Charis recalled Celia's party and Steve's Glenn Miller collection. She particularly remembered 'American Patrol' and 'In the Mood' and mentioned them to Ken.

"'Moonlight Serenade' is on the back of 'American Patrol'," said Ken. "How about 'Pennsylvania 65000' and 'Little Brown Jug'?"

"I don't know those," she admitted.

Ken raised his eyebrows: "You don't know what you're missing. *Do* go and see the film. It isn't *all* music. There's a lot of romance too, if that's what you like. *That* part didn't interest me much, of course. I just let it wash over me and waited for more music."

Charis relayed this conversation to Maggie and Leo.

"Oh yes. It's on at the Regal," Leo said. "Why don't we go?"

"I'd *love* to," said Maggie promptly. "My brother Bernard told me it was great."

"How about you, Charis?"

"*Me?* I didn't think you meant me too."

"Yes, of course you too. We'll talk about it later," said Leo.

Once he had finished his duties on the door, Tom danced exclusively with Charis. During the last waltz, unhindered by smooching, she had plenty of opportunity to observe Leo and Maggie dancing cheek to cheek and, far more surprisingly, Ronnie similarly engaged with Rosemary. Nick, meanwhile, was dancing with Miranda, but at the end Celia's group all left together so that it was impossible to speculate on individual pairings, apart from Babs and Steve who were inseparable.

At the very end Leo said, "I'm taking Maggie home in my car tonight. Can I give you a lift, Charis?"

Leo tilted the front passenger seat forward so that she could climb into the back of the small Austin, while Maggie settled herself comfortably in the front, relaxed and contented. In less than five minutes they were at Charters Lea Station.

"Drop me off here, please, Leo," said Charis. "This is very near where I live."

"Well, if you're sure," said Leo. "Now about that film: I'll ring Maggie early in the week, and then the two of you can make arrangements to suit you both and we'll all go together."

Charis was impatient to meet Maggie at school the following Monday morning: "What was Leo like?" she asked.

"If you mean what I *think* you mean, the answer is *gorgeous*," said Maggie.

Charis was curious to know more, but was afraid of sounding too inquisitive, despite her close friendship with Maggie. Nevertheless, she persevered: "How far did . . . ?" she began.

"How far did he go is what you want to know, isn't it?" said Maggie, with a chuckle.

Charis blushed, and giggled.

"Well, how far did Banjo go with *you*?"

Charis had never divulged the events of those two well-remembered evenings to anyone, not even to Maggie: "Far enough to be pretty exciting," she admitted.

"OK, you'll know what I mean when I say Leo was exciting too," said Maggie, "but I'm not going into further details. My name's neither Pam Sperry nor Polly Phillips."

At that point Wendy appeared.

"Are you better?" they asked her in unison.

"Yes, I'm fine now, but I felt *rotten* over the weekend, and about missing Holyoaks. What happened?"

"Leo took me home in his car," said Maggie triumphantly, and we're going to the Regal one day this week with Mitch to see *The Glenn Miller Story*."

Wendy looked a little crestfallen: "Was Ronnie at the club?" she asked.

"Yes. He wanted to know where you were. He said you were charming, and hoped you'd soon be feeling better."

Wendy's eyes immediately lit up: "Do you think he'll be there this week?" she asked.

"You can never tell with Ronnie," said Charis, and she was pleased, though not surprised, when Maggie, with her usual good sense, avoided all references to Miranda Gates. "Ken Purchiss asked about you too," said Charis.

Wendy raised her eyebrows: "I'm not interested in him," she said firmly, "only Ronnie."

Charis, Maggie and Leo saw *The Glenn Miller Story* on the Wednesday evening. The girls loved the romantic side of the film, weeping at the end when the ill-fated plane went missing, but Leo's main preoccupation was with the music. They all agreed that the Miller tunes were wonderful, but they were positively mesmerised by the scene in a Harlem nightclub when Louis Armstrong played 'Basin Street Blues', blowing into his trumpet with such joyful abandon that Charis thought his cheeks looked like balloons about to burst. Then there was Gene Krupa attacking the drums like a maniac, producing such an intoxicating rhythm that it was impossible to sit still, and most of the cinema audience burst into wild applause. Charis had never experienced anything like that before, enjoying it even more when she guessed how much her mother would have disapproved.

That week everything seemed to be happening. When Charis returned from school the day after seeing the Glenn Miller film, Grace met her in the hall, all smiles: "I'm sure you'll be thrilled," she said. "Mrs Walsh came in this afternoon and brought a great pile of clothes that Beverley doesn't want any more. Most of them are very nice indeed — good colours, and nothing too garish or common-looking — but you know how extravagant that girl is. She was simply tired of them and they would have gone to a jumble sale if Mrs Walsh hadn't thought of you. I've put them in your room. Go and have a look."

Charis did not share her mother's enthusiasm entirely, as she had mixed feelings about other people's cast-offs, even those previously owned by fastidious Beverley Walsh, but when she saw the mixed array of pretty dresses, skirts and summer blouses lying on her bed she began to feel excited at the prospect of wearing so many different outfits, and examined each one with a critical eye.

She immediately discarded two dresses in dismal colours, but there was a crisp-looking skirt in cornflower-blue and white gingham, a blouse in a matching shade of blue and three dresses which were simply perfect.

She tried them on, twirling in front of her wardrobe mirror with growing enthusiasm. Her favourite was black and sleeveless, liberally scattered with sprigs of minuscule pink rosebuds and green leaves. It had a flared skirt with an emphasised waistline, and looked quintessentially feminine. Another dress, also full-skirted, had lavender and white stripes, with a plain lavender belt, and a third was in pale-green cotton with small, white polka dots and charming little puff sleeves.

"I just love these," she said when Grace joined her in the bedroom. "I shan't be able to decide which one to wear on Saturday."

"Well, you have a few more days to make up your mind," said Grace. "Maggie and Wendy are going with you again this week, I hope."

"They certainly are," Charis replied, feeling her spirits soar.

Charis, Maggie and Wendy were sitting on the sun-warmed asphalt of the school playground, relaxing and trying to get a tan in the May sunshine.

"Isn't it *hot*?" said Maggie. "I wish we could wear something cooler in the summer. Trust Stella Maris to come up with this uniform. I mean, who in their right mind would wear a tie in this weather? It's amazing they don't make us wear our berets in the summer too."

The summer uniform at the convent consisted of light-grey skirts and short-sleeved white blouses, but in the winter charcoal-grey tunics replaced the skirts, and the blouses were long-sleeved Viyella. In summer and winter alike, each girl wore a tie in one of four house colours; each house named after a female saint. It was blue for St Agnes, gold for St Catherine, red for St Faith and green for St Helena. Maggie and Wendy were in St Catherine's, and Charis was in St Faith's. The school badge bore the letters S and M in light-blue, intertwined beneath a golden crown on a background of dark-grey, and was attached to the breast pockets of the light-grey summer blazers, with a smaller version for their winter berets.

"It's all probably meant to be a penance," Charis said. "I don't know whether or not it's true, but I've heard that the nuns wear sacking under their habits, so perhaps they think we ought to feel uncomfortable too."

"*Sacking?*" Wendy was shocked. "*Surely* not?"

"It wouldn't surprise me," said Maggie. "Anyway, *I'm* not a nun, and I don't like feeling all hot and sweaty," and with that she pulled off her tie and undid the top button of her blouse.

"Better not let the Rice Pudding see you like that," Charis warned. "You know the rules."

"I'm resting in peace," said Maggie irreverently. "Don't nag."

While enjoying their sunbathing session they opened their Biology textbooks, balancing them on their knees as they endeavoured to revise for the GCE exam which was now uncomfortably close at hand.

"I wonder if we really *will* get a question on amoeba," Maggie mused.

"Probably not. It'd be just our luck," Charis replied. "I know everything there is to know about amoeba, don't you?"

"Intimately. I'm also pretty well genned up on veins and arteries. I only have to close my eyes to see that diagram we drew with the red bits for arteries and the blue bits for veins."

"How about ears? I'll always remember those funny little bones inside," said Wendy.

"Hammer, anvil and stirrup, you mean?"

"Yes, that's right. Oh, isn't this sunshine super? If only we weren't in school."

"I know. Never mind. It's Friday and tomorrow's *Saturday!* I wonder what'll happen at Holyoaks this week," said Maggie.

Charis had been wondering that herself. "We'll have a super time, I'm sure. I'm *so* glad you two joined. It's made such a difference."

Maggie beamed: "Not half as glad as I am," she said with a laugh. "My life has certainly perked up these last few weeks."

In the end it was Beverley Walsh's puff-sleeved, pale-green dress with the polka dots that won the day. It was a perfect spring evening of gentle, lilac-scented warmth, with flowering cherry trees frothing against a cloudless sky and gaudy tulips standing erect as guardsmen. There was no need to wear a coat, but Charis draped a cardigan round her shoulders in casual fashion against cooler temperatures later in the evening.

Leo was taking Maggie directly from her home to Holyoaks in his car, so Charis met Wendy alone at the station and walked with her to St Jude's hall.

She looked sweet in her cream dress, but was dreadfully nervous: "Supposing Ronnie isn't there," she said for the umpteenth time. "I shan't be able to *bear* it. I've been thinking about him non-stop."

"Don't worry," said Charis, also hoping secretly that he *would* be and that, if only for a little while, the evening would bring her into contact again with this fascinating, enigmatic young man, who had the uncanny power of transforming a commonplace event into a special occasion.

It was Audrey Duffy's turn to collect the subs, so Tom was free and already waiting for Charis. Leo and Maggie joined them within a few minutes, and Ken Purchiss, sitting with a group on the opposite side of the hall, promptly asked Wendy for one of the early dances. Charis kept her eyes fixed on the entrance, watching out for Ronnie who, when he finally arrived, hovered nonchalantly in the doorway smoking a cigarette, and allowed some twenty minutes to elapse before asking her for a dance.

"Where's Miranda this week?" Charis enquired, partly out of personal curiosity and partly because of concern for Wendy.

"Haven't a clue," said Ronnie airily. "I don't keep tabs on her."

"But you were with her last week."

"Hold on," said Ronnie, frowning. "I was *with* her, was I? And what does that mean?"

"Well, you danced with her a lot, and you were sitting together most of the evening."

Ronnie laughed: "You're assuming too much, Charis," he said. "I'm a free agent and so is Miranda. You've probably heard that we used to go out together, and so we did, but that was some time ago."

Charis was mortified, wishing fervently that she had held her tongue.

"Luckily Miranda and I see eye to eye on most things," Ronnie continued. "We had our fling, as you might say, over a year ago, and I dare say we'll always be friends, but anything more serious is on hold, at least for now. There, does that satisfy your curiosity?"

"I shouldn't have asked. It was none of my business,"

"Forget it," said Ronnie. "You're my friend too, aren't you?" He smiled at her, his dark, expressive eyes crinkling at the corners.

"I hope so." She curled up inside with happiness.

Ronnie squeezed her hand: "Well, why don't I come and sit at *your* table this week and start a few more rumours?"

"Oh, yes *please!*"

After that the evening was transformed. Charis, Maggie, and Wendy joined in every dance, switching partners all the time between Leo, Ronnie and Tom. Charis caught Ken Purchiss staring hard at Wendy many times, and he took advantage of every opportunity to pursue her when there were snowballs or excuse-me dances.

Maggie was several inches taller than Ronnie, which caused a lot of merriment when he partnered her: "You're a peach," he said in front of the others, "but it's like dancing with a poplar tree."

"Gee, thanks," said Maggie in her best American drawl.

"Come on, Wendy," said Ronnie. "You're just the right height for me." At the end Tom said, "Can I walk to the station with you tonight, Charis?"

"Yes, OK," she replied, aware that she sounded half-hearted and ungracious, but not caring very much.

In the cloakroom Wendy said breathlessly, "Ronnie's taking me *home*. I can hardly *believe* it."

"I *thought* he seemed very attentive," said Maggie. "Aren't *you* the lucky one!"

"Well, you're lucky too. Leo's *so* nice."

"I know. How about you, Mitch?" asked Maggie.

"I'm going with Tom."

"At *last*! I wondered if he'd ever get round to asking you."

"I'm absolutely *thrilled*," Charis replied sarcastically. "Oh well, see you on Monday."

SIX

As May melted into June, Charis observed her friends and their relationships with mixed emotions — Maggie surprising her more than anyone. She and Leo were utterly enraptured with one another — holding hands at every opportunity, and gazing moonily into each other's eyes, particularly while dancing. Maggie had entered a magical world of her own, finding school work increasingly irksome, and even beginning to wonder whether she should leave that summer instead of becoming involved in sixth-form studies.

"But you always said you wanted to take GCE at Advanced Level," Charis reasoned with her. "I thought you were keen on catering. You'd need Domestic Science, at least."

"That was before Leo," said Maggie, making it sound as reverential as 'BC'. "Now I only want to cater for him."

Charis was mystified by the change in her friend, missing some of the confidences they had once shared, which now appeared reserved for Leo's ears alone.

Ronnie, having taken Wendy home on that one occasion, did not appear at Holyoaks for the next three Saturdays, leaving her unhappy and restless. Although Charis still coveted him herself, she felt in some way responsible for Wendy's disappointment, and tried to explain to her when they were alone that Ronnie apparently didn't wish to be tied to anyone in particular.

"But he's so *wonderful*," Wendy protested. "I want to go out with him *so* much. Why did he take me home that time if he didn't like me?"

"He *did* like you," said Charis, "but I expect he didn't want you to get too serious, and perhaps he thought you might."

"Do you think it has anything to do with Miranda?" asked Wendy.

"How did you find out about her?" asked Charis, aggrieved after she and Maggie had so carefully tried to avoid mentioning her name in Wendy's presence.

"Pam Sperry told me. She said Ronnie and Miranda used to be inseparable. Perhaps they still are. Perhaps he only wants her."

"No he doesn't. They're just friends, that's all."

"Pam said Miranda is absolutely stunning," Wendy went on, "and that Ronnie only goes in for beautiful girls."

"Don't pay any attention to Pam," said Charis, thoroughly annoyed that anyone could be so tactless. "The very fact that he took you home shows that he was interested — *is* interested. The next time he comes to Holyoaks try to act casually. He won't appreciate it if you behave with him like Maggie does with Leo, but those two are living in their own little world at the moment. Try flirting with someone else just a bit, then Ronnie will see you're not taking him too seriously, and he'll like you even more."

Wendy gazed at Charis as though she were the Source of All Wisdom, which made her feel quite important. Only a short time ago, Charis had been looking to Celia for advice, but now it was her own turn to hand it out.

Celia had taken to travelling to school by train in the mornings in order to meet Mark Earle on his way to Guy's Hospital, so Charis had been seeing less of her than before. Celia and Mark's relationship was developing steadily, but they seldom patronised Holyoaks, preferring Young Conservative functions, dances at the Starlight Ballroom, or their favourite haunt — Warbridge Jazz Club.

"There's a jazz number called 'Doctor Jazz'," Celia told Charis one day. "So that's Mark's new nickname. Appropriate, isn't it?"

Charis still enjoyed the atmosphere at Holyoaks and the weekly opportunity it provided for meeting someone more interesting than Tom, who had taken to walking with her as far as Charters Lea Station, where he would catch a bus to his home in Ockley. He had never even kissed her properly, yet his interest in her was obvious, like the time when the Midsummer Ball was first announced at Holyoaks: "We have one every year," he said. "Do you think you'll be able to go?"

"I might," Charis replied, "but it's too early to decide yet. How about you?"

"Well, as admin officer, I'm tied up with the general arrangements, selling the tickets and so on, so I'll certainly be there," said Tom, "but I'd like to think you'd be going too. Will you let me know soon?"

"Do you still see that young man we met at the hospital — Tom, wasn't it?" Grace asked one Saturday evening when Charis was getting ready for Holyoaks.

"Every week," Charis said, making it sound as routine as it certainly was.

"Hasn't he asked you out yet?"

"No, but I don't think I'd want to go out with him much, anyway," said Charis, remembering the uneventful walks to the station, when he had progressed no further than pecking her hastily on the cheek.

Grace sighed: "I did hope he might," she said. "I took to him from the outset, and so did your father, but I expect his studies come first. I don't suppose Tom wants to get too involved with a girl when he has important exams and his career at stake."

"He's awfully dull," said Charis. "I just dance with him, that's all."

"The trouble with you, young lady, is that you don't recognise a good, sincere, worthwhile boy when you meet one. Why don't you make the first move and ask him home to tea one day?"

"*Mummy!*" Charis cried, appalled. "I *couldn't* do that. How could you even suggest it?"

"I'm only thinking of you," said Grace. "I'm sure you'd like to have a steady boyfriend, but sometimes you have to meet them halfway, you know."

"Just leave me alone," said Charis, running upstairs to the haven of her bedroom and slamming the door behind her, never guessing that the evening ahead was to mark a turning point in her life.

It was the second Saturday in June, and warm sunshine had persisted all day, fading into a balmy evening as Charis stepped into the lavender and white dress which had once belonged to Beverley Walsh. She could not decide whether it looked more mauve than blue, but it was a very becoming shade. Her hair, freshly trimmed again by Mr Forbes and regularly enlivened with Golden Haze colour rinses, looked clean and neat, the little fringe tickling her forehead pleasantly.

Pam and Roger were planning to be at Holyoaks that week, and there was a possibility that even Celia and Mark might put in an appearance. In the event, most of Celia's group arrived in dribs and drabs, and a little later than everyone else, Banjo Wilkinson showed up with a supercilious-looking Polly. By then Charis had grown indifferent to them, so their presence did not affect her as much as it had in the recent past.

"That" Charis said to Maggie, "is the infamous Banjo."

"Oh-ho!" said Maggie. "Isn't he *fat!*"

"Wide is the way I'd have described him. A wide boy in *every* sense."

Wendy, as usual, was apprehensive about the evening and whether Ronnie would be there — would talk to her — would take her home — or not. He *was* there, but so too was Miranda. Pam and Roger drifted over, apparently only to say hello, but Pam, oblivious to any hurt she might cause, casually pointed Miranda out to Wendy.

"Don't let him see you're upset," Charis urged, noticing when Pam and Roger had left them that Wendy was looking very distressed. "Remember what I told you: smile, and try to flirt with someone else."

"She *is* lovely," said Wendy, staring at Miranda with awe, and looking wan.

"So are you," said Maggie. "Stop moping."

The evening began with a longer than usual Paul Jones, with Tennessee

Ernie's recording of 'Blackberry Boogie' providing the link tune.
"Isn't that a bouncy song?" said Maggie. "Really cute."

"I'd better not attempt this," said Leo, "but you join in Mags."

Maggie, dressed that evening in a swirling deep-pink taffeta skirt, a
white blouse and a black waspie-waist belt, beamed at him and sashayed
over to join the large circle of girls, which was soon surrounded by another
circle of boys revolving in the opposite direction.

There was a quickstep, a St Bernard waltz, and then a samba, at which
point Charis came face to face with Banjo: "Well, well, if it isn't cuddly
Charis," he said with a wink. "How's life? How's your mother? I say, can
you do this thing?"

She shrugged her shoulders and made a valiant attempt at matching the
catchy rhythm to steps of her own. Banjo's efforts made him look like a
circus clown, she thought, but he was a born comedian and everyone in
the vicinity was laughing at his antics, including Polly, who was herself
putting on a creditable show with Nick Buchanan nearby.

A foxtrot; a Gay Gordons; a waltz; a veleta — Charis danced with
Ronnie; with Ken; with Nick; even with Celia's Doctor Jazz. It was a real
ice-breaker, at the end of which everyone was hot, laughing and happy.
Rejoining Maggie, Leo and Wendy, who had danced the final sequence of
the Paul Jones with Ken Purchiss, Charis noticed two boys she had not
seen before standing just inside the doorway.

Both were good looking; both wore sports jackets, open-necked shirts
and cravats; both were smoking cigarettes. The taller of the two (although
by only a fraction) had curly, dark hair and even features; the other had
tawny hair, a neat nose, a generous mouth with nicely-shaped lips, and
suntanned skin. Banjo and Polly spoke to them at once, and Nick waved to
them from across the hall.

"Who are *they*?" asked Maggie admiringly.

"I've never seen them before," said Charis, equally impressed.

"While you're all cooling down," Greg was saying, "let me remind you
once again about the Midsummer Ball at Mundy Park College. There are
still plenty of tickets available, but if you want to be sure of getting any, I
suggest you see Tom about them soon. They're six shillings each, and that
includes excellent refreshments. There'll be a live band too — Mack's
Merrymakers — and the ball begins at seven o'clock."

"Are you going, Mitch?" asked Maggie.

"Not without a partner," said Charis, feeling a trifle forlorn. "It's fine
for you and Leo, but not much fun for the likes of me."

"How about Tom? I thought he'd asked you."

Charis pulled a face: "Nothing's settled yet."

"It would be a means of going, wouldn't it?"

"I suppose so," said Charis, but the prospect of a whole evening with
Tom as her sole partner was unappealing.

As dancing resumed to the strains of the song, 'Happy Days and Lonely Nights', Charis was in a state of reverie, staring fixedly at the floor, but when she finally looked up, released from daydreaming, she saw the two newcomers heading in her direction. The dark one promptly asked Wendy to dance, and the one with the tawny hair asked Charis.

Almost immediately she was aware of a faintly woody, smoky scent and the dry warmth of the hand which held hers as they began to dance.

"I'm Rick," he volunteered brightly. "I don't like dancing with strangers, so tell me your name?"

She did so.

"Charis? How unusual. I don't think I've ever met anyone called that before."

"I'm not surprised. Neither have I."

"I liked your version of the samba."

"I hadn't a clue what to do."

"It was an inspired attempt, then. You've got a good sense of rhythm. Do you happen to know any variations to the quickstep — the fishtail, for instance?"

"Only slightly."

"I've been wanting to have a go at it. Are you game to try?" Rick's feet fishtailed skilfully, and at least Charis did not trip over them.

"Good. We'll try that again when we're round the other side of the floor, shall we? Show old Banjo how professional we are."

He laughed.

"You obviously know him," said Charis.

"*Everyone* knows Banjo, don't they?" said Rick. "At least, they do at my school. He's larger than life, isn't he?"

"You're at Eden House too, then?"

"Where else?"

"Which form?" She wondered how their ages tallied.

"Upper fifth. How about you?"

"I'm in the fifth form too. Five Alpha. We don't have uppers and lowers at my school."

"Which is?"

"Stella Maris."

"*Really!* My sister used to go there."

"What was her name? Maybe I knew her."

"Teresa Woodrose. Tessa."

Charis thought for a moment, and then recalled a slim, willowy girl, some three years her senior, who had left the sixth form the previous year.

"Yes, I do remember her. Where is she now?"

"Beavering away at a teacher-training college in Birmingham. We don't see much of her these days."

"Do you have any other sisters or brothers?"

"'Fraid so. Twins, aged ten. Holy terrors, the pair of them. How about you?"

"No, there's only me," said Charis.

"Have you sat any GCEs yet?" asked Rick.

"Not yet. My first one's on Tuesday."

"Mine too. This is like the calm before the storm, don't you think?"

"Yes. I'm dreading the exams. Dreading the results even more."

"Aren't we all?" said Rick. "Still, never mind. It's Saturday, the night is young, and I must say I'm beginning to like you."

Back with her friends once more, Charis quizzed Wendy about the other boy.

"Adrian," said Wendy. "Isn't he nice-looking? He has the most perfect teeth I've ever seen."

They stole surreptitious glances across the room to the table where Rick and Adrian were sitting. They had lit fresh cigarettes and were puffing away, eyes narrowed against the smoke.

"Listen, Wendy," said Charis. "Next time there's a snowball or an excuse-me I think I'm going to ask Rick. I like him. Why don't you do the same with Adrian? It's your chance to show Ronnie how footloose and fancy-free you are."

"Well — I *might*," said Wendy.

"You're a real couple of conspirators," Maggie laughed, lolling back in her chair against Leo's protective arm. "Those two poor boys won't stand an earthly once you get your paws on them."

"Take your partners for an elimination waltz," Greg called.

Ken Purchiss, seizing his opportunity, marched purposefully across the hall and asked Wendy to dance. Leo and Maggie promptly followed them while, surprised and gratified, Charis saw Rick heading her way once more.

"Are you feeling lucky tonight?" he asked.

"Not specially," she said. "I never win anything."

Ruby Murray's plaintive voice began singing 'Softly, Softly'.

"I'm tired of that song. Aren't you?" said Rick. "It's so sugary and sentimental, and it's been around far too long. Actually, I don't like songs much at all. I'm a jazz man myself."

"Oh, you too?"

"I belong to the Jazz Record Club at school. We meet on Thursday evenings."

"I heard about that. Tom Potterfield told me."

"Old Potty? He hates jazz. He's a classical-music buff. I say, how long has he been taking the money at the door?"

"Not long. It was decided at the AGM, so he's on the committee now."

"Is he a friend of yours?" Rick asked.

"Well, sort of. He usually dances with me a lot, but not so much when he's on duty, like this week."

"Good. I'm glad I chose tonight to come here, then," said Rick as the music stopped.

Greg had divided the hall into four quarters with hastily drawn chalk lines. The quarters were designated Hearts, Diamonds, Clubs and Spades, and Charis and Rick found themselves in the Diamond section when the music stopped. Greg asked someone to cut a pack of cards, whereupon a club was revealed, eliminating twenty-five per cent of the dancers.

"So far, so good," said Rick.

When he smiled, Charis was reminded of the engaging, funny grin of a playful puppy. It truly lit up his face, including his eyes, which were honey-brown. She noticed also that his teeth were strong and white like nut kernels. 'He's *very* attractive!' she thought, feeling increasingly drawn to him.

They were saved again when the cards were next cut, but their luck finally ran out at the third attempt.

"Oh well — you can't win 'em all," said Rick, "but it was fun anyway," and returned to his table to relight the cigarette he had temporarily stubbed out.

"How about some refreshments, Min?" said Leo in his best quavery Henry Crun voice when the elimination waltz ended.

"Right-o, buddie," Maggie responded on cue as Minnie Bannister. "Shall we get them, Mitch? What does everyone want?"

"I'll have a photograph of a bath bun, and some of that sinful orangeade," said Leo, prolonging the Goonery.

As they waited in line at the kitchen counter, Rick joined the queue behind them. "What's on offer here?" he asked.

"Tea, orangeade, lemonade, biscuits, buns — that's about it."

"It's too hot for tea," he said.

"I thought it was supposed to cool you down," Maggie volunteered.

"Old wives' tale," he said, with his playful puppy grin. "I'd like two iced lemonades, please," he added, addressing a plump, earnest-looking girl, who was on kitchen duty that week.

"We don't have *iced* anything," she said somewhat acidly. "Just ordinary lemonade out of a bottle."

"That'll have to do then," said Rick. "How much?"

"Fourpence each."

"See you later, girls," he said, as they carried off their refreshments and he strolled back to Adrian with the lemonade.

"Interesting, isn't he?" said Maggie.

"Very!" said Charis, following him with her eyes.

At around nine-thirty there was a snowball, during which Wendy — one of the first girls to be chosen — had an opportunity to ask Adrian for a dance, but was just pipped at the post by another girl, so she asked Ken instead. Just then Tom emerged from the lobby, finally relieved of his duties at the door, and it wasn't long before a further partner change brought him to Charis. Longing to dance again with Rick, she felt curiously agitated, and hoped Tom would not monopolise her for the rest of the evening.

"It's been very busy out there tonight," he said. "I can't remember when so many people turned up."

"It's been a super evening," said Charis. "There's so much more atmosphere with a crowd like this."

"I've sold a lot more tickets for the ball," Tom went on. "Have you decided yet whether you're interested?"

She was tempted to say yes, but at that fateful moment Greg stopped the music and called for a final change of partners. "I'm still not sure," she said as, temporarily released from Tom, she walked directly towards Rick who was beckoning her.

"Let's do another fishtail," he said and, confident now, Charis followed his flashing feet. "You're good," he said. "I like dancing with you. Most girls I've danced with haven't got the hang of that variation."

When the snowball ended, Greg told everyone to carry on dancing to Maggie's record — 'Earth Angel' Unusually, someone on the stage had turned down the hall lights — a practice normally reserved for the last waltz — and Charis felt a wonderfully sensuous thrill as Rick drew her closer to him, folding both his arms round her as they danced slowly in the semi-darkness.

'Earth Angel' was one of the most popular records around just then, sung by the Crew Cuts to the kind of tune designed to create an atmosphere of smouldering desire. Rick didn't talk, but long before the record ended his smooth cheek was against hers and she was aware once more of that woody-scented smokiness.

From the corner of her eye Charis saw Ronnie smooching with Miranda, but she was no longer envious; no longer concerned about Wendy; just happy for them, and even happier for herself. Maggie's head was resting against Leo's shoulder and he was nuzzling the back of her neck where her flaxen hair curled in wispy strands. It was as if all the ingredients of youthful passion were simmering in a steamy cauldron to concoct a heady brew of burgeoning sexual awareness and anticipated fulfilment.

When 'Earth Angel' ended, Greg Duffy, clearly sensing that everyone wanted to retain and enjoy the atmosphere for as long as possible, said quietly, "Keep your partners. It's time for the last waltz."

The hall was now in almost total darkness as Greg selected the David Whitfield recording of 'Cara Mia' — a song which had been very popular a few months earlier.

Banjo and Polly were dancing so close together that it was positively indecent. His hands were roving up and down her back, finally coming to rest just under the curve of her bottom. The next moment they came to a standstill in the darkness at the back of the hall and were kissing hungrily. Remembering vividly how Banjo had kissed her, Charis was tingling with pent-up desires, until Rick stopped too and, in a magical, unforgettable moment, she felt his sweet breath on her cheek before his lips met hers and his warm, moist tongue gently parted them and lingered inside her mouth.

His kiss, probably lasting no longer than seconds, seemed to go on for ever, and afterwards he held her tightly against him and kissed her forehead, her eyelids and then her lips once more. Finally, he began to sing along softly with David Whitfield, and then, looking directly at her, he said, "I know you're Charis, and it's a nice name, but since they're playing 'Cara Mia' and this is the first last waltz we've ever danced together, I think I'll call you Cara from now on instead."

He kissed her again and again, and she responded eagerly, fascinated, charmed, completely captivated by this engaging young stranger.

All too soon the lights came on and Father Kellow joined Greg and Audrey on the stage as usual for the closing prayer.

"How odd!" Rick whispered. "It doesn't seem quite the thing to go all religious after *that*."

"I know," Charis whispered back. "That's how I always feel, but it *is* a church club."

"Then they shouldn't encourage all that necking," said Rick with a grin. "However, I'm not complaining."

When everyone had chorused the required amen, Rick said, "I *can* see you home, can't I?"

"Of course," said Charis, floating on clouds of bliss.

In the cloakroom Maggie gave her a knowing look and a warm smile. "Poor old Tom," she said. "You didn't notice him, did you? I could tell you were miles away, but he was watching you all the time, and he looked awfully miserable."

"Did he?" said Charis, feeling mildly guilty. "No, I *didn't* see him, but can you blame me?"

"Not at all," said Maggie. "That's life, isn't it? Good luck, Mitch. I think you've struck gold tonight."

"Where's Wendy?" Charis said, suddenly missing her.

"She left early. Ken tried very hard to interest her, and I think he asked to see her home, but she rushed off early on her own. She was quite upset."

"Oh *dear* — about Ronnie, of course."

"She's dotty about him, but it looks as though he's still hooked on Miranda, after all."

"I'm afraid so," said Charis. "Poor Wendy."

Outside the hall, Rick was waiting for her, smoking a cigarette. It was a balmy, beautiful evening, not yet fully dark despite being past ten o'clock, the sky still tinted with the last peachy-purple vestiges of sunset.

Rick took her hand and squeezed it. "As I may have mentioned already, I'm glad I came over here tonight," he said. "I very nearly didn't, but

Adrian persuaded me."

"I'm glad too," she said. "Why haven't you been here before?"

"I live at Flackston. Adrian and I already belong to a club there, but he fancied a change of scene tonight, and we'd heard about this one from some of the chaps at school."

Flackston was a wealthy residential area, some ten stations down the railway line from Charters Lea. Charis had never before met anyone who actually lived there, which added even more to Rick's mystique.

They walked hand in hand, stopping now and again to kiss in the casual manner of old friends, instead of with the mutual passion of their first embrace. This seemed entirely natural and in keeping with their surroundings, and Charis began to feel that she had known Rick for years rather than for just a few hours, so familiar had he become in so short a time.

Strolling down Wednesbury Road, Rick said, "How about tomorrow? Could we meet?"

Charis hesitated, wondering what time he had in mind, and knowing she would be expected to attend church in the morning. "I'd like to," she said, "but I couldn't see you until the afternoon."

"Church?" he enquired.

She nodded.

"I understand. It's the same for me, but I'll tell you about that another time. Shall we say three o'clock then? I'm not sure of train times, but I'll meet you at the station as near to three as I can make it. I dare say you know a few places round here where we could go."

"Can you give me your phone number, just in case I can't make it for any reason?" said Charis, immediately anticipating trouble with Grace.

"It's Flackston 7239, but it's in the phone book under Woodrose, C. E. if you forget," said Rick.

They said goodnight without kissing again.

'Just as well,' thought Charis, 'as we're right outside my house and Mummy could be watching.'

Moments later, her suspicions were confirmed: "Who was that rather good-looking boy?" said Grace. "No, I *wasn't* spying on you. I just happened to be by the window as you got to the gate."

Charis was too happy to be annoyed by this unconvincing explanation. "Rick Woodrose," she said, savouring his name with great pleasure. "He lives over at Flackston, but he wants to meet me tomorrow afternoon. He'll be at *church* in the morning," she emphasised.

Grace immediately smiled: "Rick? Oh, Richard, I suppose. That's a nice name. Which church does he go to?"

"Oh honestly, Mummy, I didn't ask him. I've only just met him."

"He seems a better type than that Wilkinson fellow, at least," she said.

"You don't mind my going out with him then?"

"No. I like the look of him, and I'm *very* glad he goes to church," said Grace.

The next day Charis hurried up the road to meet Rick as arranged. He was already waiting for her in the sunshine outside the station, dressed in fawn trousers, a short-sleeved creamy-white sports shirt with a golden-brown tie, and smoking a cigarette. Over one arm he was carrying the bracken-coloured jacket which he had been wearing the previous evening.

He kissed her on the cheek. "Where are we going, Cara?" he asked.

"I can only think of the park," she replied. "Will that do?"

"Sounds fine to me," said Rick as, hand in hand, they wandered off down Coniston Avenue.

"*Did* you go to church this morning?" he asked later.

"I certainly did."

"Which one?"

"St Luke's at Ockley."

"You're not a Catholic, then?"

"No. Why?"

"Well, going to Stella Maris, I thought you might be, that's all," said Rick.

"How about you?" she asked.

"A Catholic, though somewhat lapsed I fear," he said with a sardonic smile.

Charis was surprised, although she wondered why she should be, considering that at least eighty-five per cent of the pupils at Stella Maris were Catholics, and that his sister had been one of them, and was called Teresa — a Catholic name if ever there was one. Thinking about names, Charis said, "I suppose your name is short for Richard?"

"No, actually it isn't. I'm really Patrick, but I simply *refuse* to be nicknamed Pat or Paddy. My mother's an Irish Catholic and we all have saints' names. My father doesn't believe in anything, but he goes along with whatever she wants. Non-Catholics who marry Catholics have to agree to their children being brought up in the faith, you know."

"Yes, I knew that. You said you had a younger brother and sister. What are their names?"

"Laurence and Lucy — two more saints, if somewhat obscure ones."

"If you're a Catholic," Charis said, "why aren't you at Brendan Priory?" This was a well-known Catholic boys' school in Upsvale, where Maggie's brother, Bernard, had once been a pupil.

"My father put his foot down over that," said Rick. "Eden House has a much better academic record than the other place. There were a few ructions with my mother, but she gave in eventually. I could ask you a similar question."

"What do you mean?"

"If you're a non-Catholic, why are you at Stella Maris?"

"My parents believed convents turned out good girls who were nicely behaved, in addition to being well educated."

"And is it true?" asked Rick with his characteristic grin.

"Of course it isn't," said Charis, thinking of Polly and Pam in particular. "Some of the girls I know are quite naughty, if you know what I mean."

"Somehow I don't think you're exactly a saint yourself, are you?" said Rick.

"How could you tell?" she asked coquettishly.

"I wasn't kissing a saint in the last waltz, and that's for sure," said Rick.

By then they were at the park gates and were soon wandering down the path which led to the lake. Most of the boats were out, and Charis wondered if she would see anyone she knew like, God forbid, Banjo and Polly.

"Shall we go out for a row?" said Rick.

She hesitated. "Better not. It's a bit risky," she said.

"Risky? Why?"

"Unfortunately, I can't swim."

"I won't tip you in, I promise."

The lake looked so cool and inviting that Charis was tempted, but she had been so indoctrinated by her mother about the dangers of drowning that she prevaricated: "No, not today. Some other time maybe."

"OK, then. How about an ice cream? Can you get refreshments anywhere here?"

"In the Round House," she said, relieved. "Come on. It's this way."

Soon they were sitting at red painted tables outside the circular building, overlooking the lake and enjoying vanilla cornets.

"I must have licked off all my lipstick," said Charis. "Do you mind if I put some more on?"

"Go ahead," said Rick, "although I dare say you'll need to do it again anyway before you go home."

They both laughed.

"Who was your fair-haired friend last night?" asked Rick, lighting another cigarette while Charis fumbled in her make-up bag.

"Maggie Rigg. Now she *is* a Catholic," she said, wondering why she was giving Rick this information, and feeling an irrational stab of jealousy that he had been interested enough to enquire about her.

Rick appeared to sense her slight irritation: "I'm not too keen on blondes myself," he said. "*Your* hair colour is much more interesting. She's buxom too — and tall. I like my girlfriends slim and manageable."

Leaving the Round House they headed towards the wooded area of the park, where last autumn's fallen leaves rustled under their feet and a grey squirrel leapt with amazing agility from branch to branch above them. Rick's arm was already round her shoulders, and as they neared a suitably broad-trunked tree, he pushed her gently against it and kissed her with the same passionate warmth which had so thrilled her the previous evening. After kissing several times, they clung closely together cheek to cheek, and he stroked her hair gently.

Once again she detected a woody smokiness, mixed with faint scent, and sniffed his skin with sensuous pleasure. "You smell of scented smoke," she said softly. "It's lovely. What is it?"

He laughed: "Cigarettes, more likely than not. But it could be mixed up with the soap my mother makes us use. I think its called sandalwood."

"Whatever it is, it's gorgeous," said Charis, taking another sniff.

"Shush. Let me kiss you again," he said, and she abandoned herself to the sheer delight of his warm, sensitive lips and clean-tasting tongue. "When can I see you again, Cara?" he asked.

"Soon. As soon as possible."

"Tuesday?"

"But we start exams that day."

"I know, but it's too late now to do any serious revision, and we shan't be at school in the evening, shall we?"

"My Tuesday exam is Art, anyway," said Charis. "First thing in the morning."

"I have German in the afternoon," said Rick, "but it would be nice to think I could see you in the evening after that particular ordeal."

"I'd love to," said Charis.

Walking away from the copse, Rick brushed loose pieces of tree bark from her clothes. "We don't want to give anything away, do we?" he said. "What we do together is *our* secret. Speaking of which, do you want to redo your make-up? I *said* you'd have to, didn't I?"

Laughing gaily, they sat on a park bench while she searched for her lipstick.

"I like you a lot, Cara," said Rick.

"I like you too," she replied.

Rick squeezed her hand tightly and pecked her on the cheek.

At school, Charis refused to be drawn into giving details of her Saturday-evening walk home with Rick, or her Sunday date with him. She knew now how Maggie had felt when she had asked similar questions about Leo, and realised with glowing pride that her personal relationship with Rick was already special and very private.

"I *knew* you'd struck gold. I *said* so, didn't I?" said Maggie, pleased. "Rick's awfully good-looking, and doesn't he dance well?"

All day long Charis was agitated about the exams, over the moon about Rick and even faintly, unnecessarily, anxious in case, inconceivably, she should lose this new-found delight for whatever reason. These fears were enhanced by the sight of Wendy, who had clearly not been sleeping well, and looked as though she was about to dissolve into tears.

"I feel lousy," said Wendy. "I don't think I've ever felt so rotten before. I could hardly bear to watch him dancing with that Miranda. I was *aching* for him, and I can't think about anything or anyone else."

"If it's any consolation, I know exactly how you feel," Charis said sympathetically.

"How *can* you?" Wendy snapped in a very uncharacteristic fashion.

"Very easily," Charis replied. "Don't you remember a similar thing happened to me with Banjo? He took me home twice, and then abandoned me for Polly because I couldn't go to the Boat Race."

"Yes, but Banjo isn't a nice person. Ronnie *is*, or hadn't you noticed?"

"Of course he's nice. I liked him the first time I ever saw him, Wendy, but you can't *force* someone to go out with you if they don't want to. I know it's hard to take, but you'll just have to."

"Ken Purchiss seems very interested in you, Wendy," said Maggie helpfully. "I mean, look how he kept dancing with you and asking to take you home on Saturday. Why don't you give him a chance?"

"The same reason Mitch avoids Tom Potterfield. He's *dull*, and he doesn't appeal to me," said Wendy with considerable venom.

"There's no answer to that," said Maggie.

Charis was thankful the exams began with Art because it let her down lightly. It was in three separate parts: figure drawing, plant drawing and painting a picture from imagination, and the first part was figure drawing. A girl from the fourth form had been chosen to sit, and Sister Clare, the Art mistress, arranged her in a suitable pose on a dais. The exam lasted for two hours, at the end of which Charis thought she had made a fairly good attempt, although she knew her drawing would be nothing like as good as Bernadette O'Malley's. Bernadette usually shared the bottom-of-class position with Angela Doyle, but she was truly gifted at art, and everyone envied and admired her obvious talent.

Charis could barely wait to go home and prepare for her date with Rick.

"Don't you want any dessert?" Grace asked, after Charis had first picked at, and then left, most of a tasty shepherd's pie.

"I'm not hungry," she said. "I can't eat anything else."

If Grace guessed the reason, for once she refrained from commenting. It was another balmy summer evening. The windows were open and the scent from the Farrow's newly mown lawn came drifting inside, mingling with the heady perfume of the philadelphus bush growing near the back door, which Grace insisted on calling orange blossom.

Charis changed out of her school uniform and into Beverley Walsh's blue and white checked skirt, which she wore with the matching blue blouse and a shiny white necklace. She tidied her hair, put on powder, rouge, lipstick and mascara, and finally dabbed a little Evening in Paris on her pulse spots. Clutching a cardigan and a small handbag she said a hasty goodbye to Grace and Hugh, and hurried up the road to meet Rick. She waited less than five minutes, and when he emerged from the station he greeted her with, "*Guten Abend, meine Liebe*," grinning widely, before clicking his heels together and bowing smartly.

"Sorry. My German's non-existent, so I don't know how to answer you," said Charis, amused by his antics, "but how was the exam?"

"Grim as hell," said Rick. "How about the Art?"

"Fair to middling."

"Well, they're both over now and we've got the whole evening together," said Rick cuddling her. "Where are you taking me tonight?"

"Could you bear the park again?"

"Only if you'll let me take you out on the lake."

"Oh, Rick. Suppose I fall in?"

"You *won't*. Anyway, I'm a strong swimmer, so I'd rescue you. In fact, I meant to tell you I'm in a swimming competition soon. Will you come and cheer me on?"

"Where will it be?"

"At the Warbridge Baths."

"I'll come if I possibly can," Charis promised, automatically remembering Grace's aversion to swimming pools with the risks they carried, at worst of catching polio; at best verrucas.

Reticently, Charis followed Rick to the boathouse.

"Can we take a boat out?" he asked the grumpy man who was in charge.

"Two bob for 'alf an hour," the man said. "Two and six for an hour. Number 8's free. Mind how you go, now, and no larkin' about."

Rick climbed into the little boat, holding out his hand to steady Charis as she clambered nervously aboard. Rick rowed strongly and they were soon in the centre of the lake with a peaceful view across the rippling water. It was pleasantly cool, although the water was a murky, brownish green, with the characteristic odour of hidden pond life.

Shortly afterwards Charis noticed two rough-looking Teddy boys with DA hairstyles heading in their direction in another boat, and was terrified they would purposely bump into them and tip them into the water.

"Whatcha doin' out 'ere?" one of them shouted to Rick. "You can't row for toffee. Wanna swap boats, darlin'? You'll be safer with us."

"Oh, Rick, I'm scared," said Charis.

"Take no notice," said Rick confidently. "They're just showing off."

The Teddy boys rowed alongside them, the two boats almost touching. "Out for a bit of fun, are yer, darlin'?" one of them said with a nasty grin. "Bet you won't get much fun with 'im."

"Push off," said Rick.

"Push off? Push off? Who're you tellin' to push off?" said the other one. "Right 'oity-toity twit, ain't yer?"

"Hoi there, Number 10. No bumping boats. Any more of that and I'll 'ave you good and proper." It was the boatman.

After a few more taunts, to Charis's immense relief, the Teddy boys finally gave up and rowed off in the opposite direction to pester another couple, and Rick and Charis were able to enjoy their final ten minutes on the lake, although she was uneasy all the while and thankful when her feet were on terra firma once more.

By then the sun was setting, but it would be a while before darkness fell.

"What time does the park close?" Rick asked the boatman.

"Nine-thirty sharp," he said.

"We've got almost an hour, then," said Rick. "Come on, Cara, let's go for a walk in the woods."

Charis had only a faint recollection of the little hut by the fence at the back of the woods, half hidden by hawthorn and holly, but Rick spotted it at once: "How convenient," he said. "Do you suppose there are seats inside?"

There *were* seats of a kind in the form of rickety benches, a few of them broken.

"Never mind," said Rick. "This one looks reasonably safe. Let's sit down, shall we?"

After kissing her for about ten minutes, Rick slipped his hand inside her blouse and cupped her left breast gently. It was a beautiful sensation, different from her experiences with Banjo, who had been over-eager and somewhat rough.

"You don't mind, do you?" Rick asked.

"No, not with you," she whispered.

"Have you done this with anyone else, then?" he asked.

"Just one other person," she admitted reluctantly.

"Banjo?"

"Yes. How did you guess?"

"It wasn't a guess. He told me in a roundabout way," said Rick.

Charis was dumbfounded: "If you knew, why did you ask?" she said crossly, all the beauty and enchantment of the moment evaporating in an instant.

"I meant *apart* from Banjo," said Rick. "After all, he doesn't count, seeing that he's tried it with every female for miles around."

"And he honestly told you all about me?"

"Not *all* about you, but enough for me to guess how far he went."

"How *dare* he!"

"What does it matter?" said Rick. "You're *my* girlfriend now, not Banjo's. That's all in the past. There, there." He stroked her face with soothing, gentle fingers.

"Oh, Rick," she murmured. "You won't let Banjo spoil anything, will you?"

"Of course I won't," said Rick, his hand now resting on her knee. Little by little, it crept under her skirt and fondled her thigh, and, when she did not stop him, his fingers finally strayed inside her briefs. "Banjo didn't do *this*, or *this*, did he?" Rick whispered. "Open up a little for me. Please, Cara."

Charis obeyed him without a murmur.

The sensation made her tense every muscle. It was the first time in her life that she had ever experienced anything so intimate and she was at once thrilled, scared, delighted, yet overcome by anxiety and pent-up emotion. Was this, then, how *everyone* behaved? Pam and Roger? Maggie and Leo? Miranda and Ronnie? *Celia?* She could never ask; would never tell them. It was a secret; an amazing, unexpected, glorious secret and would remain so.

Rick's exploratory fingers lingered tantalisingly inside her before he finally stopped, leaving her damp, tense, slightly sore, but incredibly happy as they kissed and cuddled conventionally again.

"That was wonderful, Cara," said Rick. "You're a great girl. I wouldn't have done that with just *anyone*, you know? I really mean that. It's simply because I want to go steady with you. Honestly. How do you feel right now?"

"Very shaky," she admitted, "but happy. Yes, happy."

"And do you want to go steady with me too?"

"You *know* I do," she replied.

Charis's favourite month had always been April, but now and for ever afterwards it would be June. She could not remember when she was last so happy — probably never. She wanted to smile all the time, even though she was in the middle of the GCE examinations and knew she had paid far less attention to revision than she should have.

The English Literature exam was looming, but on the day before she had leave of absence from school because she had no exams. Neither, it so happened, had Pam, so the two girls took their set books and their notes to Coniston Park in the afternoon, ostensibly to study.

The park was looking at its summery best as they headed towards the lake. Well-tended borders on either side of the path were ablaze with red, apricot, pink and cream roses, scenting the warm afternoon air with extravagant fragrance, while the trees and shrubs were still freshly green, not yet coated with the greyish film which usually descended in late July — the unwelcome herald of summer's decline. It was hardly a suitable place in which to concentrate on school work, surrounded as it was by too many human distractions as well as natural beauty. The antics of passers-by were always absorbing, and Charis guessed she would be certain to relive her own recent, intimate memories, but the invitation to join Pam there earlier that day had been too tempting to miss, and it had been a while since they had spent any time together.

Grace, inevitably, had questioned the wisdom of going out with Pam on the day before such an important exam. "She isn't even working on the same set books as you," she said, "so how can you help one another with revision?"

"If I don't know *my* set books by now, I never will," said Charis. "Anyway, Miss Ingle told us to relax and not get too worked up about things."

Charis was confident of doing well in English Literature and English Language, her best subjects, but Pam's interest in *any* school work was minimal. She had already had a job interview with a firm in London and was waiting to hear from them.

"They offered me four pounds, ten shillings a week," she said. "Not bad, I suppose, for a start."

It sounded a paltry sum to Charis, but she made no comment about it. Instead she asked, "Did they say anything about passing your GCEs?"

"Well, they'd like me to have English and Maths because I'll be doing clerical work, but they didn't sound too fussy. Coming from a grammar school helps, I suppose — particularly a convent."

Wendy, who was also leaving school that summer, had applied for a job as a vet's receptionist, which was also quite poorly paid, but she liked the nature of the work involved which, to her, was more important than the money. Charis, Maggie and Celia, along with very clever girls like Morag McDonald and Louise Heron were all staying on at school to do sixth-form work and to become prefects — a thought which filled Charis with dismay: "If it was just lessons, I wouldn't mind the prospect of the sixth, but trying to keep the juniors in order when I'm on dinner duty will drive me crazy."

"It would me too," said Pam. "I've always thought the staff should do that kind of thing. Thank the Lord I'm leaving."

By now they were at the lakeside, which was deserted. A line of empty boats, tied to one another, bobbed about on the water. The only sounds of life came from the nearby play area, where mothers were pushing their toddlers back and forth on swings, or bouncing them on see-saws amid screams of delight.

"This is the third time this week I've been here," Charis said.

"With that Rick character, I suppose. He's good-looking, isn't he?"

"*I* think so."

Charis hoped Pam would not ask too many questions, but, luckily, her preoccupation with her own affairs was paramount.

"Do you realise Roger and I have been going out for twelve weeks?" she announced proudly. "Ever since the Boat Race, in fact."

"So have Banjo and Polly," said Charis.

"Polly worries me," said Pam. "She's so reckless."

Charis raised her eyebrows: "With Banjo, you mean?"

"From what she implies, they've been taking risks."

Charis was very shocked. Such behaviour was rare amongst people of their age and it was the first time she had heard of anyone she knew infringing the unwritten rules. Unwilling to believe the worst, even of Polly Phillips, Charis found herself defending her: "She's probably exaggerating. I know you like her, and she's your friend, but she's always been a bit of a show-off."

"I hope you're right," said Pam. "I mean, *Roger* can be naughty enough, but so far we haven't done anything to worry about."

Charis shivered, reliving the intimate details of her recent date with Rick, although she knew that she too had absolutely no cause for concern. Reluctant to dwell on Polly and Banjo's dubious activities, she changed the subject: "Oh, let's sit down here and get on with some work. If we talk about boys all the afternoon we'll never do anything else."

"Who wants to?" said Pam, but nevertheless she joined Charis on the park bench, opened her notes on *Wuthering Heights*, and even read a couple of sentences before Charis noticed her eyes straying across the gently rippling lake.

SEVEN

Exactly a week after their first meeting, Rick called for Charis at her home so that they could walk down to Holyoaks together. He arrived early and, desperately wanting Grace and Hugh to approve of him, she invited him indoors. He looked perfect in her eyes, wearing a fawn and green lightweight tweed jacket, white shirt, green tie and beige flannels. His tawny hair was neatly cut; his skin evenly tanned.

"This is Rick," she announced proudly.

Once preliminary greetings had been exchanged between them — confidently by Rick; a little self-consciously by Grace and Hugh — the conversation, in typically English fashion, turned to the weather.

"It's too hot for me," said Grace, "but you look as though you've been sunning yourself, Rick."

"I've had plenty of time in between exams," said Rick, "and I go swimming too, whenever I can."

"Charis tells us you're at Eden House," said Hugh shyly. "How are your exams going?"

Rick pulled a rueful face, followed immediately by his playful puppy's grin. "So, so," he said, "but I still have several more to take, so I'm trying not to think about them too much."

"No, of course not," said Grace. "You need to relax a bit after all that hard work, and so does Charis. Well, off you two go and enjoy yourselves. Perhaps you'd like to come to tea sometime," she added as an afterthought.

"Thanks very much. I'd like that," said Rick.

Charis was delighted by her parents' obvious approval, particularly that of Grace, from whom an invitation to tea was certain proof of acceptability.

At Holyoaks that evening there was renewed talk about the forthcoming Midsummer Ball, for which Leo had already bought tickets for himself and Maggie. It was held annually on the Friday nearest to Midsummer's Day which, that year, coincided with the exact date: 24th June. The venue was to be the large gymnasium at Mundy Park College, and invitations had been extended to other youth organisations in the area. Charis was with Rick, Maggie, Leo and Wendy, whom she and Maggie had finally cajoled into returning, despite her despondency over Ronnie, when Leo raised the subject once more.

"Sounds interesting," said Rick. "Shall we go, Cara?"

"I'd love to, but it's choir practice on Fridays," she replied.

"Couldn't you miss it for once?"

"Probably, but I don't want my mother to go mad about it, and she might easily do that."

"Well," said Rick, "supposing I get the tickets tonight and then, if you can't go, I'll sell them to Adrian."

'If it had been Banjo,' thought Charis, warming even more to Rick, if that were possible, 'he would have just kept them and taken someone else instead.'

"How about you, Wendy?" Maggie asked solicitously.

"I can't go without a partner," said Wendy. Ken Purchiss, who had so unsuccessfully tried to woo her the previous week, was absent.

"Yes you can. You can come with us. There are bound to be masses of people there. It'd be a great chance for you to meet someone."

"I don't know," said Wendy. "I might be a wallflower all the evening, and I'd hate that."

"Oh come on, Wendy. Nothing ventured, nothing gained," said Maggie. "Anyway, she won't be a wallflower, will she Leo?"

"Certainly not. Not with that lovely silky hair and that trim little figure," said Leo.

"I say, do you mind?" said Maggie. "You're not supposed to notice things like that about my friends."

Leo laughed, putting an arm round Maggie and hugging her. "I'll get you a ticket, Wendy," he said. "Don't worry, we'll look after you."

When Leo and Rick had gone off to buy tickets from Tom, Maggie said, "I've just thought of something. If other youth clubs are invited, do you think your funny little friend Colin might be there?"

"Oh, Lord, I hope not," said Charis, aghast. "He still can't dance, as far as I know, and I don't want him hanging round me."

"Rick might be jealous," said Maggie.

"He couldn't be. Not of Colin. They're simply poles apart."

"You've fallen for Rick in a big way, haven't you?" said Maggie.

"There's never been anyone like Rick," said Charis, smiling serenely in sheer contentment.

During one of the popular snowball waltzes later in the evening, Tom danced with her: "I suppose you'll be going to the ball with Rick now," he said, looking glum.

"Yes, I will," said Charis as kindly as she could, not wanting to hurt him.

"I hoped you'd be my partner," he said. "I really did."

"Honestly, Tom, I wasn't sure if I'd be able to go at all when you first mentioned it," said Charis. "I'm sorry, but Rick and I have been out together a few times now, and one thing led to another."

"Yes, so it seems," said Tom, and Charis could not fail to note the faint bitterness in his voice.

"Leo and Maggie and Wendy will be going too," Charis prattled on, trying to lighten the conversation. "Wendy hasn't got a partner. You could dance with her." Immediately she regretted her words.

"Thanks, but no thanks, Charis," he said. "Please don't try to matchmake on my account. It was you I wanted to take."

"Oh, Tom, I *am* sorry," she said, and, although Tom held no fascination for her, she felt curiously proud and elated by the realisation that she now had two definite strings to her bow.

"What was all that about?" asked Rick as he and Charis finished off the snowball waltz together. "Old Potty looked daggers at me when I bought the tickets, and he didn't seem to be enjoying himself very much when he was dancing with you just now."

"It's a bit awkward," she said. "I think I told you he used to dance with me a lot, and it seems he wanted me to be his partner at the ball."

Rick frowned: "Oh, he did, did he? Well, tough luck. He left it too late. You're *my* girlfriend now, that is unless you'd *prefer* to get tied up with him."

"Oh, Rick, don't be silly. You *know* that's not what I want," she said. "Come on. Smile at me."

In an instant the puppy-like grin appeared. "Let's do the whisk at the next corner," he said, squeezing her hand. "I want everyone to see I've chosen the best dancer in the room."

The next afternoon they returned to Coniston Park and, as usual, Rick was smoking.

"How many do you smoke a day, Rick?" asked Charis.

"Too many. At least ten, I suppose," he admitted. "Haven't you ever tried?"

"No. My mother *hates* the smell of smoke in the house and she'd go mad if she saw me smoking. My father used to, but he gave it up."

"Do you want to have a go?" asked Rick. "You can try one of mine if you like."

The experiment was not a huge success. She choked on the smoke, which also made her eyes smart. Rick laughed, but Charis said, "I don't think I'll try that again, thanks all the same."

"Just as well," said Rick, puffing away happily. "You don't want to get addicted, and, to be honest, I don't much like to see girls smoking."

"It looks so sophisticated, though," said Charis. "I mean, *everyone* smokes in films, don't they? Women as well as men."

"Yes, I suppose they do, but if I were you I wouldn't copy them," said Rick.

Hand in hand, they approached the tennis courts, where several people were playing unimpressive matches.

"They'll never make Wimbledon, and that's for sure," laughed Rick. "I wonder who'll win the singles titles this year. Maybe Drobny and Little Mo again, like last year."

"I think Little Mo is marvellous," said Charis. "She's won the title three times, hasn't she? I wonder if she'll make it four in a row."

"We'll have to wait another couple of weeks to find out," said Rick. "You know, Cara, we could play tennis sometimes for a change, couldn't we? Are you any good at it?"

"Not really," she confessed. "Are you?"

"I like to think so," said Rick. "All my family are keen tennis players, so I might be able to help you improve your game if you'd like me to. Let's think about it, shall we?"

"How is that boy at your school who broke his arm playing tennis?" Charis asked, suddenly remembering.

"Paul Williams? How did you know about him?"

"Tom was visiting him when my grandma was in Halstead General. We met in the lobby."

"Good Lord! He's better now. Back at school, but he won't be playing tennis this year, I shouldn't think."

Leaving the tennis courts behind them, they headed towards a pathway and an inviting seat shaded by a lime tree.

"I *love* the scent of lime blossom," said Charis, taking a deep breath of its honeyed sweetness. "Let's sit down here, and then you can tell me some more about your family."

"What else do you want to know? *Why* do you want to know?" asked Rick, sitting beside her and resting his arm along the back of the seat.

"I want to know everything about you," she confessed. "Am I being too inquisitive?"

"Of course not. Well, here goes, but stop me if you get bored. There's my father, Charlie. He's forty-nine and a stockbroker. He met my mother in London in the thirties. She was working in an office as a secretary, but she used to sing with a band in the evenings at a dance hall he used to go to. She was very pretty, and Irish, as I told you. They started going out together, and they got married in 1936. Tessa, my sister, was a honeymoon baby; at least that's what they say!" Here Rick laughed naughtily. "Two years later I came along, for better or worse," he continued, "and then there was the war. My father was in the army and away for most of the time. When he came back, Tessa was eight and I was six, and the year after that the twins were born, so you see my mother was a good, dutiful Catholic having four children. That's one of the things I don't go along with, actually."

"What do you mean?"

"Not being allowed to practise birth control," said Rick. "I suppose I shouldn't admit that, seeing that I've been raised as a Catholic and pretty well indoctrinated, but I do think it makes more sense to limit families, particularly when there isn't much money — not that money was a problem for my family."

Charis had been brought up in a home where the subjects of sex and procreation and anything to do with either were taboo, so she wondered why she wasn't painfully embarrassed by this conversation, yet, somehow, with Rick it seemed perfectly natural and easy.

"What does your mother think about your views?" she asked.

"Oh, heavens, I haven't told her. I like peace and quiet whenever possible, and my mother has a fiery temper to match her hair. She doesn't need to know. I still go to Mass to keep her happy, even if I do have some doubts."

"What do you mean 'to match her hair'? Is she a redhead or something?"

"Like a fox — or should I say a vixen? Yes, red hair runs in our family. Tessa's the only dark one of the younger generation. She takes after Dad, but the twins are bright ginger, and my cousin Bryony is a redhead too."

"Bryony? What a pretty name. It's a wild flower, isn't it?"

"She's a wild flower, all right," said Rick with a laugh.

"Is she an only child like me?"

"Well, not exactly. She has a half-sister, Gabrielle, who's about eight years older. Their father, Dermot, is my mother's brother. You see his first wife, Roisin, died soon after Gaby was born."

"That's very sad."

"Yes, but it was a long time ago, of course."

"What's your mother's name?"

"Shelagh, spelt S H E L A G H. How Irish can you get?"

"I didn't know you could spell it like that," Charis admitted. "I mean, I didn't know that was the Irish way." She turned to look at him. "Your hair has a reddish tint too," she said, stroking it where it grew at the back of his neck.

"And so does yours, actually," said Rick, "only it isn't quite so noticeable. Yours is more golden, but there are some auburn bits where the sun shines on it."

"Yours is nice to touch," said Charis. "Clean and curly."

"Like something else I could mention, but I won't," said Rick with a wicked grin. "You're quite a sensual person, aren't you?"

"Am I?" She flirted with him, using her eyes.

"You know you are, and so am I," and he kissed her firmly on the lips to prove the point. "What else do you want to know before I rush you off to the woods to have my wicked way with you?" he asked.

She giggled. "Tell me some more about jazz," she said. "I don't know much about it, but I loved *The Glenn Miller Story*."

"That's dance-band music — swing," said Rick. "The *real* jazz in that film was Louis Armstrong playing 'Basin Street Blues'. Do you remember it? I've got the record at home, as a matter of fact."

"*Have* you? I thought that was one of the best parts of the film. Well, the most exciting anyway. I liked all the Glenn Miller music too, though."

"It's very smooth and easy to listen to, but jazz — real, traditional jazz — is more down to earth and, what's the word? Honest, perhaps. It's rougher, brasher, unrefined. The only way to find out about it is to listen. You'll have to come over to my place and hear my records some time. I'm building up a good collection."

She wondered whether Grace would veto a visit to Rick's house. She *longed* to be allowed to go, but somewhere at the back of her mind there lurked a nagging suspicion that Grace would refuse.

"What's the matter, Cara? You look a bit sad all of a sudden," said Rick.

"Sad? No, how could I be?" she said. "That's the last thing in the world I'm feeling."

"Come on. We've talked enough. Let's go and have another look at that little hut in the woods," said Rick, and she needed no further persuasion.

I LOVE RICK

These words appeared at random throughout the pages of Charis's school rough-work book. She had also compared their names to find out whether they were compatible:

PATRICK JAMES WOODROSE
CHARIS LAURA MITCHELL

You were supposed to score out each shared letter, and scan through those remaining, reciting the mantra: 'Love, like, hate, adore'. At the end of the exercise Charis was gratified to discover that Rick loved her and she adored him, so they were surely meant for each other.

Maggie did the same with her name and Leo's, which worked out as Leo adoring her and she liking him: "Oh well," said Maggie, with a shrug, "at least we don't hate each other."

Charis often compared Rick with Ronnie and Banjo, analysing her feelings for all three of them. It was Ronnie's fascinating appearance which had appealed to her at the outset, mingled with the first stirrings of sexual awareness which he had awakened so gently and perhaps unwittingly. The tactful way in which he had handled the embarrassing situation with Grace after Celia's party, and his apparent continuing concern for her welfare and happiness now marked him as a friend for whom she was certain she would always feel warmth and affection, but nothing deeper now that she had Rick.

Banjo's blatant advances had flattered her and bolstered her ego to such an extent that, falling so soon from her exalted perch as his latest conquest, had been all the harder to bear. But whatever else, and despite his disreputable character, he had fanned the embers of dormant passion, kindled by Ronnie, until it had become a volatile flame.

Rick, exciting, amusing, good-looking, warm-hearted and dependable, embodied the better characteristics of the other two and much more besides because he apparently reciprocated her feelings for him. She felt like a flower which had been in bud with Ronnie, unfolded with Banjo only to be blighted by the frost of his rejection, and was now in full bloom, with its petals opened to the sunshine of Rick's affection.

Last-minute revision for the remainder of the GCE examinations meant that Charis and Rick were unable to meet again until the evening of the Midsummer Ball. To her great relief, Grace not only gave her approval to the occasion, on condition that Charis apologised in advance to the organist of St Luke's for missing choir practice, but also bought her a very pretty pair of earrings. They were small pink roses made of china, complete with little green leaves, and as she had already decided to wear the dressiest of Beverley Walsh's cast-off frocks — the black sleeveless one scattered with rosebuds — the earrings were a perfect match, and she thanked her mother warmly.

"Well, you've been working very hard at your exams," said Grace, "so Daddy and I thought you deserved a little present. I must say we both like what we've seen of Rick, and we want you to enjoy the ball."

So far Charis had refrained from mentioning that Rick was a Catholic, as she knew that Grace — the diehard Protestant — would not be too pleased. All too often Charis had heard her mother deprecating the strictness of the Roman Catholic religion, with its rigid obedience to the Pope and unswerving belief in various dogmas which were not obligatory in the Church of England, and she dared not risk saying anything which might jeopardise her perfect relationship with Rick. It was fortunate, too, that Grace had not pursued the question of where he went to church, and Charis was keeping her fingers crossed that the subject would not arise.

Conveniently, the last GCE exam — apart from the final section of Art — took place on the 23rd June, so Midsummer Day itself was one of relaxation and the minimum of school work.

During the lunch hour Bernadette O'Malley came running up to Charis and Maggie. "I've just heard some super-spicy, amazing news," she said breathlessly. "You'll never guess what."

"Tell us, then," said Maggie. "Don't keep us in suspenders."

"Miss Ingle's getting married," she announced. "Isn't it *super*?"

The two girls exchanged astonished glances.

"What else do you know?" Charis demanded. "We need details."

"Nothing else. I only just heard from Glenda in Five Beta. Miss Ingle told them in the English period just before lunch."

"We've got English this afternoon. We must find out more then," said Maggie. "Mind you, I'm not surprised. She's such a lovely person. Not like a teacher at all."

Charis had never forgotten that long-ago interview with Irene Ingle, who had so encouraged her and helped her to discover her potential. She had never divulged the details to anyone, and had no intention of doing so now, but then a bleak thought struck her: "Do you suppose she'll leave?"

"We'll soon find out. I hope not, but you can never tell. She'll probably want to start a family," said Maggie.

Charis remembered Rick's remarks about his mother being a good Catholic because she had borne four children, and Maggie's mother had given birth to an amazing seven. Charis, though, was an only child, and Grace had always shrunk from discussing anything of that nature. 'Maybe that's why she isn't keen on Catholics,' thought Charis, wondering why the idea had not occurred to her before.

"Good afternoon, girls," said Miss Ingle, entering Five Alpha at two o'clock, a faint smile quivering on her lips. The class stood up, as usual, and joined in an Our Father. "If you could just see your faces," Irene Ingle said with a laugh after the prayer, as she surveyed the twenty-five or so girls seated before her, watching her every move. "You're all thinking, 'Is she going to tell us more?' Be honest now."

They all laughed.

It was Maggie, of course, who took the plunge: "We'd *love* to know, Miss Ingle," she said. "I hope we aren't being too nosey."

"Of *course* you are," said Miss Ingle, "but that's only natural, so I'll put you out of your misery. After all, you've always been my best class, and the exams are all but over." They sat in hushed silence, waiting for Miss Ingle to begin. "I've known Peter a while," she said. "We met at university. He asked me to marry him at Easter, and we've been engaged since then, but I purposely didn't wear my ring, and I didn't want to tell any of you because of your exams. I wanted you to concentrate on your studies rather than letting your imagination run riot about me. I know exactly what girls of your age are like. *Anything's* preferable to using your brains — even aimless speculation about your English mistress's private life!"

There was laughter, then someone asked about the ring.

"It's a sapphire and diamond cluster," said Miss Ingle. "I'll show you some time, but so far I've only worn it when I'm away from school."

"What will your new name be?" asked Bernadette, emboldened since Maggie had broken the ice.

"Wolsey. Like the ill-fated cardinal, or nylon stockings, if you prefer."

More laughter.

"Will you be leaving, Miss Ingle?" Charis asked shyly. She longed to know, yet dreaded the answer.

"Not until Christmas. I'll be with you for one more term, and then we expect to spend some time in France. Peter teaches too, and he fancies trying his hand at teaching French children how to speak English."

"When are you getting married?" asked Louise Heron.

"On the sixth of August in Cromer — that's my home town — nuptial Mass at eleven o'clock."

"I wish we could come, but of course we can't," said Maggie.

"I shall rely on your prayers instead," said Miss Ingle. "Now, girls, that's enough about me. This afternoon I'm going to read you a short story by Katherine Mansfield, and then we shall discuss it in some detail."

"See you tonight at the ball, Mitch," called Maggie in the highest of spirits as they left school that afternoon, "and Leo and I will call for you at six-thirty, Wendy. OK?"

Charis travelled home with Pam that day. "What did you think about Miss Ingle's news?" she asked her.

Pam sniggered. "I wonder if she's had a trial run."

"Oh *honestly*, Pam, I shouldn't think Miss Ingle's like that."

"No? How would you know? She wouldn't be the first, anyway. Most people do it when they're engaged — if not before."

Charis abandoned the subject in exasperation, but found Pam's remarks depressing, feeling excluded from the great secret of 'going all the way'. Since Pam had become so close to Polly, she had changed from the bubbly, pert young schoolgirl she used to be into a mirror reflection of the bolder girl, using even heavier make-up than before and dressing provocatively. Charis wondered, not for the first time, how Pam and Roger behaved when they were alone and whether, like Polly, Pam had been taking risks, but she dared not ask.

She was glad when she could escape indoors to reflect in solitude on the less disquieting aspects of Miss Ingle's forthcoming wedding, and the imminent Midsummer Ball.

Rick arrived at six-fifteen. He was wearing the smart dark-green blazer of Eden House with its distinctive gold, green and red badge, a green tie, an immaculate white shirt and a pair of light trousers. Charis could easily have flung her arms round him and kissed him hungrily there and then, but prudently refrained.

"You look gorgeous. What a sophisticated dress," he said. "You smell good too."

He noticed everything, even Aunt Bee's Elizabeth Arden Blue Grass perfume, which she had let Charis borrow for this special occasion.

"What time is this ball supposed to end?" asked Grace, emerging from the living room.

"Ten-thirty, I believe," said Rick, "but these things can go on a bit longer sometimes. Don't worry, Mrs Mitchell, I'll make sure Charis gets home safely, and there'll still be time for me to catch a late train back to Flackston."

"Thank you, Rick." said Grace. "By the way, I meant what I said about coming to tea. How about Sunday week?"

"Sounds fine," said Rick. "What time would you like me to turn up?"

"Say three o'clock," said Grace. "That's when you've been meeting Charis, isn't it?"

"Usually, yes. See you a week on Sunday, then," he said. "I'll look forward to it."

"Thank goodness you didn't call me Cara in front of my mother," said Charis as they walked up the road to the station. "I meant to warn you about that. She wouldn't approve at all. She doesn't like nicknames. She would be absolutely *livid* if she knew some of my friends call me Mitch."

Rick laughed: "I'm not all that surprised. You have such an unusual name that it seems a shame not to use it. Don't you mind being called Mitch?"

"I wasn't too sure at first, but I got used to it."

"Well, I wouldn't have called you Cara at your home, anyway," he said. "After all, it's a term of endearment. Not the thing to say in front of a girl's parents."

"I thought my mother was going to fuss about me getting in early," said Charis.

"You're scared of her, aren't you?" said Rick. "She just needs careful handling, that's all."

"You don't know her," said Charis. "So far you haven't done anything she'd disapprove of."

"Haven't I?" said Rick wickedly.

"She doesn't know about *that*!" Charis laughed.

"Your father tends to keep in the background, doesn't he?" said Rick.

"He doesn't have much choice," she replied.

It was six forty-five by the time they reached Mundy Park, four stations away from Charters Lea. Already the High Street was full of young people heading towards the college, amongst them Banjo and Polly on the opposite side of the road.

"Oh its *them*," said Charis tetchily. "She lives near here, so I suppose he's just picked her up."

"You certainly have a down on Banjo, don't you?" said Rick. "He's not *that* bad."

Charis bristled immediately: "He wasn't at all nice to me," she protested. "I can't *bear* him."

"He collects girls like a bee collects honey," said Rick. "He just can't help it. It's part of his make-up. He used to give us blow-by-blow accounts

131

of his conquests."

Charis blushed. "What did he say about me?"

"As far as I can remember, just a number."

"A number?"

"Yes. He had a code of one to ten. One was a kiss; two a cuddle; three a touch; four . . ."

"Don't go on. I get the picture," she said, turning even redder. "I hope he didn't exaggerate."

"Oh Cara, don't be cross. I didn't know you then, did I? Anyway, when I realised who you were, at least I knew you weren't a complete prude, and what we do is nice, isn't it?"

His engaging grin made her forget her grievances and she smiled back at him, but could not resist an acid little dig at Polly: "I wouldn't mind betting she's scored ten."

Rick raised his eyebrows. "I wouldn't know about that. Banjo hasn't been so forthcoming lately," he said. "But she certainly looks a fast little number."

The four of them converged at the entrance to the college.

"Ho ho!" said Banjo. "A night out on the tiles tonight, eh? Don't drop your glass slipper when midnight strikes, will you, sweetie?"

"If she does, I'll be there to pick it up," said Rick.

"Well, don't do anything I wouldn't do," said Banjo over his shoulder.

"Which gives you *plenty* of scope, believe me," Polly sniggered suggestively.

As usual, she was wearing vivid, shiny lipstick, and her naturally long eyelashes, thickened with heavy black mascara, fringed her prominent pale-green eyes. Her Japanese-doll black hair, with its seductive fringe, was glossy with a blue-black sheen, and her electric-blue satin dress was so tight that it clung to her as voluptuously as a second skin.

Charis clutched Rick's hand tightly, feeling gauche, timid and totally outclassed by Polly, who looked at least twenty with her shapely figure and confident style. Even the rosebud-patterned dress, which Charis had so loved, looked juvenile now, and she found herself hating Polly for having such an adverse effect on her spirits.

Tom and Audrey were sitting in the entrance lobby of the college, checking tickets — tearing them in half and instructing everyone to keep the other, numbered, halves because there was to be a raffle during the evening. Charis wondered whether, had she agreed to accompany Tom to the ball, *she* would have been sitting next to him instead of Audrey and whether, in view of his duties on the door, they would have danced much anyway. 'I'm so glad I didn't rush into saying yes to him,' she thought. Tom glanced briefly at Charis and Rick, offering only a perfunctory greeting.

The gymnasium had been set out in a similar style to Holyoaks, with tables arranged along both sides. These were spread with pink tablecloths and decorated with small vases of cheerful garden flowers, while the wall bars which overlooked the tables were intertwined with variegated ivy, to give the impression of a leafy bower. It looked fresh, summery and pretty.

"Here we are!" Maggie called out to Charis and Rick from a table halfway down the gym. Then, as they approached, she said, "Is that the dress you told me about, Mitch? I *love* it, and doesn't it suit you well?"

Maggie had chosen her yellow frock again, her pink and white skin as fine and flawless as ever; her make-up understated. Leo, in a neat grey suit, was sitting down with his gammy leg stretched out.

"Where's Wendy?" asked Charis.

"Spending a penny. She won't be a mo," said Maggie.

Mack's Merrymakers were tuning up on the stage. They wore smart red jackets and bow ties with white shirts and black trousers, and their music rests and the drum bore the letters MM in bright red. The master of ceremonies glanced at his watch as seven o'clock approached.

Wendy's entrance was startling. Standing at only five foot two, she was often overshadowed and outclassed by taller, more flamboyant girls, but tonight, with high-heeled cream shoes adding inches to her height, she was clearly trying to make a positive statement about herself. She was wearing a sleeveless scarlet dress with matching lipstick and a delicate touch of mascara, and had knotted a long scarlet, cream and gold chiffon scarf loosely around her waist, so that it floated gracefully as she walked.

Maggie and Charis exchanged glances, both observing their respective boyfriends' reactions.

Leo said, "What was all that about being a wallflower, or did I dream it?"

Wendy fluttered her eyelashes, smiling confidently, and Charis found it difficult to reconcile this self-assured young lady with the familiar, timid-little-schoolgirl image, which she normally portrayed.

"What a pity Adrian's not here," said Rick. "He loves girls in red. He'd be dancing with you all the evening."

"Aren't we lucky, Rick?" said Leo. "Here we sit with three of the most gorgeous girls in the room."

"Absolutely," said Rick. "Just look at all those envious glances."

"Have you seen Polly?" Charis whispered to Maggie at a convenient moment.

"Couldn't miss her," said Maggie. "Very common; very tarty!"

Maggie's confidence and robust approach to most of life's problems restored Charis's spirits once more, and she soon forgot about Polly and Banjo, concentrating instead on enjoying the evening ahead with Rick and her other friends.

The ball had attracted crowds of young people from various youth organisations in the area, but fortunately none of the Greenfinches from St Luke's had turned up. This was hardly surprising since membership had dwindled alarmingly, with very few people of Charis's age even attending the church. The old group, which had included Alan Decker and Desmond Hoyt, had long since been disbanded, the current one comprising mostly thirteen and fourteen-year-olds. Although Charis still sang in the choir, she judged everyone at St Luke's to be poles apart from the Holyoaks crowd, and she planned to keep it that way.

Glancing round the gym, Charis could see most of Celia's friends grouped together, and then Pam arrived with Roger and joined Polly and Banjo. Greg Duffy was sitting with Father Kellow and a few other St Jude's people from an older age group, while Ken Purchiss was with his usual run-of-the-mill Holyoaks cronies.

"Good evening, all," said the MC. "Welcome to the Midsummer Ball. I'm sure you'll all agree with me that the girls tonight look simply *ravishing* — good enough to eat — and it's going to be a wonderful evening, so let's start as we mean to go on and get going with a nice cheerful quickstep. Take your partners, please."

The band struck up with a lively rendering of 'Ready, Willing and Able', and Rick and Charis took to the floor straight away, incorporating the variations which they had now perfected. Her full-skirted dress swirled out gracefully, and she rather hoped it was revealing her frilly pink petticoat.

"Did you mean what you said about Adrian just now?" she asked as they danced.

"What? Liking girls in red? Oh yes, he does, but I was only joking about dancing all the evening with Wendy. He's been going steady for some time now with a girl from the other club."

"You never told me much about that place," said Charis, not sure if she really wanted to know.

"Didn't I? Well, I don't go any more. Not now I've met you. It was attached to a church, of course. Aren't they all?"

Charis longed to ask how many girls he had taken out from there, but dared not do so.

"Your church?" she asked.

"Heavens, no. We don't have that kind of club at St Vincent de Paul."

For no particular reason, she asked him Adrian's surname.

"Dawlish. We used to think we'd form a business partnership one day. Don't you think Woodrose and Dawlish sounds imposing?"

"Very. I can just see your names in lights over a department store or something. How did you meet him? Is he a Catholic too?"

"No, he isn't. I've known him for ages because we live near each other. We're roughly the same age, so we've gone to the same schools and grown up together."

"Why did he come to Holyoaks with you that night if he already had a girlfriend?"

"She was away for the weekend with her family, so he was at a loose end and a bit lonely. Like me, he'd heard a lot about Holyoaks from Banjo and some of the others."

Ronnie Costello arrived as they were returning to their table. He was accompanied by Miranda and a young man Charis had never seen before, so her curiosity was immediately aroused. The stranger was taller than Ronnie; his hair almost as dark, but straight and smooth, whereas Ronnie's was crisp and curly. The three of them joined Celia's group and, as usual, everyone's eyes were on Miranda, including those of the MC. Like Polly, she was wearing a slim-fitting dress, but hers was an elegant ice-blue, an altogether quieter shade than Polly's, and, because she was so petite, she looked dainty, fragile and charming.

"I know most of you have brought your own partners tonight," said the MC, "but there are still some of you on your own, so let's have a snowball to get everyone dancing. By the end of the evening I want to see *everyone* with a partner. We can't have a Midsummer Ball without some romance, now, can we? Tonight may be the luckiest night of the year for some of you. In a moment I'll be choosing someone to start off the snowball with me, and by the time the waltz ends we'll all know a little more about one another."

"Guess who he'll choose first," said Maggie.

"No need. He's already on his way," said Charis, as the MC strode purposefully towards Miranda. Appropriately, the band began to play the tune 'Changing Partners'. Miranda danced beautifully, smiling up at the MC, and talking easily with him until the music stopped.

Pam was the next girl to be chosen by the MC, but Charis was far more interested in the dark-haired youth who had arrived with Miranda and was now dancing with her. The opportunity to find out more came a little later when Ronnie partnered her in the snowball, Rick already having been chosen by another girl.

"Every time I see you these days you're looking radiant," said Ronnie. "How's your love life?"

"Just perfect," said Charis.

"I knew something was just around the corner for you. Didn't I tell you so? You look very happy with — Rick, is it?"

"Yes, it's Rick, and I'm terribly happy. He's wonderful. And how's *your* love life, or shouldn't I ask?"

Ronnie smiled a little ruefully. "I have a hunch that something's just around the corner for me too," he said mysteriously.

"Ronnie, can I ask you something?"

"You can always ask, but you may not get an answer," he replied.

Charis took the plunge: "Who is that fellow who arrived with you and Miranda?"

"Is that all? Well, that's none other than the new man in Miranda's life: Jackie Wiseman's brother Tony. Not all that new, actually; they've been going out for a while."

"*Have* they? But I thought . . . "

"You thought I'd gone back to her, I know," said Ronnie. "But didn't I tell you our relationship ended ages ago, although we're still close friends and probably always will be."

"Do you mind about it?" asked Charis, wondering whether she had overstepped the mark.

"That would be telling," said Ronnie as the music stopped for the final change of partners, and Charis was reluctantly forced to ask a hesitant Father Kellow to dance the last sequence of the snowball with her.

It was a very lively and entertaining evening. Rick stayed close beside Charis throughout, dancing just once with Wendy but a little more often with Maggie — partly out of politeness, but also because Leo couldn't dance all the numbers and it gave Maggie the chance to take to the floor and display her exuberant style.

Long before the interval Ronnie approached their table and asked Wendy to dance, after which, much to her delight and that of Charis, he joined them and continued to partner Wendy for the rest of the evening.

In the interval the MC announced that buffet refreshments would be available in the smaller hall to the right of the gymnasium.

"Come on," said Rick, addressing Leo and Ronnie. "Let's be really gallant tonight and wait on the girls."

"Aren't you glad you decided to come tonight, Wendy?" said Charis when the boys had left them to join the queue.

"I still can't quite believe it," said Wendy. "I never expected him to *be* here, let alone dance with me all the time."

"You just don't understand your potential," said Maggie. "I'm *always* telling you that men go for petite girls like you. It brings out their protective instinct."

"But Miranda's here. I don't understand what's been going on. I thought they were back together."

"They're just friends," Charis explained. "They *did* go out for a long time. You knew that. I don't know why they stopped, but that's all in the past, and she's tied up with Jackie Wiseman's brother now."

At that moment Tom passed their table. Feeling a little sorry for him, yet at the same time secure in the knowledge that she was with Rick, Charis smiled up at him brightly.

"Enjoying yourselves?" he asked with a half smile.

"Yes — Lovely — Super," the girls replied as one.

"I've finished on the door now. Do you think you could spare me a dance later on?" he said.

"If Rick doesn't mind. I'll ask him," she said firmly.

"Oh well, if it's like that, don't bother," said Tom.

"I'm free for all the quicksteps," Maggie volunteered in her usual bouncy, friendly way.

"I'll bear it in mind," said Tom before stalking off.

"He's absolutely crazy about you," said Maggie. "Poor old thing. Why is life so *difficult*? I mean, he's a very nice fellow, but he just doesn't have Rick's panache, does he?"

"What do *you* know about Rick's panache?" said Charis, which sent the three of them into one of their regular giggling fits.

The food was very good. There were sandwiches with assorted tasty fillings, potato salad, sausage rolls in shortcrust pastry, cold sausages on sticks, cubes of cheese and pineapple, crisps, nuts, tomatoes and slivers of refreshingly cool cucumber.

The drinks were all non-alcoholic, which Leo found a little irksome because he was older than the others. "I could do with a nice cold beer," he complained. "That's the penalty I pay for mixing with juveniles."

"I like *that*!" said Maggie. "You weren't too worried about mixing with a juvenile on the way home the other night."

"Just joking, sweetheart," said Leo, "but I'd still love some beer."

"There's fruit salad and ice cream still to come," said Rick, handing out plates, paper napkins and plastic cutlery, while Leo and Ronnie arranged the food on the table so that everyone could help themselves.

"No ham sandwiches for me, thanks," said Maggie. "Midsummer Day, or not, it's still a Friday and that means no meat."

"You're *very* disciplined, aren't you?" said Rick, enthusiastically biting into a sausage roll. "I'm afraid I stopped worrying about all that nonsense some time ago."

"It isn't nonsense," Maggie protested. "If you're a good Catholic, you're supposed to obey the rules."

"Who said I was a good Catholic? *I* didn't," said Rick.

"Come on, Maggie. Live and let live," said Leo.

"Sorry. After all, who am I to judge?" said Maggie, with a contrite smile for Rick.

The raffle was drawn during the interval. Someone from another club won the first prize — an elaborate basket of mixed fruit.

"Isn't that always the way?" said Maggie. "I hoped it would be someone we knew."

The second prize, a large tin of luxury biscuits, went to Babs Randle.

"Third and last prize ticket coming up now," said the MC. "Number 47. Who's been lucky this time?"

"It's *me*!" Rick exclaimed.

Everyone applauded as he went up on stage to be presented with a decorative box of chocolates, which he promptly handed over to Charis. "Don't eat them all at once," he warned. "You'll get spots."

Dancing with Rick in the second half of the ball, Charis suddenly remembered that Aunt Bee and Vanna would be spending the day at her home on the same Sunday as the one on which Grace had invited Rick to tea. She told him, and asked him if he minded.

"Why should I?" he said, relaxed and smiling. "I like meeting people, and if they're your relations I'm sure they're nice."

"Aunt Bee's lovely. Everyone's fond of her. My grandma's a sweetie too, of course, but, like I said, she had a fall a few weeks ago and had to go to hospital, so she's still a bit shaky walking."

"Poor old lady," said Rick.

"She's much better now, but the other thing is she's rather deaf."

"Don't worry," said Rick. "I'll speak with my very best diction. How's this? Rick is here, loud and clear."

"You *are* funny," said Charis.

"And you're extremely tempting tonight in that very enticing dress. I'm beginning to wish we were in our little hideaway in the woods." He nuzzled her ear, making her shiver in a most delicious way.

"Little Wendy is so happy she can't stop beaming," said Rick later. "Have you noticed?"

"I know. She has a tremendous pash on Ronnie. I hope he doesn't break her heart."

"You can never tell, of course, but he seems a considerate sort of chap. You know him better than I do. What do you think?"

"*No one* knows Ronnie completely, but he's always been sweet to me."

"Oh, *has* he? Tell me more."

"Not now, Rick. It was nothing, anyway, and a long time ago."

"Just as long as you meant sweet *to* you and not sweet *on* you," said Rick. "I don't take too kindly to rivals."

"If you only knew," said Charis, overwhelmed by such a flood of desire for Rick that she was on the verge of telling him she loved him to distraction, but she stopped herself just in time.

"If I only knew what?" he prompted.

"Oh, nothing. Just hold me tight," she said, and he needed no further encouragement.

As the ball drew to its close, the MC said: "Before you all start getting *too* lovey-dovey, let's have something really lively. Make some big circles and we'll have a hokey-cokey."

Everyone joined in zestfully, all the way from the comparatively slow beginning to the noisy, chaotic ending.

The hokey-cokey was immediately followed by 'Knees Up, Mother Brown' and, in a flash, everyone was chanting the cheeky, raucous song with as much verve as any dyed-in-the-wool Cockney.

'Mummy would be *horrified*,' Charis thought gleefully, as she sang as loudly as anyone else in the vicinity.

Then the MC said, "Now get into straight lines, eight across, for the palais glide."

"I've never got the hang of this one," Charis admitted.

"It's easy," said Rick. "Just watch what I do."

He was right, of course, and Charis was soon in step with everyone else, and greatly enjoying it.

Finally, the band launched into a noisy conga, and everyone formed themselves into the traditional tail which twisted all round the hall and even went outside via the lobby and then back through another door.

Flushed with the exertion, and supremely happy to be surrounded by all her good friends, Charis thought it one of the most marvellous evenings of her life.

"Ladies and gentlemen," the MC was saying. "I hope you'll all agree it's been a great evening."

"Hear, hear," everyone shouted enthusiastically.

"But all good things must come to an end, and I'm afraid this is it. Take your partners, please, for the last waltz."

The band played soft romantic music, and the lights were dimmed.

"You're lovely and I've never seen you in such high spirits," Rick whispered as they danced cheek to cheek.

"I'm so happy I could *burst*," she whispered back, and he hugged her closely against him, his lips against her hair.

The first Sunday of July marked one of the rare occasions when Grace and Hugh were obliged to miss morning service at St Luke's. To make amends they went to communion at eight o'clock instead, and so Grace felt justified in spending the rest of the morning preparing for Aunt Bee and Vanna, who were coming to lunch. Charis had been far too tired to join her parents at the early service that day, after a particularly energetic evening at Holyoaks with Rick, and was glad to have a valid reason for not attending church at all.

"Just as long as you don't make a habit of it," Grace said as she peeled potatoes in the kitchen. "Make yourself useful now by shelling the peas for me."

Charis sat on one of the kitchen chairs, a colander on her lap, a newspaper spread on the kitchen table, and was soon working her way through a large pile of Yorkshire Blues, which, Grace claimed, were the best peas to be had.

Hugh was spraying the roses against greenfly, and a wave of affection for him swept over Charis as she watched him through the open kitchen door. As each neat little row of green peas fell through her fingers into the colander her thoughts turned to Rick, who was actually coming to tea and would therefore be meeting not only her parents properly for the first time, but also Aunt Bee and Vanna. Life had become so smooth and happy recently that Charis could not help marvelling at how her fortunes had changed in the space of a few short weeks — it was nothing short of miraculous.

Aunt Bee and Vanna arrived soon after eleven o'clock, both suffering from the heat of that glorious July day. Hugh directed them to deckchairs on a shady part of the lawn, helping Vanna to sit down, and making sure they were both comfortable with cushions. Then Grace brought them the cups of tea they always craved, no matter how hot the weather.

"So we're meeting your young man today, are we?" said Vanna, refreshed after a few sips. "I hope we'll like him."

"I'm *sure* you will, Vanna," said Charis.

"How long have you known him now, pet?" asked Aunt Bee. "A month, is it?"

"No, not quite. Just over three weeks." Charis had taken to counting each day since Rick had burst into her life like a miser checking a hoard of gold coins.

Grace had made some of her special cakes and pastries, and it was finally decided over Sunday lunch that they would have afternoon tea in the garden.

"What about wasps and flies, though?" queried Aunt Bee, for whom all insects were a perpetual torment. "They'll be after the jam, and that's for sure."

"I'll keep them off you," Charis promised, greatly in favour of eating alfresco.

"I shall have to wear my hat," said Vanna. "I can't abide the sun on my head."

"That'll be all right, Mother. No one will mind."

"I'll take the kitchen table outside, then," said Hugh. "It's a pity we haven't got a proper garden table, but even if we had, it would only get dirty outside in all weathers."

"How about chairs?" Grace began calculating: "Let's see, there'll be six of us. Two kitchen chairs and four of those upright canvas ones from the shed, I suppose."

Once the lunch dishes had been washed and stowed away, Hugh carried the table outside and arranged the chairs, while Charis took her aunt on a tour of the garden. It was looking at its summery best with masses of multicoloured antirrhinums, yellow and orange marigolds, sweet scented mignonette and mixed pansies with their velvety brown faces. These occupied the front of the border, while tall blue spikes of delphiniums and towering hollyhocks with frilled pink and crimson flowers hugged the fence, invaded by bumblebees.

"I *am* looking forward to meeting Rick at last," said Aunt Bee. "He sounds such a nice boy."

"Oh, he *is*," Charis said, with shining eyes. "He's wonderful."

"You certainly enjoyed yourself at that ball with him, didn't you?" said Aunt Bee, who had already been briefed about it on the telephone.

"Oh yes. It was marvellous, and Rick was so attentive. I mean he was with me all the time apart from one or two dances with Maggie."

"Didn't you think he would be, then? After all, he took you there as his partner."

"I know, but if it had been Banjo . . . " Charis had told her aunt *almost* the full story about him, omitting only the intimate details.

"You were properly let down by that silly fellow, weren't you?" said Aunt Bee. "But he wasn't worth upsetting yourself over."

"It was humiliating, though. He made me feel so silly and unimportant."

"He certainly didn't do much to boost your confidence. You needed someone like Rick all along. I'm so glad you've met him."

"I still can't get over Ronnie going off with Wendy again," Charis mused. "That was the biggest surprise of the evening."

From the house came the distant chime of the front doorbell.

"That'll be Rick!" Charis sped off to let him in, heady with excitement.

The early part of the afternoon was a resounding success. Rick behaved beautifully, his easy confidence and charm endearing him to everyone. He fetched and carried tea things from the kitchen for Grace, complimented her on her scones and pastries, and handed round plates and cups of tea. He spoke slowly and distinctly to Vanna, without making it obvious that he knew she was deaf, and asked her several sensible questions about her fall and stay in hospital. As for Aunt Bee, Rick chattered away with her on a variety of topics, including tennis, in which they found they had a common interest.

Just then, exactly as Aunt Bee had predicted, a squadron of wasps dive-bombed the table, attracted by the strawberry jam.

"Help!" she shrieked, waving her hands frantically in the air and trying to duck out of their way.

"This might do the trick," said Rick, promptly producing a cigarette packet and a box of matches. "Would anyone mind?" he asked, glancing quickly at everyone seated round the table.

Grace looked surprised and mildly disapproving, but she said nothing as Rick began attacking the wasps with expertly aimed exhalations of smoke.

"Thanks for coming to my rescue," said Aunt Bee. "Years ago I'd have done the same, but I don't smoke any more. It used to give me a tickly throat."

"What a shame," said Rick. "I don't like to admit it, but I'd hate to give up cigarettes."

"I often think how silly it is that I'm called Bee when I loathe all flying insects," she laughed, when the wasps had finally dispersed.

"If you don't mind my asking, is your name short for Beatrice?" asked Rick.

"Yes, that's right. I don't care for it at all, as a matter of fact, so I suppose Bee is the lesser of two evils."

"It's the same with me," said Rick, "although I don't *dislike* Patrick. It's a decent enough name, I suppose, but I'd hate to be known as Pat or Paddy."

"*Patrick?*" Grace interjected sharply. "I always thought your name was Richard. Are you Irish, then?"

"*Half* Irish," said Rick, looking quizzically at Charis, as though surprised she had not told her family before.

After a moment's slight awkwardness at the table, Aunt Bee said lightly, "You know, when Charis first mentioned that you were called Rick, I immediately thought of *Casablanca*."

Charis and Rick looked at her in complete puzzlement.

She laughed. "Of course, you're too young to remember," she said. "It was a marvellous wartime film with Humphrey Bogart and Ingrid Bergman. Humphrey Bogart's character in the film was called Rick. You'll have to make a point of seeing it if they ever show it again."

Despite Aunt Bee's timely intervention, Grace seemed less relaxed and certainly less cheerful for the rest of the afternoon. The cakes and pastries dwindled significantly, two pots of tea were drunk, and only a couple of spoonfuls of strawberry jam were left when Hugh posed the question which Charis had so carefully avoided: "We know you go to church, Rick, but which one would that be?"

"St Vincent de Paul at Flackston," said Rick without hesitation.

Grace's eyebrows shot up ominously. "Oh, so you're a Catholic as well?"

"Yes, I am. Born and bred," said Rick, and then went on to tell them a little about his parents' mixed marriage.

"Are you a — what do they call them in your church — an altar boy, is it?" asked Hugh.

"Not any more. My little brother Laurie is, though. He looks just like the angel he isn't when he's up there."

Hugh smiled a little warily. "They start them off much earlier in your church than in ours, I believe," he said. "I suppose it's because most children in the Church of England aren't confirmed until they're about fourteen, and they don't take communion until after that."

"Is that so?" said Rick. "I never knew that. Catholic children make their first communion around the age of eight. It's a great occasion, of course. Confirmation comes later on, when they're about twelve."

Aunt Bee and Vanna sat quietly, not joining in the conversation because they were extremely erratic churchgoers, and knew nothing whatsoever about Catholicism. Grace, too, remained silent in a way which Charis found disconcerting, so she was relieved when her mother finally gave a discreet little cough and said, "Well, I think I'll clear the table now."

"Can I help, Mrs Mitchell?" said Rick at once.

"No, it's all right, thank you. Stay out here with Charis and I'll see to all this."

"I've had enough of the sun," said Vanna. "I think I'll go inside now."

"We'll have to be going home soon, anyway," said Aunt Bee. "We've really enjoyed meeting you, Rick. Hope to see you again before long."

"Goodbye, young man," said Vanna. "Take care of yourself now, and Charis."

Aunt Bee helped Vanna out of her chair while Grace began collecting the dirty plates, and the three women disappeared indoors. Hugh watched them with a look of wistful melancholy in his eyes which Charis had often noticed before, but she had never been able to discover its cause.

"Your garden looks a picture, Mr Mitchell," said Rick. "Do you look after it all yourself?"

"Oh yes, I really enjoy gardening," said Hugh, looking happier. "In fact, it's my favourite hobby. I have an allotment too, you know."

"I suppose you grow lots of vegetables, then? I'm afraid my father doesn't like gardening at all, but my mother loves flowers so she potters about in the borders. Fortunately we have someone to help with the heavier work or else the garden would be a shambles."

"Is it large, then?"

"Pretty big, I suppose."

Charis invited Rick to see the other end of the garden, so he stood up to follow her, and Hugh went indoors.

"Is there some problem about my being a Catholic?" Rick asked when they were out of earshot.

"I'm not sure. I *hope* not, but I didn't mention it to them before, just in case."

"It doesn't make any difference to us, does it?" he said. "I mean, I'm not in the least concerned about you being a Protestant."

"People are funny. My mother definitely has something against Catholics, but I've never found out why."

"Yet she sent you to a Catholic convent. How odd! I know the reason you told me, but even so if she was *that* prejudiced she wouldn't have risked sending you there in case you were brainwashed."

The Farrows were in their garden too: Mrs Farrow sitting under a tree in the shade, and her husband hoeing a flower bed close to the fence where Rick and Charis were talking.

Proud and happy to have Rick by her side, and at peace with the whole world, Charis called out, "Hallo, Mr Farrow. Isn't it a nice day? This is my friend, Rick."

"Good afternoon, sir," said Rick politely.

Mr Farrow, clearly peeved at being interrupted, straightened up, rubbed his back, and looked at them uncomfortably, mumbling only a half-audible response before resuming his hoeing, whereupon Rick pulled a face and she stifled a giggle.

Later in the day, when Charis was alone with her parents, Grace said accusingly, "Why didn't you tell us Rick was a Catholic?"

"It didn't occur to me."

"Does it matter all that much?" asked Hugh, bravely.

"Perhaps not *now*."

"What's *that* supposed to mean?"

"Well, you appear to be very keen on each other. I think he's charming, most polite and helpful, and well educated too, but if you were to get serious . . ."

"Oh, leave off, Grace," said Hugh. "They've only been going out for a little while. You make it sound as if they're about to get married."

"Don't be silly," said Grace. "All I'm saying is I wish he wasn't a Catholic. And I wish he didn't smoke either. That's a habit I can't abide. Otherwise, he's nice enough."

As she listened to her mother's remarks Charis felt an uneasy twinge of disquiet, as though a faint shadow had fallen across the previously unbroken sunshine of her friendship with Rick.

EIGHT

Much to Charis's relief Grace made no further mention of Rick's religion which, Charis now realised, could be a thorny subject in the future and one which was also creating problems for Maggie.

"My parents like Leo a lot," Maggie told Charis in confidence during a lunch hour towards the end of the summer term, "but he isn't a Catholic, and that's so important to them. I suppose it's important to me too, but they keep *on* about it."

"My parents like Rick but they wish he *wasn't* a Catholic. Why does it have to matter?"

"I don't know much about Protestants, but Catholics are like Jews, I suppose. They expect their children to marry into the same religion."

"But who said anything about marrying?" Charis protested. "We're only sixteen. We shan't be getting married for *years*."

Maggie looked unusually grave and wistful. "Leo's nearly twenty-one, don't forget, and he's getting serious — *really* serious. For example, when I told him where we were going on holiday this year — a self-catering place in Swanage, actually — he said he'd book up there too, somewhere near where we'll be staying. He said he didn't want us to be apart even for two weeks."

"I see what you mean about getting serious," said Charis, "but it surely doesn't mean that he's set on marrying you?"

"I think it does," said Maggie. "Not yet, of course, but he talks about the future a lot. I said I thought I was much too young to consider even getting engaged, but he wants to buy me an eternity ring, at least."

"Oh, *Maggie!*" Charis was amazed by this news, pleased for her best friend, yet alienated because she had suddenly crossed the invisible borderline between high-spirited youthfulness and responsible maturity, leaving Charis far behind.

"I love my parents and I'd hate to upset them," Maggie went on. "They've always wanted me to go into the sixth form and then on to university if I'm clever enough, but I don't think I really *need* a degree if I decide to go in for catering, and now I'm almost certain I love Leo too and I don't know *what* to do. I don't want to lose him. We're right together, somehow; like you and Rick."

"Is that really how you see us?"

"You behave as though you've known each other all your lives. It's wonderful," said Maggie.

"Does Wendy say much about Ronnie?" asked Charis. "She's always been closer to you than to me, and she never opens up about him when I'm around."

"That could be because you used to be so keen on him yourself, and she feels sensitive about it," said Maggie, "but we're all having problems these days." She sighed before continuing: "Wendy dotes on him, but did you know he has Latin American blood?"

"I often wondered if he was foreign because of his name," said Charis.

"Costello isn't foreign, though, is it? It's Irish, I think," said Maggie, "but his mother came from Argentina originally and some of her people live in Spain."

"That accounts for his exotic appearance," said Charis. "How fascinating!"

"Wendy's parents don't think so," said Maggie. "They have a strong bias against foreigners, for some reason, and they've made it clear to her that they don't approve. Ronnie's going to Spain while Wendy's family are on holiday in Wales, so the whole thing could easily fizzle out, and Wendy is feeling very glum and unsettled."

"Better shut up, Maggie," said Charis. "She must have finished her lunch earlier than usual. She's on her way over to join us."

Rick and Charis were in the back row of the Regal Cinema in Upsvale, where subdued lozenge-shaped lights held aloft by art deco figures were emitting a gentle glow. Two usherettes were walking backwards down the aisles, torches poised aloft over trays of ice creams and soft drinks, and the cinema organist had risen above the stalls to play jaunty interval music.

"Fancy a choc ice?" asked Rick.

"No, thank you. Too messy to eat in here. I usually end up dropping most of it on my skirt. I'd prefer orange squash."

"OK. I'll be back."

They poked straws through foil-covered holes in the plastic cartons and sucked thirstily, watching a blue haze hovering over their seats as smoke from Rick's cigarette mingled with that from scores of others being smoked all around them.

"You know, it's time you met my family, Cara," said Rick, putting his arm round her shoulders when they had finished their drinks. "You said you wanted to know all about them and, after all, I've met yours now, so fair's fair."

"I hope my mother won't make a fuss if I come over to your place," said Charis.

"Why on earth should she? She's met me. She likes me, doesn't she?"

Charis sighed: "I know, but I just have this hunch that she might be difficult about it. She'd want to make sure your mother was there, for example."

Rick laughed: "Of *course* she'd be there. She wants to meet you. Shush . . . the main film's just about to start."

All the way through *A Kid for Two Farthings* Charis was troubled by her underlying thoughts, despite enjoying the whimsical storyline of the film.

On the way back to Charters Lea Rick said, "How about coming over on Saturday before we go to Holyoaks?"

"You *know* I'd love to."

"But you're still worried about your mother? Well, why don't I ask her tonight when we get to your house?"

Full of trepidation Charis rang the doorbell, standing on the step with Rick squeezing her hand to give her confidence.

Grace opened the door. "You're back early," she said. "How was the film?"

"It was very unusual," said Rick. "I think you might enjoy it, Mrs Mitchell."

"Come in for coffee, then, and tell me about it," she said.

"It's very nice of you, but I don't think there's time. The next train leaves in fifteen minutes and I have to get home now," said Rick. "But what I really wanted to ask you was could Charis come over to tea at my house on Saturday?"

Charis saw the expected small frown hover between Grace's eyebrows. "Will your parents be there?" she said, sharply, just as Charis had predicted.

"Oh yes, of *course*," said Rick. "They very much want to meet Charis, and so do the twins. I thought that afterwards we could go straight on to Holyoaks from my house."

"Well, if you're quite sure. It isn't that I don't believe you, Rick, but it just isn't the thing for a girl to go to a boy's house when his parents aren't there. I'm sure you know that."

"That's exactly how my parents feel," said Rick evenly. "I assure you, they *will* be there. You can ring them to check, if you like."

"That won't be necessary," said Grace. "I trust you."

Charis and Rick exchanged relieved glances, and Rick said, "See you on Saturday then, Charis. I'll come over for you around two-thirty."

Sandon Avenue, Flackston, was edged with wide grass verges and flowering shrubs, the pavements constructed from small buff-coloured paving bricks, fitted together in a herringbone pattern. Rick's house, like all the others, was large and detached.

As they approached it Rick said, "Flackston Manor isn't far away and the grounds are open to the public. The fields stretch for miles. I'd love to take you there. We'd be beautifully private — far better than in our little hut in the woods."

"Shall we go there later today, then?" Charis said, anxious for an opportunity to have Rick all to herself after sharing him with his family.

"There won't be time. I want to play you my jazz records and then we'll be having tea, but we'll go tomorrow, shall we? We needn't tell anyone. It'll be another of our little secrets."

"I can't wait," she said.

Most of the windows of Rick's house were wide open, and from one of them came the sound of a female voice singing 'Under the Bridges of Paris'.

"That's my mother," said Rick. "I told you she was a singer, or at least she *used* to be, but she doesn't sound in the least like Eartha Kitt, does she? Come to think of it, *no one* sounds like Eartha Kitt. That lady's a definite one-off."

Unlike Charis, Rick already had his own house key, and let her into a spacious hall, somewhat reminiscent of Celia's at Tamarisk Villa.

"Ma! It's me!" he called. "Where are you? Charis is here."

"Just a tick," a friendly voice replied from upstairs, amidst little scuffling noises, and then Shelagh Woodrose ran lightly downstairs in her bare feet, wearing a beige dress with a brown leather belt. "You'll have to excuse me, Charis," she said. "I can't find my slippers anywhere. I've been wandering around like this for the past couple of hours."

Rick's mother looked amazingly young in comparison with Grace. She had short, bobbed auburn hair and wide, clear eyes that were more green than blue. Her skin was very fair; her bare arms covered in pale freckles.

"Isn't Pa back yet?" asked Rick. To Charis he explained: "He's been playing golf."

"He won't be long," said Shelagh. "The twins are in the den. If you want to play Charis your records, I'll have to chase them out of there."

"No, don't worry, *I'll* do it," said Rick, marching off into the room Charis assumed was the kitchen.

"You go to Stella Maris, don't you?" Shelagh said. "Do you remember my daughter, Teresa?"

"Yes," said Charis, "but I never spoke to her. She was older than me, so our paths never really crossed."

"Come and see her photo. It's in here. Which house are you in?"

"St Faith."

"Tessa was in St Helena — the green one. Most appropriate as we're Irish."

Shelagh beckoned Charis into a large, comfortable lounge with a settee and armchairs covered in blue-grey moquette, and a thick carpet patterned in understated colours. The photo brought back memories of the older girl playing netball with the senior team and singing in the school choir. How strange it seemed to Charis that in those days she could have had absolutely no idea that at a future date she would be going out with Tessa's younger brother.

"It's a very good photo," said Charis.

"She would have been two or three years older than you, I suppose," said Shelagh, "but even two years makes a lot of difference when you're young. I should know. Perhaps Patrick told you my husband Charlie's *ten* years older than me. I was eighteen when we met, and married at twenty. He seemed ancient to me at the time, but the gap closed considerably as we got older."

"I suppose it would," said Charis, trying to recall Rick's comments about his parents' marriage. She thought he'd said they were married in 1936, which made Shelagh Woodrose around thirty-nine now.

"Would you believe it?" said Shelagh. "My slippers were in here all the time." She bent down and fished out a pair of soft suede mules, half hidden under the settee, grinning at Charis as she slipped them on.

Charis was still working out the difference in age between Shelagh and Grace when there was a commotion in the kitchen, and the next moment two children burst into the room with the speed and noise of twin tornadoes.

"Rick's turned us out of the den," said the boy. "I was trying to finish my aeroplane. 'Tisn't fair."

"And I was in the middle of a magic colouring picture," said the girl. "He jogged me and made me spill the water."

"Quietly now, children," said Shelagh. "Where are your manners? We have a guest — Patrick's friend, Charis. Say hello, now."

The twins looked her up and down and then grinned engagingly.

"Hello, Charis," said the girl. "I'm Lucy."

"And I'm Laurie," said the boy. "Haven't you got a funny name? I say, do you love my brother?"

Charis blushed fiercely.

"Laurie!" said Shelagh. "You do *not* ask questions like that, and you do *not* make personal remarks about other people."

"I bet she does love him," he continued unabashed. "I bet they're all lovey-dovey and soppy."

"That's quite enough, Laurie," said Shelagh. "I'm warning you!"

Rick saved the moment, raising his eyes to heaven and flashing Charis his special grin. "You should just see the mess in the den, Ma," he said. "When will you two horrors learn to keep the place tidy? Now I've got to take Charis down to an absolute pigsty."

"You'll put your things away this minute," Shelagh ordered. "You've had the den to yourselves all day, and it's Patrick's turn now. Hurry up now. After that you'll have to get ready to go to confession. It's no use pulling that mournful face either. The sooner you go, the sooner you'll be home again, and there are sugar-backs for tea."

"Oh, *YUM!*" said Laurie.

The colour of the twins' hair reminded Charis of red roof tiles. Lucy's had a centre parting and was tied in two pigtails; Laurie's was parted on one side, curly and unruly, and both their faces were liberally freckled. They raced outside again, and Shelagh sighed after their departing backs. "Saints preserve us," she said. "When will they grow up and learn how to behave?"

Presently, Charis followed Rick into a wide, rambling garden. "Do they *really* have to go to confession?" she asked, shocked.

"Certainly," said Rick with a grin. "They jolly well need to."

"Seriously, though?"

"They're receiving Holy Communion at Mass tomorrow, that's why," said Rick. "Ma is very strict about these things."

"Do *you* go to confession, Rick?"

"Sometimes."

"When did you last go?"

"Not since I met you."

Charis was silent, wondering whether he would have to confess his frequent exploratory intimacies with her.

"I know what you're thinking," said Rick. "I can read you like a book. I don't know whether I'm breaking any rules, but *I* think you only have to confess things your conscience tells you are wrong, and nothing I've done with you feels wrong to me. Does it to you?"

"I'm not sure," said Charis, "but that doesn't mean I want to stop."

"Good. That's settled then," said Rick. "Come into the den. This is where we all let our hair down, within reason. My only problem is that Ma won't let me smoke in here. She says the fumes take too long to clear and it's a fire risk."

The den was large, light and bright, with plenty of windows. An old sofa, covered in patterned cretonne, and several elderly, wicker basket chairs with floral cushions had been placed at random around the room, and four tall white-painted chests stood side by side against one wall.

"Mine's the end one," said Rick. "Lucy's is next to it, then Laurie's, and Tessa's is at the other end, only there isn't much left in hers any more. Hopefully, I'll take it over soon."

"What a good idea!" said Charis, fascinated. "What do you keep in them?"

"Pens, papers, paintboxes, souvenirs, letters, gadgets, books — anything we like," said Rick. "We can lock them if we want to, but Ma keeps the keys in case we lose them — in case the *twins* lose them, I should say — so there isn't much point in bothering."

A lopsided table leaned against another wall, covered in an olive-green chenille cloth. "Just let me prop up its wonky leg," said Rick, "and then we can listen to my records." He pushed an old book underneath the table leg, and then produced a portable record player and a pile of gramophone records from a corner cupboard. "Pa had someone run an electric cable down here from the house," said Rick. "It's great because we can use the den in the winter too, *and* I can play my records."

"How super!" said Charis. "I'd love to have somewhere like this to escape to."

"I wouldn't be without it," said Rick. "Sit down, Cara. I'll join you in a moment."

She perched on the edge of the sofa while Rick rummaged through some 78s, selecting four of them. "The autochange takes eight," he explained, "but I don't always trust it, and these records are precious. The first one's 'Basin Street Blues' because you said you enjoyed it in that film, and the others are by Kid Ory, Sidney Bechet and Bunk Johnson."

The names meant nothing to Charis, but the combination of Rick's strong influence, the uniqueness of the occasion, and the wild magic of the music that flowed from the trumpets, trombones and clarinets of those jazz giants had her converted within a few minutes.

"How *fantastic!*" she said.

Rick was clearly gratified that she approved. "Now I'll play you some records by English bands," he said. "They're good, but personally I don't think they'll ever quite equal the real old New Orleans jazzmen. See what you think."

They listened to some Humphrey Lyttelton, Chris Barber and Ken Colyer records, all of which Charis loved, unable to say with complete honesty whether or not she preferred them to the earlier recordings. The fast tunes were so vital, alive and happy, whereas the slow blues numbers were soulful and expressive of hidden emotions which touched a chord deep inside her.

"Have you ever been to Warbridge Jazz Club?" she asked suddenly.

"At the Outhouse? No, I haven't. Why?"

"I've heard about it from some of my friends. Celia, for instance. You haven't met Celia, have you?"

"I don't think so."

"She often goes there with her boyfriend Mark, and other friends of hers. They think it's great."

"I've heard it has a dubious reputation. It isn't licensed for alcohol but it's very near a pub, so most people go over there in the interval and drink too much. I think there have been a few fights too."

"Celia's never mentioned any trouble like that," said Charis.

"No? Well, I don't suppose it happens regularly. There's a jazz club in Flackston too. I've been there with Adrian once or twice. It's miles away from any pubs so it's about as harmless as Holyoaks from that point of view, but the music's good. I'll take you some time if you like."

"You know I'd love to go. Do you think my mother would let me?"

"There you go again. Stop worrying about your mother. Just leave it to me. I'll persuade her. You'll see."

When Charis had listened to all Rick's records he put them back carefully in their paper covers and stowed them in the cupboard, along with the record player. Then he rejoined her on the sofa, put his arm round her and kissed her fondly on the lips, but very lightly and not in his usual passionate way. "Why are you so nice?" he said.

"I can't help it," she answered with a laugh. "I could ask you the same question, of course."

"You know, Cara, I went out with other girls before I met you. You must have guessed that. But most of them were awfully kind of shallow. You're not like that. You *think* about things, and you can be serious as well as light-hearted. I like talking to you — as well as all the other things we do."

"*Patrick!* Tea's up!" Shelagh called from the back door.

"Quick, Cara, put on a little bit of lipstick before we go in," Rick instructed. "Ma's very fussy. She wouldn't like to think we'd been necking in the den. Your mother would be surprised just how particular mine is about things like that." He winked at her, and she followed him back inside the house.

By then Charlie Woodrose had come home. He was a large man with dark hair greying at the temples, and expressive brown eyes, very much like Rick's. He wore glasses with tortoiseshell frames, and was in the act of removing his tie when they appeared. "So you're Charis," he said, holding out his hand. "I'm Charlie. Please call me that. None of that formal Mr Woodrose business. Is it a deal?"

"Yes, all right," said Charis, warming to him at once.

"The same goes for me, of course," said Shelagh. "I meant to tell you. Just Shelagh will be fine."

"Can we call you Charlie and Shelagh too?" asked Laurie cheekily.

"Certainly not, you young pup," said Charlie. "We'll have a little respect from you for a few more years yet, if you don't mind."

Laurie giggled.

"I expect you'd like to wash your hands, Charis," said Shelagh. "Rick, you can use the downstairs cloakroom. Show Charis where the bathroom is, will you, Lucy?"

It was a cool, shady room with a light-blue enamel hand basin and bath. The curtains were made of good-quality floral towelling in pastel shades of blue, lavender and green. As soon as she used the round disc of soap Charis was aware of the delightful scent of sandalwood, which was so much a part of Rick, and inhaled its fragrance rapturously.

Charis was pleased that she soon felt comfortable and at home with Rick's family, who chattered naturally amongst themselves as though they had known her for years and were not standing on ceremony just because she was there.

"What penance did you get, Laurie?" asked Shelagh.

"Two Our Fathers and a Glory Be," said Laurie.

"And you, Lucy?"

"Three Hail Marys," said Lucy.

Charlie rolled his eyes heavenwards, pulling a face, and Charis remembered Rick telling her that his father was not interested in religion.

"Have you said them properly?" Shelagh demanded.

The twins nodded, looking pious.

"I wonder," said Shelagh. "Never mind, we'll talk about that later. Let's have tea."

Lucy was asked to say a simple grace, and then everyone sat down round the tea table. The sugar-backs turned out to be what Charis had hitherto known as iced buns. From then on she resolved to call them sugar-backs too.

"Have you heard about Bryony's party, Patrick?" Shelagh asked as they munched moist sandwiches filled with tinned red salmon and cucumber.

"I knew she was thinking about having one," said Rick. "Is it all settled?"

"She was waiting to know definitely when Danny's ship was sailing. I was talking to Hattie on the phone today and the next cruise begins soon, so it looks like the party's fixed for next Saturday."

"Explain to Charis," said Charlie. "The poor girl must be baffled by all these strange names."

"I've already told you about my cousins, haven't I?" said Rick.

"You mentioned them once, I think, but tell me again."

"Bryony and Gabrielle — Gaby; their father is Dermot Mayo — Uncle Motto — and Aunt Harriet, known as Hattie, is Bryony's mother and Gaby's stepmother."

"Dermot's my brother," said Shelagh.

"Oh yes. I remember now," said Charis.

"Danny is Bryony's boyfriend," said Shelagh. "He's in the merchant navy."

"How *exciting*!" Charis held romantic notions about sailors and the sea.

"Dermot is a director of Garnet and Mayo Cruise Lines," Charlie explained. "The company holds an annual dinner and dance in London, and that's how Bryony met Danny. He works in the purser's office on one of the liners."

"She's batty about him," said Lucy.

"She's just batty," said Laurie, washing down the remains of a sandwich with a large gulp of lemonade. "And her hair's *brilliant* red. It's even gingerer than *ours*."

"Don't be so *rude*, Laurie," said Shelagh. "And there's no such word as 'gingerer'. You have to say 'more ginger'."

"I think it's lovely," said Lucy. "I wish mine was like hers, and then we'd look like sisters."

"Don't be so *daft*, Luce," said Laurie. "She's our cousin. Why should you want to be her sister instead? You're an idiot."

Shelagh waved a deprecatory finger at Laurie. "Bryony will be in touch with you," she said, turning to Rick. "I'm sure you'll be invited too, Charis."

"*Will* I?"

"Of course you will, noodle," said Rick affectionately. "You don't think I'd go without you, do you?"

Once again Charis felt as though she were bathing in the sunshine of Rick's warmth, enhanced now by his family's friendly acceptance of her.

Before they left for Holyoaks Shelagh Woodrose said, "It's been so nice meeting you, Charis. You'll come back another time, won't you?"

"Thank you very much. I'd love to, and thank you for the tea. I've had a lovely afternoon."

"Take care of her, now, Patrick," said Charlie.

"Do you ever *kiss* him?" asked Lucy, wide-eyed.

"*Lucy!*" said Shelagh.

"Of *course* she does," said Laurie, who proceeded to make kissing sounds as he ran upstairs out of his brother's way. "Bye," he called down. "Kiss, kiss, kiss."

"Sorry," said Lucy, blushing. "I shouldn't have asked you that question, and Laurie doesn't mean to be rude. I *do* like you, Charis. Next time I'll show you all my dolls."

"I'll look forward to that," said Charis, smiling at Rick's quaint little pigtailed sister.

Later that evening at Holyoaks Greg Duffy announced that the club would be closed during August so that evening's meeting would be the last until September.

"I didn't know about that," said Charis, at once feeling woefully deprived.

"Well, next Saturday evening's taken care of if we're going to Bryony's," said Rick, "and then I'll be away for a couple of weeks. When I come back it'll be the end of August, and then Holyoaks will be back in business, so it won't be *that* bad."

Charis gazed at him in disbelief, his throwaway statement taking the wind even further out of her sails. "You're going away?" she repeated, aghast. "Why didn't you tell me before?"

"We *always* go away in August — to Ireland," said Rick. "I suppose I take it so much for granted that I didn't think of mentioning it. It's a family tradition. The Mayo grandparents live in County Kerry, on the Dingle Peninsula. Bryony's going too, but I don't know about Tessa, or Gaby for that matter."

Charis felt the ominous, prickly precursor to tears in her eyes: "I can't bear it," she said heatedly. "I'll miss you so terribly."

"Oh, Cara, don't be blue. I'll miss you too. You know I will, but I can't *not* go. Aren't *you* going away sometime?"

"Not this year," she said morosely, remembering a dismal holiday in Bexhill the previous summer, after which Grace had said it would be a long while before anyone would persuade her to go away again; it was a waste of money *and* she didn't want to put Dizzy into a cattery again as he'd come home with fleas.

"It's only for two weeks," said Rick coaxingly. "Come on, let's enjoy tonight and tomorrow. They say it's going to be very hot, and I'm taking you over to Flackston Manor, remember?"

She gave him a wan smile, trying her utmost to be cheerful, although her heart felt leaden as they rejoined Maggie, Leo and the others.

The next day, Charis walked casually to the station, as though she were meeting Rick there as usual, but instead she caught a train to Flackston.

He was waiting for her, smoking a cigarette, and hugged her before leading her to a bus stop where a single-decker was waiting.

"That's lucky," he said. "These buses don't run all that frequently."

A sweeping paved driveway led up to the main entrance of Flackston Manor, but Rick walked past it and turned down a narrow lane to the left of the mansion, bordered by hedgerows which were knotted with brambles and starred with dog roses. Further down the lane a mellifluous fragrance hung in the air.

"Honeysuckle," said Charis, breathing deeply. "Look, isn't it beautiful?"

Together they examined its pink and cream tongues and inhaled its unique rich perfume.

"Almost as good as your Blue Grass," said Rick sniffing her neck. "It *is* Blue Grass, isn't it?"

"Yes, but it's my own this time. Aunt Bee bought it for me."

"Wear it to Bryony's party, won't you?" said Rick. "And your black dress with the little flowers."

"You like that one, don't you?"

"Oddly enough it's my favourite," said Rick.

"Why oddly enough?"

"Well, black can be a dreadfully mournful colour, can't it? But that dress really suits you. Perhaps it's because of the pink flowers."

"Do you remember what I was wearing the night we met?" asked Charis.

"Mauve stripes, wasn't it? Very pretty. Very demure. Not at all sophisticated."

"You didn't seem to mind about *that*."

"I liked the look of what was inside it," said Rick. "You were frowning, miles away, when I asked you for that first dance, but as soon as you smiled it made all the difference in the world. There was something different about you that attracted me straight away, but of course I didn't know what you were *really* like then."

"My mother always says it's character that counts; not looks. But *I've* always thought looks are all you have to go on to begin with. I mean, there has to be a starting point, doesn't there? I never thought anyone would notice *me*. I always thought I was terribly ordinary."

"I wouldn't describe you as ordinary, Cara. I'd say you were unusual. I mean, you're not a classic beauty, but you don't need *me* to tell you that. You don't look tarty like that Polly character, or even your friend Pam. You have the most beautiful eyes, you know — deep and expressive and the colour of the sea on a wild day. I've seen seas like that off the Irish coast."

"Oh, Rick — how lovely," said Charis. "I suppose my eyes *are* quite nice, but I used to think my ears were my best feature."

"Your *ears*? How funny. Let me check," said Rick, and turning her towards him he nibbled her earlobes, making her squirm and shiver.

Presently, arms entwined, they came to a gap in the hedge and an open field where scarlet poppies, purple vetch, richly scented clusters of creamy meadowsweet, and red and white clover mingled with tall nodding grasses.

"Let's sit down?" said Rick, spreading his sports jacket on the ground. "I told you it would be a lot more secluded here than in the hut in the woods. As far as I can tell there's no one around for miles."

In a moment they were lying amidst the aromatic grasses and wild flowers, exchanging lingering kisses while Rick unbuttoned her blouse, pushed up her skirt and began fondling her all over in the special, familiar way she had grown to expect and enjoy. With his exciting, mysterious male body in such close proximity, she felt such a passionate yearning for him that she almost threw caution to the wind and touched him as intimately as he was touching her, but her courage deserted her at the last moment. It was surely up to him to make the first move; to invite her. It was different for boys, she thought. They always took the lead in such matters, and if she were to touch him, uninvited, he might consider her fast and brazen. In any case, she had no idea what do, nor what he might expect of her, so she lay back quietly on her grassy bed and enjoyed his caresses.

Soon they were both perspiring freely, for it was a hot, humid afternoon.

"Steamy, isn't it?" he whispered, extracting a handkerchief from his trouser pocket and mopping first her forehead and then his own. Leaning on one elbow he broke off a long blade of grass and tickled her face with it, gazing down at her so that all she could see was his tanned face with its frame of tawny hair against the backdrop of a pastel-blue sky. "Just at this moment I feel all kinds of mixed-up things," he said.

"What sort of things?"

"Odd, happy, muddled, tempted — very tempted, as a matter of fact.

How about you?"

"Odd, happy, muddled, scared."

"Scared? Of me?"

"Of both of us. Of what might happen."

Rick kissed her, but gently that time. "Don't be scared, Cara. I'm not the type to take risks. Can you imagine how ghastly it would be for both of us and our families if we did and we were unlucky? Who knows what we'll do eventually if we stick together, but just now you don't have to worry, I wouldn't dream of getting you into trouble, even though I've often imagined how thrilling it would be to go all the way with you. There, are you shocked?"

"No, because I've thought of it too," she said, blushing at so blatant an admission.

"It'll be something really wonderful to look forward to in the future, won't it?"

Charis felt faint with joy at the implication behind his words, and savouring the sudden, sweet solemnity of the moment she said in hushed tones, "I can't imagine anything more perfect."

Rick kissed her gently. "I think I love you, Cara," he said.

"I'm *sure* I love you," she replied.

On the way to the dinner party the following Saturday, Charis kept wondering what lay in store. In one respect it was like the day of Celia's party, but then she had been alone, unsure of herself and terribly apprehensive. Now, confident because of Rick's support, the only similarity with eight months ago was the minor ordeal of meeting strangers.

"Bryony's a crazy girl, but you'll like her," Rick assured Charis when she asked him for a description of his cousins. "She's dying to meet you. Gaby is more serious, but then, as I told you, she's older and wiser. She's just got herself engaged to Giles, so he's bound to be there too." They were walking down a broad tree-lined avenue in Flackston, not too far from Rick's home, when, "This is it. The Magpies," he said.

A tall holly hedge shielded an imposing house built of honey-coloured brick with an unusual green-tiled roof. On either side of double gates stood stone pillars, each mounted with the sculpted birds which had given the house its name.

"It's huge," Charis said in awe.

"I suppose it is," said Rick. "It's just that I'm so used to it. Come on."

Their feet scrunched on the gravel driveway, and they heard music coming from a downstairs room.

"I bet that's Bryony's latest record," said Rick. "'Mezzy's Tune', I think she said it was. She's mad on Humphrey Lyttelton."

He rang the bell, and within a moment the door was opened by Bryony Mayo, who greeted them in a cultured voice with a charming, distinctly

Irish lilt, "*Wonderful!*" she cried. "Come *in*, darlings. Apart from Danny, you're the first to arrive."

Charis would never forget that moment. She tried not to stare, but she had never met anyone so theatrically striking.

Bryony's hair framed her face like a burnished auburn halo. Thick and frizzy, it sprang away from her white forehead in uncontrolled waves, with little tendrils clinging to her temples. Her greenish-blue eyes were fringed by eyelashes darkened with mascara, and her neatly arched eyebrows were pencilled in reddish-brown. Orange-red lipstick enhanced white teeth with the merest suggestion of a gap between the two front ones, which served only to add to her charm. She literally *shone* in a flared dress of shimmery pale golden satin, which perfectly complemented her colouring.

"It's grand meeting you at last," said Bryony, standing a short distance away to appraise Charis. "I've heard so much about you, and you're more than welcome. Let me look at you more closely. Oh, isn't your hair nice? It looks really manageable, and a pretty colour too. Mine is quite impossible."

"I've always wished mine was naturally curly," Charis replied, "and yours is a really striking colour."

"Oh, *thank* you," said Bryony. "Come upstairs and I'll show you where to leave your cardy. Rick, darling, go and talk to Danny, there's a love. He's in the lounge."

Bryony's bedroom reminded Charis of pictures she had admired in glossy magazines. The wallpaper was patterned geometrically in shades of peach, apricot and cream, while the doors, window ledges, picture rails and skirting boards were glossy with cream paint. The bed was covered with a fitted apricot bedspread, on which lay a frilly cushion, edged with cream lace. The early-evening sun, slanting through the window, illuminated an array of amber jars and bowls on the dressing table and a charming painting of a red squirrel on the wall over the bed.

"What do you think of my teddy bears?" asked Bryony, pointing to the chest of drawers in the far corner. "I've been collecting them all my life."

Charis guessed there must have been about twenty bears in all: some large; some small; some elderly and battered; others new and pristine.

"Aren't they heaven?" Bryony continued. "Cuddle them if you want to. *I* do — frequently — especially when Danny isn't available." At this she giggled prettily.

"They're all adorable," said Charis, choosing a large comfortable-looking specimen from the back row, "but I think this one's my favourite."

"My third birthday present," said Bryony. "Isn't he a pet? Of course, they all have names. This one's Charlie, because it was Uncle Charlie — Rick's father — who gave him to me, at least in principle. He was actually away at the war at the time, but the idea was his."

"Isn't your room beautiful?"

"Oh, aren't you kind?" said Bryony. "Just throw your cardy on the bed, and feel free to come up here whenever you want. If you need the loo, it's just down there on the right, with the bathroom next door."

"Thank you very much."

"Just before we go downstairs, and in case I don't get a chance later, I must tell you how glad I am Rick's met you," said Bryony. "He's a dear and I love him lots, so I like him to be happy, and he *is* happy with you. His last *serious* girlfriend was a disaster, but that's a secret between you and me."

Disarmed by this magnetic girl, who never seemed lost for a word and was already prepared to exchange confidences, Charis dismissed the remark about Rick's former girlfriend for now. At the same time, with growing admiration, she resolved to note Bryony's behaviour throughout the evening so that in future, if necessary, she might emulate it, for Bryony was the kind of girl she had always yearned to be.

Downstairs, Rick was chatting to a rosy-cheeked young man with light-brown curly hair.

"Charis, this is Danny McCormack," said Rick.

"Do you really work on a ship?" Charis asked him shyly.

"That's right," said Danny. "In the purser's office. I go back to sea on Wednesday for a short spell of cruising, but in September we sail for Australia, and then I shan't be back until December."

"And I shall be absolutely bereft," said Bryony. "What am I going to do without you, honey?"

"Somehow I think you'll survive," said Danny. "Here, Charis, try some of this," and he handed her a glass of chilled fruit cup.

"Danny, play 'Mezzy's Tune' for Rick," said Bryony. "I'd like to know what he thinks of it."

The catchy music flowed once more. Charis loved it, resolving to make it her next record purchase.

Rick was non-committal: "Typically Humph," he said. "It's named for Mezz Mezzrow, of course."

"Not that tune, *again*, darling." A deep, cultured, female voice came from the direction of the doorway, and Charis turned to see a statuesque woman, elegantly dressed in a black evening gown.

"Mummy! You look *divine!*" said Bryony. "Do come over and meet Charis. Where's Daddy?"

"Just checking his bow tie. He won't be a moment."

As Harriet Mayo approached, Charis was aware of exquisite perfume, flawless make-up and perfectly manicured dark-red fingernails.

"Hello, darling," she said. "We've heard so much about the girl with the unusual Christian name." She eyed Charis up and down. "Charming," she continued, "and such a pretty frock. I do hope you enjoy this evening. Motto and I have a theatre-and-dinner date tonight, so I'm afraid this is hello and goodbye, but I'm sure we'll meet again. Oh — here *is* Motto. Darling, say hello to Rick's friend Charis."

Dermot Mayo in his formal evening attire looked well groomed and affluent, the perfect complement to his glamorous wife. His greying hair still retained a faintly sandy hue, but Harriet's, by contrast, was dark and dramatic-looking against magnolia-petal skin.

"Well now," he said, extending his hand to Charis. "You've surely picked a winner here, young Rick."

"Thanks, Uncle Motto. That's what *I* think."

A moment later a slender girl, with a frilly apron tied round her waist, put in an appearance. Charis guessed she was in her mid-twenties, with dark auburn hair styled into soft face-framing waves. She was closely followed by an older man who had rolled up his shirtsleeves.

"Sorry to disappoint you all," said Harriet Mayo with a husky laugh, "but you see we're not leaving you to your own devices. Gaby and Giles have very kindly volunteered to serve dinner to all you young things, and they'll be keeping an eye on you afterwards to make sure you don't break the house rules."

"What are those?" Charis whispered to Rick.

"You'll find out. Aunt Hattie and Ma have similar ideas, I'm afraid."

Bryony's four remaining guests arrived together just before Dermot and Harriet left for their evening engagement. Charis remembered Adrian Dawlish from his one visit to Holyoaks. Tonight, though, he was accompanied by his girlfriend, Anna, a foreign-looking girl with high cheekbones and dark hair tied back in a long single plait, at the end of which danced a splendid red satin bow.

"This is Sally, one of my oldest pals," Bryony said before kissing the other girl on both cheeks. "And this is Graham. They've been going steady for *months*."

"You make it sound really unusual," said Danny.

"In my experience it *is*," said Bryony.

Sally was as ordinary as Bryony was remarkable. Small and plump, she was wearing a simple blue dress with a white collar. Her mousy hair looked clean and shiny, and she had happy blue eyes and a friendly smile.

"We'd better be on our way, Hattie," Dermot said, and, after general goodbyes, the Mayos drove off in an impressive silver Bentley.

"Didn't Mummy look gorgeous tonight?" Bryony remarked to her half-sister.

"But then, doesn't she always?" said Gaby.

Giles and Gaby left the rest of the party in the lounge and returned to their duties in the kitchen.

"Charis wants to know the house rules," said Rick. "Do you think we should tell her?"

Everyone laughed.

"Mummy's terribly fussy about what goes on here," said Bryony. "I'm never allowed to have Danny here on my own, so we can never have a good old necking session. It's most frustrating, isn't it, honey? Just as well she doesn't know what we get up to when we're out. Daddy's even worse in a way. He wraps me in cotton wool and always wants to know exactly where I'm going and how long I'll be. Sometimes I can't believe I'm sixteen. I might as well be ten."

"Charis has trouble with her mother, too," said Rick. "She has to ask permission about almost everything, don't you, Cara?"

"It's the same for most of us," said Sally. "Isn't it, Anna? It's much more difficult being a girl."

"We have so much more to lose," said Bryony with a wicked grin and her eyes shining. "Did I hear you calling Charis Cara, or did I imagine it, Rick?"

Charis blushed.

"You heard correctly," said Rick. "What of it?"

"Nothing. Darling, Cara, Cherie, they're all the same, aren't they? And mavourneen, of course, but that's rather a mouthful even though it's so Irish and romantic. Actually, I think Cara's the nicest."

Later, Gaby ushered them all into the dining room. The table was set for a formal dinner party; the centrepiece a silver bowl filled with mixed rosebuds already beginning to open. At first Charis was surprised that there was no tablecloth, an unthinkable omission in her own home, but it soon occurred to her that covering such a beautiful walnut table with anything other than the eight leaf-green fabric place mats, gleaming cutlery and crystal glassware, would be wholly inappropriate.

Giles produced two bottles of white wine, uncorked them and stood them in ice buckets on a side table. "A quarter of a bottle each won't hurt you, I'm sure," he said, "and I'm here to make sure no one cheats!"

The first course was iced asparagus soup, which was new to Charis, so she sampled it gingerly before deciding it was very good. Chunks of crusty French bread lay in a basket alongside a small dish of chilled butter pats, fresh from the refrigerator.

"When are you off to Ireland?" asked Sally as the meal got under way.

"Thursday," said Bryony. "The day after Danny sails."

"Are you all going?" asked Graham.

"Most of us," said Bryony glancing at Rick. "Uncle Charlie, Auntie Shelagh, Rick and I and the twins are going in Uncle Charlie's car and doing the Fishguard/Rosslare crossing. Daddy and Mummy are flying over next weekend, but we still don't know about Tessa, do we, Rick?"

"Well, this friend of hers wants her to go to Spain, but Ma and Pa aren't too keen on the idea in case the accommodation isn't satisfactory. They've heard all kinds of sorry tales about young girls running out of cash and getting stranded in foreign countries, and you *know* what parents are like," said Rick, giving Charis a meaningful look.

"All the same, I'd *adore* to go to Spain," said Bryony. "All that flamenco and hot weather and — *passion!*"

Danny exploded with laughter: "Passion!" he mocked. "Probably all you'd get out of Spain would be a gippy tummy and sunstroke, and I've been there so I know what I'm talking about."

"I couldn't watch a bullfight," said Anna, wincing. "It's just too cruel and bloodthirsty."

"Nor me."

All the girls were agreed on this.

"But we hunt foxes," said Rick, "so who are we to criticise?"

"Well, I'm not going to Spain, so there's not much point in dwelling on it," said Bryony. "It's back to the Emerald Isle again for me." A moment later she added, "What a pity you're not coming with us, Charis. You'd love it: beautiful sandy beaches; high cliffs; fuchsia hedges; friendly people . . . "

"And rain, rain and more rain," Danny interrupted.

"Don't spoil my eloquent description. It's the rain that makes Ireland so green, and it doesn't rain *all* the time, does it Rick?"

"Soft weather they call it over there," said Rick, "and when the sun comes out everything sparkles."

"Maybe next year, Charis," said Bryony.

Such an idea had never even remotely crossed her mind. "Who knows?" was all she dared reply, overwhelmed by the implications.

"How about Gaby and Giles?" asked Adrian.

"Giles can't take time off just now," said Bryony, "so Gaby is holding the fort here, but they'll probably come over for a weekend at least."

"Are you talking about us?" said Gaby, entering with Giles to collect the soup plates.

"How did you guess?"

"Walls have ears."

Moments later Giles and Gaby carried in a tray of individual lemon sorbets, served in delicate little glasses shaped like flower trumpets; the sorbet forming the centre of each. "To cleanse the palate, as they say," said Gaby.

The main course consisted of sliced cold chicken, ham and tongue served with a mixed salad dressed with oil and vinegar. This was another idea new to Charis. Grace had never dressed a salad in her life, apart from supplying salad cream in a bottle for anyone with a taste for it.

"Enjoying yourself?" Rick asked Charis quietly, with an affectionate smile.

"*Loving* it."

The conversation ranged from jazz to exam results (expected in about ten days' time), to holidays once more and, finally, when they were all mellowed by their modest allowance of wine, to future ambitions.

"A secretary," said Anna. "I'm starting a Shorthand and Typing course at Mundy Park College in September so I'm already on my way."

"Nursing. Nothing else but that for me," said Sally, "but I'm working for Advanced Level first."

"Directing a company with old Rick here," said Adrian. "We always said we'd do that, didn't we? Dawlish and Woodrose, or vice versa."

"What did I tell you?" said Rick, looking at Charis.

"Don't ask me why, but I fancy teaching," said Graham.

"How about you, Charis?"

"I haven't made up my mind yet. I'm expecting to try for university but that's as far as I've thought."

"Tell Charis *your* ambition, Bryony," urged Sally.

"To sing professionally. That's what I'd really like," said Bryony without hesitation. "Added to that, I'd like to be an entertainer on a ship. Seeing the world, *and* singing — what could be better? That's what I'd really like."

"On *Danny's* ship?"

"On *any* ship."

"I didn't know you sang," said Charis.

"Oh yes. I've always adored singing. I take after Auntie Shelagh."

"Are you going to sing for us tonight, Bryony?" asked Anna.

"If you'd like me to. If you could all *bear* it, and if Gaby will play the piano for me."

"Talking about me *again*?" Gaby laughed, entering once more with a large cut-glass bowl of fruit salad and a jug of cream.

"We want Bryony to sing. Will you play for her, *please*?"

"Certainly, I will. Just as soon as dinner's cleared away."

After dinner the girls renewed their make-up in Bryony's luxurious bedroom, and then trooped downstairs to the main lounge, which was dominated by a grand piano. Gaby was already at the keyboard, leafing through a bundle of sheet music, with Bryony peering over her shoulder.

"*That* one first," said Bryony, "and then those two. That'll probably do. They won't want to listen to me *all* the evening."

Rick and Charis claimed one of the settees, where they sat as close to one another as possible, holding hands. Anna sat on Adrian's lap, leaning back against him in an armchair. Sally and Graham chose the floor, with their backs propped up against another settee, and Danny and Giles stood by the window, proudly watching their girlfriends, the talented Mayo sisters.

Gaby played a few notes of introduction and then Bryony began to sing in a strong, melodious voice, filling the room with the evocative words of 'Blue Moon'. Dusk had fallen, and Charis knew without a doubt that this was another of those moments in her life that she would never forget. A great surge of happiness welled up inside her, not just because of Rick, but because all these outgoing young people had accepted her so readily in a way that Celia's group never had. There was something so warm, so generous about Bryony that Charis harboured a hope that they might become good friends. How wonderful it would be to come to this lovely house frequently, she thought, and to *belong* as an extension of Rick's family. Her head swam, her imagination running riot as she listened to the plaintive song.

Bryony followed 'Blue Moon' with 'Love is the Sweetest Thing' and 'The Nearness of You', both of which had the desired effect, and soon, along with everyone else, Rick and Charis were kissing and cuddling in the semi-darkness.

"House rules! House rules!" Giles called out teasingly after about five minutes' laxity. "Come on now. Lights on, and no more necking!"

"Oh *spoilsport!*" cried Bryony. "You might at least have given me a chance to have a little session with Danny. After all, everyone else was enjoying themselves while *I* was providing the atmosphere. You really are mean. What would you say if someone stopped you spooning with Gaby?"

"Hypothetical question, since we're adults and engaged to be married," said Giles. "It makes all the difference in the world, so stop being cheeky, kid sister-in-law-to-be."

Bryony pulled a face.

"Sorry, everyone," said Gaby. "To be perfectly honest, I'm very much on your side, but don't tell Mummy and Daddy I said so."

"It's not good for you to get all sexually worked up at your age, anyway," said Giles with a grin.

"Sexually worked up! Fat chance with you around," said Bryony.

"Oh, come on, let's heat up the tempo another way and play some of your jazz records," said Giles.

It wasn't long before the record player had been turned up to full volume, and everyone's feet were tapping to the persistent beat of New Orleans jazz, which continued non-stop, until Gaby served coffee and biscuits at ten o'clock.

Charis was truly reluctant to leave, but at ten-thirty Rick insisted on taking her home: "We don't want to upset your mother, now, do we?" he said sensibly.

"You *must* come over again, Charis," said Bryony. "When we're back from Ireland and Danny's on leave next time I'll organise another party. Would you like that?"

"I'd love it. I just can't wait, and thank you for a simply marvellous evening."

On the train going home with Rick, Charis said, "What *incredible* people. I never thought I'd meet anyone like them. Your aunt and uncle are so frightfully glamorous, and Bryony's sensational. I'd really like to think she was one of my friends."

"She's mad, but she obviously likes you too. If she didn't, you'd have known pretty soon. She always says what she thinks. Absolutely honest."

Stopping in a shop doorway near Charters Lea Station for a brief cuddle and a few of his specially wonderful kisses on the way home, out of the blue Rick said, "Do you think you still love me, Cara?"

"Any reason why I shouldn't?" she replied fondly, and they clung together, wrapped in a sheltering cloak of mutual happiness.

The following day was the first Sunday in August and, in the early afternoon, just after lunch, Charis was lounging in her bedroom reliving every moment of the dinner party. She had spent so long describing it to her parents that she had been very late to bed, and then too animated to sleep properly, and even now she was still feeling drowsy.

Although Rick and the Mayos were uppermost in her mind, Charis was also thinking about Irene Ingle, who was now Irene Wolsey following her marriage in Cromer the previous day. Charis was over the surprise of the whole thing now, and hoped her English teacher was going to be very happy. She expected to hear more about the wedding when she was back at school, as Mrs Wolsey would not be leaving until Christmas.

Charis often wondered what it would be like to be married, and Maggie's serious relationship with Leo had given her even more food for thought lately. Marriage sounded so permanent, so adult, so scary. She regarded Rick as her steady long-term boyfriend but not yet as her future husband, which seemed a remote idea when they were only sixteen.

Still feeling tired, or perhaps just lazy, Charis was sending Dizzy into paroxysms of delight as she stroked and tickled him behind his ears. In the background the exhilarating sounds of traditional jazz were blaring from the old wind-up gramophone as she took advantage of her parents being at the far end of the garden and, hopefully, out of earshot. Charis had bought Sidney Bechet's version of 'Joshua Fit the Battle of Jericho', along with 'Sister Kate' by Bunk Johnson, both on Rick's recommendation, and enjoyed them so much that she had played them over and over again. Unfortunately, neither Grace nor Hugh shared her enthusiasm, complaining about the noise, which was impossible to quieten because the old gramophone had no volume control.

"What the Farrows must think I dread to imagine," Grace had scolded one day. "Dreadful, noisy, common old music. It makes me feel ashamed to think that it's coming from *our* house."

"The boys from Eden House think it's wonderful," Charis told her, "so it just shows how old-fashioned you are."

"Don't be so *rude*," said Grace.

"Well, it's true," said Charis, sulkily. "They don't think it's common at all, so why should you?"

"We've always liked *good* music," Hugh explained. "We hoped you would too. Jazz isn't our cup of tea at all."

"You just don't understand it," said Charis passionately.

"We don't want to, thank you," said Grace in her most irritating voice.

By way of a compromise Charis was allowed to play the records occasionally, provided that she kept the windows and door of her bedroom firmly shut, but if the music went on for longer than about fifteen minutes at any one time, she was liable to be in trouble.

Since meeting Rick, Charis had come to know Flackston quite well. Now, very soon, she would be going there with him once more to their special place, bewitched by his appealing face and puppy-dog grin, and feeling more attractive and desired than she would ever have believed possible. All the same, her happiness was clouded by the knowledge that his holiday in Ireland was looming and would part them, if only for a short time. After today she might perhaps see him once more, but then he would be gone.

Later that afternoon they returned to Flackston Manor. They followed the same pathway leading into the open fields surrounding the manor, walking hand in hand, and stopping every now and then for a lingering kiss.

"I saw Bryony at the eleven o'clock Mass today," said Rick. "She said how much she liked you, but you knew that anyway."

"My head's still spinning after last night. It was a marvellous party."

"There'll be more of them. Bryony loves parties, and you'll always be included now. I'm not sure what'll happen about Danny, though. Bryony's sure to feel lonely when he sails for Australia, and somehow I don't think she'll be content to hang around waiting."

"I'd wait for *you*," Charis said firmly. "I wouldn't want *anyone* else."

"It's easy enough to say," said Rick. "I know you mean it now, and I feel exactly the same about you, but if we were in their shoes it might not work out that way, even for us. Out of sight, out of mind, and all that."

"How about absence making the heart grow fonder?"

"Well, those two proverbs cancel each other out, don't they? Who knows which one is nearer the truth?"

"When you're in Ireland will I be out of sight, out of mind?"

"Of course not, noodle. It won't be long enough for that, and I'll be writing to you — at least once," he promised with a grin.

"Can I write to you as well?"

"Of course. If you really want to."

"Rick, can I ask you something?"

"Fire away."

"I don't know if I should, because Bryony said it was our secret — hers and mine, I mean — but I don't like keeping things from you, and it was *about* you."

"Oh, glory!" The playful puppy's grin returned and he stubbed out his cigarette on the sandy path.

"She said something about your previous serious girlfriend being a disaster."

For a moment Rick was silent, then, "Well, she was right about that, I suppose," he admitted.

"Who was she? What went wrong?"

"Do I *have* to tell you? I'd prefer to forget all about it, actually."

"No, you don't *have* to, but I can't help being curious."

"*Women!*" said Rick. "OK, I'll tell you, but no searching questions and no long, miserable silences afterwards. Don't forget, this is our last date for a while, and I want it to be a happy one."

"Only tell me what you want to, and I promise not to brood."

"Well, OK. Her name was Shirley. I met her at the Starlight Ballroom in Upsvale."

"I didn't know you'd ever been there. That's where Pam and Polly used to go before they met up with Roger and Banjo."

"It was the first time I'd been. I'd only just learnt how to dance and I wanted some practice. Anyway, I met this girl. She was very vivacious and amusing. Older than me as it happened, but that didn't bother us. We went out for a while and had a lot of fun until I discovered she was two-timing me. She'd had another boyfriend all along, but he was doing national service so he was away a lot. She led me right up the garden path but, as I said, it was fun while it lasted. As soon as I found her out I dropped her like the proverbial hot potato. Bryony never liked her. Perhaps she suspected what I was too stupid to guess."

While he was speaking, Charis's mind ticked like a time bomb as she recalled the only other Shirley she had ever known: the Shirley with dark bubble-cut hair in the square-dance team at St Luke's Church Hall; the Shirley who had been Alan Decker's girlfriend, and had unknowingly caused Charis considerable envy and anguish in what seemed an eternity away but was, she realised with a measure of shock, only two short years ago. For a moment she remained silent, but her burning curiosity triumphed in the end.

"It couldn't possibly have been Shirley Croft, by any remote chance, could it?" she said.

Rick stared at her, wide-eyed.

"I don't believe it. Yes, it was. You don't *know* her, do you?"

"Only by sight. I've never even spoken to her, but I certainly knew her boyfriend."

"Tell me more."

"His name was Alan Decker and he used to go to my church. He and Shirley were going out together two years ago. I haven't seen either of them for simply ages. In fact, I'd almost forgotten all about them until now."

"Small world, isn't it?" said Rick, lighting another cigarette. "I wish I hadn't told you now. I wish Bryony hadn't said anything. That's the only trouble with her. She talks *far* too much for her own good, or anyone else's."

A stream of horribly jealous thoughts flooded Charis's mind: 'Did *she* teach him how to kiss the way he does? Did he get *all* his experience from her? Did he touch her the way he touches me? Did he bring her *here*? How far did they go? All the way? Oh, please not. Did she meet his parents? Did he? Did she . . . ?' Valiantly brushing aside these agonising imponderables, Charis said, "Well, I know about it now, and I'm not going to sulk. I shouldn't think I'll ever see either of them again, so there's no harm done, and I shan't hold it against you."

"You won't? Oh, I was hoping you *would*," Rick teased, regaining his good humour as quickly as he had lost it. "Come on, Cara, let's stop talking nonsense and get down to some serious business. Race you to our special spot. I bet we've made the grass permanently flat there, don't you?"

NINE

The GCE results came out a few days after Rick and his family had left for Ireland. Charis had done well, passing in English Language and Literature, Maths, Latin, Biology and Art, but failing in French and History. She was elated because she had been promised an electronic record player if she passed at least six subjects. This had been a family decision of epic proportions, arrived at after much juggling with the housekeeping. The deal had been clinched when Aunt Bee and Vanna declared they would be more than happy to be included, and so the record player was to be a joint gift from all the family.

Pam Sperry telephoned later that morning: "How many did you pass?" she asked.

"Six. I failed two," Charis told her. "How about you?"

"I got Maths, Geography and English Language, but I failed English Lit. Anyway, what does it matter? I've left school, so I couldn't care less."

"Do you know Celia's results?"

"She passed everything except French."

"How odd. I failed French too. I thought Celia would have done better in that."

"How about Maggie?" asked Pam.

"She's away in Swanage, so I haven't heard. I'm itching to know."

"Are you doing anything this morning?"

"Not really."

"Come up to the Zanzibar then. I'll call for you in a quarter of an hour."

It was much quieter at the café on a weekday morning than at weekends when many of the local youngsters still made it their rendezvous. Today, only a few housewives and elderly ladies sat drinking coffee, either singly or in pairs, and two bus inspectors, wearing peaked caps, were enjoying a quick cuppa and a cigarette in the furthest booth.

"I shan't be able to do this much longer," said Pam. "I'm starting work the week after next, and I have to go in some Saturday mornings too."

"I'd *hate* that," said Charis.

169

"I'm not too thrilled," Pam admitted, "but it'll be worth it to earn some money. I can't wait to be independent." Pam took out a packet of cigarettes and a box of matches.

"I didn't know you'd started smoking," Charis said.

"Didn't you? Well, I haven't seen much of you lately. Roger smokes, of course, and I picked up the habit from him. Do you want one?"

"No thanks. I tried it once but it made me choke."

"It takes practice," said Pam, exhaling smoke through her delicate nostrils. Her nails were very long but the red varnish on them was chipped. Nevertheless, Charis thought she looked extremely sophisticated as she held the cigarette between her first and second fingers, knocking off the ash into a little silver tray on the table.

"How *is* Roger?" Charis enquired.

"Fine. Lucky for me he's not going away this year. He's taking next week off so we're going out for some day trips together before I start work the Monday after."

"What about Polly?"

Pam pulled a face. "That was one of the reasons I wanted to see you today," she said.

"Really? Why's that?"

"Do you remember I told you she'd been taking risks with Banjo?"

"I'll never forget. I was shocked."

"You'll be even more shocked now, then. She's late. She should have had the curse six days ago, but she didn't, and now she's nearly going frantic."

"Oh, *Pam*!" Charis's stomach churned at the enormity of the news. For a moment she imagined the same thing happening to her, and the sheer dread of breaking it to her parents — especially Grace.

"She's been so *stupid*," said Pam. "It was no good telling her to be careful. She slept at Banjo's house one night when his parents were away. Can you *imagine*? She told her parents she was staying with me, but luckily I didn't have to cover up for her because Polly's parents didn't ask any awkward questions. They've always given her a pretty free rein. I mean, *my* parents are fairly easy-going, but compared with Polly's they're martinets. Of course, it takes two to tango, and Banjo should have had more sense, but he keeps his brains in his pants, as you probably know."

Charis blushed. "He didn't get very far with me," she admitted.

"He would have tried before long," said Pam.

"I wouldn't have let him," said Charis firmly. "I'd be *much* too frightened. Wouldn't you be?"

"I've never been out with him, so I don't know," said Pam. "Roger's another story, of course. No, don't look so concerned. *We* haven't gone all the way *yet*, but he keeps trying to persuade me, and if we keep going out together for much longer I'm sure we shall. I want to know what it's like. Polly says it hurts a lot the first time, but after that it's great."

"But Pam, supposing — well, I mean now that Polly may be in trouble — wouldn't you be scared of — of getting pregnant?"

"Not with Roger. He knows what he's doing. He isn't a fool like Banjo. Anyway, he keeps a packet of French letters in his pocket. I've seen it."

Charis was horribly shaken and perturbed by the turn of this conversation: "But I've heard those things don't always work, and if they didn't, how could you ever tell your mother that you were expecting a baby?" she whispered as they were sitting within earshot of an old lady in the next booth.

"I don't know," said Pam. "It's something I try not to think about."

"What will Polly do?"

"Wait a bit longer, I suppose, and then she'll have to see a doctor."

"Does Banjo know?"

"She hasn't dared tell him. She acts as though she couldn't care less about him, but I think she does and she doesn't want to lose him."

"Do you think that's why she took chances?"

"Definitely."

They sat in silence for a while, trying to visualise how they would cope in such an unbearable situation.

"What about you and Rick?" Pam said after a while.

"*What* about us?"

"*You* know what I mean. How far have you two gone?"

"We haven't done anything to worry about," said Charis, "but I don't want to talk about it. What Rick and I do or don't do is very private."

"I'll bet it is," Pam said with a suggestive snigger.

"You always make everything sound so grubby. Rick's really special. We're very close."

"He isn't any more special than anyone else," said Pam. "He just *seems* that way because you're as nuts about him as Polly is about Banjo."

"Oh, it's no good talking to you," said Charis, standing up abruptly, and feeling vexed and worried by Pam's attitude. "I think I'll go home."

"Please yourself," said Pam. "Be good. And if you can't be good, be careful," she added as a parting shot.

When Charis saw the letter from Rick with the Irish stamp she ripped it open impatiently. Her first observation was that he had not written the full address, and that the postmark was so blurred as to be illegible. Then she noticed that the letter began 'Dear Charis' — not darling; not dearest; not even Cara — but then she thought he was probably playing safe in case her parents saw it:

Dear Charis,
Here we are again, back with the Mayo grandparents and doing all the
things we've been doing since we were little. The sea has been pretty
rough sometimes, but we've all been bathing even so. Tessa came with us
in the end. The Spanish holiday didn't come off, so she brought her friend
over here instead.

('I wonder what *she's* like,' thought Charis, instantly suspicious.)

She's a reasonable sort of girl, and fits in with everyone quite well but,
like you, she can't swim, so she's been marooned like a beached whale
watching us instead. We've been to some dinner parties which were a bit
stuffy and elderly. My grandparents know all the well-heeled local families,
so we always have to do the rounds and then they're invited back here.
I found some second-hand jazz records in a junk shop. They were pretty
ancient, but they sound good on the radiogram, which cuts out all the
scratches if you turn up the bass and turn down the treble. I'm dying for
you to hear them. You must come over to my place as soon as possible
after we get back and then we can have a session!

(Charis smiled as she read the implication behind the exclamation mark,
and felt trembly inside anticipating their reunion.)

We've been playing tennis a lot. We had a mixed-doubles tournament. Pa
and Aunt Hattie beat Uncle Motto and Ma, and Bryony and I beat Gaby
and Giles — yes, they did come over for a weekend, and it was sunny
enough to play. Pa and Aunt Hattie won overall, though. Bryony's game
isn't all that strong, and Pa is terrific on a hard court. The twins can't play
properly yet, of course, but they practice a lot and I think they'll be good
eventually. Tessa and Marion (that's her friend) played a few matches. In
fact we've all played one another at one time or another in singles. It's
been good fun, but we've been short of men, as you can gather, so I haven't
had many challenging games.
How are you? I've been thinking about you, of course, and looking
forward to seeing you again. Please give your parents my good wishes,
and also your grandma and Aunt Bee.
Until I see you, Charis,
Love from Rick.

There was a discreet kiss underneath his name, so nothing, surely, to which
Grace could possibly take exception. At the very end was a PS:

My GCE results came through. I passed everything. Hope you were successful too.

"I've had a letter from Rick," Charis announced at the breakfast table. Hugh had already left for the sorting office, and Grace had finished eating and was studying the front page of the *Daily Mail*.

"Oh, good," she said vaguely. "How is he?"

"Having fun in Ireland. Lots of swimming and tennis, he says. He sends you and Daddy his good wishes, and he mentions Vanna and Aunt Bee too."

Grace lowered the newspaper. "I must say he's more polite and thoughtful that most boys of his age," she said. "I always fancied Tom Potterfield as a partner for you, as you know, but so far I can't complain about Rick. The only thing I'm not happy about is that he's a Catholic, and I still worry about the class difference too. I mean, living at Flackston in a big house like that, and having those swanky relations."

"They aren't a *bit* swanky," Charis protested, "and I still can't understand why you object to Rick's religion. After all, he goes to church, so what does it matter which one?"

"I know it's good that he's a churchgoer," said Grace, "but the Catholics are terribly strict. You must have found that out already from school and your friend Maggie, perhaps. I don't like the way they interfere with married people's lives either."

"How do you mean, Mummy?"

She hesitated, a faint blush warming her pale cheeks. "Well — I don't know how to put it — but, as your father's not here, it's the way they expect people to have lots and lots of children. I've always thought that was something very private indeed. Nothing to do with the church, to my mind, and fortunately *our* church doesn't preach about things like that. Most Catholic families I've known have always been huge, so that speaks for itself."

For Grace this was such a long speech on a topic which, until now, she had always shunned, that Charis felt like applauding. "I know Maggie's one of seven, and Rick is one of four, but his Uncle Dermot only had two children, one with his first wife who died, and one with Rick's Aunt Hattie, and *he's* a Catholic," she said, "so why do you think that was?"

"I have no idea," said Grace, becoming flustered, "and I don't want to discuss it any further. All I'm saying is that I'm quite happy about you going out with Rick for the time being, but if you were to get too serious and want to get married in the future, that would be a very different kettle of fish."

"It's much too soon to even think about anything like that," said Charis, concerned nevertheless that another little cloud had appeared on the horizon.

173

"Just remember what I've said, and always, *always* behave yourself when you're with him. Promise me now."

"Yes, of *course*, Mummy," said Charis dutifully.

Those who were to join the sixth form at Stella Maris were asked to meet Mother Ambrose at the school on a Friday afternoon towards the end of August.

Maggie rang Charis about it as soon as she returned from Swanage.

"Maggie!" Charis exclaimed, delighted that she was back in circulation. "Did you have a good holiday? How's Leo?"

"Everything was fine," said Maggie, sounding happy. "I'll tell you all about it when I see you, but I'm dying to know about your results."

Charis told her. "How about you?" she asked.

"You'll never guess," said Maggie, "but I passed everything. I could hardly believe it. My parents are over the moon, and so am I because I really didn't work all that hard."

"That's fantastic! Congratulations!"

"Are you going to this sixth form meeting?" Maggie asked.

"Yes, of course. I'll see you there on Friday."

Fifteen girls from Five Alpha and two, most unusually, from Five Beta would soon become first-year sixth formers. Predictably, these included Celia, Morag McDonald and Louise Heron, the latter bringing news to the gathering which intrigued everyone.

"I was on holiday in Cromer with my parents just at the time Miss Ingle was getting married," she said. "If you remember, she didn't tell us the name of the church, but we managed to find out from the local paper, so we went along and saw everything."

"What was it like?"

"What was she wearing?"

"What did you think of her husband?"

"It was a white wedding. She looked beautiful," said Louise. "Her husband — Peter Wolsey — is tall and good-looking. I took some photos. You can see them later if you like."

"Were there bridesmaids?"

"Yes. Two little girls. They wore white dresses too, but they had pink sashes and they carried pink and white posies, whereas Miss Ingle carried an all-white bouquet."

"What else?"

"It was a nuptial Mass, of course. There was just one hymn: 'O Perfect Love'. I threw confetti over her afterwards, so she certainly knew I was there and she smiled at me very nicely, so I'm sure she didn't mind."

"Trust Louise," said Maggie in a whisper. "Always *in* on everything."

"I know," said Charis, "but at least we'll be able to see the photos."

"Shush! Here comes the Rice Pudding," said Maggie, as Mother

Ambrose sailed into the room, her black habit swishing as she walked.

"Good afternoon, girls."

"Good afternoon, Mother."

"First of all, I want to congratulate you all on some excellent results. You've done tremendously well, a real credit to the school, and only a few of you will need further coaching to resit a few exams. I don't think any of you need worry unduly. I'm certain you'll pass at the second attempt. Let me see, now. Celia and Charis both failed French, didn't you? Ah, yes, and so did you, Nancy. You three will have special tuition twice a week in Room 31. Some of you failed Latin, so the same will apply to you, but those who failed History won't need to sit that again necessarily, unless you particularly want to read it at university, but I'm not aware that anyone does."

Mother Ambrose went on for several more minutes, outlining additional duties which the sixth formers would be expected to undertake, and the particular subjects each of them would be aiming to pass at Advanced Level — Charis's being English Literature, French and Latin. Maggie was to take Maths, Biology and Domestic Science, in view of her ambition to go in for catering, or perhaps to become a dietician.

"We shan't be sharing any classes, then," said Charis ruefully.

"No, but we'll still be in the same form, and don't forget we'll have our own common room where we can relax. It'll be fun," said ever-optimistic Maggie.

When the short meeting was over, two young novices served tea and biscuits, and the girls chattered noisily amongst themselves.

"Tell me about Swanage," Charis urged.

"Do you mean Swanage, or would you rather hear about Leo?" Maggie said with a laugh.

"Both, I suppose."

"Well, he stayed at a guest house not far away from our self-catering place, just as he said he would. It was nice because I saw him every day, and he fitted in very well with my family. He was awfully good with the children — all five of them. They *adore* him, especially Carmel and Timmy, our two youngest."

"How do your parents feel about him now?"

"Much better, I think, but they still keep on about him not being a Catholic. That's the only thing I'm worried about. After all, I can't *make* him convert, but he did come to Mass with us in Swanage, so I keep hoping."

"Have you heard about Polly Phillips?"

"No. *What* about her?"

Charis whispered the unthinkable news, at which Maggie visible winced. "I still can't believe how silly Polly's been," Charis continued. "I don't like her one little bit, but I do hope it isn't true."

"My mother would be so terribly disappointed in me if anything like that happened," said Maggie. "I think I'm very lucky because the situation isn't likely to arise with Leo. We think along the same lines, and I trust him."

"I feel that way about Rick. Nothing whatever to worry about, but we still have a wonderful relationship."

"Oh yes, so do *we*," said Maggie. "Spicy enough to be exciting, but fairly innocent when all's said and done, and we definitely shan't go all the way until we're married. We've made a pact."

Charis went on to tell Maggie about Bryony's party, the people she had met there, Rick's holiday in Ireland and the letter he had sent. "He comes home *TOMORROW*," she ended exultantly. "I'll be seeing him on Sunday, and I just can't wait."

In preparation for Rick's return Charis washed her hair on the Saturday evening and chose her outfit for the next day with great care. Some time before, she and Grace had gone round the July sales in Upsvale, where they had bought a pretty skirt in pale-green glazed cotton, going for a song. Then Aunt Bee had given Charis a pound note to buy something to wear with it, and she had seen the very thing in a small shop in Charters Lea: a dainty, white blouse with an overall pattern of daisies, their petals faintly tipped with pink, their leaves a fresh green, and fastened all down the front with little green buttons.

"Very pretty; a bit flowery for church, though," said Grace when Charis appeared in her new outfit on the Sunday morning.

Not wishing to cross Grace on that day of all days, Charis refrained from making the logical observation that few people would see what she was wearing at church anyway since her outdoor clothes would be hidden under her choir robes.

The service was short, and there were some cheerful hymns like 'He Who Would Valiant Be', 'God of Mercy, God of Grace' and 'Bright the Vision That Delighted', which nearly made Charis laugh aloud because the first line was one of Aunt Bee's favourite quotations whenever they were out together and happened to see someone dressed in vivid colours. She could be so funny and irreverent, often picking out lines from hymns like that at appropriate moments. On odd occasions she had even been known to hum, 'O Happy Band of Pilgrims' or 'Fight the Good Fight' under her breath, when Grace and Hugh had been having a mild argument, which always reduced Charis to a fit of the giggles.

After church it was home on the bus to a traditional Sunday dinner of roast lamb, mint sauce, roast potatoes and runner beans, followed by blackberry and apple tart and custard. Afterwards, scarcely able to contain her excitement, Charis flew upstairs, powdered her nose, tidied her hair and applied Apple Blossom Pink, the latest in Woolworth's range of lipsticks, which toned very nicely with the daisy blouse.

Moments before she was due to leave, the telephone rang. Grace answered it and called Charis to come down and talk to Pam.

'Oh bother, bother, bother!' thought Charis. 'I really don't want to.'

The two girls had not spoken since the episode at the Zanzibar Café, so Charis did not know what to expect.

"Are we still friends?" asked Pam.

"Yes, of course," said Charis somewhat curtly.

"Only, after you stormed out of the Zanzibar that day, I thought I'd seriously offended you."

"I've forgotten all about that now. What did you want to tell me?"

"Mainly about Polly. Is it all clear your end? I mean, is anyone likely to be listening in?"

Charis glanced round, but there was no sign of either Grace or Hugh: "It's all right. Tell me."

"She's OK," said Pam. "She's *so* relieved. It happened on Thursday, so she didn't even have to see the doctor after all."

"Thank goodness," said Charis, genuinely pleased. "Do you think she's learnt her lesson?"

"I *hope* so, but knowing Polly I wouldn't bet on it. She'll be so thankful she hasn't got to break the news to Banjo that they'll probably have a riotous reunion, and who knows *what'll* happen then," said Pam.

"Has he been away too?"

"Yes. I forgot to tell you. He's been on holiday with some chap from his school most of the time she's been so worried. They've been touring Scotland, trying out that dreadful old car Banjo bought. Probably trying out the local talent as well!"

"Very likely," said Charis. "Well, thanks for telling me. I hope your new job works out all right. You start tomorrow, don't you?"

"Yes. I'm feeling a bit wobbly, but I'm looking forward to it."

"Pam, I *must* go now. I'm meeting Rick in about five minutes. I'll ring you during the week."

"What did *she* want?" asked Grace. "She doesn't usually ring on a Sunday."

"Oh, just to tell me about starting work tomorrow. If I don't leave now, I'll be late, so goodbye, Mummy, bye, Daddy," and she was gone.

As Charis closed the front gate she was irritated to see Arthur and Emily Farrow walking very slowly up Wednesbury Road several yards ahead of her. He was decked out in a panama hat and a light summer jacket, and she was wearing a floral dress and a blue straw hat. It was an awkward situation because Charis had neither the time nor the desire to stop and speak, so she crossed over the road to avoid them, running most of the way to the station, where Rick — darling, darling, Rick — was waiting for her in the sunshine.

He looked utterly irresistible, and she was overwhelmed by a tidal wave of love. His arms and face were gloriously tanned, as was his neck, revealed by a light-yellow sports shirt, casually unbuttoned at the top.

He opened his arms to give her a bear hug and a long, penetrating, wonderfully satisfying kiss. "I've really missed you, Cara," he said. "Let me look at you. What a pretty new outfit. You look good enough to eat."

"You're so *brown*. You must have had good weather."

"Mixed. Well, you know what Ireland's like — still, there was more sunshine than usual, and what with swimming, and the outdoor life generally, it would be difficult *not* to get a tan."

"It's been horrid without you," said Charis, "but now you're back everything's perfect again."

"Did you get my letter?"

"Yes, but you didn't put a proper address so I couldn't write back, and I forgot to ask you before you went away."

"I thought I'd given it to you, but never mind, that's all in the past now. What have you been doing? I hope you've been faithful."

"*Rick!*" Charis exclaimed. "What do you *think*? Of *course* I have. How about you?"

"Faithful in that I haven't been carrying on with anyone else the way I do with you, but not faithful in absolutely *every* sense because I did dance quite a lot with Tessa's friend Marion at a couple of local hops."

Jealously nibbled at her heart. "I wondered," she said coolly, "when you mentioned her in your letter, I wondered straight away."

"Don't get all huffy," said Rick. "There was nothing to it, honestly. She's older than me too — Tessa's age."

"That didn't bother you when you were going out with Shirley Croft," Charis remarked sharply. "I got the impression you were pretty keen on her even if she *was* older than you."

"Cara, what is this? We're not going to fight are we? I've been so looking forward to seeing you. Don't spoil it."

"I'm sorry," she said. "I didn't mean to be ratty, but most of this month I've been feeling awfully unsettled one way and another: everyone going away; you and I being split up; not being able to chat to Maggie on the phone; no Holyoaks (not that I'd have gone without you); waiting for the GCE results; dreading the sixth form; and being really shaken about Polly Phillips."

"Polly Phillips?" said Rick. "Why should you have been concerned about her?"

"Everything's OK now, but there was a distinct possibility that she was in trouble."

"Trouble?"

"Yes. You know — pregnant."

Rick whistled. "Heavens!" he exclaimed. "I suppose I'm not altogether surprised, knowing old Banjo's reputation, and she's certainly a naughty little minx too. You can tell just by looking at her. It wouldn't surprise me at all if he wasn't her first, and she definitely wasn't his."

"How do you know?"

"Stories get round at school. People talk. You can't stop gossip, and it's often true. I even heard he chanced his luck with a married woman once. Tried very hard to seduce her, I believe, and he led us to believe she encouraged him, but her husband found out and stepped in."

Charis remembered Celia telling her about Banjo and her mother. Could Frances Armitage *really* have led him on, Charis wondered. Life was beginning to seem much less innocent than she'd imagined it to be in her childhood. Polly going all the way with Banjo; Pam planning to do the same with Roger; but Banjo and Frances Armitage? Surely not. The story had been told her in confidence so she did not press Rick further.

He cuddled her. "It looks as if we're on our way to the park," he said as they strolled down Coniston Avenue. "Is that what you intended?"

"I suppose so. I hadn't really thought about where we'd go. I just wanted to see you again."

"You're right about August," said Rick. "It can be a disturbing month. We're so used to being at school, aren't we? Slogging away at lessons, and just having the weekends to ourselves. Then comes the long holiday and everything's topsy-turvy. Never mind. It's over now and things will soon get back to normal."

"I can't imagine the sixth form ever being normal," said Charis. "We have to do dinner duty and all kinds of horrible things like that."

"That's just part of growing up," said Rick. "Responsibilities, leadership and all that. But I'm not in the least worried about anything. I intend to cope with whatever's thrown at me."

"You're so *confident*. I wish I could be."

"You will be one day," said Rick. "Half the battle is *acting* confidently, you know, even if you don't feel it. I suppose I shouldn't say this, but I think your mother tends to smother you, and won't allow you to be your own person."

"You're probably right."

By then they were inside the park, where the afternoon sun sent their shadows slanting across recently mown grass.

"How *serious* we are today," said Rick. "Why don't we sit down and enjoy ourselves in the sunshine for a little while?"

Carefully, Charis smoothed the folds of her pale-green skirt on the grass around her, but once Rick had settled himself he pulled her down beside him so that he could kiss her properly. After their enforced separation, the sensation of his warm, sensitive lips and his sweet-tasting tongue coalescing with hers was immensely satisfying. It was almost as wonderful as the first time he had ever kissed her in the dimness of the hall at Holyoaks that June night over two months ago.

"Oh, Rick, I've missed you *so* much, and I do love you," she murmured blissfully.

"And I love you too," he whispered back, nuzzling her ear. "We must visit our little hut in the woods soon," he added huskily.

"Why's that?"

"Why? Because you have such an inviting row of little buttons on your pretty blouse and I want to try them out."

They lay on the grass for about ten minutes, simply kissing and cuddling to rediscover their pleasure in each other.

Finally, Rick said, "Shall we make a move?" and, standing up, he helped her to her feet.

As they dawdled over the grass towards the lake, arms entwined, Rick said, "You haven't told me about your exam results. How did you get on?"

"I failed French and History, but I passed all the others, thank goodness. I need French for Advanced Level, but I shan't bother taking History again. It was never my best subject."

"Well done! Bryony only passed Music and Art, but that didn't surprise anyone. Those are the only things she's interested in. It isn't that she's stupid, but she won't work at anything if it doesn't appeal to her."

"Weren't your aunt and uncle cross?" asked Charis, trembling to think how Grace, in particular, would have reacted in similar circumstances.

"Cross? Oh, no, they were resigned to it, and she's terribly spoilt. Always has been. I expect she'll get some temporary job for the time being, but she's set her sights on this singing business."

"It makes a change from teaching or nursing anyway," said Charis. "I wish I knew what *I* wanted to be, but I still don't. Maggie's always been keen on cooking, so she's planning to go in for catering. She'll stay on in the sixth for Advanced Levels and then go to a domestic-science college."

"Is she still seeing Leo?"

"*Seeing* him? They're practically married," Charis laughed.

"Just as well she's domesticated, then," said Rick. "No good getting married unless you know how to cook."

"The way to a man's heart is through his stomach, you mean?"

"Yes, but that's not the *only* way, Cara," he replied, giving her a huge wink. "Come on. I think you know the way to *my* heart, so let's go and see if you remember."

The little hut was, as usual, deserted.

"Lucky for us," said Rick. "But surely we can't be the *only* people in Charters Lea who've discovered this place."

The kissed; they hugged; he fondled her breasts, and even pulled up her skirt for a little while to caress her intimately, but they were cautious of being spotted by passers-by, because of the time of day.

They stayed in the hut for some twenty minutes and then Rick said, "Oh, Cara, it's *so* good being with you again."

"We've certainly made up for lost time, haven't we?" she replied breathlessly.

"I don't know about you, but I fancy something cool to drink now," said Rick at last. "How about going to the Round House and getting some lemonade or something?"

Charis powdered her nose, put on some lipstick and smoothed her skirt.

"Can I borrow your comb?" Rick asked, and ran it through his short, tawny hair.

"Your hair never looks untidy," said Charis enviously. "I wish mine was naturally curly."

"If it was, you'd want it straight," said Rick grinning like a puppy, as usual. "All women are the same — never satisfied — my mother; Tessa; Bryony; you."

"I couldn't believe it when Bryony said she wished her hair was like mine," said Charis. "I thought hers was positively *gorgeous*."

"*She* doesn't think so. Hates the colour; hates it being frizzy. It's as I say: women are never satisfied — at least not with their hair."

Later, they sat in the Round House as on their first Sunday afternoon together in June. Then, their relationship had been brand new and they had been exploring uncharted territory. Now, familiar and happy together, Charis could only hope and dream about the golden future which surely stretched ahead. So infinitely exciting was this thought that she sighed involuntarily with sheer contentment.

They exchanged fond smiles.

"Happy?" he asked.

"Blissfully," she replied. "Are you?"

"The same," he said.

It was nearly five o'clock when Charis went home, having left Rick at the station. As she walked up the front path she was surprised to see the door ajar, but a moment later it opened wide and Grace stood there wearing an expression of such anger and ferocity that Charis was startled. "Come inside quickly and close the door," said Grace coldly. "I've never been so ashamed in my entire life. To think that my daughter, *my* daughter, could behave in the way you've been behaving this afternoon."

"What . . . ?" Charis began.

"Don't stand there looking like a little innocent," said Grace, "and don't try to pretend that you don't know what I'm talking about. You've been *seen*."

"Seen?" In a flash, Charis thought of the little hut, and was filled with dread. Surely, *surely*, no one had spied on her and Rick in there. It couldn't be possible.

"Yes, *seen*. Lying on the grass in the park, rolling around with *HIM*. I could murder him. I've entertained him here. I trusted him, heaven help me. I trusted *you*, too, and you've let me down."

By then Charis was trembling, fears multiplying by the moment.

Grace continued, her voice rising, her usually pale cheeks flushed: "Lying on the grass like some common little guttersnipe, and letting him kiss you that way. Disgusting! Absolutely disgusting! You can't have any shame. You can't have any decency to behave like that in a public place. I shall never be able to hold up my head in this road again. To be told by my neighbours that my daughter has been misbehaving in the park. Oh, the disgrace of it."

"Which neighbours?" said Charis, still unable to believe what was happening.

"The Farrows, of course. They were walking in the park this afternoon when they saw the two of you rolling around on the grass. As soon as they came back they made it their business to tell me. Horrible, smug, holier-than-thou people. They made me feel *terrible*, as though it was somehow my fault."

"How *could* they be so mean?" said Charis, recalling in a mist of confusion that she had seen them earlier that afternoon as she had left the house. "It wasn't like you said at all. We weren't doing anything wrong."

"If you don't think it's wrong, then there's something radically wrong with your morals," Grace barked. "Look at your skirt; all creased. Yes, *and* grass stains too. You can't explain *them* away. I wonder what else you've been getting up to these past weeks. It makes my blood run cold. If you could behave like that in our local park, what on earth have you been doing further afield? That's what *I'd* like to know."

"Nothing! Nothing!" By now, Charis was so close to tears that her voice was quavering.

"I don't believe you," said Grace icily. "You've been over to Flackston; to his home; to his cousins' home. What went on there?"

"I told you. Nothing!"

"Don't you shout at me, my girl. I'm beginning to think you're no better than that girl from the cottages at the top of the road who got into trouble. Her poor mother was beside herself when she found out. Never for a moment did I imagine *my* daughter was in that kind of danger, but now I wonder. The only thing I have to thank the Farrows for is alerting me to your behaviour, and if that boy has been taking advantage of you he'll have to answer to me."

"Rick and I have *never* done anything like that. Rick has very fixed ideas about — that sort of thing." Charis faltered, discomfited by her mother's fury.

"Oh yes, I'm *sure* he has," she said scornfully. "All he ever thinks about, probably. If he could encourage you to behave in the way you've been carrying on today, he can't be much good. And he's a *Catholic*! So much for *their* precious ideas about morals!"

Charis burst into tears: "You don't understand," she sobbed. "You make it all sound so sordid, and it *wasn't* like that at all. We love one another, and I don't care what you say — we never, never did anything wrong."

"Love! Love!" Grace scoffed. "You don't know the meaning of the word. It's obvious that all the two of you understand is *sex*, and all that kind of nastiness. Well, that's it," she continued, even more coldly. "It's over."

"What do you mean?"

"You and him. I can't bear to mention his name. It's over. You're *never* to see him again."

Charis gasped at the enormity of her words, and for the moment could not take them in. She gazed at her mother in total disbelief, but her glare was steely.

"I mean it," she said, and, turning her back on Charis, she stalked into the living room and closed the door.

Charis fled to the comforting privacy of her bedroom, where Dizzy was curled up on the bed. Flinging herself down beside him and burying her face in his warm fur, she sobbed as though her heart would break, while Dizzy, sensing human grief, nuzzled her, making funny little trills as though offering sympathy. This so touched her that her tears increased until her eyes were swollen, and she was assailed by waves of nausea. Unable to come to terms with the events of the past few ghastly minutes, or to accept Grace's chilling ultimatum, she could not think ahead. She was numb with grief and paralysed with fear of Grace's power over her.

Hugh had been working on his allotment for most of the afternoon, but as soon as Charis heard his key in the door she ran downstairs and flung herself into his arms.

"Whatever is all this about, sweetheart?" he asked gently, stroking her hair.

"It's Rick," she sobbed. "Mummy won't let me see him any more. Please make her change her mind. *Please*, Daddy."

"There, there, sweetheart," he murmured soothingly, "It can't be that bad, surely. What happened?"

Grace emerged from the living room, still looking pale with anger. "*I'll* do the talking," she said. "We can't trust our daughter any more; nor that young devil she's been going out with. *That's* what's happened. The only good thing about this whole matter is that hopefully I've stopped it before it's gone too far."

"I think we'd better talk this over," said Hugh. "All three of us together."

"It won't make any difference," Charis sobbed. "You know *her*. She won't listen to my side of it, so it's no good."

"She's right about that," said Grace. "There's no more to be said. It's all over. Finished."

Hugh held up his hands in a hopeless kind of gesture and followed

Grace back into the living room. As for Charis, she returned once more to the sanctuary of her bedroom, unable to decide what course of action to take, but desperate to think of *something*. Could she go to Aunt Bee? She guessed not because, along with Vanna, she would be upset, possibly take Charis's part and cause even more family dramas. Her mind raced for a long while until she suddenly thought of Maggie, and knew she was the only person in the world she wanted to be with.

Softly, cautiously, Charis sneaked out of the house without her parents knowing, taking with her just enough small change for her fare, and hurried to the station. There she caught a train to Halstead, where she asked a passing stranger to direct her to Maggie's road as she was unfamiliar with the area.

Maggie lived in a terrace of large, dismal Victorian houses with very small front gardens. Some were neat; others unkempt, with litter lying jumbled in long, rough grass. Maggie's simply comprised a concrete square containing the one item each house had in common — a battered metal dustbin. Knocking at the front door, which was sorely in need of a coat of paint, Charis had no idea what would be the outcome of her impulsive action. Indeed, she was finding difficulty in thinking at all as she waited anxiously for the door to open.

When it did she was confronted by a fair-haired, plump woman of about forty, dressed in a flowered crossover pinafore and cradling a toddler in her arms, with another child clinging to her skirt. "Yes?" the lady said, looking puzzled. "Who are you? What do you want?"

"I'm Charis," she explained. "Maggie's friend from school. The one she calls Mitch."

"Oh, *Mitch*? Hallo, dear. Maggie's always talking about you," said Mrs Rigg, "but you look as though you've been crying. Whatever's the matter? Are you in some kind of trouble?"

Her tears immediately began to flow all over again, startling the two toddlers, who looked as though they, too, might burst into tears at any moment.

"Pauline!" called Mrs Rigg. "Come and help me a moment, will you, love?"

A blonde child of about nine years old, and very much like Maggie in appearance, clattered down the stairs and gaped at Charis.

"Look after Carmel and Timmy for a few minutes, will you, Pauline, please?" said Mrs Rigg, and then, taking Charis's arm, she led her into a lofty old-fashioned room, where sagging armchairs were cluttered with faded cushions, and closed the door behind them. "I'm sure it's Maggie you want to talk to," she said kindly, "but she's out just now with Leo, and my boy, Dominic. They won't be long, but would it help to tell me what this is all about?"

Charis needed no further encouragement. She was soon pouring out all

184

her anguished bitterness towards Grace, and her inconsolable sadness over losing Rick. When she had finished, Mrs Rigg stayed deep in thought for a little while, and then said, "It's very difficult for me to take your part and criticise your mother, dear, and it wouldn't be right for me to do that, but you're so dreadfully upset, and I hate to see anyone so unhappy. Do your parents know where you are?"

"No," Charis sobbed.

"Well, I think I'd better let them know right away," said Mrs Rigg. "No, don't worry, you needn't go home yet. Wait till Maggie gets here, and then we'll see. I expect she'll go with you in Leo's car. Now, what's your phone number?"

Charis sat back against the dusty, lumpy cushions, trying with the greatest difficulty to control her tears. The room contained a crucifix, a statue of Our Lady of Lourdes with pink and white plaster roses at its feet, and a flamboyant picture of the Sacred Heart. On the mantelpiece, on either side of a large noisily ticking clock, stood a pair of ugly china dogs which, Charis suspected, were not genuine Staffordshire and which, even if they were, she did not care for. It was an entirely different house from her own, and yet at that moment the shabby room was the most comforting place in the world.

Mrs Rigg returned a little later with a cup of tea and some biscuits, on a plate which did not match the cup and saucer. "I've spoken to your mother," she said, "and I've told her that you'll be brought home safely a little later. It's all right. She wasn't cross, just relieved that you were safe."

"I'm surprised she cares," said Charis bleakly.

"Of *course* she cares," said Mrs Rigg. "I'm sure it's because she cares so much that she acted the way she did today. You're her only child, aren't you? All she has. That makes you very special in her eyes; much more so than if you had a lot of brothers and sisters, like Maggie."

"But she just doesn't understand," Charis protested. "Rick and I *weren't* doing anything wrong."

"I only wish I could help you, dear. Only you know what really happened," said Mrs Rigg looking distant and sad, "but it wouldn't be my place to come between you and your mother. Mothers are given special graces, you know, to guide their children until they're old enough and wise enough to make their own decisions, and I think you'll realise that as you get older. When you're twenty-one it will be a different matter. You can do what you like then, within reason, of course. Now, drink your tea and try to calm down. Maggie won't be long, I'm sure, and I must be getting on with the children's supper and putting them to bed."

By the time Leo, Maggie and her younger brother, Dominic, arrived some thirty minutes later, Charis had her tears under control, but when Maggie hugged her and, for the first time ever, gave her a big kiss on the cheek, she began weeping all over again. Maggie banished Leo and

Dominic to the back room, and listened intently while Charis related her story for the second time that day.

"I just can't believe it," said Maggie gently, when she had finished. "How *could* she have sided with your neighbours against you? They must be horrible people to spy on you like that and tell tales, and they've obviously made it all sound much worse than it was. I mean, *I* know Rick; *Leo* knows Rick; we *all* know Rick. He's a lovely fellow, and you've been so *happy*. Oh, Mitch, are you *quite* sure about what your mother said?"

"She always means what she says, and she said it was finished. I can't bear to think I'll never see him again." Charis burst into fresh floods of tears.

"Does Rick know about this yet?" asked Maggie.

"No."

"Well, wouldn't you like to speak to him? You can use our phone if you want to."

"I don't think I can. I'm too upset."

"Well, let me then. I'll start off and then you can talk to him afterwards." Maggie dialled Rick's number, and standing beside her Charis heard her say, "Hello, Rick. This is Maggie. Yes, *Maggie*. Charis is here with me, but I'm afraid she's in frightful trouble with her mother. It's bad news for both of you and she's terribly upset."

Charis longed to hear Rick's response, but could not.

Maggie continued: "Charis wants to talk to you but she really is in a state. That's why I thought it best to speak first." Putting a hand over the mouthpiece, Maggie turned to Charis. "Ready now?" she said. "Rick's asking for you," and handed over the telephone.

"Cara, whatever is it?" He sounded very concerned.

"Oh, Rick," said Charis with a catch in her breath, "it's so awful. I can't ever see you again."

"*What!* You can't see me again? But *why*?" When she had broken the news to him Rick said, "None of this makes any sense to me at all. What's the matter with your neighbours? They must be monsters. As for your mother, well, words fail me. I don't think I can trust myself to speak." He sounded very angry.

"But what about *US*?" said Charis. "What are we going to do?"

"What *can* we do? I know what I'd *like* to do. I'd like to come over this very minute and have the whole thing out with your mother. However, that's clearly a non-starter. I can't think straight right now. Unfortunately, if you're unlucky enough to be stuck with an impossible parent, there isn't an easy way out."

"But I *love* you," Charis cried. "I can't believe I'll never see you again. I can't bear the thought of it."

"I know, Cara, and I love you too, but this is a very tricky situation. I think we ought to calm down and think this through when we're less keyed up. It could be that your mother will relent, although I doubt it from what you've told me."

"I need to see you, though, Rick. We *must* meet somehow. We've got to talk. When can we?"

"I don't know," he said.

"Holyoaks starts again next Saturday. Will you be there?"

"Can't see much point in that," he said bitterly. "If we kept meeting and going out without telling your mother, you'd never be able to relax, and nothing would ever be the same again, would it?"

"What shall we do, then?"

"Wait and see, I suppose. Give it time. I still haven't got used to the idea yet. It's been a shock for me too. Let's have a break for a little while and then who knows what may happen? I suppose your mother just *might* change her mind about me in due course, but she certainly isn't going to at present, is she?"

"No. She was *adamant*," said Charis miserably.

"A break's the only answer, then," said Rick. "Don't you agree?"

"If that's what you want."

"It's not what I *want*, but I think it's all we can do, don't you?" said Rick.

"Is it goodbye, then, Rick?"

For a moment he was silent, then, "For the time being, yes, I suppose it's got to be," he said. "Goodbye, Cara. Take care of yourself. Try not to be too upset."

The library at Stella Maris was peaceful as Charis sat in the corner by the window overlooking the recreation ground. The books were dusted regularly by priggish little monitors from the first forms who, eager to ingratiate themselves with the staff, regularly volunteered for mundane tasks of this nature. Despite their outwardly pristine appearance, Charis found most of the books intensely dull: the works of the metaphysical poets; Gibbon's *Decline and Fall of the Roman Empire*; Shakespeare's plays (of course); most of Jane Austen's novels; Lives of the saints and scores of books on a variety of religious themes; English translations of *The Iliad* and *The Odyssey*, but none of the modern novels she really enjoyed.

From a raised pedestal in a space between the shelves, the benevolent gaze of St Joseph fell upon her, reminding her of a Religious Education period in the fourth form when one of the nuns had told the class that they would be wise to pray to St Joseph for guidance in finding a suitable husband when the time came, and novenas to the Blessed Virgin in aid of all kinds of special intentions were also recommended.

Someone had placed a jar of dahlias at the feet of St Joseph, their vibrant colours clashing horribly, so Charis imagined this too must be the work of one of the juniors, since no one with any kind of mature taste would have mixed magenta with scarlet and yellow. She visualised the disdainful expression which would appear on her mother's face if confronted by so gaudy a display, yet, in her present mood, Charis would probably have sided with the flower arranger, if only to oppose Grace.

In the opposite corner of the library, Morag McDonald and Louise Heron sat quietly making notes, text books open on the table in front of them. Charis knew she should be studying too, but concentration that day, as on most days, was difficult. In thirty minutes' time it would be her turn to supervise the first and second forms as they ate their school lunches — a chore she detested — although Celia, and particularly Maggie, took such sixth-form duties in their stride. Charis supposed looking after younger children came naturally to Maggie, whilst Celia's aloofness and decidedly chilly glare struck fear into the hearts of most of the eleven and twelve-year-olds, who dared not misbehave in her presence.

When the library clock had sneaked round to eleven-fifty Charis headed towards the sixth-form classroom and stowed her unread text books in her desk. She took a small cosmetic purse out of her case, called in at the nearby cloakroom, washed her hands, combed her hair and dabbed her nose with the remnants of a creme puff compact, before setting off for the canteen.

It was a depressing room with three sets of trestle tables and benches running down its entire length. At the far end, dinner ladies, dressed in ugly green overalls, stood ready to offload the contents of huge metal canisters on to waiting plates once the long lines of pupils had been admitted. The school canteen always reminded Charis of the famous 'Please sir, I want some more' scene in *Oliver Twist*. She had never eaten there, preferring always to bring packed lunches from home, but it never failed to amaze her how so many pupils could stomach the unappetising food served there day after day.

"Hello, Charis, love," called Mrs Cheney, the head dinner lady, smiling cheerfully as she stirred the contents of one of the metal containers. "Your turn today, is it? The best of British luck!"

Soon a revolting smell combining cabbage and cooking fat filled the room, and the canteen doors opened to admit a line of giggling, jostling juniors.

"No pushing! *Quietly* now!" Charis shouted as loudly as she could.

Some of the juniors simply stared at her; others ignored her; but one — a cheeky little brat with flaxen curls and a retroussé nose — stuck out her tongue.

"What's your name?" Charis demanded, bracing herself to take the action which was so clearly required.

"Find out," said the brat.

Charis felt physically sick, wondering how to deal with such insubordination. She guessed that Celia and Maggie would know exactly how to cope, but then the situation probably would not have arisen in the first place had they been on duty.

"Don't worry, I *will*," she promised. "You'll get at least one conduct mark for your bad behaviour."

"Who cares?" said the brat, and pulled a face which made all her cronies collapse into giggles. Charis could happily have slapped her but, instead, she turned her back and stalked off to supervise another part of the queue, trying to maintain a dignified demeanour.

Twenty minutes later, all the children were seated and clearly engaged in a competition to see which of them could gobble the unpleasant meal in the fastest possible time. Charis was supposed to make sure there were no breaches of table manners, but she was too miserable to care. Why, she wondered, had she ever decided to stay on at school? Lucky Pam; lucky Wendy; lucky everyone who had escaped from this imprisonment to freedom.

Released at last, Charis joined Maggie in the sixth-form common room, where they opened their packed lunches.

"What's the name of that revolting child with the fair hair and turned-up nose in One Beta?" Charis asked, inspecting the pink luncheon meat inside her sandwiches.

"You must mean Janice Cox, I think. A real little horror, that one."

"I've a good mind to report her to her form mistress. She was incredibly rude to me today."

"That wouldn't do much good," said Maggie. "She'd *really* have it in for you then. The best thing to do is ignore her. After all, most of the time she's only trying to get attention."

"I hadn't looked at it that way," Charis admitted, full of admiration for sensible, down-to-earth Maggie.

"When are you seeing Miss Ing — sorry, Mrs Wolsey?" Maggie asked, munching a cheese sandwich.

"Immediately after school. Four o'clock."

"What will you tell her?"

"I'm not sure. Most of it, probably."

"I wonder what she'll say."

"I'll soon find out, but I'm rather dreading it."

"I'm not surprised. Still, she's easy to talk to and you've always liked her, and she's married now — that may make a difference."

"Oh, Maggie. Why can't it be June all over again? I do so wish it could be."

"It's no good wishing, Mitch. Life isn't like that. You can't go back, and you can't go forward, you just have to live in the present. I mean, I wish I could go forward about four years, and then I'd probably be safely married to Leo, provided my parents had got used to the idea by then."

"But they've softened up a bit, haven't they?"

"Oh yes, but there's still a long way to go before they'll be completely happy. If only Leo would become a Catholic, that would make a big difference."

"Do you think he will?"

"I don't know, but I'm working on it."

At four o'clock Charis tapped on the door of Room 31. This was the smallest of all the classrooms, situated on the top floor and used only by sixth formers who were receiving special coaching, but it was Irene Wolsey who had suggested this venue, and now Charis heard the familiar voice inviting her to step inside, and there was no escape. "Sit down, Charis," she said. "I have to admit I'm puzzled, but here I am, so you'd better tell me why you wanted to speak to me."

While Charis related the full sequence of her relationship with, and parting from, Rick, Irene Wolsey listened in silence, concern and sympathy apparent on her face.

"My dear girl," she said eventually, "I'm so sorry about all this. It's a very sad little story, but tell me, have there been any further developments?"

"No. We haven't been in touch, and I still feel so lost without him. Sometimes I think I'll never be happy again. He was so terribly important to me. I know it sounds silly, but I truly loved him. I'm *sure* I did, and I think he loved me too."

"It isn't at all silly, Charis," said Irene Wolsey. "Sixteen is a wonderful age. It's when most people fall in love for the first time, and it's also when most people have their first taste of heartache too. I know *I* did."

"*You*, Mrs Wolsey? Did you really?"

"Oh yes, indeed, and very unhappy I was too for a long while afterwards. But eventually the wounds healed, and look at me now — a happily married woman with a lovely husband who I didn't even know existed when I was sixteen."

"But I don't suppose it was your mother's fault."

"No, but perhaps it's better that way in some respects. At least the break-up of your relationship was nothing to do with either you or Rick directly, and in a strange kind of way you may eventually find that comforting."

Charis was quiet for a moment. "I hadn't thought of it that way. It would be like preserving what we had for ever, wouldn't it?"

"Yes, it would, but, Charis, however carefully you guard that precious memory, you must also learn to lock it up and get on with your life. You're much too young to shut yourself away and pine for Rick. Do you still go to the club where you met him, for instance?"

"Oh no. I just can't bear the thought of it."

"I can see it would be sad and difficult for you, Charis, but I think you ought to be brave and go back. After all, it's one of the few places where you can have a change of scene and a chance to relax, and you wouldn't be alone, would you? I mean Maggie and her boyfriend still go there, don't they?"

"Not every week, but, yes, they still go."

"Well, think about it, Charis."

"But what about my mother, Mrs Wolsey? What do you think about her? Don't you think she was wrong?"

Irene Wolsey hesitated. "Like Mrs Rigg, it wouldn't be at all proper for me to criticise your mother," she said, "but I think, in all fairness, she shouldn't have reacted quite so strongly to your neighbours' tale-bearing. She could at least have given you an opportunity of defending yourself, listened to your side of the story, and perhaps granted you both a second chance."

Charis smiled wanly at what seemed like a hollow victory.

"I'm touched that you should have wanted to confide in me," said Irene Wolsey, "and, of course I remember our conversation a couple of years ago. You were very different then, and I'm sure Rick has played a large part in helping you to gain confidence in yourself. But, Charis, you have all the years stretching ahead of you and there will be other romances, you know, probably *many* more, and don't forget the prospect of going on to university. That would be the time for you to make the break from home and begin a life of your own. It would be a great opportunity, and something to aim for, wouldn't it?"

"Yes, Mrs Wolsey."

"I hate having to ask you this, and I suppose it's none of my business, but I feel it's my duty to make certain about something. I know from what you've told me how deeply attached to Rick you were, and he to you, but can you give me your word of honour that nothing of a more intimate nature occurred between you? Kissing and cuddling is one thing, but anything more would be very serious. You *do* realise that, don't you?"

"Yes, I do," said Charis, wondering if the way Rick had fondled her would count as very serious in Mrs Wolsey's eyes, or whether she had meant going all the way. She would never know, for she had no intention of divulging the very special and private memories which were hers and Rick's alone.

"Good. I'm relieved," said Irene Wolsey. "How are things at home now?"

"Frosty. My mother and I are still barely on speaking terms."

"Take my advice," said Mrs Wolsey, "and make it up. I have a feeling that she may have been so upset by what she saw as the neighbours' criticism of *her*, that she justified herself by punishing you. Try to look at it through your mother's eyes, Charis. Do you think you could bring yourself to do that?"

"Perhaps."

"Good. As for the future, working hard at school will help take your mind off your present unhappiness. Go back to your club with an open mind, and just take one day at a time. Eventually you'll start feeling happier, believe me."

Donning her school blazer, Charis left Stella Maris and headed towards the bus stop and home, thanking providence for Irene Wolsey who, for the second time in her life, had come to her rescue, lifted her spirits and helped to restore her faith in the future.

TEN

September ended, October began and life in the sixth form continued inexorably, dinner duty remaining Charis's weekly penance. Scarcely a day went by when she did not think of Rick, but as the amount of homework to be completed increased significantly, and the sixth formers were expected to engage in unsupervised study during their free periods each day, she was obliged to curtail her memories and ever-present sense of loss. It was a very different routine from the old days in Five Alpha, but as the weeks went by she gradually accepted it.

Additional coaching in French took place on Mondays and Wednesdays, Charis and Celia being joined by Nancy Morrison, an earnest girl with straight brown hair, whose attractive, warm brown eyes saved her from being plain and had earned her the nickname Nutmeg.

The lessons were conducted by Sister Gertrude, who tried to make them as interesting as she could to soften the blow of having to stay for an extra hour after school. One of her pet ideas at the start of each session was to unroll a large, busy, coloured picture, which the girls had to describe in French.

One Wednesday it was a beach scene, where a family was enjoying a picnic. Charis had always been self-conscious when obliged to speak French, and when she was asked to begin she was immediately stumped. After a few moments of uncomfortable silence, during which she racked her brains and blushed hotly, she said hesitantly, *"C'est un — une —* oh, *what's* a picnic, please, Sister? I've completely forgotten."

"Can anyone help?" asked Sister Gertrude.

Nancy looked blank but Celia said, "Isn't it *un pique-nique*, Sister?"

Charis and Nancy thought this highly improbable and giggled, but, "Quite right," said Sister Gertrude. "There, that wasn't so difficult, was it, Charis?"

She felt a complete idiot, silently said *'Merde'*, a satisfying word she had learnt from Pam, and, still blushing, wondered yet again why Celia hadn't passed the exam the first time round. But at least her own written work was almost up to standard now and the oral section of the exam carried only a small percentage of the total marks.

When the three girls had each taken a turn at describing the picture, Sister Gertrude gave them a passage written in French which they were to translate into English: "I'll give you half an hour," she said, "so work hard at it, please, and when you've finished that we'll have some dictation."

At last the extra coaching was over and they were free to go home.

"I'd like to leave school next year," Celia suddenly announced at the bus stop.

Charis was very surprised: "*Would* you? You mean you don't want to try for university after all?"

"I can't see much point," said Celia. "I've discovered that I'm not all that studious, and the thought of another year at school and then three more at university doesn't appeal to me now. Babs is enjoying her job so much that it's made me envious."

"What would you do instead?"

"I like the idea of the travel business," said Celia. "Maybe working for an airline or something."

"Do you mean as an air hostess?"

"I don't know if I have what it takes to be accepted for *that*," said Celia. "They have terribly high standards, but there are other possibilities — ground staff, for instance. Or perhaps if I worked for a travel company, I'd have more opportunities to go abroad. That's why I'm anxious to pass French, and I'm trying to learn Spanish too."

"Are you teaching yourself, then?"

"Well, not exactly. Ronnie's mother, Rosa, speaks it fluently, so she's been helping me."

"Oh yes, I heard she was from South America. Argentina, wasn't it?"

"That's right — Buenos Aires."

"What's she like?"

"Very excitable, small and glamorous. She has black hair which she wears in a bun, and honey-coloured skin like Ronnie's."

"Does Ronnie speak Spanish too?"

"He *can*, but he doesn't make much of it. You know how secretive he is."

Charis sighed, envying Celia her lifestyle. Rosa Costello sounded almost as fascinating as her son, and she wanted to know more about them both: "What's Ronnie doing now?" she asked. "I suppose he's left school?"

"He's at Warbridge Art College," said Celia. "He's always been keen on painting."

"That fits," said Charis. "He even *looks* like an artist."

"I suppose he does, now you come to mention it."

"I'll never forget how surprised I was when I first heard him call your mother Fran after your party," said Charis.

193

Celia laughed. "Most of my friends still call her Fran. She encourages them, but Ronnie was always one of her favourites, and he's fond of her too, I think."

"I couldn't imagine *my* mother ever agreeing to anything like that."

"It isn't all that usual, though," said Celia. "I mean, none of us call Pam's mother Jane."

Charis thought of Shelagh and Charlie Woodrose and how, the first and only time she had met them, they had asked her to use their Christian names. She sighed again, something she did all too frequently.

"That was a big sigh. What's the matter?" Celia asked.

"Oh, just thinking."

Later, Charis said, "Do you still keep in touch with Miranda?"

"I haven't seen her lately," said Celia. "Don't you think that once people start working there's a rift between them and those of us still at school? I do."

"Yes, I suppose you're right. Take Pam, for instance. I've only seen her in the distance. We haven't even had a chat on the telephone for ages."

"We can't even meet at the Zanzibar any more," said Celia. "Wasn't it awful about the fire?"

"Dreadful, but thank goodness no one was hurt. My father heard it was caused by an electrical fault." Charis had been shocked by the incident and awed by the sight of the blackened, roofless building.

"Perhaps it'll reopen once it's been rebuilt," said Celia, "but it'll never be quite the same again."

"Now that Pam works most Saturday mornings, I don't suppose I'd have gone there on my own anyway," said Charis.

"I'm worried about you," said Celia.

"Worried? About me?"

"Well, you don't seem to want to *do* anything any more. You used to enjoy Holyoaks. At least, I thought you did."

"I loved it," said Charis, "but things have changed. I couldn't face going there without Rick. That's why I haven't been back."

The bus turned into the Charters Lea Station precinct, and they stepped off.

"You wouldn't consider Warbridge Jazz Club for a change, I suppose?" said Celia, as they walked down Wednesbury Road.

"That reminds me of when you first asked me along to Holyoaks," said Charis, "but this time I don't think there's a hope in hell of my mother agreeing. She's absolutely dead set against anything to do with jazz."

"What if Maggie and Leo were to go along as well?" said Celia. "Think about it. Your mother approves of them, doesn't she?"

"She approves of you, too."

"Does she? I'm flattered," said Celia with an amused little smile. "Well, if you were to go and come home with a group, she couldn't object, surely?"

"Oh yes she could," said Charis, "but I'll work on the idea."

That evening there was a phone call from Aunt Bee who, after a preliminary chat with Grace, asked to speak to Charis. "Hello, pet," she said. "How are you?"

"Exhausted after extra French," Charis told her. "The school day's long enough without all that."

"I'm sure it is, but forget about that for now. I wondered if you'd like to pop up to London with me on Saturday."

"London? Why? What about the shop?"

"Gladys has offered to look after it for me in the morning, and then spend the afternoon with Vanna, so I've got a free day," she said. "I thought we could look round the Oxford Street shops, have some lunch at a Corner House, perhaps, and then go to the pictures."

"What's on?"

"There's a film called *Summer Madness*."

"Who's in it? What's it about?"

"Katherine Hepburn and Rosanno Brazzi. It's a love story set in Venice, with lots of beautiful scenery. What do you think? Would you like to come with me?"

"Yes, I'd love to," said Charis, adding as an afterthought, "Does *SHE* know?" Since Grace had forbidden her to see Rick, Charis had refrained from calling her Mummy, either in direct conversation or when referring to her in conversation with others.

"I've just mentioned it, so that's all right. I'll meet you at Upsvale Station, on the platform at ten o'clock."

It was fun exploring the Oxford Street shops, with Aunt Bee making jokes about her somewhat rotund figure, and hugging unsuitable dresses against her ample bosom just to make Charis laugh. In reality, Aunt Bee always wore well-cut dresses which minimised her faults, but had a poor eye for colour, sometimes mixing caramel with fuchsia-pink, or donkey-brown with royal-blue, combinations which made Charis wince.

"You *can't* wear those colours together, Auntie," she had admonished on more than one occasion.

"Can't I, pet? Well, thanks for telling me. I thought they looked rather nice."

At the Tottenham Court Road end of Oxford Street, almost opposite Bourne and Hollingsworth's, Charis noticed a shop selling dress materials. Dominating the window was a large sign which read:

Make Your Own Fully Circular Felt Skirt.
No Hemming Required.

"Look at that, Auntie," said Charis. "I've read about felt skirts in *Woman's*

Own. They're all the rage at the moment. Don't you think they're super? I'd love to have one."

They went inside to investigate and saw bales and bales of felt in every conceivable colour. After admiring them for a while Aunt Bee said, "I'd like to buy you what's necessary and make one up for you. You need cheering up, and clothes usually do the trick, don't they? What colour do you fancy?"

The range of pretty colours was tempting, but Charis opted for black, mentally teaming it with her sweaters, and knowing it would serve her well for the approaching winter. Thus, the matter was promptly settled and they left the shop in a buoyant mood.

Aunt Bee was rarely cross, although she had barely been able to conceal her anger over the Rick affair. Grace had told her about it initially, but when Charis had given her own side of the story in a snatched moment of privacy, there was no doubting whose side her aunt was on.

At lunchtime, as they sat at a table in Lyons Corner House eating a mixed grill, Aunt Bee said, "It isn't often we're alone, is it? I've been wondering about you such a lot. Are you still sad about Rick? Silly question — I'm *sure* you are."

"I simply *ache* for him," Charis admitted. "Sometimes I don't think I'll ever get over him."

"I was so sorry for you, pet," said Aunt Bee. "There wasn't much I could do, though. Although Grace is my sister, and I love her very much, I've always known there was no arguing with her, and she was in such a fury about what happened."

"I told Mrs Wolsey all about it in the end," said Charis. "I didn't know who else I could confide in except you, but I didn't want to involve Vanna, and it's so difficult to get you on your own."

"I'm glad you had someone," said her aunt. "We all need a confidante sometimes."

"Now that we *are* alone for once, Auntie, can I please ask you something that's been bothering me, and that I couldn't possibly have asked Mrs Wolsey?"

"Of course you can. Fire away."

"Well, it's about Rick and me. That day in the park when the Farrows saw us lying on the grass, we really were only kissing and cuddling, but there were other times when it was more than that . . ." Here Charis blushed before continuing: "I mean, we were never silly enough to take any risks or anything, but we had some pretty close moments, if you know what I mean."

Aunt Bee smiled gently. "You wouldn't be normal unless you did, pet," she said. "I suppose you're asking me if it's wrong, and all I can say is that *if* it is then about ninety-five per cent of the world's population is at fault. Rick was a sensible young man. I could tell that straight away when I met him, and you have your head screwed on the right way too, I'm sure. The only trouble is that when you're as fond of someone as you two were, those close moments as you call them are sometimes difficult to control, and it's all too easy to get carried away. Thank goodness you didn't."

"Have *you* ever felt like that, Auntie?"

"Good gracious me *YES!*" she exclaimed. "You may be surprised, pet, but I've certainly had *my* share of close moments."

"Oh, *Auntie!* Have you really?"

"Most certainly. Don't forget, I was *engaged* once upon a time, and one of these days I'll tell you about Henry Gander too, not to mention Mr Sackville."

"Who on earth was Mr Sackville? I've forgotten."

"The man who fancied me when I first started work in London. You know, when I come to think of it, I wouldn't be surprised if Mummy stopped you seeing Rick because she was terribly worried you were starting to take after me — or even Uncle Freddy, for that matter."

At this, Aunt Bee burst into peals of such merry, infectious laughter that Charis was soon giggling uncontrollably, amused at having her suspicions about Aunt Bee's past confirmed, at least by innuendo. They laughed for so long that a couple of fierce-looking, classy ladies at a nearby table began staring at them disapprovingly over their coffee cups.

Even though Charis adored her aunt, she felt lonely inside the cinema without Rick as they sank into the plushy red seats and adjusted their eyes to the darkness of the auditorium and the activity on the big screen.

There was a crazy Tom and Jerry cartoon; the news, including items about London recently being declared a smokeless zone, and the beginning of independent television; strings of adverts and a trailer for (in Charis's opinion) yet another boring western 'shortly to be screened at this cinema'. Eventually *Summer Madness* began, and they relaxed as they watched the charming offbeat love story unfold amidst the architectural splendours and romantic atmosphere of Venice.

"I *did* enjoy that," said Aunt Bee afterwards, mopping her eyes with an embroidered handkerchief. "I hope you did, pet."

"It was lovely," said Charis, "but I thought the characters were a bit old to be so lovey-dovey."

"Perhaps they were, judged by your young standards, but it's never too late to fall in love and enjoy a bit of romance, you know."

"It's been a super day, Auntie," said Charis, as they travelled home on the train. "Thanks for everything, including my skirt. How long do you think it'll take to make-up?"

"Not long. You shall have it asap," Aunt Bee promised as the train drew to a halt at Upsvale and she stepped out, wrapping her donkey-brown autumn coat round her and clutching her capacious handbag and the carrier bag containing the precious black felt.

Charis waved to Aunt Bee, who waited on the platform until the train moved off again. Then she sat back in her seat to reflect on the pleasant day she had spent in her aunt's warm and comforting presence.

She failed to notice anyone else at Upsvale Station, so it was a complete surprise when someone sat down beside her and a familiar soft voice said, "Hello, Charis."

"*Ronnie!* I was *miles* away. You gave me quite a shock," she said, astonished but delighted to see her one-time hero once more after a lengthy absence.

"Sorry. I didn't mean to startle you," he said. "I saw you waving to someone. Who was that?"

"My aunt. We've been in London all day."

"Spending money, no doubt. Clothes?"

"Only some material for a skirt. I don't earn any money yet, and although my aunt's very generous, I don't expect her to buy me lots of clothes, but she often does, even so."

"Aren't you lucky to have someone like that? A kind of fairy godmother."

"Yes. She's very special," said Charis.

They sat quietly for a while as the train juddered through a tunnel. Then Ronnie said, "Celia told me about you and Rick. I thought the whole episode was awfully sad, and so unnecessary. I must have a very soft centre, I suppose, but I had a tremendous urge to get in touch with you — just as a friend, you understand. Wasn't that odd?"

"Oh, Ronnie," said Charis, amazed and touched. "I do wish you could have. It would have helped, I know. I was terribly lonely, and my mother made me feel guilty and grubby, even though there wasn't anything to feel guilty or grubby about."

"I suppose I shouldn't say this, but I think your mother is still living in the first decade of the century. She doesn't see that times have changed, and the same goes for those ghastly neighbours of yours. They were unbelievably narrow-minded and mean. A kiss and cuddle in the park? I mean, what's so dreadful about that?"

"I know. Don't remind me," said Charis, "but the worst part of all was being cut off from Rick so completely and so suddenly. I wasn't given a second chance, and my mother certainly didn't want to hear my side of the story."

"So you haven't seen Rick since?"

"No, not once. Sometimes I've thought he was angry with me for not standing up to my mother. Do you think he could have been?"

"Hard to say."

"He was always telling me not to worry about her reactions, and he reckoned he could cope with her and persuade her to let me go places with him. It worked, too, because he could charm the birds from the trees, and both my parents liked him very much before all hell broke loose that day."

"If it's any consolation, which I doubt," said Ronnie, "things have been pretty bad for me, too, of late. My father, despite some pretty dyed-in-the-wool ideas about how *I* should behave, is carrying on with his secretary and, needless to say, my mother is devastated. The atmosphere at home was awful for a long while, but now he's left and moved in with his floozie, things aren't quite so bad there."

"I'm terribly sorry," said Charis, "particularly for your mother."

"She's better off without him," said Ronnie bitterly. "My old man's *always* been a rotter. I don't know why I'm telling you all this, but he got my mother pregnant when she was very young, and only married her because her father threatened to make trouble for him. Yours truly was the result of that unhappy union. Not many people know that, but somehow I trust you to keep it under your hat. Fran and Celia Armitage know, but they're very discreet."

Charis felt honoured to be party to Ronnie's secrets, and surprised at the turn the afternoon had taken. "What do you think will happen?" she asked.

"If my father hadn't left home, I think I would have had to instead," said Ronnie. "But I'm happy enough there with my mother, and I can't help feeling responsible for her now."

"Thank you for trusting me," said Charis. "Celia told me your mother was teaching her Spanish, but she never mentioned anything personal."

"No. She wouldn't have," said Ronnie. "She's a very good friend, and so are you now, only a little less so because I don't know you so well yet."

"The only thing Celia told me was that you were at Warbridge Art College," said Charis.

"That's right. I left school in the summer and got a deferment from national service for the time being. Did I ever tell you that art's the only thing I've ever wanted to go in for?"

"No, but I seem to remember Banjo mentioning that you didn't want to go into your father's firm. I'm not at all surprised that you want to be — are — an artist. You look like one."

Ronnie smiled.

"Ronnie, can I ask you something?"

"Fire away."

"Well, it's about Miranda. What's been happening to her?"

"Everything's gone round in a circle," said Ronnie. "A bit like that film *La Ronde*, but I don't suppose you ever saw that."

"No, but Pam did. I heard all about it."

"Miranda went out with Tony Wiseman for some time, but it seems, like Banjo and Roger in the past, he wanted more from her than she was prepared to give. I know Miranda like the back of my hand, and she has very strong views. I really thought it was going to be a serious affair. That's why I dropped out of her life in the summer and tried to get her out of my mind. Your little friend, Wendy, was a sweet girl and she looked so radiant that night at the Midsummer Ball that I thought she might be the answer, but she wasn't, as you undoubtedly heard."

"Her parents were difficult, too, weren't they?"

"Yes. They didn't approve of my mixed blood, or my prospects for that matter. Well, they were entitled to their opinion, but I knew it wasn't going to work even before that."

"Because of Miranda?"

"Of course. The last thing I wanted to do was to make Wendy unhappy, but I simply couldn't forget Miranda. She was in my mind all the while, and it just wasn't fair to Wendy."

"And now?"

"It's strange I should have met you this afternoon, because only this week Miranda and I decided to get back together again — seriously this time. She's one of the warmest people I've ever known — wonderfully sympathetic and caring."

"And beautiful to look at," Charis added, feeling a small twinge of envy.

"That too," said Ronnie. "When I was going out with her before, I painted her portrait. She was a great sitter — very patient. I used to go over to her home because it was difficult to organise things at mine. Her parents are very understanding people. She takes after them."

Charis was so absorbed in this fascinating conversation that she failed to notice the train stopping at the usual string of stations. Now, looking up, she saw dark-green and white paintwork, a well-kept shrubbery and a couple of silver birch trees overlooking a brick wall which backed on to the railway line: "Heavens, we're at Charters Lea already," she said, aggrieved that the journey shared with Ronnie was at an end.

"So we are," said Ronnie. "I suppose you've got to rush off home now, have you?"

"Unfortunately, yes."

"Look," he said. "I don't know why, but I've always felt oddly protective towards you. Let me give you my phone number, and if you ever want a sympathetic ear, or you're feeling miserable, or simply want to have a friendly chat, just ring me. Would you like that? Would it help? My mother won't mind at all, and once I've told Miranda the circumstances, neither will she."

"It's awfully nice of you," said Charis. "I don't know what to say."

"Well, don't say anything. Just think about it," said Ronnie, handing her a scrap of paper on which he had hastily scribbled the number. "And try to keep smiling, won't you?"

"Thanks awfully, Ronnie. Goodbye," she said.

"*Hasta la vista*," said Ronnie.

On a wet Saturday afternoon in October, Charis glanced distastefully at the grimy plastic cover of her library book as she lounged on the settee in the living room. Sometimes she wondered why she bothered to belong to the local library when the books were so often grubby, but it was a welcome form of escapism to lose herself in a novel, and her pocket money would not stretch to new paperbacks as well as gramophone records. Today, though, the contents of her book were considerably less absorbing than speculation about the evening ahead when, after a lapse of twelve weeks, she was returning to Holyoaks with Maggie and Leo. The dread of visualising herself in that familiar hall without Rick was tempered by the smallest twinge of excitement that at last she would be back in circulation once more after her self-imposed exile.

Dizzy was curled up in a ball, fast asleep in one of the armchairs, his tail wrapped round his pink nose, oblivious to the miserable weather, in the way of all cats. Hugh, relaxing in the other armchair, was glancing at his latest post office staff magazine, dropping off to sleep now and again and waking with a start as the booklet fell into his lap, while Grace sat upright at the gate-legged oak table writing a letter. The only sounds in the room were Hugh's occasional snores, and the rustle of Grace's high-quality azure writing paper.

The sudden shrillness of the telephone bell shattered the quietude, startling Dizzy, rousing Hugh, and causing Grace to look up sharply from her writing pad. Charis volunteered to answer it, glad of the chance to escape momentarily from the claustrophobic gloom, and gladder still when the caller turned out to be Pam.

"Haven't seen you for *ages*," Pam said. "Are you doing anything?"

"Nothing at all. I'm bored to tears."

"Why don't you come down for a chat, then? Are you going out tonight?"

"Yes I am, actually, but I could come for an hour or so I expect."

"Will you have to ask?"

"No doubt. Hold on a mo."

Returning to the sepulchral living room, Charis put the proposition to Grace.

"Pam? It's a long while since you've heard from her," she said. "All right, then, but don't forget you're going out later."

"As if I would."

"And be home in time for tea."

Pam, relaxed and as pretty as ever, opened her front door. "Come on in," she said brightly. "Hang your raincoat here and leave your umbrella in the stand. We'll go upstairs to my room and play some records, shall we? We can talk at the same time. My folks are out so we don't have to worry about them."

Pam's room was a colourful place, defying the greyness of the afternoon. A huge bunch of scarlet paper poppies erupted from a blue vase; the window seat was padded with cushions made from bright floral cretonne to match the curtains; the bedspread was the colour of a summer sky, and the miniature replica of a chest of drawers on the dressing table housed, Charis imagined, Pam's ever-growing collection of cosmetics.

The garden, observed from a distance through rain-streaked windows, reminded Charis of an Impressionist painting, the rich colours of autumn merging into a washy blur. Closer scrutiny, however, revealed a battalion of chrysanthemums, a little bowed now in the rain despite being staked, and sturdy pyracantha and cotoneaster bushes, peppered with bright berries. The lawns were littered with leaves, and a few pink and red geraniums were still putting on a brave show, as though unwilling to be lifted for their indoor winter sojourn.

Turning away from the window, Charis complimented Pam on her cheerful room, but, even as she spoke, she was comparing it with Bryony Mayo's, for ever imprinted in her memory, along with visions of a friendship that was never to be.

"Well, what have you been doing lately?" Pam asked, brightly.

"Enjoying my new record player. Working pretty hard at school. Going to a film with my aunt in London. Not much else."

"Which film?"

"*Summer Madness.*"

Pam pulled a scornful face, which made Charis wish it had been something more racy.

"Don't you go to Holyoaks any more, then?"

"I'm going tonight, as a matter of fact. It's been twelve weeks since I was there. It's taken me a long time to pluck up courage, and even now I'm dreading it."

"Do Maggie and Leo still go?"

"Yes, most weeks, and they'll be there tonight, thank goodness. But I'll probably be a gooseberry. They're so lovey-dovey it just isn't true."

"How about Wendy?"

"No, she gave it up after she left school and stopped seeing Ronnie."

"Her parents didn't approve of him or something, wasn't that it?"

"They didn't want their daughter going out with someone with foreign blood. How *stupid*!" Charis was indignant about it. "They didn't care a fig about his nice personality. They were just so prejudiced."

"You always liked him, didn't you?"

"Oh yes, very much." Charis was finally ready and proud to admit it, but had no intention of mentioning the satisfying, private and totally unexpected conversation she had recently held with him.

"Dare I ask? Have you heard from Rick at all?"

The very sound of his name was like being stabbed with a sharp needle. "No," Charis replied dully. "What would have been the point after that ghastly day? He knew as well as I did that he couldn't confront my mother again, so we didn't have much option but to stop seeing one another."

"Your mother is still terribly strict with you, isn't she?" said Pam. "Fortunately mine's much more relaxed, but my father tends to fuss. He's still not sure whether or not he likes Roger, for instance, and I bet he wonders what we get up to and how far we go."

"And how far *have* you gone, or shouldn't I ask?"

A wicked grin lit up Pam's pert little face. "We've actually *done* it," she said, with a note of triumph. "Twice, actually, just the other day in the back seat of Roger's car. I was longing to tell you."

Charis was speechless.

"Don't you want to know about it?" Pam continued.

"I'm not sure. You worry me."

"There's nothing for *you* to worry about. Leave that to me. Anyway, I *told* you Roger knows what he's doing. It was super — at least it was the second time.

"How about your mother?" Charis said. "Do you think she knows?"

"Between you and me I'm sure she *guesses*," said Pam. "Actually, I think she's envious, and wishes she was in my shoes."

"Oh, *PAM*! I can't imagine *my* mother *ever* enjoying that kind of thing, not even with my father."

"She *might* have, once upon a time," said Pam, "but she's probably forgotten all about it now."

"I'd be very surprised if you were right. She just isn't the type."

Pam's sexual adventures dominated their conversation for most of the afternoon, but they also continued comparing their respective mothers, until Charis changed the subject by asking Pam how she was enjoying her new job.

"It's fun," she said. "I've met some friendly people, and my boss is nice. He flirts with me like mad, and pinches my bottom when he gets the chance. It doesn't bother me. He says my work's OK, and it's great getting paid and having my own money at last. I'd hate to be back at school."

"Lucky old you." Charis felt envious. "By the way, how's Polly? What's her latest news?"

"Still with Banjo, but they had a big row because she suspected he'd been out on the tiles while he was up in Scotland. Knowing Banjo, he probably had, but Polly played him at his own game, went to the Starlight Ballroom and let someone take her home. She told Banjo and he was hopping mad and wildly jealous. They didn't speak for over a week, but he must be crazy about her because he actually sent her a bunch of flowers to make things up. I mean, can you imagine *Banjo* doing something romantic like that?"

"Totally out of character. Celia said once that he'd never get serious about anyone, but he seems to have met his Waterloo with Polly, doesn't he? I still get all churned up inside when I think how close she came to disaster. Do you think they still go all the way?"

"Almost certainly. I mean, once you've tasted forbidden fruit, it's hard to stop. Still, I think they're a lot more careful these days. She told him about the scare when it was all over and it gave him a big shock."

Charis wondered secretly and with an uncomfortable little inner quiver when it would be *her* turn to sample forbidden fruit, but she dismissed the disturbing thought by asking Pam where she and Roger went for entertainment.

"Oh, here and there. Cinema, dances, Holyoaks now and again. We've even been to the Young Conservatives a few times and, of course, Warbridge Jazz Club. We go there more than anywhere else, really. You ought to come."

"That's what Celia said the other day, but I can't see it happening."

"Let's listen to some of my jazz records, anyway," said Pam. "I'm collecting them with a vengeance. Roger gave me a few, and he found some old ones in a shop in Charing Cross Road, and some more at a jumble sale. He tells me which ones to look out for, and I've already bought some of those. How many records have you got now?"

"Ten. My parents and Aunt Bee and my grandma treated me to one each when they bought me the record player, and I've spent most of my pocket money on the rest. I bought several that Rick recommended and I listen to them a lot. It's so nice being able to turn the sound down so that my mother doesn't get ratty."

"We shan't have to worry about that this afternoon. We're on our own so we can turn up the volume as loud as we like."

A moment later Pam's bedroom was filled with the exuberant sounds of Kid Ory's Creole Band, followed by a soulful blues number: "'Blue for Waterloo' — Humphrey Lyttelton," Pam said.

Charis lolled back against the window seat as poignant memories of Rick's den came flooding back: "Isn't that a sad tune? It's lovely, but it makes me want to howl."

"Blues are supposed to, aren't they? Oh, come on, cheer up. Here's one for your mother," and Pam laughed naughtily as she picked out a record with a red Good Time Jazz label.

Soon Charis was giggling delightedly as she heard a joyfully raucous voice belting out a jazz number called 'Mama Don't Allow'.

The trombone, banjo, bass and clarinet were mentioned in turn in the vocal, after which individual jazzmen performed spirited solos illustrating their virtuosity. The record ended with a reference to George playing his clarinet even though Mama didn't allow it.

"Who's George?" Charis asked.

"George Lewis. He recorded it in 1950. Not all that long ago, really."

"It's *gorgeous*. I'd *love* to have it. I'd play it secretly when my mother was being difficult. It would make me feel so much better, and I *must* go to

Warbridge Jazz Club sometime too. I wonder how I can wangle it."

"Well, if you need any help just let me know."

When the records were exhausted Pam said, "Let me show you my newest purchase." Opening her wardrobe door, she lifted out a very full midnight-blue, ballerina-length felt skirt.

Charis fingered it admiringly, glad that for once Pam had not outsmarted her in knowing about, and owning, the latest fashion. "It's felt, isn't it? I've got one too. There's a shop in London where they'll cut it out for you in a circle, and all you have to do is fix the waistband and the zip and whatever. You don't even have to hem it. I saw it when I was in London with Aunt Bee, so she bought it and made it up for me. Where did you get yours?"

"Barkers in Kensington," said Pam. "Mine was ready-made. What colour did you get?"

"Black." Charis was proud of this. "Plain black."

"Black? You don't usually wear black."

"I know, but I thought it was high time I did. I'd do *anything* for a change these days."

"*Anything?*" said Pam with her usual wicked grin.

"Well, *almost* anything," Charis conceded.

By the time Charis left Pam's house the rain had stopped. Chatting to her old friend and listening to her jolly records had raised her spirits, but she dwelt on the news Pam had told her about Roger with a mixture of envy and anxiety and, in an effort to forget it, she tried to concentrate on the forthcoming evening at Holyoaks after so long an absence.

When Hugh opened the front door of her house Charis detected a fishy smell emanating from the kitchen and wrinkled her nose: "Not another cod's head, is it, Daddy?"

He grinned, his afternoon of considerably more than forty winks clearly having revived him. "No. Kippers," he said.

Charis pulled a face.

"Hurry up now, Charis," Grace called from the kitchen. "It's nearly teatime."

The oblong dining-room table had been spread with a checked seersucker cloth and laid with the pale-blue tea service. A crusty French loaf had been cut into wedges, buttered and displayed on one of two large plates, while its twin held half a shop-bought fruit cake and some Cadbury's milk-chocolate-covered jam rolls wrapped in blue and silver foil.

"I haven't had time to bake this week," Grace confessed, "but I always think Baxters' cakes are nice."

She set kippers in front of Hugh and Charis, and then brought in her own plate and joined them at the table. Charis studied the kipper, its colour reminding her of tan shoe polish. She much preferred the richer, oilier flavour of herrings, especially ones with hard roes, but today the kippers weren't too salty, the crusty white bread and butter pleasantly complementing their unique flavour.

"I suppose you'll be wearing your new felt skirt tonight?" said Grace, pouring tea.

"Of course."

"Are your friends calling for you, sweetheart?" asked Hugh.

"Yes, Daddy. In Leo's car."

"I hope Tom Potterfield is at the club," said Grace. "I always thought you should have encouraged him more."

Charis glared at her mother, barely able to suppress the scornful words which sprang to her lips. Instead, she swallowed too large a piece of kipper and nearly choked on a small bone, which made her splutter and her eyes water.

"Be *careful*, child," said Grace. "You're as bad as Bee. I've never known her to eat any kind of fish without having trouble with the bones."

"Have a drop of water," Hugh advised. "It might help."

At last tea was over and Charis began to prepare for the evening. She found to her annoyance that the backs of her nylon stockings were splattered with mud after walking down to Pam's house in the rain, but she only possessed two other pairs, one of which had been washed and was still damp, and the other had a ladder in the foot. Undaunted, she dampened a piece of cotton wool, ran it over the Lux soap in the bathroom and washed off the marks with a modicum of success.

Back in her bedroom Charis lifted the beautiful black felt skirt off its hanger and stepped into it, enjoying its smooth texture and the way it swirled over her petticoat. Her red and white jumper brought back memories of her first visit to Holyoaks and meeting Banjo, but she still loved it and felt smart when wearing it.

As she buttoned her raincoat she heard a car pull up outside and guessed it was Leo's. The vague possibility that Maggie and Leo might not be seeing her home afterwards if she happened to meet someone eligible, prompted her to pick up her umbrella, which had been drying in the hall, and gave her a minuscule spark of hope — the first she had experienced since parting from Rick.

"Remember us to Tom if you see him," said Grace as Charis was leaving, which was enough to make her want to slam the front door loudly, but she just managed to restrain herself.

Maggie stepped out of the front seat of Leo's little Austin and tilted it forward so that Charis could climb in the back. "How do you feel about tonight, Mitch?" she asked.

"A bit weird."

"Never mind. We're with you. I'm sure it'll be OK."

Charis wondered if anyone would dance with her.

"I know someone who will," said Maggie.

"Who?"

"Tom, of course. He'll probably go wild with joy at seeing you again."

"Oh, don't *you* start. You sound just like my mother. For some reason she's been trying to fix me up with him from the very first time she saw him."

Leo, half concentrating on his driving, half listening to the conversation, laughed at this remark. "That's because she'd feel you were safe with him," he said.

"She'd be right," Charis agreed, "but who wants to be *that* safe? Anyway, I was safe with Rick, only *she* didn't think so."

"Ah yes," said Maggie. "*We* know that, but think how wildly attractive Rick was. Your mother probably thought you'd be tempted more easily by someone who looked like that. Poor old Tom is so ordinary by comparison, isn't he?"

Charis was adamant in her reply: "There *isn't* any comparison. No one will ever be like Rick."

Driving up to the familiar hall, and remembering her last visit there in July, made Charis feel horribly shaky, but Leo and Maggie jollied her along, and soon they were standing by the entrance desk facing Audrey Duffy.

"Haven't seen you for ages," she said. "What have you been up to?"

"That would be telling, wouldn't it, Mitch?" Maggie answered brightly, winking at Charis, who managed to force a grin, grateful for her friend's loyal support.

"I *love* your skirt," said Maggie later. "Isn't it *super*?"

"You should get one too."

"No. It wouldn't suit me, I fear. I'm too big. But it looks wonderful on you."

Maggie's flaxen hair, recently trimmed, curled softly round her face and neck, enhancing her rose-petal skin. She had always been a nice-looking girl, but Charis thought her friend's appearance had blossomed amazingly since knowing Leo. Unfortunately, her wardrobe, like Charis's, was fairly limited due to lack of funds and, that evening, under a very ordinary pinafore dress, she was wearing a powder-blue jumper which Charis had not seen before.

"It's the one I've been knitting," said Maggie. "I told you about it the other day."

Once they were inside the hall Charis looked round anxiously for any sign of Rick. The dancing had already begun, and she saw Tom waltzing with a short girl with a sallow complexion, who was wearing a tight jumper which looked as though it had shrunk in the wash.

The dance soon ended, and then the voice of Jimmy Young singing 'The Man from Laramie' started Maggie's feet tapping.

Leo said, "Oh, drat my leg. I *wish* I could dance quicksteps with you. I know how you love them."

"Not to worry. I love you more than I love dancing, honey," said Maggie. "I'm happy just being with you."

The envious ache, which had become so familiar to Charis, eased fractionally as she saw Tom heading in her direction. He was wearing a heathery Harris-tweed jacket, grey flannels and a pair of highly polished black shoes. "I just can't believe my eyes," he said, "but even if you're just an illusion, will you dance with me anyway?"

Charis granted him a small, prim smile. She recalled the first time she had danced with him way back in March, and wondered why he looked different. Then she noticed he was wearing new glasses. His old wire-framed ones had been indelibly stamped 'National Health Service', but these had smart, tortoiseshell frames, making him look older, even more intelligent and really quite imposing. His lips were still dry, but no spots or traces of spots marred his complexion now.

He danced with his customary verve, and when they had travelled the length of the hall he said, "You were wearing that jumper the first time I saw you. I thought you looked wonderful then, and you still do."

"Thanks."

After a moment or two's silence he went on, "I'm not going to pester you about Rick, or probe into why you haven't been down here since the summer, but . . . "

"Thanks again," Charis interrupted tersely.

"I'm sorry," said Tom. "Trust me to put my foot in it. Let me start again. I'll change the subject. What are you doing at school? You *are* still at school, I presume?"

"Yes, but sometimes I don't know why. I'm not enjoying the sixth form at all."

"Why not?"

"Oh, it's not the *work*. It's things like having to do dinner duty. I simply *hate* that."

"So would I," he admitted, "but fortunately we're spared such horrors at Eden House."

Just then, Greg Duffy stopped the music: "Just to make things a bit more interesting, this will be a competition dance," he said. "So if anyone *isn't* dancing, now's the time to find a partner. There are valuable prizes at stake."

"What on earth's a competition dance?" Charis asked.

"Wait and see," said Tom.

Soon, almost everyone took to the floor. Charis noticed the girl in the shrunken jumper who had been dancing with Tom earlier, and asked him her name.

"That's Valerie Blyth. She's fairly new. In fact there have been several newcomers since the summer. It happens every year, and it's a good thing because there's always a need to swell our numbers but, all the same, it means the whole atmosphere of the club changes."

"It's certainly different," Charis agreed, "and there are a lot of people I don't know."

"Well, you know *me*," said Tom, smiling.

"Keep your partners, please," Greg called. "This time I want to see how your foxtrots are progressing."

"I still can't do this properly," Charis admitted. "Can you?"

"Not really, but we'll try, shall we?"

Several couples left the floor at once, but at least Tom and Charis kept time with the music, taking the long, sweeping strides which the dance demanded.

They also attempted a sailor's hornpipe and an Irish jig, both of which caused a great deal of general merriment, but when Greg announced a tango they finally conceded defeat and Charis returned to her table alone.

Almost at once the exciting words and rhythm of 'Hernando's Hideaway' filled the hall. This was a song from the musical *The Pajama Game* which had become very popular in recent times.

A few brave couples attempted the exaggerated steps with the requisite set expressions on their faces.

"Just *look* who's having a go," said Maggie. She nodded towards the far end of the hall, where Charis was surprised to see a strange girl, with an enviable mane of black hair, performing an entirely creditable tango with Ken Purchiss.

"Who's *she*?"

"Don't know her name," said Maggie. "But she's been coming here with Ken for the past few weeks."

Charis was dazzled by their performance: "They're brilliant. I wonder where they learnt."

The final competition dance was a jive. Four of the five couples who had attempted the tango left the floor, but once again Ken and his partner opened out and gave it their all. At the end they were cheered and applauded and, breathless and shiny with perspiration, made for the stage to receive their prizes. Ken's was a case designed for holding gramophone records, and the girl was given a dressing-table set of brush, comb and mirror, all displayed in a see-through box on a bed of ruched rose-pink satin.

"I'd give anything to be able to dance like that," said Charis.

"So would *I*," said Maggie.

"That last dance — the jive — is that what they do at jazz clubs?"

"I don't really know. Something like that, I suppose," said Leo, "but I shouldn't think it's all so fast moving. I mean a blues rhythm is much slower, isn't it?"

With admirable nonchalance Charis raised the subject which had been at the forefront of her mind for so long: "Celia was saying we ought to go to Warbridge Jazz Club some time."

"Who's 'we'?" asked Maggie.

"You and Leo, maybe Celia and Mark, me and anyone else we know who might be interested."

Maggie glanced at Leo. "You wouldn't be able to do much jiving, would you, honey?"

"No, but I'd enjoy the jazz. You don't *have* to jive. I've heard that lots of people never do. They just go to listen."

"What would your mother say?" asked Maggie. "I can't see her being very keen on you going to a jazz club."

"She wouldn't be," Charis agreed, "but if I told her we were going in a group she just might give in."

"Particularly if Tom was included," Leo said, casually.

Charis was about to object when the sense of Leo's words hit her with a vengeance. The thought that she might be prepared to use Tom for her own selfish ends crossed her mind momentarily, but she dismissed it quickly and begin to formulate a plan.

Maggie laughed: "What's going on behind that innocent expression?"

"Nothing," Charis lied.

Later there was the customary Paul Jones, when her first partner was Ken Purchiss, who danced the quickstep with as much polish as in the earlier numbers. She complimented him on winning the competition dance and asked him where he had learnt the tango and the jive.

"A place over at Warbridge," he told her. "I've been going to ballroom classes since the summer."

"Who's that girl you were dancing with?"

"My girlfriend, Avril," he said proudly. I met her there, so we've been learning together, and we've been to the Starlight Ballroom too."

"You put on a terrific show."

"Thanks. By the way, how's Wendy?"

"Working for a vet. I only hear about her through Maggie these days."

"Is she tied up with anyone?"

"Yes, she is. It started when someone brought an injured dog to the surgery, and he took a fancy to Wendy right away."

"The dog?"

"Ha, ha. Sorry to disappoint you, but, no, it was its owner — a rather nice young man."

"I don't blame him," said Ken. "I fancied her myself, as you know, but she just wasn't interested in me. She only had eyes for Ronnie Costello, didn't she? Anyway, that's all in the past, and I've got Avril now. Aren't I the lucky one? I always hankered after a brunette anyway."

Tom claimed Charis for the next proper dance, and stayed with her for the rest of the evening. She kept glancing at her watch, dreading the last waltz and the memories it would evoke, and hoping against hope that Greg would not play 'Cara Mia', which would have been unbearable. She was relieved when he selected a new record by Ruby Murray, which held no memories for her, so while she danced with Tom she tried to negate all emotion, and guessed she was dancing woodenly.

When the lights were turned off Tom made no attempt to kiss her, but, much to her surprise, he held her closer than usual and for a while they were awkwardly cheek to cheek. Even this limited proximity irritated her because his spectacles got in the way, but she suffered in silence, and, when the lights came on again, there, true to form, was Father Kellow on the stage, ready to conduct the dismissal prayer.

"Can I walk you home, Charis?" Tom asked.

She agreed as casually as she knew how and sauntered off to the cloakroom with Maggie.

"Well?" said Maggie.

"Yes. He's seeing me home. As if you didn't know."

"Better than being on your own, though," said Maggie. "Tom's been after you for ages. I bet he's thrilled to bits."

"Well, *I'm* not. I couldn't care less."

"I think the rain's stopped for good. Shall we walk?" said Tom when they met outside the hall, so they set off along the familiar road to Charters Lea Station.

Halfway there Tom clutched her hand awkwardly and said, "Would you like to come to a concert with me next week?"

"A *concert*?" she said, feeling anything but excited. "What kind of concert?"

"Classical music, but nothing too stuffy. I think you'd enjoy it."

Secretly she doubted this, but the idea which had been simmering in her mind since Leo's throwaway remark earlier in the evening led her to pursue the conversation: "Where is it?"

"At the Coronation Hall."

This was a modern building in Upsvale, only two years old and used for various kinds of entertainment.

"I've never been to a concert," Charis admitted.

"Now's your chance, then," said Tom. "Will you come? I'd be only too pleased to take you. It's on Thursday. It starts at seven o'clock. What do you say?"

"OK, Tom. Thanks."

"That's just wonderful," Tom replied with a glowing smile, and then leaned towards her stiffly and, for the very first time, kissed her very quickly on the lips with a complete lack of passion.

ELEVEN

Charis lost no time in telling her parents that Tom had brought her home from Holyoaks and invited her to a concert, whereupon Grace's face lit up like a beacon. "At *last!*" she exclaimed. "He's most suitable for you — nice, serious-minded, polite, sincere. How *lovely!* You *are* going to the concert, aren't you?"

"I suppose so," Charis muttered.

"Try to sound more enthusiastic," said Grace. "It was very kind of him to invite you."

"But I don't know if I really *like* classical music," Charis protested.

"That's only because you don't know enough about it," said Hugh, reasonably. "A concert will be a good way to start, and I expect it'll be light music."

"I'm sure it'll be frightfully dull whatever it is."

"Go with an open mind," Hugh advised, "and you may be pleasantly surprised."

When Tom called for her he was wreathed in smiles and wearing a navy-blue raincoat. "More rain," he said cheerfully. "Never mind, I've got an umbrella. Are you bringing one?"

"Of course," she said.

"You could share mine," said Tom.

"That wouldn't work. From past experience one or the other of us would end up getting soaked."

"It would be me," said Tom. "I'd keep all the rain off you, of course."

"Well, it won't be necessary. Let's go, shall we?"

Grace and Hugh were hovering between the living room and the hall, uncertain whether or not to emerge, but Tom caught sight of them just before Charis shut the door. "Hold on a moment, Charis," he said. "I'd better just have a word with your parents." He smiled and greeted them as though they were long-lost friends: "How nice to meet you again," he said. "I do hope you've been keeping well."

"Yes, thank you, Tom," said Grace. "And you?"

"Oh, I'm fine, thanks," he said. "I've so much been looking forward to taking Charis to this concert."

"I expect she's told you it's her first," said Hugh. "I hope she won't be put off by anything too heavy."

Making sure she could not be seen by Tom or her parents, Charis pulled a face.

"I'm sure she'll enjoy it," said Tom. "I made certain the music would be suitable."

They left their raincoats in the Coronation Hall's ample cloakroom, and in exchange were given tickets by a plump lady attendant with a bored expression and purply-pink rouged cheeks.

The orchestra was already tuning up as they took their seats, and Tom handed Charis the programme outlining the evening's entertainment. "You'll recognise most of it," he promised, and, indeed, she did, although she had never before been able to put names to some of the familiar pieces of music.

In the interval they had coffee, and mulled over the first half of the concert.

"I liked 'The Carnival of the Animals'," said Charis. "I'd heard bits of it separately, like 'The Swan', but I never knew they all belonged to the same suite. It was easy to imagine the animals while I was listening to the music — oh, and they used to play the music from the 'Jewels of the Madonna' on *Children's Hour* on the wireless years ago. It was the signature tune for one of their serials — *Ballet Shoes* or *The Bell Family*, I think. I can't remember which, but I'd forgotten all about it until tonight."

In the second half Charis felt uncomfortable when Tom reached for her hand and held it determinedly until the end of the concert. Their palms grew more and more clammy and sweaty, and she longed to pull away, but stoically endured his hot fingers intertwining with hers until the final triumphant burst of the '1812 Overture' released her, and she was able to fumble for a nice, dry handkerchief.

"Well, what's the verdict?" Tom asked her on the way home.

"I really liked it."

"You're not just saying that?"

"No, of course not. It was nice music. Easy to listen to, and nothing went on for too long, but . . . "

"But?"

"Oh nothing, but I have to admit I still prefer jazz. I mean I simply *adore* jazz."

Fortunately, Tom did not look too disappointed: "It's possible, of course, to be like our Music master at school and appreciate all kinds of music, but I wonder if you'll still be so keen on jazz when you're thirty?"

"I'll *always* be keen on jazz," Charis insisted. It was, after all, for ever linked with Rick in her heart, for he, more than anyone else, had fired her with his infectious enthusiasm and introduced her to some of its leading protagonists.

Outside her house Tom kissed her briefly on the cheek and arranged to meet her at Holyoaks in two days' time, after which she thanked him for the evening and hurried indoors out of the rain.

Maggie met Charis at Stella Maris on the following Monday morning, looking more than usually animated. "Leo's planning a record evening," she said. "It'll be a very small, cosy and exclusive gathering. Just four of us, in fact. You and Tom; Leo and me. How about *that!*"

"Me and *Tom?*" said Charis. "Oh, for goodness' sake, Maggie. You're getting as bad as my mother, trying to push Tom and me together."

"Well, who else is there?" asked Maggie reasonably.

Charis sighed: "If only . . . " she said.

"As if I didn't know, but it can't be Rick, now, can it?"

"Of course not, but — oh, Maggie, we could all have had such a good time. Can you imagine what fun it would have been? What *bliss!*"

"I know," said Maggie, "but it's no good having regrets. If you keep on mooning about Rick you'll never go out with anyone else and, as I'm always trying to tell you, there are *plenty* more interesting fish in the sea."

"The trouble is, Tom just isn't my kind of fish."

"But he's the only one swimming in your direction at present, isn't he?" said Maggie, "so don't be awkward. Say 'Yes' and we could have a nice enough evening, don't you think?"

Tom was predictably delighted to have an opportunity of spending another evening with Charis, and Grace, of course, wholeheartedly approved. Maggie, Leo and Tom could do no wrong in her eyes, and she had also been singing the praises of Maggie's mother ever since Mrs Rigg had phoned to tell her that Charis was safely at their house on that fateful August day.

Leo lived in Upsvale, quite near to Aunt Bee and Vanna, but in a quiet cul-de-sac away from the main shopping parade. His parents were elderly in comparison with Maggie's, or even Charis's, but then Leo was older than them so it was hardly surprising.

Mr and Mrs Crewe greeted Maggie warmly with kisses and hugs as though she was already their daughter-in-law. They were a small, cuddly pair, unlike tall, lanky Leo, although his elder married sister, June, was said to be the very image of her mother. Charis watched the display of affection between Leo's parents and Maggie impassively, remembering that Maggie's parents were less enthusiastic about Leo because he wasn't a Catholic.

"And you must be Charis," said Mrs Crewe. "We know Tom from church, of course, but we haven't met you before. Well, make yourselves at home, my dears. We shan't interfere with your evening. We'll be safely tucked away in the other room watching television, so you can listen to your records for as long as you want. You won't disturb us, I'm sure."

"Tom probably won't like our kind of music," said Maggie, "so if he gets bored, we'll send him in to watch television with you."

Everyone laughed.

"It isn't that I don't like it," said Tom. "I just prefer classical music, that's all."

"We know. We know," said Leo, "but don't forget the offer stands if you get desperate."

Leo's radiogram was housed in a large oak cabinet. He switched it on, opened the lid, and stacked some records on the autochange. In a moment the room was filled with music of a depth and tone which thrilled Charis with its quality and richness. Most of Leo's records were recent popular tunes.

"We're playing the jolly ones first," Maggie explained. "Then we'll have your jazz records, Mitch, and later on — well, wait and see."

Eddie Calvert's 'Cherry Pink and Apple Blossom White' brought a flavour of South America as his trumpet soared and swooped up and down the scale, accompanied by exciting Latin rhythms. This was followed by Rosemary Clooney singing the jaunty 'Where Will the Dimple Be?'.

"Another of my mother's favourites," Maggie said. "As I told you once before, she likes anything to do with babies."

Next came Sammy Davis Junior singing 'Something's Gotta Give', and Jimmy Young's 'The Man from Laramie'.

"Isn't it funny how he copies the Americans and sings *'specialty'* instead of *'speciality'*?" Tom observed when the record was halfway through.

"Speciality would have too many syllables, though," said Leo. "It wouldn't scan."

"Anyway, it's an American song about an American, so it's only right for him to sing it their way," said Charis.

"I rest my case," said Tom.

'The Yellow Rose of Texas' came next, followed by 'Hernando's Hideaway' which reminded them of the competition dance when Ken Purchiss and black-haired Avril had put on such an unexpectedly professional performance.

"They learnt the tango and all those other dances somewhere over at Warbridge," said Charis. "Ken told me so. *Everything* happens at Warbridge," she added, thinking of the jazz club and trying to sound knowing and mysterious, although her remark was unfortunately lost on the others.

"Wait till you hear my newest record," said Leo. "It's like nothing *I've* ever heard before. See what you think."

It dropped with a loud plop on to the seven others piled below, and a moment later Bill Haley's 'Rock around the Clock' catapulted them into a brand-new musical dimension, blasting them with its wild exuberance, so that even Tom's feet were tapping to this compulsive new rhythm.

"What *is* it, Leo?" Maggie asked, her eyes shining.

"The very latest craze from America. It's called rock and roll."

"It makes me want to get up and dance right this minute," said Charis. "I just can't sit still. Don't you just *love* it, Maggie? I *must* buy it next time I have some spare pocket money."

"What a pity we can't dance in here," said Maggie.

"There isn't nearly enough room," said Leo apologetically. "I hadn't planned on dancing, but I suppose I could have pushed the furniture back a bit."

"Never mind. Let's hear *your* records now, Mitch," said Maggie.

"Sorry, Tom," said Charis, hurriedly opening a carrier bag and handing them over to Leo. "I'm afraid you won't like these at all."

"Don't apologise. I'm not complaining," said Tom.

Throughout the evening he kept looking at her admiringly, in a way she was beginning to find irritating.

Charis had brought nearly her entire collection of jazz, which had grown considerably now that she spent three-quarters of her pocket money each week on records. Grace and Hugh had agreed that five shillings a week was sufficient for her present needs, but Aunt Bee had doubled it to ten, which left three or four shillings for sweets, lipstick and other minor necessities.

Charis's latest purchase was the George Lewis record of 'Mama Don't Allow', which she had first heard at Pam's house that wet October afternoon.

"We certainly get the message," said Maggie. "I bet you don't play that one when your mother's in earshot."

"Too true," said Charis with a giggle, "but isn't it *fun*?"

Tom sat quietly, tapping his right foot in time with the beat, but making no comment as record followed record, and George Lewis's clarinet gave way in turn to Humphrey Lyttelton's trumpet, Sidney Bechet's saxophone, and the trombones of Kid Ory and Chris Barber.

As the familiar jazz music blared out, amplified so dramatically in Leo's little room, Charis began feeling happier, though still wishing desperately that Rick was with her instead of poor, uninspiring Tom. It was then that she made up her mind to take the plunge: "Why don't we all go to Warbridge Jazz Club some time?" she said brightly, as if the thought had only just struck her.

Leo and Maggie exchanged glances, probably remembering the last occasion when she had raised the subject.

"I've been wanting to go there for *ages*," she continued, "but — like the record says — I didn't think my mother would allow me to. Anyway, as I may have mentioned to Maggie before, if several of us went together she just *might* give in, so how about it?"

"Well, Leo?" Maggie pressed.

"OK by me," he said. "I've often wondered what that place was like."

"Tom?" Charis asked, dazed by her audacity.

"Left to my own devices, it's the last place on earth I'd want to go to," said Tom. "But for you — yes. Yes, I'll come with you."

"Oh, that's just great. I could *hug* you," said Charis, instantly regretting her words.

"Go ahead," said Tom, looking pleased, so she had no option other than to give him a light squeeze.

"When shall we go, then?" said Maggie. "We'd better arrange it now or it'll be Christmas before we know it."

"It'll have to be when I'm not on door duty at Holyoaks," said Tom. "How about Saturday week?"

"Suits us, doesn't it, Mags?" said Leo.

"And me," said Charis. "Gosh! I just can't *wait*."

"You'll have to persuade your mother first, don't forget," said Maggie.

"For once, I think it'll be OK," said Charis.

"Don't say OK . . ."

"It's so *common*."

Maggie and Charis exploded into giggles at the umpteenth repetition of their mimicry of Grace, while Tom looked baffled, and Leo merely indulgent.

Later, after they had drunk coffee and nibbled ham and tomato sandwiches and potato crisps, Leo said, "Now for the closing session," and deliberately switched off the main light, leaving only a small table lamp which gave off a subdued, mellow glow. Once again he loaded the radiogram with records and then, taking Maggie's hand, sat her on his lap on the settee. Charis lolled in one of the two armchairs on either side of the electric fire, while Tom sat upright in the other, making no attempt to join her nor inviting her to join him.

This time the records were sentimental love songs, and Charis's earlier happy mood dissolved into melancholy as the familiar ache and intense longing for Rick washed over her yet again. It made it worse knowing that Leo and Maggie were spooning on the settee, although she was polite enough not to stare, and tried instead to concentrate on the electric fire with its imitation coals and leaping artificial flames, always revolving in the same direction and making the same flickering pattern.

Each time the record changed, Charis held her breath in case 'Cara Mia' should be the next. Perhaps Maggie had briefed Leo in advance, or perhaps he did not even own that particularly poignant reminder of Rick, yet 'Earth Angel' and 'Let Me Go, Lover' were so emotionally charged that it was hard to listen without feeling tearful.

When it was time for Leo to replenish the records, Maggie slid off his lap.

"What on *earth's* the matter with you two?" he said with a laugh as he saw Charis and Tom occupying the twin armchairs. "You look like a couple of bookends. How much *more* encouragement do you need, for goodness' sake, Tom?"

"Shut *up*, Leo," said Maggie.

"Sorry," said Leo, "but, honestly, Tom, why don't you let your hair down a bit? You only live once, you know."

When the records were organised once more, Leo turned off the table lamp as well so that the only light in the room now came from the electric fire, and it was then that Tom made a move: "Come and sit on my lap, Charis," he whispered.

Groaning inwardly, she was soon perched uncomfortably on his bony knees, sitting upright to avoid being too close to him.

Tom, though, was emboldened enough to tilt her backwards so that she was leaning against his shoulder. Then he put his face close to hers and his tortoiseshell spectacles knocked against her cheekbones. "You're lovely," he whispered in her ear.

She suppressed a desperate urge to giggle but said nothing, waiting for the inevitable kiss. When it came it was as arid and unexciting as ever, and she wished the evening could soon be over.

Some fifteen minutes later Leo switched on the lights again, and saw Tom and Charis occupying the same armchair. "That's better," he said.

Maggie began fiddling with her hair and powdering her nose. "That was a really nice evening, honey," she remarked. "Didn't you think so Mitch? Tom?"

Charis was quick to agree as she clambered off Tom's lap with great relief and began tidying her hair in front of the mirror.

Tom stood up too. "Most enjoyable," he said. "We'll have to do it again sometime. Perhaps you could all come round to my house."

Determined to remind him of his earlier promise, Charis said, "That would be nice, Tom, but we'll definitely go to Warbridge Jazz Club first, won't we?"

"Your mother permitting," joked Leo.

Charis knew she must choose exactly the right moment for confronting Grace about the jazz-club idea. It was essential that she should be in a good mood, which was a rare occurrence in the dank days of November, which she particularly disliked.

The opportunity arose unexpectedly when Charis came home from school one day, having forgotten that Grace had been out with Violet Leyton.

"Aren't you going to ask me how I enjoyed myself?" said Grace.

"Why? What have you been doing?"

"You are a complete scatterbrain," said Grace. "I told you this morning that I was going out shopping with Vi. Don't you remember?"

"Oh yes, now I do," said Charis. "I've been so busy at school I quite forgot."

"It was such a bright, sunny day. Warm, too, for November. We had lunch in Warbridge, went round the shops and I bought a nice hat. It was very reasonable and a becoming style too. Let me show you." She scurried into the living room and emerged wearing yet another head-hugging hat in fawn velour which, Charis had to admit, suited her mother well, both in shape and colour.

"Very nice," said Charis. "When will you wear it?"

"To church next Sunday, I expect. It'll go very well with my brown coat."

"I hadn't realised you were going to *Warbridge* today," said Charis.

"It made a nice change from Upsvale. There are some interesting little shops in Warbridge. Vi bought some gloves and some stockings, and we really enjoyed ourselves."

Charis felt her heart pounding as she prepared to ask the fateful question: "Were you anywhere near the town hall?" she began.

"Fairly near, I suppose. Why?"

"I was thinking about the Outhouse," Charis continued. "That's not far from the town hall, is it?"

Grace raised her eyebrows: "The Outhouse? Do you mean that horrible place that's painted black all over? What made you think of that?"

"It's been on my mind a lot lately because of Warbridge Jazz Club," said Charis, treading with the utmost caution. "That's at the Outhouse, you see, and Tom, Leo and Maggie said they'd like to go there sometime. Of course they'd like me to go too, but I wondered what you thought about it."

"*Tom* wants to go to that awful place?" said Grace. "That doesn't sound like Tom."

"Honestly, it *isn't* an awful place at all. Even Celia goes there, and so do lots of people from Holyoaks. Just because they play jazz doesn't mean it's not respectable. I mean, if I went with Tom and Leo and Maggie, what could possibly go wrong?"

Grace frowned. "I don't like the thought of my daughter going to somewhere like that. It sounds absolutely decadent, and I'm sure it's full of Teddy boys."

"Teddy boys don't like traditional jazz. They only like modern stuff, so they wouldn't be there. Oh, *please*. It would be such fun, and you know how much you like Tom. I'd be perfectly safe with him and the others."

"Well, I don't know," said Grace, beginning to weaken. "I'm not at all happy about it. We'll see what your father says when he comes home."

Hugh, of course, did not share Grace's misgivings, agreeing that little harm would come to Charis if she were in the safe company of her three respectable friends and so, to her intense delight, her longed-for visit to the jazz club was approved.

The November evening was clear and cold; the night sky pierced with thousands of stars; the moon a brilliant disc against the inky blackness. Tiny specks of frost glinted on blades of grass, fallen leaves and on the bonnet and windscreen of Leo's car as Charis sat in the back seat mulling over the unexpected turn of events which had led to her being *un*-accompanied by Tom, yet still on her way to Warbridge Jazz Club.

"Poor old Tom," said Maggie. "What did he say?"

"It's tonsillitis. He could hardly speak," Charis explained, "but he was very sorry to be missing out, and he hoped we'd all enjoy ourselves."

"How did you square things with your mother?" asked Leo.

"She was terribly sorry Tom was ill, and at first I thought she'd stop me from going. I was surprised when she gave in, but the deal was that I was to come straight home in your car, Leo, with Maggie, door to door."

"Well, that's no problem," said Leo. "Meanwhile, let's go all out for a great evening."

The Outhouse was a long, low building with a flat roof and brick walls which were, as Grace had observed, painted uniformly black. All the windows were firmly shuttered so that it was impossible to peep inside, lending the establishment a satisfying air of mystery. It was open six nights a week, Mondays being given over to young, inexperienced jazz musicians and Tuesdays and Wednesdays to better-established bands who had nevertheless not yet found real fame and fortune. Thursdays, Fridays and Saturdays were the most popular evenings, featuring bands which had turned professional and were well known.

"Who's on tonight, Leo?" asked Maggie.

"Boss Clarrie and the Beale Street Blue Notes," he replied. "They're pretty good, I believe."

A flashing green neon sign just over the entrance read 'Warbridge Jazz Club — Six Nights a Week — 7.00 p.m. to 11.00 p.m.' — and as Leo pushed open the black-painted wooden door they heard the exuberant sounds of a Dixieland rag, somewhat muted because the entrance lobby was separated from the main hall by strong double doors and heavy velveteen curtains.

A thin man with beady eyes was seated in a very small kiosk to the left of the entrance. "Are you members?" he asked offhandedly.

"Not yet," said Leo, "but we're interested in joining."

Within five minutes all three of them were in possession of green membership cards bearing their names, addresses and registration numbers.

"You have to show these whenever you come here," said the man. "It's five shillings to join, and half-a-crown each time afterwards."

Leo paid up and they left their outdoor clothes with a heavily made-up woman, with long blood-red fingernails, who was in sole charge of a cloakroom filled with rail after rail of mackintoshes and duffel coats.

Drawing aside the dark curtains and pushing open the heavy double doors, they were engulfed in a wave of noise and heat, and an assortment of odours of which smoke, perspiration and stale perfume were the most easily identifiable. The hall was smaller and hotter than Charis would have believed. The walls were painted black and glistened with condensation, the only light coming from the square platform serving as a stage. At first it was difficult to see anything clearly, rather like entering a darkened cinema or a cave, but their eyes soon grew accustomed to the gloom and Charis saw that the walls were decorated with enlarged black-and-white photographs of jazz musicians, lit dimly from above by heavily shaded light bulbs.

Boston (Boss) Clarrie and the Beale Street Blue Notes were a seven-man band, identically dressed in dark-blue trousers and shirts, with sky-blue cravats. Perspiration beaded the foreheads of the trumpet, clarinet and trombone players fronting the band and blowing into their instruments with great gusto as they performed their own raucous, uninhibited version of 'Tiger Rag'. The stage jutted out into the hall, surrounded on three sides by crowds of admiring fans pressed tightly together and gazing up at the band with rapt expressions on their faces.

Charis noticed that many of the girls were wearing tight drainpipe trousers, and greatly envied them this practical, yet undeniably sexy, attire. Others, though, wore skirts, so her black felt skirt and famous red and white sweater were perfectly in keeping.

"Here's another little number you all know," Boss Clarrie announced when 'Tiger Rag' ended. "It's called 'Maple Leaf Rag'. OK boys, take it away."

The hall was soon throbbing all over again as trumpet, clarinet and trombone first competed with one another, then gave way so that each could play solo in turn. The double bass, banjo, and drums provided a stimulating background rhythm, whilst the fingers of the man on the honky-tonk piano skittered up and down the keyboard as though possessed of a life of their own.

Charis, Leo and Maggie mingled with the crowds packed round the stage, simply listening to the music and enjoying the verve of the musicians, whilst behind them, those who wished to jive were giving free rein to their energy.

"How about a drink, girls?" Leo suggested after the first few numbers. "This place is as hot as hell."

"I don't want alcohol," said Maggie. "Just some orange squash for me, please."

"I don't think they sell alcohol here anyway," said Leo. "It isn't licensed. How about you, Charis?"

"I don't know. Perhaps Pepsi-Cola."

"Right," said Leo, "I'll be back in a sec."

The next tune was a blues, during which the dancers moved in a particularly sensual fashion, perfectly expressing the emotions which frequently smouldered inside Charis. She longed to join in, but without a partner it was impossible, so she simply tried to find satisfaction in watching the others as they gyrated to the soulful music.

Charis could never remember how many more numbers the band played before the evening took a completely unexpected turn, but it was shortly after the boisterous 'South Rampart Street Parade' that someone said, "Don't I know you? It's Charis Mitchell, innit?"

Turning round sharply she came face to face with Alan Decker. "I don't *believe* it," she said.

"Me neither," he replied. "I didn't know you was a jazz fan. I'd never 'ave thought it."

"It's my first visit," she told him, "but I've been keen on jazz for months."

"Well, fancy that," said Alan, his face creasing up in the Bisto Kid smile she well remembered. "This calls for a celebration, but it's not too easy to celebrate 'ere. They 'aven't got what it takes."

"What do you mean?"

"No alcohol. Luckily, though, the pub's just over the road — 'ow about it?"

"Oh, I don't know. I've never been inside a pub."

Alan roared with laughter: "Well, there's always a first time. Later, perhaps. What you doin' these days? You don't still go to St Luke's, do you?"

"Yes, I do. Nothing's changed much," she said.

"*You* 'ave," said Alan. "Last time I saw you, you was just a kid. *Now* look at you — all grown-up, and very attractive too."

Charis was grateful for the darkness because she knew she was blushing. "Are you still doing national service?" she asked him.

"Yup, but not for much longer. I'm due to finish in March."

"Aren't you going to introduce us, Mitch?" said Maggie.

"*Sorry*," she said, feeling guilty as she had completely forgotten about Maggie and Leo. "This is Alan Decker who used to go to my church. I haven't seen him for simply ages. Alan, this is Maggie, my best friend from school, and this is her boyfriend, Leo."

"Hi there," said Alan. "Enjoying it, are you?"

"I wish it wasn't quite so *hot*," said Maggie.

"That's all part of it," said Alan. "Come to this place and you either catch a cold or lose one. If you've already got one you sweat it out before the evening's over. If you 'aven't got one, someone's sure to be generous and pass on theirs."

"How revolting!" said Maggie. "But the music's great."

"I'd like to sit down," said Leo. "My leg's playing up a bit."

"Not much chance, I'm afraid," said Alan. "No one sits down. There ain't room. 'Owever, I was just saying to Charis, 'ow about coming over to The Old Grey Mare for a drink? It'll be the interval soon, anyway."

"What happens in the interval?"

"They play records. Most people go over the road for a pint."

"How do we get back in again?"

"You get a pass at the door."

Inside The Old Grey Mare it was warm and smoky, but nothing like as hot as the jazz club. Alan settled them into a secluded corner of the saloon and ordered drinks at the bar.

"Let me help you carry them," Maggie volunteered.

Leo was resting his leg, and, much to her shame, Charis simply hadn't thought of offering.

Charis had Merrydown cider; Maggie a lemonade shandy; Leo a pint of best bitter; and Alan a pint of Guinness, dark as a Christmas pudding and topped with its characteristic half inch of creamy froth, which soon transferred itself to his upper lip, giving him a blond moustache.

Leo and Maggie thanked him for their drinks, and Maggie quizzed him for a while about national service, comparing his experiences with those of her brother, Bernard. After a while, however, Leo and Maggie turned to one another to engage in a private conversation which, Charis suspected, was specially designed to allow her to talk more intimately with Alan.

"So, 'ow's the old church?" he said. "Don't suppose I'll ever go back, but I still 'ave a soft spot for it."

"I'm still in the choir," said Charis. "As I told you, nothing's changed very much at all."

"What about your mum and dad? They OK?"

"Yes, thanks. How about yours? I heard they moved away."

"That's right. They're up near Coventry now. Me dad changed his job, but I've still got contacts 'ere, like me old aunt and uncle. When I'm on leave I stay over with them more often than not. More fun than Coventry."

"Did you keep up with Desmond Hoyt?"

"Old Des? No. Lost all touch with 'im. We was never that pally. 'E was too brainy for me. All work and no play."

"What happened to that girl he was going out with? Penny Reed, wasn't it?"

"Long story that. Soon as Des went off to Durham, old Reg Bradley got 'is foot in the door. 'E'd always fancied 'er any'ow. Shirl told me all about it. Remember Shirl?"

"Yes."

"Well, Reg was a right dirty old man. Ten years older than Penny, and before you could say knife she was in the club?"

This was a term Charis had not heard before.

"Club? Which club do you mean?"

Alan roared with laughter: "The Puddin' Club, of course. Baby on the way."

Charis blushed a deep crimson. "How *awful*," she said.

"Could 'ave been worse, I s'pose. 'E married 'er and they moved away. Don't know where they are now. Shirl lost touch. Cigarette?"

"No, thanks. I don't smoke."

"Sensible girl. Expensive 'abit, and bad for your lungs."

Looking at him, with his national serviceman's cropped hair, a wave of nostalgic warmth washed over her as she recalled the juvenile crush she had once had on him. Intrigued by the news about Reg and Penny, she longed to be updated on Shirley Croft, who had not only once been Alan's girlfriend, but had also two-timed Rick, and her curiosity finally overcame her: "I often think about the old days. Do you remember the square-dancing?" she began.

"As if I could forget," Alan laughed. "Honour your partners; honour your corners; do-si-do; promenade; allemande; God, don't it all sound old-fashioned now?"

"Compared with the jazz club, yes, but it was fun at the time."

"I s'pose so."

"You mentioned Shirley. What happened to her?" Charis prompted, ashamed of her duplicity.

"Old Shirl? I'm still goin' with 'er," said Alan. "It's been a *long* time. *Too* long, p'r'aps. We've been engaged for the best part of a year, but 'eaven knows when we'll get married — if ever. She still lives at Ockley. That's what I meant by contacts. She's another one of 'em — the main one, you might say."

"*Engaged!*" exclaimed Charis. "Where is she tonight, then?"

"Down with flu," said Alan. "Poor old duck. Still, we don't spend every minute of every day in each other's pockets. We 'ave an understanding — if you know what I mean — and it's not much fun for 'er when I'm away. We go our own way a bit, so it's my turn to be out on the tiles tonight."

"It's mine too," said Charis. "The person I was supposed to be with tonight was ill too."

"'Is loss, my gain, then," said Alan. "'Ow's your drink?"

"How long does the interval last?" said Leo, finally turning away from Maggie. "It's nice here, and thanks for the drinks, but we'd like to get our money's worth from the jazz club."

"Course you would. We'll go back soon. 'Ow about another pint first, Leo? More shandy, Maggie?"

"No, thanks," they both replied. "If you don't mind, I think we'd rather go back now."

"OK. Fine by me," said Alan. "Drink up, then, Charis."

In the seclusion of the pub's ladies' room Maggie said, "We're a bit worried about you, Mitch. Don't let him take you home, for goodness' sake. We promised your mother, so don't let us down."

"I've known Alan for *years*," said Charis. "Anyway, he's engaged to someone. He's not very likely to want to take me home."

"Don't be too sure," said Maggie. "I saw the way he was looking at you."

Charis giggled. The cider had already gone to her head and was making her feel beautifully relaxed, and flattered that Alan's mild attentions had been noticed by her friends: "Oh, don't be an old spoilsport, Maggie," she chided. "I can take care of myself. Anyway, I want to try jiving, and if he asks me to I'm not going to miss the opportunity of *that*."

"Well, suit yourself, but don't forget *we're* taking you home, that's all."

"Stop fussing!" said Charis.

Back at the Outhouse the last interval record had just ended, and Boss Clarrie and the others were emerging from the curtains behind the stage. This time they were accompanied by a slim girl wearing a tight skirt and an even tighter sweater in the same dark-blue as the band's outfit, a sky-blue square knotted at her neck.

"Great! That's Cindy Slade, their blues singer," said Alan. "She's not always with 'em, but we're in luck tonight. What a figure! Wow!"

"I'd like you all to give a big hand to Cindy," said Boss.

"I'd like to give her two," said Alan with a cheeky smirk, but the hall had already erupted with cheers and clapping, and Cindy was flashing a dazzling smile at her assembled fans.

"And now we'll start off the second half with that great old favourite the 'Saint Louis Blues'."

"Come on, Charis," said Alan. "Let's do this one together."

She found it surprisingly easy to emulate the movements of the other dancers, and it was so dark anyway that any mistakes she made would have gone unnoticed. The cider she had drunk, and Alan's attentiveness, gave her added confidence, and she was soon in her element.

Cindy Slade, despite her slight build, had a powerful voice, perfectly attuned to jazz, and the words came over with a considerable depth of emotion. Alan's eyes met Charis's, holding them with a challenging stare, and she responded provocatively, her shoulders and hips moving in time with the rhythm of the blues.

In the all-enveloping gloom she lost sight of Maggie and Leo who were, she supposed, closer to the stage, while she and Alan were in the crowded centre of the hall.

"You're doin' just great," he said. "You like dancin', don't you?"

"I love it," Charis agreed, "but this isn't like anything I've ever done before."

"You'll be comin' back for more," he said. "Mark my words — you'll be back."

Further fast jazz numbers followed, and then another blues, during which Alan pulled Charis so close against him that they stayed virtually stationary, and she was thrillingly conscious of his powerful male anatomy.

"Let's go outside, babe," he whispered hoarsely, and she allowed him to lead her into a shop doorway near the Outhouse, where it was mercifully dark. "It's been a *great* surprise seein' you 'ere tonight," said Alan. "I'd never 'ave believed you'd grow into such an excitin' girl. Do you remember when I used to wink at you in the choir?"

"Of course," she said. "You used to excite *me* when you did that. I had a real crush on you."

"You did? I never knew. Are you warm enough?"

"This sweater's nice and thick, but it's an awfully cold night."

"Let me warm you up, then. Come 'ere. Come and be nice to Al," said Alan, and wrapped her in his strong arms.

His lips were wet and tasted of cigarettes; his tongue was forcefully penetrating; his breath hot and beery. Charis responded with such enthusiasm that, in a husky voice, Alan said, "Who taught you to kiss like *that*, babe?" and then his large hands found their way under her sweater and he began to fondle her like Banjo, like — Rick.

It was the first time anyone had touched her since Rick, and the first time she had even wanted anyone to do so, and yet she felt horribly guilty; as though she were being unfaithful to Rick's memory.

A moment later she was aware of Alan fumbling with the front of his trousers, and then he was guiding her hand inside his fly. "See what you're doin' to me, babe," he said.

At first she felt elated to be marking a new page in her limited catalogue of sexual experience, but almost at once she realised it was a mistake. She had longed to touch Rick in exactly that way, but had never been invited by him to do so, nor taken the initiative herself, so why was she allowing herself to besmirch his memory.

"What's wrong?" Alan breathed in her ear as he sensed her reluctance. "You're all tensed up. You don't mind this, do you?"

"No, it isn't really that," she murmured. "It's just old memories."

"Someone special, was it?"

"Someone I loved."

"What 'appened? Tell Al all about it." He zipped up his fly, stopped caressing her, but still held her close, his breath steamy against her hair.

"It's a long story."

"We've all been through it, babe, you know. But if it's over, you should let it go. Honest, you should. A girl like you needs lots of love. You're 'ungry for it. I guessed that by the way you kiss, not to mention the look in your eyes."

"It's too soon, though. I can't forget him."

"Tell me all about it another time. There'll be another time, won't there?"

"I don't know. What about Shirley?"

"I told you. We 'ave an agreement. Don't worry about Shirl."

Charis said nothing.

"Look, babe," said Alan, "when I'm on leave I usually come down 'ere to let off steam. I'll tell you what we'll do. If you and I are 'ere on our own, we'll carry on from where we left off tonight, which could be *magic*. If Shirl's 'ere, of course, I know you'll 'ave the sense to keep your distance, and if *your* boyfriend's 'ere, I'll do likewise. 'Ow's that? Is it a deal?"

"OK," said Charis, confused and shivery, "but can we go back inside now, Alan? I'm *freezing*."

"Sure," said Alan, "but 'ow about me seein' you home? I've got me motorbike round the back in the parkin' lot."

"No. I'm sorry, but you can't do that," she said. "It isn't that I wouldn't like you to, but it's all arranged with Leo and Maggie."

"That's disappointin'," said Alan as they re-entered the Outhouse, "but not to worry, there'll be another chance, and keep your pecker up about your 'someone special'. You may find it'll all work out right."

"Thanks for a wonderful evening, Alan," said Charis. "I don't know when I last had such a great time."

"Thank *you*," said Alan, "'tisn't often I find me past catchin' up with me like that. Oh, look, 'ere's your friends makin' sure I 'aven't sold you into the white slave trade. It's OK, folks, she's quite safe, and I'd best be off. Nice meetin' you all. Be seein' you."

"No need to ask if *you've* enjoyed yourself," said Maggie on the way home.

"You'd better not look *too* enthusiastic when you get in," said Leo, "otherwise your mother will smell a rat."

"I shall say it was all rather tame," said Charis. "Oh yes, and I'll probably say how terribly I missed Tom."

"You're a case, Charis," said Leo, "but you needed a bit of fun. I hope meeting that guy tonight won't lead you into any trouble."

"I shouldn't think so," she said, but at the same time the possibility of a clandestine relationship with Alan Decker suddenly seemed eminently desirable, and she smiled a naughty little smile all to herself in the back of Leo's car.

On the morning when Charis was due to sit the French exam for the second time, she woke up feeling under the weather and with a decidedly painful neck, which was lumpy and achy when she pressed it just below her ears.

"Take an aspirin," advised Hugh, who regarded aspirins as the universal cure-all.

"For goodness' sake take *two* if they'll help you get through this exam," said Grace. "Of all the days to be ill this is just about the worst."

The aspirins certainly helped, but Charis's head felt muzzy all day and she wished she were anywhere but at school — preferably tucked up in bed.

Luckily, she had been putting much more effort into her French homework that term, and the extra coaching at school must have helped too, because she found the exam easier to cope with than the one she had taken in June. Even so, she was profoundly thankful when it was over and she could go home to nurse her illness.

"I wonder if I've got mumps," she said to Celia on the bus.

"Are you sure you've never had it?" Celia replied.

"Positive. I only had measles and whooping cough. I didn't even get chickenpox."

"You were lucky. Chickenpox was foul."

They laughed at the unintentional pun, but Charis jogged her neck in the process, which made her wince.

"You'd better let your doctor have a look at you," said Celia.

"I suppose I had. What a bore."

Grace was worried and sent Charis off to the surgery on her own. She hated doctors' surgeries and as she sat there, glancing at the other patients and wondering what was wrong with them, she kept swallowing to test her throat, and pressing her painful neck.

The practice was run by a lady doctor who rang a bell when she was ready for the next patient, and it was up to everyone to remember whose turn it was. Charis thought it would make more sense if the seats were occupied in strict order instead of everyone sitting at random, but that was too much to hope for.

Eventually it was her turn. The doctor was sympathetic — examining her tender neck, looking down her throat, and taking her temperature. "You have a slight glandular infection," she said. "I'll give you a special gargle, and you must have plenty of hot drinks. You needn't stay away from school, but if you don't improve in the next day or two, come back and see me again."

Despite the gargle and hot drinks Charis soon began to feel worse, developing such a sore throat that Grace insisted on a further visit to the doctor.

That time tonsillitis was diagnosed, and Charis left the surgery with a prescription for penicillin tablets and a tonic. The tablets were large and yellow, and had to be sucked instead of swallowed. They tasted sweet and lemony, but made her tongue so sore that eating any food soon became unbearable. Then she began to run a temperature, so Grace summoned the doctor to the house.

"You again, young lady," the doctor said with a grin. "You *are* having a rough time, aren't you? Let's take another look at you."

The thermometer showed that her temperature had climbed to a dramatic hundred and three degrees, and she could barely speak.

"M & B tablets," said the doctor. "Those should do the trick, and you can take codeine too. At the same time I want you to drink four to five pints of water a day."

Charis was aghast.

"I know it sounds a lot," laughed the doctor, "but M & B tablets can make you a wee bit depressed, so the water will wash them through you and counteract the problem."

Once Grace had seen the doctor off the premises, she joined Charis in the bedroom. "November!" she declared with a note of exasperation. "I've always thought it the most miserable month of the year anyway."

Charis had heard this complaint many times before and waited for the familiar follow-up.

"It's the month of death," Grace continued right on cue, "starting with All Saints' Day. Not that I'm criticising that. It's a beautiful festival with such lovely hymns, but it's followed by All Souls' Day and Remembrance Sunday, and I'm sure more people die in November than any other month. Then there's the prospect of fog, and dark, cold evenings, and, as if all that isn't bad enough, you have to go and get tonsillitis."

"I couldn't help it," Charis croaked. "I probably caught it from Tom."

"I'm not so sure about *that*," said Grace. "Much more likely you picked it up at that place. I wish I'd never agreed to you going there. It was asking for trouble. Who knows how many germs were lurking there and being spread about by all those strangers?"

Charis keep quiet, partly because it hurt to talk, but mostly because she wanted Grace to leave her alone so that she could go on reliving the thrilling events of the evening at Warbridge Jazz Club.

"You'd better take one of these tablets," said Grace. "Come on now, swallow it quickly and drink plenty of water. You heard what the doctor said."

"Couldn't I have orange squash instead?" Charis pleaded. "Water's so *boring*."

"Next time I come upstairs I'll bring some," Grace promised. "There's only one thing I'm thankful for, and that's that you managed to take your French exam before all this happened."

"I know, but I was feeling rotten that day and my neck was hurting dreadfully. I hope I passed."

"So do I, child. So do I," said Grace, plumping up the pillows and straightening the sheets. "Now try and go to sleep. I'll leave the orange squash on the bedside table for you when I come back."

As soon as Charis heard her mother's departing footsteps she reflected that perhaps she was suffering for her sins. Yet she had no regrets whatsoever, and would happily have endured tonsillitis all over again as a fair price for such a sparkling evening.

As for the time she had spent with Alan Decker — a secret to be kept from her parents at *all* costs — she had little doubt that she would be tempted to go along with his suggestion, although she had no idea when she would next be able to visit Warbridge Jazz Club.

'And as for that Shirley,' she thought to herself, 'why should I care about her? If Alan's two-timing her with me, or anyone else for that matter, it's all she deserves. After all, she was doing exactly the same with Rick.'

Rick. Remembering him stirred all the old longings again: 'I'll never forget him,' she vowed, 'but if I still truly loved him I suppose I wouldn't have let myself get carried away by Alan Decker. Rick and Alan are *poles* apart, but I don't know if I'll ever see Rick again, and sometimes I feel so lonely and out of things.'

At the same time she had to admit that Alan's sexy behaviour in the shop doorway had roused her considerably; had been amazingly therapeutic and had perhaps set her on the first rung of the ladder she would have to climb before memories of Rick finally lost their power to cause her heartache.

TWELVE

Irene Wolsey's leaving celebration was due to take place the day before the school broke up for the Christmas holidays. There had been a collection which had raised enough money to buy her a coffee set. Edwina Rawlings (the head girl), was charged with the task of buying it from Noble's, the big department store in Upsvale, and invited Louise Heron and Celia to help her in the selection. Having made their choice, they displayed it to the rest of the sixth formers in the common room.

"What do you think?" Edwina asked, unwrapping the tissue paper from some of the small cups, which were in two shades of fawn, the lighter colour on the inside.

"Very pretty," said Morag McDonald.

"We thought those colours would tone with any table linen she might have," said Celia, as everyone crowded round making admiring noises.

"I think they're dull," Maggie whispered to Charis. "I've seen sets just like that in blue, green and pink. Trust them to choose brown."

"Still," said Charis, "it's true what they say. They *will* tone with everything, won't they? It would be awful if they clashed with her colour scheme."

"We don't worry about things like that at *our* house," said Maggie, a trifle scornfully. "Nothing matches for long. With all our brood, things are getting broken all the time."

"Well," Louise was saying, "now you've all seen them, we'll wrap up the box in some nice paper ready to hand over to Mrs Wolsey on Thursday."

"Yes, we'd best put them out of harm's way now," said Edwina. "It's nearly time for the carol practice, anyway."

"Have you put up your Christmas decorations yet?" Charis asked Maggie as they walked down to the music room.

"We're doing them tonight when my dad comes home," said Maggie. "He and Bernard are the only ones who know how to fix the fairy lights, and Bernard won't be home on leave in time. Dominic *thinks* he knows all about electricity, but he's only ten so Mum won't let him near anything.

231

Pauline and Lizzie have been making paper chains for days, but they keep coming unstuck. The trouble is they don't paste them properly, and Mum and I can't be supervising them all the time."

"My mother won't have paper chains," said Charis. "Daddy and I like them, but she thinks they're tawdry and just one more thing to collect dust. We usually have balloons, though."

"Balloons wouldn't last two minutes with us," said Maggie. "Dominic takes great delight in bursting them, I'm afraid."

"I hate balloons when they've been hanging around for too long and shrivel up," said Charis. "They feel revolting, like jelly that hasn't quite set."

The whole school was taking part in the concert, which had become a tradition at Stella Maris. The well-known carols would be sung by everyone in unison, but each form had been rehearsing less familiar ones, which they would be performing individually.

The sixth form's was 'The Coventry Carol', and Mrs Baker, the Music mistress, was stressing the importance of light and shade in their singing: "It's meant to be a lullaby," she said, "so most of it should be sung softly. However, when you come to the verse about Herod the King you must raise the tone to *forte* to give the impression of anger and fury."

"Did you hear about Annabel Callaghan?" Maggie whispered to Charis in the safety of the back row.

"What about her?"

"She's been chosen to sing the first verse of 'The Holly and the Ivy', unaccompanied."

"*NO* talking at the back there," said Mrs Baker. "*Really*, girls, this is no time to be carrying on a conversation."

"Sorry, Mrs Baker," they said simultaneously.

"Ready now . . . " said Mrs Baker, and began to play a few introductory chords on the music room's ancient upright piano.

Charis had sung 'The Coventry Carol' so many times in the choir at St Luke's that now, as she joined in with the others, she allowed her thoughts to stray. Maggie's remark about Annabel Callaghan singing solo had at once reminded her of Bryony Mayo. Rick and Bryony were inextricably linked in her thoughts, as they had been ever since the party at The Magpies, and it was rarely that she remembered one without the other. Instinct told her that, had her relationship with Rick continued, friendship with Bryony would have been guaranteed, for the cousins were obviously close, and Bryony's complimentary remarks about her, she felt sure, had not been thrown away lightly. There had been something so glamorous and desirable about the Mayos and their lifestyle that it had made her long to be more closely associated with them. The Woodrose family too, whilst more down-to-earth than the Mayos, had left her with a portfolio of poignant memories, which made her separation from them all the harder to bear.

"Any more cards for me?" Charis asked when she arrived home that afternoon.

"Yes," said Grace. "One or two, I think. They're on the table by the Christmas tree."

The first was an amusing one from Leo. The next bore unfamiliar writing, and she was gratified to find it had come from Ronnie and Miranda. There were also cards from Patsy and Ruth from St Luke's but, sadly, nothing from Rick. Charis had debated for days whether or not to send one to him, but, although she longed to, she had been reticent about making the first move. 'There's still time for one to arrive,' she thought, although she remained doubtful.

Later that evening Charis began attaching her Christmas cards to lengths of red velvet ribbon, later to be hung on either side of the fireplace. As well as those from the family, there was a snow scene dusted with silver glitter from Pam, and a silly red-nosed Santa Claus with a dopey-looking reindeer from Colin Crisp. Much to Charis's relief he had at last given up pursuing her, having switched his allegiance to a very young girl, new to St Luke's and clearly smitten by him, but in sending to Charis she took it to mean that they remained friends. Tom had chosen a large, shiny card depicting Christmas roses, and had simply written *Love from Tom* which, unfortunately, left her unmoved.

"Oh, bother!" said Hugh mildly as all the Christmas tree lights suddenly flickered and went out. "I suppose that's another dud bulb. We really ought to buy a new set of lights."

"It won't start a fire, will it?" asked Grace anxiously.

"Of course not," Hugh assured her. "Just leave it to me. I'll fix it somehow."

"I'm nervous of electricity. It's so easy for a fire to start, and the needles on that tree are drying up already. Are you *sure* those lights are safe?"

Charis groaned softly to herself, for similar exchanges between her parents at this time of year were as seasonal as Christmas pudding. "If we ever *do* get new lights, there won't be much left to talk about, will there?" she said.

"Don't be so *cheeky!*" said Grace.

Mother Ambrose, having led the usual prayers at morning assembly, turned towards the members of staff behind her on the stage: "And now for a special announcement," she said. "Mrs Wolsey, will you step forward, please."

Irene Wolsey, her golden hair brushed into its usual neat pageboy bob, was wearing a heathery tweed costume over a mauve blouse. She looked mildly embarrassed, but maintained her composure as she joined the headmistress at the lectern.

"It's a sad day for us, indeed," said Mother Ambrose, "but our loss is,

I'm sure, France's gain. We wish you and your husband every happiness and success across the Channel and we'll always be more than delighted if you should ever come back to visit us or, indeed, to work here in the future."

"What about babies?" Maggie hissed in Charis's ear.

Charis dug her in the ribs: "Shut *up*, Maggie," she admonished.

"Just a thought," Maggie whispered back.

"And now," Mother Ambrose continued, "we have a little surprise for you."

Proudly bearing the large parcel wrapped in green and silver paper and festooned with silver ribbons, Edwina, Celia and Louise mounted the stage, bowed politely to the headmistress and presented Irene Wolsey with her gift.

"This is a tremendous surprise," she said. "I don't know how to thank you all. You've been incredibly kind."

"Aren't you going to open it, Mrs Wolsey?" Mother Ambrose urged gently. "I'm sure everyone would like you to."

Soon the coffee set was revealed in all its splendour.

"It's simply perfect," said Irene Wolsey. "What a clever choice. Thank you all so *very* much. I shall miss you enormously, even though I'm looking forward to my new life in France. I've thoroughly enjoyed my teaching days here, and I'll never forget the friends I've made amongst the staff and pupils of Stella Maris."

"Three cheers for Mrs Wolsey," called Edwina Rawlings. "Hip hip . . . "

"Hoo*ray*."

When the cheers had subsided, Mother Ambrose said, "We shall close this morning's assembly with hymn number 6 in your books."

Mrs Baker played the first line by way of introduction, and then everyone began singing:

> See amid the winter's snow,
> Born for us on earth below,
> See, the tender Lamb appears,
> Promised from eternal years.
>
> Hail thou ever blessèd morn,
> Hail redemption's happy dawn,
> Sing through all Jerusalem:
> Christ is born in Bethlehem.

It was one of Charis's favourite Christmas hymns, but as she sang the familiar words she noticed Irene Wolsey dabbing at her eyes with a handkerchief, and was close to tears herself.

Celia was waiting for the bus at Charters Lea Station when Charis joined the short queue on the last day of term, so they travelled to school together for the first time in a while.

"You usually go by train these days, don't you?" said Charis. "Where's Mark?"

"Home for the Christmas vacation," said Celia, while Charis was annoyed with herself for not having been smart enough to realise.

"Have you been back to the jazz club any more?" Celia asked later.

"No, there just hasn't been a chance," said Charis. "My mother was convinced I caught tonsillitis there, which didn't help, and now she'd only be likely to let me go if Tom was taking me, and he doesn't much want to."

"How do you get along with Tom?"

Charis pulled a face. "He's OK," she said, "but I can't say I'm keen on him. I don't suppose I'll ever be. I mean, he isn't going to change, and I just find him awfully — ordinary."

"Yes, I know what you mean," said Celia. "He isn't very exciting, but he's a steady kind of fellow. I'd say he was pretty dependable. He wouldn't be the type to let you down."

"I'm sure you're right about that. Well, I'll be seeing him on Saturday at the Holyoaks Christmas Party. Will you be there?"

"Possibly," said Celia, "but Mark may have other plans. Which reminds me, Charis, I meant to mention this before, but somehow I forgot. Pam and Roger and most of my friends are coming round to our house on Christmas Eve, around eleven o'clock in the morning, for mince pies and coffee. If you're free, *do* join us."

"What a lovely surprise!" said Charis. "Thank you very much."

For the rest of the day visions of returning to Celia's elegant home filled her mind. It would be the first time she had been back there since the party over a year ago.

"I wish you were coming too, Maggie," she said in the lunch hour.

"She wouldn't invite *me*," said Maggie. "I've never been all that friendly with her. Anyway, I'll be in demand at home on Christmas Eve, helping Mum with the children. You have no idea what it's like having a big family, with everyone wanting everything at once, and Bernard will be home too."

"Will you go to midnight Mass?"

"Oh *yes*," said Maggie. "I couldn't possibly miss that. It's an absolute *MUST*, and this year Leo's coming with Bernard and me, so it'll be even more special. Mum and Dad and the children will go on Christmas morning while I get on with preparing dinner."

"Is Leo having Christmas dinner at your house?"

"No. He and his mum and dad are going to his sister's, but he's coming round in the afternoon when we open the Christmas tree presents."

When Charis returned to the sixth-form classroom after lunch she found a small white envelope on her desk. Christmas cards had been exchanged earlier that morning, school work having been all but abandoned, so it was a surprise to find yet another one awaiting her: "Oh look," she said. "It's from Mother Ambrose."

"I've got one too," said Maggie.

"So have I," said Morag.

"She sends to everyone in the sixth form every year," said Nancy. "My sister told me so."

"Good old Rice Pud," said Maggie.

"How nice of her," said Charis, putting it inside her school case along with the ones from her friends, which she planned to add to those she had already fixed to the length of red ribbon.

The carol concert started at two o'clock in the school hall. It began, as Maggie had correctly predicted, with Annabel Callaghan's unaccompanied singing of the first verse of 'The Holly and the Ivy', after which everyone joined in the chorus and remaining verses.

The first of the individual carols was 'Come to the Manger', sung by forms One Alpha and Beta together.

"They look like the Holy Innocents," said Maggie. "Little perishers."

"Even that wretched Janice Cox looks angelic," said Charis, "and we *all* know what she's really like."

The second, third, fourth and fifth Alpha and Beta forms sang their special carols in turn, separated from one another by various popular Christmas hymns sung by everyone. The sixth form's rendering of 'The Coventry Carol' was the last of the specially rehearsed pieces, followed by the whole school joining in 'Adeste Fidelis'.

"I'm more in the mood for Christmas now," said Charis when the concert was over. "Aren't you, Mags?"

"Absolutely," said Maggie, "and we've got the Holyoaks Christmas Party tomorrow too. Should be fun."

Irene Wolsey was standing near the school's exit to bid a final farewell to individual pupils as they left the building for the start of the Christmas holidays. Charis and Maggie approached together, and she held out her hands to them. "Goodbye, Maggie," she said. "Good luck with the catering. Maybe you'll be running a restaurant some day, and I'll be sure to pay you a visit. And, Charis," she continued, allowing Maggie to walk on a little way, "keep up the good work with your studies, won't you, and at the same time don't forget there's someone out there waiting for you. I'm *sure* of it. You'll know who it is when the time is right."

"Thank you for *everything*, Mrs Wolsey," said Charis, growing more emotional and weepy by the minute. "I'll never forget you. Goodbye."

"Goodbye, Charis. Off you go, now. Maggie's waiting for you."

Christmas decorations had transformed Holyoaks. A large tree stood in a tub on the stage, its lights cleverly flashing on and off. Prominent red cards spelling out MERRY CHRISTMAS EVERYONE had been strung up overhead, multicoloured garlands criss-crossed the hall, and plump bunches of balloons billowed in each corner.

"I wish I wasn't on the door this week," said Tom when he and Charis arrived together. "I think I'll resign from this job. I'd much rather be dancing with you."

"But you're so good at counting the money and balancing the cash. You never make any mistakes," said Charis, dreading the thought of being obliged to partner him in every dance each Saturday evening. "They'd miss you terribly. I don't think they'd *let* you resign."

"Steve Parish has a much better deal," said Tom. "I mean, if I were treasurer I could be with you all the evening and still have a finger in the financial pie."

"Well, Steve won't always be treasurer, and you might get his job next year," she said. "If you quit now, though, they might not give you the opportunity."

"You could be right, I suppose," said Tom, taking up his position behind the cash desk. "Oh well, see you later."

Charis was wearing her famous black felt skirt with her white polo-necked jumper with the green and blue diamond design. Pearl earrings from Woolworths, which looked smart despite being surprisingly cheap, completed her ensemble along with a few dabs of Blue Grass perfume and her black high-heeled shoes.

Maggie and Leo had already arrived.

"No home-made paper chains here, you notice," Maggie remarked wistfully. "Most of ours are drooping already and they keep breaking too. *One* year I suppose we'll we able to splash out and buy some proper ones, but at least it keeps the children out of mischief having something to make."

Greg and Audrey Duffy had assembled a selection of secular seasonal music and had already played 'White Christmas' and 'Jingle Bells'.

"I hope someone dances with me," said Charis. "Tom's on the door tonight, and it looks as though most people are paired off."

Before long the party was in full swing, Greg starting it off in the best possible way with a Paul Jones.

"Come on, Mitch," said Maggie. "You don't mind if I join in this, do you, Leo?"

By the end of the Paul Jones, Charis had danced with Ken Purchiss and three energetic but unfamiliar youths, and returned to her table out of breath, yet somewhat deflated.

Just as she sat down Maggie said, "Oh look, Ronnie and Miranda have just arrived."

Ronnie was in a dark suit, white shirt and red tie, and Miranda in red velvet, her black hair sleeked forward in its usual wispy face-framing fronds.

"Made for one another," Leo remarked.

"Yes, aren't they?" Charis agreed, her pleasure at seeing Ronnie mingling with an overwhelming desire to experience for herself the settled kind of happiness which he and Miranda were so obviously enjoying. She watched them heading in her direction, marvelling at the charisma which always surrounded them, but of which they themselves seemed completely unaware.

"May we join you?" Ronnie said. "We were hoping we'd see some friendly faces. This place has changed so much. Hardly anyone we know comes here any more."

Miranda smiled charmingly at everyone.

"Delighted," said Leo. "Do you know, in all the time I've known you, Miranda, we've never sat at the same table before."

"He's just admired you from afar," said Maggie, which made everyone laugh and feel at ease.

Having an extra couple at the table made it easier to join in with more dances, and soon they had all danced with one another. Now, at last, it was Charis's turn with Ronnie.

"I'm *so* glad you're here tonight," she confided.

"How nice of you to say so. Why tonight particularly?"

"Because Tom's on the door, so I'm more or less on my own."

"Do you mean to tell me you're actually going out with Tom after all this time?" said Ronnie with a chuckle.

"Please don't tease me about it."

"As if I would, but I think I know pretty well how he rates with you."

"At least it stops me from feeling lonely," said Charis, knowing that she sounded wistful and perhaps a bit sorry for herself.

"Someone as nice as you shouldn't be lonely," said Ronnie. "It makes me sad to think you might be."

"Does it really?"

"Of course. By the way, did you get our card?"

"I meant to thank you. It was very nice of you."

"I wanted you to know we were thinking about you," said Ronnie. "I haven't seen you since that day on the train, and you never rang me, so I thought you must be OK. Are you? *Really* OK, I mean."

"I'm surviving," said Charis, "but life still isn't as much fun as I'd like it to be. I had tonsillitis last month, but I *did* go to Warbridge Jazz Club."

"You *did*? What did you think of it?"

"Fan*tas*tic," she said. "Sometime I'm going back, but it won't be all that easy."

"Your mother?"

"How did you guess?"

Ronnie laughed gently. "Same old problem," he said.

Between that dance and the next, Audrey Duffy visited each table handing out Christmas crackers from a large basket. While she was doing so, Greg Duffy said, "The next dance is a Christmas elimination special. Every cracker should have a paper hat inside, and I want to see everyone wearing one. Positively *no* exceptions."

Irreverent comments were thrown at him from all sides as the lights were dimmed and the hall was filled with the sounds of giggling, further rude remarks, loud snaps as the brightly coloured crackers were pulled and, afterwards, much crumpling of crêpe paper.

Charis had never much enjoyed making a fool of herself, and wearing stupid paper hats was not high on her list of amusing activities. However, there appeared to be no available option, so when Leo had pulled the other end of her cracker she faked enthusiasm for the paper hat inside by saying, "Great! It matches the green in my jumper."

Just then, someone covered her eyes from behind, startling her considerably. "Guess who?" said a familiar voice, though a voice unheard for many long months. It was a voice she could never forget. Turning in total disbelief she found Rick Woodrose standing behind her chair.

"Rick?" she cried. "*RICK!*"

"I think that's me," he said.

"It's *Rick!*" she exclaimed stupidly, turning towards the others. "It's Rick!"

"So it is," said Leo calmly. "Hello, stranger. Long time, no see. We'll catch up with you later. Just now we're supposed to be dancing."

"Well, Rick, what a surprise!" said Maggie with an enigmatic smile, drifting on to the dance floor in Leo's arms, and Charis just had time to see Ronnie whispering something to Miranda as they, too, joined the other dancers.

"Red," said Rick, extracting a paper hat from his cracker. "We can't all be lucky, I suppose, but red just isn't *me*, and it clashes horribly with *my* jumper."

"You're crazy," said Charis, half laughing, half crying, "but then, you always were."

"Come on," he said. "Don't get all weepy. Let's dance."

The dry hand holding hers; the other pressed lightly into her back; the fragrant aroma of sandalwood mixed with cigarette smoke; the neat nose, playful puppy grin and expressive eyes were all so familiar and dear that it felt ecstatic to be dancing with him again after so long a break. There were countless questions she longed to ask, yet she was strangely tongue-tied.

The music stopped. Exactly as in the first elimination waltz she had ever danced with Rick, the floor had been divided into four chalked-off areas. This time, though, the sections bore seasonal connotations, with four volunteers standing in the centre of each, respectively holding aloft sprigs of holly, ivy, mistletoe and laurel.

A pack of playing cards was cut to reveal a heart.

"Hearts are holly. Everyone in the holly section is eliminated."

More music.

Rick and Charis were eliminated when a spade found them in the mistletoe quarter.

"Oh well," said Rick. "That puts *us* out of the running yet again."

Back at the table, he lit a cigarette. "Want one?" he asked.

"No, thanks, I still don't."

They watched the rest of the elimination waltz in silence. Eventually only six couples remained, including Maggie and Leo.

"Right," said Greg when the music stopped. "The prize goes to the first couple to reach me with the guy wearing his partner's earrings."

A great scramble ensued, followed by wild applause at the end. Leo and Maggie were pipped at the post, although they made a gallant attempt, Leo tastefully adorned in Maggie's gilt earrings, which were shaped like shells.

"My! *How* well they suit you, honey!" joked Maggie when they rejoined Charis and Rick. "I should carry on wearing them if I were you."

"What have you been doing with yourself, Cara?" Rick asked when they were dancing again. "Are you going steady with anyone?"

"Not exactly."

"What's that supposed to mean?"

"It means," said Charis, "that I've had a few dates with Tom Potterfield, but I wouldn't describe him as my steady — at least not in the accepted sense."

"I saw him when I came in," said Rick. "He gave me a black look. A *very* black look, now I come to think of it."

"How about you, Rick? Have you found someone else?"

"Like you, there *is* someone," said Rick, and Charis felt an immediate sharp stab of jealousy.

"Anyone I know?" She dreaded the reply.

"You've never met her, but you may remember the name," said Rick. "It's Tessa's friend Marion — the one who came to Ireland with us."

"But she's at Tessa's college in Birmingham, isn't she?"

"Yes, but we write to each other and I've been up there for a couple of weekends."

Charis swallowed hard.

"She's a nice girl, but not a bit like you."

"Meaning?"

"Cool and restrained, not warm and co-operative like you used to be."

Charis said nothing, misery rising within her.

"Changing the subject, what are you doing over Christmas?" said Rick, "or shouldn't I ask?"

"Not much," said Charis. "I've been invited to coffee and mince pies at Celia's house on Christmas Eve, and Aunt Bee, Aunt Hester and my grandma are staying with us until the twenty-seventh."

"I never did meet Celia face to face," said Rick, "but I remember her. A cool blonde, wasn't she? Is the mince-pie do in the evening?"

"No, the morning."

"You'll probably be having more fun than me," said Rick.

"I can't believe *that*," said Charis scornfully. "Convince me."

"It's pretty bleak for our family just now," said Rick. "My grandfather on the Mayo side of the family in Ireland died a few days ago, so Ma and Uncle Motto have gone over to look after my grandmother and organise the funeral and everything, and Tessa and Gaby are there as well to represent the younger generation. The twins are staying at The Magpies with Aunt Hattie and Bryony, and Pa and I are joining them there for Christmas, but at the moment we're on our own. Apart from wanting to see you again, it was so dreary at home that I couldn't bear staying in tonight."

"Oh, Rick, I *am* sorry."

"I don't suppose we'll ever go back to Ireland in the summer again," he continued. "I can't see my grandmother living in Voyle House on her own. I expect Uncle Motto and Ma will persuade her to come over here so that she's nearer to us."

"Won't you be seeing Marion over Christmas?"

"Oh no. She'll be with her own family in Lincolnshire."

"And Bryony? How's Bryony?"

"Still as dotty as ever, and still keen on this singing idea. In fact, Uncle Motto's arranged for her to have an audition with the entertainments' officer on one of their ships in the new year, so she may get what she wants sooner than she expected, but it's all in the lap of the gods."

When the music ended, Rick escorted her back to the table.

"What's happened to Tom?" asked Leo.

Charis thought it a little provocative of him to ask just at that moment: "I don't know," she said. "It's gone nine o'clock. He usually puts in an appearance around now."

"Take your partners for a foxtrot," said Greg Duffy.

"Cara?" said Rick, holding out his hand.

When they were dancing again he said, "You couldn't care less where Tom is, could you?"

"Is it *so* obvious?"

"Patently," said Rick. "How do you like dancing with me again?"

"It's heaven," she said, whereupon Rick squeezed her hand and held her closer.

In the last waltz, with the lights extinguished, they danced cheek to cheek as though the anguished months of separation had never existed. At the far end of the hall, just as he had always done, Rick stopped dancing and gave her one of his gorgeous French kisses. Then he held her tightly against him, breathing deeply, before he kissed her again and she responded with all the pent-up passion of the last few months. No one had ever kissed her the way he did, and she doubted whether anyone ever would again.

"Cara," he whispered in her ear. "It seems a long time since that first night, doesn't it?"

"In some ways, yes," she replied. "In other ways, it could have been just yesterday."

The music faded; the lights came on; and there, as usual, was Father Kellow on the stage waiting to say the closing prayer. It was the collect for the third Sunday in Advent, followed by the blessing.

"I have to hand it to you. Your Prayer Book language is something special," Rick said afterwards. "I'm used to Latin, of course, but hearing such eloquent English makes me wonder sometimes what we're missing."

"Better not let your parish priest hear you say that," said Maggie.

"I know, I know," said Rick. "Heresy rears its ugly head, but don't you agree with me, Maggie?"

"I've never given it a moment's thought," she answered coolly.

"Get your coat, Cara," said Rick. "I don't know what's happened to Tom, and I care even less than you do. The point is *I'm* walking you to the station tonight. Agreed?"

She nodded, drowning in a sea of euphoria.

In the cloakroom Maggie said, "I can't tell you what to do, Mitch, but don't forget poor old Tom."

"He's not here," she protested. "I've hardly seen him since I left him at the door when I arrived."

"That's because he's gone off on his own. He obviously saw you and Rick dancing as though you were the only two people in the world in the elimination waltz, and when that was over he took one more look at you, and that's the last we saw of him."

"I can't help it, Maggie," said Charis. "I'm sorry if he's upset, but this is the first time I've seen Rick since August, and I need to talk to him urgently. You must see that."

"I know, I know, but I think it's pointless trying to turn the clock back. It never works."

"Don't be cross with me," Charis pleaded. "Seeing Rick is the best Christmas present I could possibly have had. Please don't spoil it."

"As if I would," said Maggie smiling ruefully. "I won't say another word, but I'll ring you sometime over Christmas."

As Charis and Rick walked slowly in the direction of Charters Lea Station, arms tightly around each other, Rick said, "I didn't know how to cope with what happened, you know. I just couldn't think straight that day."

"*You* didn't know how to cope? How do you think *I* felt? It was like the end of the world."

"I thought about you such a lot. Every day. But I didn't know how to put things right. Don't laugh, but I couldn't help thinking how ironic it was that I met you at a club run by a church dedicated to St Jude, of all people. Did you know St Jude is the patron saint of lost causes? You're supposed to pray to him in hopeless situations."

"And did you?"

"I'm afraid not, but then, as you may recall, I'm neither a very good nor devout Catholic."

"Did you tell anyone about what happened?"

"Only Bryony. She was incensed at the time because it was all so unnecessary. I mean that silly, narrow-minded pair of old busybodies telling tales about us to your *mother* of all people. It's beyond belief."

"Did Bryony have any advice?"

"Bryony? Heavens, no. She's not at *all* the Evelyn Home type. She was very sympathetic, but she soon forgot about the whole thing. She means well, but she doesn't concern herself too much with other people's problems. She's far more interested in herself. Completely egocentric."

"What did you tell your parents?"

"Just that you and I wouldn't be seeing each other any more. That it hadn't worked out."

"Were they sorry?"

"Of course. They liked you."

"I only met them once. I'd have given anything to know them better — *all* your family. They were so sweet to me."

"Gaby and Giles are getting married in April," said Rick.

"How perfect!" said Charis. "I'm sure they'll be happy."

"Marriage is a bit of a gamble in my opinion," said Rick, "but they've known one another a long while, so they've had time to make up their minds, I should think."

By then they were near the recreation area, which Charis could never pass without remembering her clumsy initiation with Banjo, but tonight it was Rick who led her over to the sheltering darkness of the oak trees.

"I really needed to see you again, Cara," he said, "that's why I took a chance on your being there tonight. I don't like unfinished business, and there were loose ends that needed to be tied up."

"Tell me, then," she said. "What are we going to do?"

He held her very close. "I've had a long time to think about things, and I've been seeing Marion too, as I told you. What you and I had in the summer was very special, wasn't it? It's something I'll never forget. Will you?"

"Not possibly. Not ever."

"It probably wouldn't have stayed like that indefinitely, though, however good it was at the time. Sooner or later we might have had a flaming row and parted company without anyone else intervening."

"We *might* have, but we didn't, so we'll never know."

"Exactly. We'll never know. All we have are our memories."

"I know that, but are you trying to tell me that we'll never go out together again? I mean, I could always try to find a way of meeting you somehow."

"I suppose you mean by telling lies to your mother? It's a thought, but I don't think it's a very sound one. Your conscience would start bothering you, so a relationship like that wouldn't last for long."

"You know, Rick, I thought you were angry with me for not standing up to my mother in the summer, and, now that I'm trying to, you don't approve of that either."

"Sooner or later you'll *have* to, but not by telling lies. You'll have to be firm at some stage, but I'd be surprised if you could ever be less than honest."

Charis sighed deeply, remembering how she planned to sneak off to Warbridge Jazz Club again secretly at some time in the future. Perhaps Rick did not know her as well as he thought he did. "I can't bear to think I may never see you again, Rick," she said. "I can't bear letting you go for good. And how about Marion? It's going to be torture imagining you doing things with her like you used to do with me? Will you *really* be going steady with her? Are you *really* interested?"

"It's much too soon to know for sure," said Rick. "She certainly doesn't set me on fire the way you used to, but, as I said, she's a nice enough girl, and I'm prepared to let things take their course. Come here, Cara. Don't get all upset."

Gently, slowly, Rick unbuttoned her coat and began caressing her in his specially gentle, tantalising, intimate way, and memories came flooding back of the little hut in the woods and the flower filled fields near Flackston Manor. His kisses, too, were so wonderful, so unmistakably his — different from Banjo's; from Alan's; from Ronnie's; and most certainly from Tom's. From time to time he brushed her cheek with his own, which was warm and smooth, but at last, although she longed for him to continue indefinitely, he stopped fondling her.

"Cara, it's terribly difficult, it's dreadfully painful, but what I'm trying to tell you is that this really is goodbye," he said, holding her gently. "I'm never coming back to Holyoaks after tonight and we must get on with our lives. We really have to, you know. Don't be too sad. Say you agree — *please*."

"If it's what you want. If you think it's the only way," said Charis, trembling violently, very close to tears and longing, *aching* to touch him the way she had touched Alan, so that she would always carry a truly intimate memory of him. She remembered the casual way Alan had encouraged her to fondle him, as though it were the most inevitable and natural thing in the world, but Rick had never behaved in such a way, and she was too afraid that, if she took the initiative now, he would guess she had already shared the experience with someone else and it might spoil everything for good. Restraining herself from so reckless an action, she simply said, "I'll never forget you, Rick. As long as I live, I'll never forget you."

"You'll find someone eventually," said Rick gently, "and, despite what you say, you *will* forget me — but I hope not altogether. I doubt very much that I'll ever forget you completely. How could I? But you do see it's got to be goodbye now, don't you? So goodbye. Goodbye, Cara Mia."

A few days after the party Maggie rang Charis as she had promised. Charis was grateful. She wished school had not broken up so early, for then there would have been distractions and conversations with her friends to take her mind off Rick and everything concerning him.

"Can you talk easily?" Maggie asked tactfully.

"Yes. It's OK. I'm on my own. My mother's out shopping and Daddy's at work."

"Tell me *all,* then. What happened?"

Charis outlined her farewell conversation with Rick, and Maggie allowed her to continue without interrupting. "Give me your honest opinion, Maggie. What do you think?" she said when she had finished.

"My honest opinion is that Rick's right," said Maggie after a slight pause. "I *know* it's hard. I *know* it's heartbreaking, but you'd already got over the worst of it. In a way, I wish he hadn't turned up on Saturday. It's just unsettled you again and opened up an old wound."

"It was fantastic seeing him, though. He looked so wonderful, but just a tiny bit older, I thought."

"Well he *is* a tiny bit older," said Maggie. "So am I. So are you. Fact of life."

After a moment Charis said, "You know, Maggie, I think I'm beginning to look at the whole thing in a new light. Although it was agony saying goodbye, spending that evening with Rick was the best Christmas present I could possibly have had, and something I'll always remember, and now that I've had a few days to simmer down I'm gradually coming round to accepting the situation."

"Thank goodness for that," said Maggie. "Leo and I were afraid you'd be dreadfully upset, get all depressed and have a miserable Christmas, but it looks as though you're bearing up pretty well."

"I'm trying to."

"Good for you. Keep it up," said Maggie.

After a few more exchanges about Christmas plans, Maggie said, "I've got some news for you too."

"Good news?"

"Mixed, I suppose," said Maggie. "It's my mother. She's having another baby."

"*NO!*" Charis was appalled. "She *can't* be. Another baby at *her* age?"

"She's not *that* old," Maggie protested.

"So you'll have another little brother or sister." Charis was shocked to think that the Rigg family would now comprise seven young children, as well as Maggie and Bernard. "Which do you hope it'll be?"

"To be honest," said Maggie, "and contrary to my strict Catholic upbringing, I wish it wasn't happening at all. My mother's worn out already, without having to worry about another baby. I try to help out as much as I can, but it's difficult when I'm at school, and this will just make everything worse."

"Poor you."

"Poor Mum," said Maggie. "Sometimes I think it was a blessing that Dad was away at the war after I was born, but she had a miscarriage once after he came home on leave, and another time there was a baby that was stillborn. If those two had lived, there would have been nine of us now, and ten with this new baby."

"You never told me that before."

"Didn't I? Well, it's all in the past. As for this latest addition, I suppose we'll cope. We always have done so far."

Grace came home soon after Maggie had rung off. She opened the front door with her key, closed it firmly, hurried into the kitchen and practically threw her shopping bag on the floor in a most uncharacteristic fashion. "Charis!" she called. "Have you seen it?"

"Seen what?"

"The For Sale sign next door. It can only just have been put up. The Farrows are on the move."

"Good riddance!" said Charis with great feeling.

"Although that's a rude remark, for once I agree with you," said Grace. "Nasty, stand-offish people. Let's hope our new neighbours will be more friendly."

Charis was sorely tempted to add, 'Let's hope they don't interfere in my affairs, either,' but, since neither the ghastly summer episode nor Rick's name had ever again been mentioned, she prudently held her tongue.

"I wonder where they're going to live," said Grace.

"Who cares?"

"Well, I don't exactly *care*," said Grace, "but I'd still like to know. Perhaps Mrs Walsh will tell me sometime."

"I think it's the best news I've heard for ages," said Charis.

"So do I," said Grace. "Let's have some coffee to celebrate, shall we, before I sort out the shopping?"

Sitting in the warm kitchen with their hands cupped round steaming mugs of Nescafé and Dizzy rubbing himself against their legs, Charis felt more at ease with her mother than for many months past, and almost — *almost* — ready to forgive her. 'Perhaps,' she thought, 'I *will* forgive her eventually, but not quite yet. It'll take me some time.' She remembered her childhood when the bond with her mother had been close and loving, though always a little restrained, and it saddened her to think that those days were gone for ever.

"Will you be seeing Tom over Christmas?" Grace asked without warning.

"I'm not sure."

"Well, didn't he say anything on Saturday?"

"I didn't see much of him. He was on the door."

"I'm surprised Celia didn't include him in the invitation for Christmas Eve," Grace continued.

"He was never one of her crowd," said Charis, "and no one thinks of us as partners."

"Maggie and Leo seem to," said Grace. "Well, it's still early days, but I wouldn't be surprised if things soon change. It would be so nice for you to have someone like him to rely on and take you out more, and you'll be seventeen next month — a lovely age for a girl."

Charis gulped a mouthful of coffee to avoid answering. She had no intention of disclosing Tom's disappearance from the party, and was determined that Rick's name should not escape from her lips in an unguarded moment. "I think I'll finish putting up my cards," she said. "I don't suppose I'll get any more, so I may as well."

"All right, dear. They'll look very pretty strung up by the fireplace," said Grace. "Perhaps I'll do something similar with ours."

It was so unusual for Grace to call Charis 'dear', or to approve of anything she did around the home, that she only just stopped herself from remarking on it, thus ensuring that peace and harmony prevailed for a little longer.

Charis arrived at Tamarisk Villa shortly after eleven o'clock on the morning of Christmas Eve. Memories of Celia's party thirteen months ago were uppermost in her mind, along with reflections on all that had happened since that far-off evening which had opened the door to so many new experiences.

A tall Christmas tree, shimmering with hundreds of tiny white lights, stood on the polished parquet hall floor, dwarfing Celia as she stood in the doorway to welcome Charis. She looked as chic and cool as ever in a light-beige woollen dress, almost the same colour as her hair, and expensive-looking gold jewellery. "Merry Christmas! Come right in," she said. "Pam's already here with her parents and Roger, and you know all the others too. We're still expecting a few more."

In the luxurious drawing room with its light carpet and cream leather armchairs, Jack and Frances Armitage came over to greet Charis before returning to their other guests. Momentarily alone, she had time to note that neither paper chains nor balloons were in evidence. Instead, a small silver Christmas tree, decked in minuscule pink, turquoise and silver balls and star-shaped fairy lights, had been placed close to the window, and clever, festive arrangements of logs, candles, holly, ivy and frosted baubles stood on the polished surfaces of suitable pieces of furniture.

Charis smiled, nodded or spoke briefly to casual acquaintances such as Nick and Rosemary, Mark Earle (Celia's Doctor Jazz), Babs and Steve, and then glanced round the room to see who else was there.

She had met Gordon Sperry only once before, and was as struck now as she had been then by his appearance. It was evident that Pam had inherited her good looks from him, for he was conventionally handsome. The director of a company which manufactured garden equipment, he was frequently away from home on business trips, and he and Jack Armitage were deep now in conversation, undoubtedly talking shop.

Jane Sperry, Charis realised for the first time, would have been quite plain without the heavy make-up and dramatic clothes which always ensured that she stood out from the crowd. Today, resplendent in a tangerine-coloured dress, she was smoking a cigarette in a long silver holder. "Merry Christmas!" she said. "What will you be doing over the holiday?"

"My grandma and two aunts are staying with us," said Charis. "I expect it'll be quiet, though. It usually is."

"I wish *I* could have a quiet Christmas for once," said Jane sulkily, exhaling smoke through her nostrils like a dragon, "but this one looks like being busier than ever. I'm expecting Roger's family, and there are four of them, plus my brother's crowd, so we'll be twelve altogether."

"You know you love entertaining. Stop complaining," said Pam, eavesdropping on the conversation. "How's life?" she asked Charis when Jane had moved on to talk to someone else. "How's Tom?"

"Life's so-so. I haven't heard from Tom lately."

"Oh! I thought you two were seeing more of each other these days. At least, that's what I heard."

"We go out now and again," said Charis, "but he isn't exactly my regular boyfriend." She had no intention of mentioning Rick, remembering that only Maggie, Leo, Ronnie and Miranda knew about their brief reunion. "How's Polly?" Charis enquired casually in order to change the subject.

Pam glanced round quickly to make sure she was not likely to be overheard. "Still in one piece, more by luck than judgment," Pam whispered, with a wink and a saucy grin.

"You don't mean . . . ?"

"Still at it, the pair of them, and Banjo still doesn't always take precautions either, according to Polly. I've given up. It's her funeral. Why should I bother myself?"

"But surely she doesn't want to risk going through all that worry again," said Charis.

"She must think it's worth it," Pam said, still whispering, "and, of course, I have to agree with her, but at least when Roger and I do it I don't have to worry."

"There's always a risk, though," said Charis.

"So what?" said Pam, then, reverting to her normal speaking voice, she went on, "Remember the last time you were here?"

"As if I could forget."

"Well, see if you remember *him*." Pam nodded towards a lanky youth who was standing by the piano chatting to Rosemary.

Charis stared, puzzled. She did not recognise this young man at all.

"You'll never believe it. *I* didn't," said Pam. "It's Teddy Clack."

"But he used to be so fat and clumsy," said Charis in disbelief, resuming her appraisal.

"I know. Amazing what a year can do, isn't it? See you later. I promised to give Celia a hand with the mince pies."

"Ronnie wants a word in your ear, Charis," said Miranda, who had just arrived.

Ronnie beckoned her over.

"You can guess what it's about," Miranda continued, "but I promise you our lips are sealed."

"Thanks. You're wonderful," said Charis gratefully. "I won't be long."

"Sweet, shy Charis," Ronnie said. "Look what's happened to you in just over a year. I wouldn't have believed it."

He kissed her on both cheeks, just as she remembered him embracing Miranda all that time ago. It made her feel really special, marking her out as one of his particular friends.

"Are you going to tell me about Rick?" he asked her in a low voice. "I've been itching to know."

She explained as briefly as possible, ending with her new resolve to make a break with the past and concentrate on the future.

"That sounds very sensible and satisfactory," said Ronnie, "but that thing you had going with Rick was extra-special, wasn't it? I don't think I'll ever forget the sizzling way the two of you used to look at each other last summer. It was riveting."

"Yes, I know, but it's just a wonderful memory now. I'm going to try not to let myself be sad about it any more."

"Good girl," said Ronnie. "Oh, look, here are the mince pies. Hot and spicy I hope, Pam."

"Just like me," said Pam, making eyes at him.

The coffee was good and strong; the mince pies sweet and fruity inside their shortcrust-pastry cases. Christmas music was playing softly in the background, and Charis felt relaxed and replete with seasonal goodwill.

"Hi, there," said a gruff, recently broken male voice. "I think I owe you an apology, even if it's over a year late."

It was Teddy Clack. No longer red-faced; no longer gawky; he towered over her, smiling nicely.

"An apology? Whatever for?"

"The firework incident," he said. "Eileen told me about your dress getting torn, and it was all my fault. If it's not too late, I'm awfully sorry about it."

"Good heavens, I'd almost forgotten," said Charis with a laugh. "How nice of you, but it's quite all right. Don't give it another thought."

"Were you able to mend it?"

"Yes, but I never wore it again anyway. I never liked it much in the first place."

This made them both laugh, and then Jack Armitage came over brandishing a bottle of Tia Maria: "How about something to liven up the coffee?" he said.

Not everyone was enthusiastic.

"It always gives me a headache," said Eileen Clack, standing hand in hand with her new boyfriend, Peter.

"I think it's sickly," said Rosemary.

"I *love* it," said Pam.

"I'd rather just have some more coffee, please," said Charis.

By one o'clock the brief social gathering was nearing its end.

"There's just one more thing," said Frances Armitage, giving her husband a mischievous wink. "While you've all been chattering away in here a bunch of mistletoe has mysteriously appeared in the hall, and positively *no one* will be able to leave without walking under it."

Standing beneath the mistletoe, and in the midst of much mild ribaldry and merriment, along with all the other girls Charis was kissed in turn by Roger, Mark, Nick, Steve, Peter, Jack Armitage, Gordon Sperry, and even briefly by Teddy Clack, but it was Ronnie's kiss which meant the most because she knew he was someone who would always be her friend.

Afterwards, everyone walked up Wednesbury Road together, calling out cheerful goodbyes and Merry Christmases to Charis as they left her at her front gate.

On Boxing Day Charis seized a rare moment of privacy to confide in Aunt Bee: "I've been dying to tell you," she whispered. "The most amazing thing happened. *Rick* was at the Holyoaks party."

Her aunt looked startled. "Whatever happened?" she asked in a low voice.

Charis told her as much as she could in the space of about five minutes, including her intention of trying to face the future without regretting the past too much.

"I'm glad to hear you say that, pet," said Aunt Bee. "I'm sure it's for the best. No use crying over spilt milk, as they say." There was silence for a moment before she added, "I'm afraid you may not like what I'm going to say next, though."

"Why not, Auntie? I never mind what *you* say to me."

"Well, haven't you wondered about Tom? About what happened to him that night? I mean, he took you to the party, and certainly meant to dance with you and see you home, and what happened? Off you went with Rick. Tom must have been awfully upset. *You* would have been, wouldn't you?"

Charis blushed, ashamed because it was so rare for Aunt Bee to criticise her that it confirmed in no uncertain terms her own privately acknowledged sense of guilt. "I could only think about Rick," she said. "Nothing else mattered that night except that we were together again. We *had* to talk and straighten things out. We simply *had* to."

"I know, pet, but don't you think you could have found a moment just to try and explain the situation to Tom."

"There *wasn't* a moment. Rick simply took over."

"So it seems. Well, think about it, pet. If you and Rick definitely won't be seeing one another again, why not try to be nice to Tom for a change. I know you think he's dull, but I expect he's a very nice fellow with more personality than you might imagine. He's probably shy, and perhaps you should give him a chance to come out of his shell. You might even be able to encourage him to have a bit more fun with you. From what you've told me, I wouldn't mind betting you're in the driving seat when it comes to kissing and cuddling." Here Aunt Bee gave one of her specially funny giggles, which was so infectious that Charis found herself breaking into a grin. "That's better," said Aunt Bee. "Don't get too serious, pet. Take life lightly. After all, you're still only sixteen."

Once Christmas was over, Charis was in the doldrums. It was always the same. Aunt Bee, the life and soul of every family gathering, along with Vanna and gentle, happy Aunt Hester, had gone home; the Christmas tree, once so festive with its array of brightly coloured baubles and fairy lights, now looked dried up and dispirited, the tinsel awry, the lights unlit. Cards which opened horizontally instead of vertically had, as usual, performed the splits on the mantelpiece and sideboard, whilst those of poor quality had simply buckled and fallen over.

"These decorations are just collecting more and more dust," said Grace. "I shall be thoroughly glad when its Twelfth Night, and if I had my way they'd all come down a long time before that."

Charis's Christmas presents had included a page-a-day diary, just like the one she had been writing up faithfully that year, a film star annual, some earrings, the usual collection of bath cubes and talcum powder, a bottle of perfume and a very pretty winter dress in deep-blue velvet with a wide matching belt, and a full skirt. This, of course, had been from Aunt Bee, but Charis was at a loss to know when she would be able to wear it, as her social life had once again fallen into a decline.

She opened the film star annual, turning the sepia pages for the umpteenth time, admiring the sultry elegance of stars such as Lana Turner, Elizabeth Taylor, Vivien Leigh and Gloria Grahame, and sighing over heartthrobs like Dirk Bogarde, Robert Wagner and Laurence Harvey.

Grace came in carrying the vacuum cleaner, and plugged it into the socket by the fireplace. "Still mooning about," she said. "Why don't you do something useful? You haven't written your thank you letters yet. You could be getting on with those."

It was the last thing Charis wanted to do, but wearisome ennui eventually drove her to agree, and she wandered off in search of her writing pad.

Stuck in the middle of the first thank-you letter, Charis begin thinking ahead to the new year and what might be in store. She had certainly not forgotten her assignation with Alan Decker, and the idea of a clandestine evening with him excited her considerably more than she guessed it should. 'I'll go back to Warbridge Jazz Club as soon as I possibly can,' she vowed. 'Somehow I'll find a way, and even if *he* isn't there, someone else interesting might be.' The telephone rang. Glad of any excuse to break off from writing her letter, she hurried to answer it: "Charters Lea 6507."

"Is that Charis? Er — er — it's Tom here."

"Tom — oh, hello." She was lost for words, embarrassed and disconcerted.

"How are you? How was your Christmas?"

"I'm OK, thanks. Christmas was OK too, but it seems ages ago now. How are you?"

"I'm not sure," said Tom.

Charis fell silent.

"Are you still there?" he asked.

"Of course I am."

"Look, Charis, I don't know how to say this to you, but at the party, you know, on the 17th, as soon as I saw Rick I guessed how you'd react and what might happen, and I felt pretty desperate. When I saw you dancing with him I just couldn't bear to stay and watch. I sensed you two would be together for the rest of the evening, so I took the coward's way out and went home."

"I behaved very badly," she admitted, making sure Grace was not listening. "I know I did. I should have spoken to you, but I just couldn't think straight. I suppose it's a bit late to apologise, but I'm sorry. I really am."

"You see, I thought we'd been making some headway, and then *he* showed up, and I felt these past few weeks had been a complete waste of time. I'm right, aren't I?"

"No, not exactly, Tom. I can only say again that I'm very sorry."

"But you and Rick? Are you starting up all over again?"

"No. It's over," she whispered, hating the awful finality of the words.

There was silence on the other end of the line for a little while before Tom said, "*Really* over? Are you sure?"

"As sure as I'll ever be."

Another silence ensued, but after a moment or two he said, "I hardly dare to suggest this, but in view of what you've just told me, couldn't we at least *try* to go out on a more regular basis?"

Charis swallowed hard. Tom fell so sadly short of her ideal, and yet she felt she owed him something for having used him for her own selfish purposes. "Well, I suppose we could," she said.

"That's encouraging," he said, sounding more cheerful, "and, if that's the case, I wonder if you'd consider being my partner at the New Year's Eve Ball at the Starlight Ballroom in Upsvale. It's still possible to get tickets. I've checked with Leo, who's taking Maggie as you probably know. I could pick you up at home, let's say at six-thirty. Please say yes, Charis. Honestly, there's no one I'd rather start the new year with than you."

Thoughts of wearing her new blue velvet dress, with Leo and Maggie there to jolly Tom along; the latter's incredible forbearance; the prospect of some fun at friendly foursomes in the future; continued success at school and *still* the thrilling possibility of a secret rendezvous with Alan Decker, flashed through her mind in a tangled, glittery mass. All of a sudden, life seemed full of promise. "Thank you Tom," she said. "I'd love to."

SUMMER 1995

As the underground train slowed down at Victoria Station, Charis prepared to meet Maggie in the main concourse.

'Dear Maggie,' she thought. 'Who would have guessed we'd still be friends after all these years?'

Maggie's parents, along with Grace and Hugh, Aunt Bee, Vanna and Aunt Hester had all sadly passed away, but Uncle Donald was still alive, in his nineties, and living in a retirement home for clergy.

Maggie and Leo Crewe, married for thirty-five years and still as blissfully happy as they had always been, were the proud parents of four sons: Paul, Aidan, Simon and David. Leo had eventually converted to Catholicism before their marriage, and they were a strongly devout and united family.

All Maggie's brothers and sisters had married, even Johnny, the youngest, who had been born in the summer of 1956. Dominic, Pauline and Carmel were all in secure partnerships, but Lizzie had not been so successful and was separated from her wayward husband. Timmy, the second youngest of the brood, had been tragically killed in a motoring accident, leaving a young wife and three small children, but the Rigg dynasty was so large and loving that his grieving family had been safely sheltered under its wing until his wife had remarried a few years later.

Ronnie and Miranda's marriage had been idyllic, though childless by design. They had kept in touch with Charis over the years, if only at Christmas, but she rarely saw them. Ronnie had made quite a name for himself as an artist, and his paintings, one of which was proudly owned by Charis, were much in demand.

Pam, after a series of wild affairs, had finally settled down, moved away and lost touch with Charis. Celia had married her Doctor Jazz and become a formidable lady, enjoying her role as a surgeon's wife, but she, too, had drifted out of Charis's orbit.

Banjo, as everyone had predicted, had finally impregnated Polly, and there had been a shotgun wedding. Charis had no idea whether or not they were still together, but she knew that Polly had given birth to a daughter towards the end of 1956.

And Charis? After a protracted, undemanding relationship with gentle, faithful Tom Potterfield, which had spanned their years at university, she had firmly resisted all his attempts to coax her into marriage. They had parted amicably when, eventually, he had found someone new, and Charis sincerely hoped that their marriage had been a happy one. True to her vow, she had met Alan Decker clandestinely on several occasions spread over five years, and it was with him that she had finally tasted the ultimate, intoxicating flavour of forbidden fruit. He had never married Shirley Croft, but, as a seasoned womaniser, Charis was only one of his many conquests, and he eventually moved on to pastures new.

Following in the footsteps of the revered Irene Wolsey, Charis had graduated in English and embarked on a teaching career. A series of partnerships with totally unsuitable men had followed the ending of her relationships with Tom and Alan, but throughout her life she had never met anyone to compare with Rick Woodrose, and neither had she forgotten him. Since that December evening forty years ago, Charis had neither heard from nor seen him, and so her treasured memories of him remained locked in a time warp.

It was Aunt Hester who had unwittingly instigated the chain of events which had led Charis to the present crossroads in her life, by leaving her the pretty little Sussex house where she had lived so happily until her death in the late 1980s. Charis, who by then was approaching the age of fifty, had always loved Aunt Hester's house and could think of nothing more desirable than living there. She was fortunate, too, in finding a suitable teaching post at a high school for girls in the vicinity, where she planned to remain until her retirement in 1999. Owning the house, along with money from the sale of 22 Wednesbury Road, and also from Aunt Bee's estate, meant that Charis was in a comfortable financial position, though lonely for her much-loved, departed relatives and for that elusive someone with whom she still wished to share her life.

News that Maggie and Leo had decided to retire to Haywards Heath in 1990 had been the happiest possible surprise for Charis, and now that they lived so close to her they soon ensured that she was treated as part of their large family.

It was at one of their crowded gatherings that Charis had met Maggie's elder brother Bernard, whom she had not seen for many years. This was hardly surprising as he had been living in the north of England since his marriage in the early 1960s. Now, though, the father of two grown-up sons and a daughter, he had been a widower for several years, and to Charis's immense surprise there had been an instant rapport between them.

And now Charis saw Maggie waiting patiently for her outside the coffee shop at Victoria as arranged. Plump, large and motherly, her hair still blonde, she hugged Charis and kissed her warmly on the cheek.

"Thanks for giving me the chance to go back for a last look," said Charis. "I had to do it, you know, for old times' sake."

"Not a bit! It's what we agreed, and I was happy to catch a later train. Anyway you're right on time, so let's get going, shall we? I can't wait to have lunch, and then to get something to wear for the great day. Bet I'll have a job finding the right size, though."

The two old friends, soon to be sisters-in-law, linked arms, and Charis, newly received into the welcoming fold of the Catholic church, anticipated her forthcoming marriage to Bernard Rigg and the nuptial Mass which would bless and seal their union.